DATE DUE

DEMCO 38-296

THE GLENCOE LITERATURE LIBRARY

The Adventures of Tom Sawyer

and Related Readings

**Glencoe
McGraw-Hill**

New York, New York   Columbus, Ohio   Woodland Hills, California   Peoria, Illinois

Acknowledgments

Grateful acknowledgment is given authors, publishers, photographers, museums, and agents for permission to reprint the following copyrighted material. Every effort has been made to determine copyright owners. In case of any omissions, the Publisher will be pleased to make suitable acknowledgments in future editions.

"Boy's Manuscript" by Mark Twain excerpted from HUCK FINN AND TOM SAWYER AMONG THE INDIANS AND OTHER UNFINISHED STORIES by Mark Twain. Copyright © 1989 by The Regents of the University of California. Reprinted by permission of the University of California Press.

"A Rescue from an Underground Mine!" excerpted from REAL KIDS, REAL ADVENTURES #6: A RAGING FIRESTORM by Deborah Morris. Copyright © 1994 by Deborah Morris. Reprinted by The Berkeley Publishing Group, a division of Penguin Putnam.

"Getting the Bugs Out of *Tom Sawyer*, An Entomologist's View of a Classic" by John D. Evans. Copyright © 1997 by John Evans. Reprinted by permission of the author.

"Sometimes I Feel This Way" by John Ciardi, reprinted by permission of the Ciardi Family Publishing Trust.

From ETHICS by Susan Neiburg Terkel. Copyright © 1992 by Susan Neiburg Terkel. Used by permission of Lodestar Books, an affiliate of Dutton Children's Books, a division of Penguin Putnam, Inc.

Cover Art: Josef Mensing Gallery, Hamm-Rhynern, Germany/Bridgeman Art Library, London/Superstock

Glencoe/McGraw-Hill

*A Division of The **McGraw·Hill** Companies*

Send all inquiries to:
Glencoe/McGraw-Hill
8787 Orion Place
Columbus, OH 43240

ISBN 0-02-818008-9
Printed in the United States of America
3 4 5 6 7 8 9 026 04 03 02 01

Contents

The Adventures of Tom Sawyer

Preface	1	Chapter 19	101
Chapter 1	3	Chapter 20	108
Chapter 2	10	Chapter 21	111
Chapter 3	15	Chapter 22	116
Chapter 4	21	Chapter 23	122
Chapter 5	29	Chapter 24	125
Chapter 6	34	Chapter 25	131
Chapter 7	44	Chapter 26	133
Chapter 8	49	Chapter 27	139
Chapter 9	54	Chapter 28	146
Chapter 10	60	Chapter 29	149
Chapter 11	66	Chapter 30	152
Chapter 12	70	Chapter 31	158
Chapter 13	74	Chapter 32	166
Chapter 14	81	Chapter 33	174
Chapter 15	86	Chapter 34	177
Chapter 16	90	Chapter 35	186
Chapter 17	95	Chapter 36	189
Chapter 18	98	Conclusion	194

Continued

Contents *Continued*

Related Readings

Related Readings   **195**

Mark Twain   **Boy's Manuscript**   short story   **197**

Deborah Morris   **A Rescue from an Underground Mine!**   true life adventure   **214**

John D. Evans   **Getting the Bugs Out of *Tom Sawyer*: An Entomologist's View of a Classic**   natural science essay   **240**

John Ciardi   **Sometimes I Feel This Way**   poem   **247**

Susan Neiburg Terkel   from *Ethics*   essay   **249**

The Adventures of
Tom
Sawyer

Mark Twain

Preface

MOST OF THE ADVENTURES recorded in this book really occurred, one or two were experiences of my own, the rest of those boys who were schoolmates of mine. Huck Finn is drawn from life; Tom Sawyer also, but not from an individual; he is a combination of the characteristics of three boys whom I knew, and therefore belongs to the composite order of architecture.

The odd superstitions touched upon were all prevalent among children and slaves in the West at the period of this story; that is to say, thirty or forty years ago.

Although my book is intended mainly for the entertainment of boys and girls, I hope it will not be shunned by men and women on that account, for part of my plan has been to try pleasantly to remind adults of what they once were themselves, and of how they felt and thought and talked, and what queer enterprises they sometimes engaged in.

Hartford, 1876

THE AUTHOR

Chapter 1

Tom!'

No answer.

'Tom!'

No answer.

'What's gone with that boy, I wonder? You Tom!'

No answer.

The old lady pulled her spectacles down and looked over them, about the room; then she put them up and looked out under them. She seldom or never looked *through* them for so small a thing as a boy, for they were her state pair, the pride of her heart, and were built for 'style' not service; she could have seen through a pair of stove lids as well. She looked perplexed a moment and said, not fiercely, but still loud enough for the furniture to hear, 'Well, I lay if I get hold of you, I'll—'

She did not finish, for by this time she was bending down and punching under the bed with the broom—and so she needed breath to punctuate the punches with. She resurrected nothing but the cat.

'I never did see the beat of that boy!'

She went to the open door and stood in it and looked out among the tomato vines and 'jimpson' weeds that constituted the garden. No Tom. So she lifted up her voice, at an angle calculated for distance, and shouted:

'Y-o-u-u-*Tom!*'

There was a slight noise behind her, and she turned just in time to seize a small boy by the slack of his roundabout and arrest his flight. 'There! I might 'a thought of that closet. What you been doing in there?'

'Nothing.'

'Nothing! Look at your hands. And look at your mouth. What *is* that truck?'

'*I* don't know, Aunt.'

'Well, *I* know. It's jam, that's what it is. Forty times I've said if you didn't let that jam alone I'd skin you. Hand me that switch.'

The switch hovered in the air. The peril was desperate.

'My! Look behind you, Aunt!'

The old lady whirled around and snatched her skirts out of danger. The lad fled on the instant, scrambled up the high board fence, and disappeared over it. His Aunt Polly stood surprised a moment, and then broke into a gentle laugh.

'Hang the boy, can't I ever learn anything? Ain't he played me tricks enough like that for me to be looking out for him by this time? But old fools is the biggest fools there is. Can't learn any old dog new tricks, as the saying is. But, my goodness, he never plays them alike two days, and how is a body to know what's coming? He 'pears to know just how long he can torment me before I get my dander up, and he knows if he can make out to put me off for a minute, or make me laugh, it's all down again, and I can't hit him a lick. I ain't doing my duty by that boy, and that's the Lord's truth, goodness knows. Spare the rod and spile the child, as the good book says. I'm a-laying up sin and suffering for us both, *I* know. He's full of the old scratch, but laws-a-me! he's my own dead sister's boy, poor thing, and I ain't got the heart to lash him somehow. Every time I let him off my conscience does hurt me so; and every time I hit him my old heart 'most breaks. Well-a-well, man that is born of a woman is of few days and full of trouble, as the Scripture says, and I reckon it's so. He'll play hookey this evening,[1] and I'll just be obliged to make him work tomorrow, to punish him. It's mighty hard to make him work Saturdays, when all the boys is having a holiday, but he hates work more than he hates anything else, and I've got to do some of my duty by him, or I'll be the ruination of the child.'

Tom did play hookey, and he had a very good time. He got back home barely in season to help Jim, the small coloured boy, saw next day's wood, and split the kindlings before supper—at least he was there in time to tell his adventures to Jim while Jim did three-fourths of the work. Tom's younger brother (or rather half-brother) Sid was already through with his part of the work (picking up chips), for he was a quiet boy, and had no adventurous, troublesome ways. While Tom was eating his supper and stealing sugar as opportunity offered,

---

1. South-western for 'afternoon'.

Aunt Polly asked him questions that were full of guile, and very deep—for she wanted to trap him into damaging revealments. Like many other simple-hearted souls, it was her pet vanity to believe she was endowed with a talent for dark and mysterious diplomacy, and she loved to contemplate her most transparent devices as marvels of low cunning. Said she, 'Tom, it was middling warm in school, warn't it?'

'Yes, 'm.'

'Powerful warm, warn't it?'

'Yes, 'm.'

'Didn't you want to go in a swimming, Tom?'

A bit of a scare shot through Tom—a touch of uncomfortable suspicion. He searched Aunt Polly's face, but it told him nothing. So he said:

'No, 'm—well, not very much.'

The old lady reached out her hand and felt Tom's shirt, and said:

'But you ain't too warm now, though.'

And it flattered her to reflect that she had discovered that the shirt was dry without anybody knowing that that was what she had in her mind. But in spite of her Tom knew where the wind lay now. So he forestalled what might be the next move.

'Some of us pumped on our heads—mine's damp yet. See?'

Aunt Polly was vexed to think she had overlooked that bit of circumstantial evidence and missed a trick. Then she had a new inspiration:

'Tom, you didn't have to undo your shirt collar where I sewed it to pump on your head, did you? Unbutton your jacket!'

The trouble vanished out of Tom's face. He opened his jacket. His shirt collar was securely sewed.

'Bother! Well, go 'long with you. I'd made sure you'd played hookey and been a swimming. But I forgive ye, Tom. I reckon you're a kind of a singed cat, as the saying is—better'n you look, *this* time.'

She was half sorry her sagacity had miscarried, and half glad that Tom had stumbled into obedient conduct for once.

But Sidney said:

'Well, now, if I didn't think you sewed his collar with white thread, but it's black.'

'Why, I did sew it with white! Tom!'

But Tom did not wait for the rest. As he went out of the door, he said:

'Siddy, I'll lick you for that.'

In a safe place Tom examined two large needles which were thrust into the lapels of his jacket—and had thread bound about them—one needle carried white thread and the other black. He said:

'She'd never noticed if it hadn't been for Sid. Confound it, sometimes she sews it with white and sometimes she sews it with black. I wish to geeminy she'd stick to one or t'other—I can't keep the run of 'em. But I bet you I'll lam Sid for that. If I don't, blame my cats.'

He was not the model boy of the village. He knew the model boy very well, though, and loathed him.

Within two minutes, or even less, he had forgotten all his troubles. Not because his troubles were one whit less heavy and bitter to him than a man's are to a man, but because a new and powerful interest bore them down and drove them out of his mind for the time; just as men's misfortunes are forgotten in the excitement of new enterprises. This new interest was a valued novelty in whistling, which he had just acquired from a Negro, and he was suffering to practise it undisturbed. It consisted in a peculiar bird-like turn, a sort of liquid warble, produced by touching the tongue to the roof of the mouth at short intervals in the midst of the music. The reader probably remembers how to do it if he has ever been a boy. Diligence and attention soon gave him the knack of it, and he strode down the street with his mouth full of harmony and his soul full of gratitude. He felt much as an astronomer feels who has discovered a new planet. No doubt as far as strong, deep, unalloyed pleasure is concerned, the advantage was with the boy, not the astronomer.

The summer evenings were long. It was not dark yet. Presently Tom checked his whistle. A stranger was before him; a boy a shade larger than himself. A new-comer of any age or either sex was an impressive curiosity in the poor little village of St Petersburg. This boy was well dressed, too—well dressed on a week-day. This was simply astounding. His cap was a dainty thing, his close-buttoned blue-cloth roundabout was new and natty, and so were his pantaloons. He had shoes on, and yet it was only Friday. He even wore a neck-tie, a bright bit of ribbon. He had a citified air about him that ate into Tom's vitals. The more Tom stared at the splendid marvel, the higher he turned up his nose at his finery, and the shabbier and shabbier his own outfit seemed to him to grow. Neither boy spoke. If one moved the other moved—but only sidewise, in a circle. They kept face to face and eye to eye all the time. Finally, Tom said:

'I can lick you!'

'I'd like to see you try it.'

'Well, I can do it.'

'No you can't, either.'

'Yes I can.'

'No you can't.'

'I can.'

'You can't.'

'Can.'

'Can't.'

An uncomfortable pause. Then Tom said:

'What's your name?'

''Tisn't any of your business, maybe.'

'Well I 'low I'll *make* it my business.'

'Well, why don't you?'

'If you say much I will.'

'Much—much—much! There, now.'

'Oh, you think you're mighty smart, *don't* you? I could lick you with one hand tied behind me, if I wanted to.'

'Well, why don't you *do* it? You *say* you can do it.'

'Well, *I will*, if you fool with me.'

'Oh, yes—I've seen whole families in the same fix.'

'Smarty! you think you're *some* now, *don't* you? Oh, what a hat!'

'You can lump that hat if you don't like it. I dare you to knock it off; and anybody that'll take a dare will suck eggs.'

'You're a liar!'

'You're another.'

'You're a fighting liar and darn't take it up.'

'Aw—take a walk!'

'Say—if you give me much more of your sass, I'll take and bounce a rock off'n your head.'

'Oh, of *course* you will.'

'Well, I *will*.'

'Well, why don't you *do* it, then? What do you keep *saying* you will for? Why don't you *do* it? It's because you're afraid.'

'I *ain't* afraid.'

'You are.'

'I ain't.'

'You are.'

Another pause, and more eyeing and sidling around each other. Presently they were shoulder to shoulder. Tom said:

'Get away from here!'

'Go away yourself!'

'I won't.'

'I won't, either.'

So they stood, each with a foot placed at an angle as a brace, and both shoving with might and main, and glowering at each other with hate. But neither could get an advantage. After struggling till both were hot and flushed, each relaxed his strain with watchful caution, and Tom said:

'You're a coward and a pup. I'll tell my big brother on you, and he can lam you with his little finger, and I'll make him do it, too.'

'What do I care for your big brother? I've got a brother that's bigger than he is; and, what's more, he can throw him over that fence, too.' (Both brothers were imaginary.)

'That's a lie.'

'*Your* saying so don't make it so.'

Tom drew a line in the dust with his big toe, and said:

'I dare you to step over that, and I'll lick you till you can't stand up. Anybody that'll take a dare will steal a sheep.'

The new boy stepped over promptly, and said:

'Now you said you'd do it, now let's see you do it.'

'Don't you crowd me, now; you'd better look out.'

'Well, you *said* you'd do it—why don't you do it?'

'By jingoes! for two cents I *will* do it.'

The new boy took two broad coppers out of his pocket and held them out with derision.

Tom struck them to the ground.

In an instant both boys were rolling and tumbling in the dirt, gripped together like cats; and for the space of a minute they tugged and tore at each other's hair and clothes, punched and scratched each other's noses, and covered themselves with dust and glory. Presently the confusion took form, and through the fog of battle Tom appeared, seated astride the new boy, and pounding him with his fists.

'Holler 'nuff!' said he.

The boy only struggled to free himself. He was crying, mainly from rage.

'Holler 'nuff!' and the pounding went on.

At last the stranger got out a smothered "nuff!" and Tom let him up, and said, 'Now that'll learn you. Better look out who you're fooling with next time.'

The new boy went off brushing the dust from his clothes, sobbing, snuffling, and occasionally looking back and shaking his head, and threatening what he would do to Tom the 'next time he caught him out'. To which Tom responded with jeers, and started off in high feather; and as soon as his back was turned the new boy snatched up a stone, threw it, and hit him between the shoulders, and then turned tail and ran like an antelope. Tom chased the traitor home, and thus found out where he lived. He then held a position at the gate for some time, daring the enemy to come outside; but the enemy only made faces at him through the window, and declined. At last the enemy's mother appeared, and called Tom a bad, vicious, vulgar child, and ordered him away. So he went away, but he said he "'lowed' to 'lay' for that boy.

He got home pretty late that night, and when he climbed cautiously in at the window he uncovered an ambuscade in the person of his aunt; and when she saw the state his clothes were in, her resolution to turn his Saturday holiday into captivity at hard labor became adamantine in its firmness.

Chapter 2

SATURDAY MORNING WAS COME, and all the summer world was bright and fresh, and brimming with life. There was a song in every heart; and if the heart was young the music issued at the lips. There was cheer in every face, and a spring in every step. The locust trees were in bloom, and the fragrance of the blossoms filled the air.

Cardiff Hill, beyond the village and above it, was green with vegetation, and it lay just far enough away to seem a Delectable Land, dreamy, reposeful, and inviting.

Tom appeared on the side-walk with a bucket of whitewash and a long-handled brush. He surveyed the fence, and the gladness went out of nature, and a deep melancholy settled down upon his spirit. Thirty yards of board fence nine feet high! It seemed to him that life was hollow, and existence but a burden. Sighing he dipped his brush and passed it along the topmost plank; repeated the operation; did it again; compared the insignificant whitewashed streak with the far-reaching continent of unwhitewashed fence, and sat down on a tree-box discouraged. Jim came skipping out at the gate with a tin pail, and singing *Buffalo Gals*. Bringing water from the town pump had always been hateful work in Tom's eyes before, but now it did not strike him so. He remembered that there was company at the pump. White, mulatto, and Negro boys and girls were always there waiting their turns, resting, trading playthings, quarrelling, fighting, skylarking. And he remembered that although the pump was only a hundred and fifty yards off Jim never got back with a bucket of water under an hour; and even then somebody generally had to go after him. Tom said:

'Say, Jim; I'll fetch the water if you'll whitewash some.'

Jim shook his head, and said:

'Can't, Ma'rs Tom. Ole missis she tole me I got to go an' git dis water an' not stop foolin' 'roun' wid anybody. She say she spec' Ma'rs Tom gwyne to ax me to whitewash, an' so she tole me go 'long an' 'tend to my own business—she 'lowed *she'd* 'tend to de whitewashin'.'

'Oh, never you mind what she said, Jim. That's the way she always talks. Gimme the bucket—I won't be gone only a minute. *She* won't ever know.'

'Oh, I dasn't, Ma'rs Tom. Ole missis she'd take an' tar de head off'n me. 'Deed she would.'

'*She!* She never licks anybody—whacks 'em over the head with her thimble, and who cares for that, I'd like to know? She talks awful, but talk don't hurt—anyways, it don't if she don't cry. Jim, I'll give you a marble. I'll give you a white alley!'

Jim began to waver.

'White alley, Jim; and it's a bully taw.'

'My; dat's a mighty gay marvel, *I* tell you. But, Ma'rs Tom, I's powerful 'fraid ole missis.'

'And besides, if you will I'll show you my sore toe.'

Jim was only human—this attraction was too much for him. He put down his pail, took the white alley, and bent over the toe with absorbing interest while the bandage was being unwound. In another minute he was flying down the street with his pail and a tingling rear, Tom was whitewashing with vigour, and Aunt Polly was retiring from the field with a slipper in her hand and triumph in her eye.

But Tom's energy did not last. He began to think of the fun he had planned for this day, and his sorrows multiplied. Soon the free boys would come tripping along on all sorts of delicious expeditions, and they would make a world of fun of him for having to work—the very thought of it burnt him like fire. He got out his worldly wealth and examined it—bits of toys, marbles, and trash; enough to buy an exchange of work maybe, but not enough to buy so much as half an hour of pure freedom. So he returned his straitened means to his pocket, and gave up the idea of trying to buy the boys. At this dark and hopeless moment an inspiration burst upon him. Nothing less than a great, magnificent inspiration. He took up his brush and went tranquilly to work. Ben Rogers hove in sight presently, the very boy of all boys whose ridicule he had been dreading. Ben's gait was the hop, skip, and jump—proof enough that his heart was light and his anticipations high. He was eating an apple, and giving a long melodious whoop at intervals, followed by a deep-toned ding dong dong, ding dong dong, for he was personating a steamboat! As he drew near he slackened speed, took the middle of the street, leaned far over to starboard, and rounded-to ponderously, and with laborious pomp and circumstance, for he was personating the *Big Missouri*, and considered himself to be drawing nine feet of water. He was boat, and captain, and engine-bells combined, so he had to imagine himself standing on his own hurricane-deck giving the orders and executing them:

'Stop her, sir! Ling-a-ling-ling.' The headway ran almost out, and he drew up slowly towards the sidewalk. 'Ship up to back! Ling-a-ling-ling!' His arms straightened and stiffened down his sides. 'Set her back on the stabboard! Ling-a-ling-ling! Chow! ch-chow-wow-chow!' his right hand meantime, describing stately circles, for it was representing a forty-foot wheel. 'Let her go back on the labboard! Ling-a-ling-ling! Chow-ch-chow-chow!' The left hand began to describe circles.

'Stop the stabboard! Ling-a-ling-ling! Stop the labboard! Come ahead on the stabboard! Stop her! Let your outside turn over slow! Ling-a-ling-ling! Chow-ow-ow! Get out that head-line! Lively, now! Come—out with your spring-line—what're you about there? Take a turn round that stump with the bight of it! Stand by that stage now—let her go! Done with the engines, sir! Ling-a-ling-ling!'

'Sht! s'sht! sht!' (Trying the gauge-cocks.)

Tom went on whitewashing—paid no attention to the steamer. Ben stared a moment, and then said:

'Hi-yi! You're up a stump, ain't you!'

No answer. Tom surveyed his last touch with the eye of an artist; then he gave his brush another gentle sweep, and surveyed the result as before. Ben ranged up alongside of him. Tom's mouth watered for the apple, but he stuck to his work. Ben said:

'Hello, old chap, you got to work, hey?'

'Why, it's you, Ben! I warn't noticing.'

'Say, I'm going in a swimming, I am. Don't you wish you could? But of course, you'd druther work, wouldn't you? 'Course you would!'

Tom contemplated the boy a bit, and said:

'What do you call work?'

'Why, ain't that work?'

Tom resumed his whitewashing, and answered carelessly:

'Well, maybe it is, and maybe it ain't. All I know is, it suits Tom Sawyer.'

'Oh, come now, you don't mean to let on that you like it?'

The brush continued to move.

'Like it? Well, I don't see why I oughtn't to like it. Does a boy get a chance to whitewash a fence every day?'

That put the thing in a new light. Ben stopped nibbling his apple. Tom swept his brush daintily back and forth—stepped back to note the effect—added a touch here and there—criticized the effect again, Ben watching every move, and getting more and more interested, more and more absorbed. Presently he said:

'Say, Tom, let me whitewash a little.'

Tom considered; was about to consent; but he altered his mind: 'No, no; I reckon it wouldn't hardly do, Ben. You see, Aunt Polly's awful particular about this fence—right here on the street, you know—but if it was the back fence I wouldn't mind, and she wouldn't. Yes, she's awful particular about this fence; it's got to be done very careful; I reckon there ain't one boy in a thousand, maybe two thousand, that can do it the way it's got to be done.'

'No—is that so? Oh, come now; lemme just try, only just a little. I'd let you, if you was me, Tom.'

'Ben, I'd like to, honest injun; but Aunt Polly—well, Jim wanted to do it, but she wouldn't let him. Sid wanted to do it, and she wouldn't let Sid. Now, don't you see how I am fixed? If you was to tackle this fence, and anything was to happen to it—'

'Oh, shucks; I'll be just as careful. Now lemme try. Say—I'll give you the core of my apple.'

'Well, here. No, Ben; now don't; I'm afeard—'

'I'll give you all of it!'

Tom gave up the brush with reluctance in his face, but alacrity in his heart. And while the late steamer *Big Missouri* worked and sweated in the sun, the retired artist sat on a barrel in the shade close by, dangled his legs, munched his apple, and planned the slaughter of more innocents. There was no lack of material; boys happened along every little while; they came to jeer, but remained to whitewash. By the time Ben was fagged out, Tom had traded the next chance to Billy Fisher for a kite in good repair; and when he played out, Johnny Miller bought in for a dead rat and a string to swing it with; and so on, and so on, hour after hour. And when the middle of the afternoon came, from being a poor poverty-stricken boy in the morning Tom was literally rolling in wealth. He had, besides the things I have mentioned, twelve marbles, part of a jew's harp, a piece of blue bottle-glass to look through, a spool-cannon, a key that wouldn't unlock anything, a fragment of chalk, a glass stopper of a decanter, a tin soldier, a couple of tadpoles, six fire-crackers, a kitten with only one eye, a brass door-knob, a dog-collar—but no dog—the handle of a knife, four pieces of orange-peel, and a dilapidated old window sash. He had had a nice, good, idle time all the while—plenty of company—and the fence had three coats of whitewash on it! If he hadn't run out of whitewash he would have bankrupted every boy in the village.

Tom said to himself that it was not such a hollow world after all. He had discovered a great law of human action, without knowing it, namely, that in order to make a man or a boy covet a thing, it is only necessary to make the thing difficult to attain. If he had been a great and wise philosopher, like the writer of this book, he would now have comprehended that work consists of whatever a body is obliged to do, and that play consists of whatever a body is not obliged to do. And this would help him to understand why constructing artificial flowers, or performing on a tread-mill, is work, whilst rolling nine-pins or climbing Mont Blanc is only amusement. There are wealthy gentlemen in England who drive four-horse passenger-coaches twenty or thirty miles on a daily line, in the summer, because the privilege costs them considerable money; but if they were offered wages for the service that would turn it into work, then they would resign.

Chapter 3

Tom PRESENTED HIMSELF before Aunt Polly, who was sitting by an open window in a pleasant rearward apartment, which was bedroom, breakfast-room, dining-room, and library, combined. The balmy summer air, the restful quiet, the odour of the flowers, and the drowsing murmur of the bees had had their effect, and she was nodding over her knitting—for she had no company but the cat, and it was asleep in her lap. Her spectacles were propped up on her grey head for safety. She had thought that of course Tom had deserted long ago, and she wondered to see him place himself in her power again in this intrepid way. He said:

'Mayn't I go and play now, Aunt?'

'What, a'ready? How much have you done?'

'It's all done, Aunt.'

'Tom, don't lie to me. I can't bear it.'

'I ain't, Aunt; it *is* all done.'

Aunt Polly placed small trust in such evidence. She went out to see for herself; and she would have been content to find twenty per cent of Tom's statement true. When she found the entire fence whitewashed, and not only whitewashed but elaborately coated and re-coated, and even a streak added to the ground, her astonishment was almost unspeakable. She said:

'Well, I never! There's no getting round it; you *can* work when you're a mind to, Tom.' And then she diluted the compliment by adding, 'But it's powerful seldom you're a mind to, I'm bound to say. Well, go 'long and play; but mind you get back some time in a week, or I'll tan you.'

She was so overcome by the splendor of his achievement that she took him into the closet and selected a choice apple, and delivered it to him, along with an improving lecture upon the added value and flavour a treat took to itself when it came without sin through virtuous effort. And while she closed with a happy Scriptural flourish, he 'hooked' a doughnut.

Then he skipped out, and saw Sid just starting up the outside stairway that led to the back rooms on the second floor. Clods were handy, and the air was full of them in a twinkling. They raged around Sid like a hailstorm; and before Aunt Polly could collect her surprised faculties and rally to the rescue, six or seven clods had taken personal effect, and Tom was over the fence and gone. There was a gate, but as a general thing he was too crowded for time to make use of it. His soul was at peace now that he had settled with Sid for calling attention to his black thread and getting him into trouble.

Tom skirted the block and came around into a muddy alley that led by the back of his aunt's cow-stable. He presently got safely beyond the reach of capture and punishment, and wended towards the public square of the village, where two 'military' companies of boys had met for conflict, according to previous appointment. Tom was general of one of these armies, Joe Harper (a bosom friend) general of the other. These two great commanders did not condescend to fight in person—that being better suited to the smaller fry—but sat together on an eminence and conducted the field operations by order delivered through aides-de-camp. Tom's army won a great victory, after a long and hard-fought battle. Then the dead were counted, prisoners exchanged, the terms of the next disagreement agreed upon, and the day for the necessary battle appointed; after which the armies fell into line and marched away, and Tom turned homeward alone.

As he was passing by the house where Jeff Thatcher lived, he saw a new girl in the garden—a lovely little blue-eyed creature with yellow hair plaited into two long tails, white summer frock, and embroidered pantalettes. The fresh-crowned hero fell without firing a shot. A certain Amy Lawrence vanished out of his heart, and left not even a memory of herself behind. He had thought he loved her to distraction; he had regarded his passion as adoration; and behold it was only a poor little evanescent partiality. He had been months winning her, she had confessed hardly a week ago; he had been the happiest and the proudest boy in the world only seven short days, and here, in one instant of time, she had gone out of his heart like a casual stranger whose visit is done.

He worshipped this new angel with furtive eye, till he saw that she had discovered him; then he pretended he did not know she was present, and began to 'show off' in all sorts of absurd boyish ways in order to win her admiration. He kept up this grotesque foolishness for some little time; but by-and-by, while he was in the midst of some dangerous gymnastic performances, he glanced aside, and saw that the little girl was wending her way towards the house. Tom came up to the fence, and leaned on it, grieving, and hoping she would tarry yet a while longer. She halted a moment on the steps, and then moved towards the door. Tom heaved a great sigh as she put her foot on the threshold, but his face lit up, right away, for she tossed a pansy over the fence a moment before she disappeared. The boy ran around and stopped within a foot or two of the flower, and then shaded his eyes with his hand, and began to look down street as if he had discovered something of interest going on in that direction. Presently he picked up a straw and began trying to balance it on his nose, with his head tilted far back; and as he moved from side to side in his efforts he edged nearer and nearer towards the pansy; finally his bare foot rested upon it, his pliant toes closed upon it, and he hopped away with his treasure, and disappeared around the corner. But only for a minute— only while he could button the flower inside his jacket, next his heart, or next his stomach possibly, for he was not much posted in anatomy and not hypercritical anyway.

He returned now and hung about the fence till night-fall, 'showing off' as before; but the girl never exhibited herself again, though Tom comforted himself a little with the hope that she had been near some window meantime, and been aware of his attentions. Finally, he went home reluctantly with his poor head full of visions.

All through supper his spirits were so high that his aunt wondered 'what had got into the child'. He took a good scolding about clodding Sid, and did not seem to mind it in the least. He tried to steal sugar under his aunt's very nose, and got his knuckles rapped for it. He said:

'Aunt, you don't whack Sid when he takes it.'

'Well, Sid don't torment a body the way you do. You'd be always into that sugar if I warn't watching you.'

Presently she stepped into the kitchen, and Sid, happy in his immunity, reached for the sugar-bowl, a sort of glorying over Tom which was well-nigh unbearable. But Sid's fingers slipped, and the bowl dropped and broke. Tom was in ecstasies—in such ecstasies that he even controlled his tongue and was silent. He said to himself that he would not speak a word, even when his aunt came in, but would sit perfectly still till she asked who did the mischief; and then he would tell, and there would be nothing so good in the world as to see that pet model 'catch it'. He was so brim-full of exultation that he could hardly hold himself when the old lady came back and stood above the wreck discharging lightnings of wrath from over her spectacles. He said to himself, 'Now it's coming!' And the next instant he was sprawling on the floor! The potent palm was uplifted to strike again, when Tom cried out:

'Hold on, now, what're you belting *me* for? Sid broke it!'

Aunt Polly paused perplexed, and Tom looked for healing pity. But when she got her tongue again she only said:

'Umph! Well, you didn't get a lick amiss, I reckon. You'd been into some other owdacious mischief when I wasn't around, like enough.'

Then her conscience reproached her, and she yearned to say something kind and loving; but she judged that this would be con-strued into a confession that she had been in the wrong, and disci-pline forbade that. So she kept silence, and went about her affairs with a troubled heart. Tom sulked in a corner, and exalted his woes. He knew that in her heart his aunt was on her knees to him, and he was morosely gratified by the consciousness of it. He would hang out no signals, he would take notice of none. He knew that a yearning glance fell upon him, now and then, through a film of tears, but he re-fused recognition of it. He pictured himself lying sick unto death and his aunt bending over him, beseeching one little forgiving word, but he would turn his face to the wall, and die with that word unsaid. Ah, how would she feel then? And he pictured himself brought home from the river, dead, with his curls all wet, and his poor hands still for ever, and his sore heart at rest. How she would throw herself upon him, and how her tears would fall like rain, and her lips pray God to give her back her boy, and she would never, never abuse him any more! But he would lie there cold and white and make no sign—a poor little sufferer whose griefs were at an end. He so worked upon his feelings with the pathos of these dreams that he had to keep swallowing—he was so like to choke; and his eyes swam in a blur of water, which overflowed when he winked, and ran down and trickled from the end of his nose. And such a luxury to him was this petting of his sorrows that he could not bear to have any worldly cheeriness or any grating delight intrude upon it; it was too sacred for such contact; and so presently, when his cousin Mary danced in, all alive with the joy of seeing home again after an age-long visit of one week to the country, he got up and moved in clouds and darkness out at one door as she brought song and sunshine in at the other. He wandered far away from the accustomed haunts of boys, and sought desolate places that were in harmony with his spirit. A log raft in the river invited him, and he seated himself on its outer edge, and contemplated the dreary vastness of the stream, wishing the while that he could only be drowned, all at once and unconsciously, without undergoing the uncomfortable routine devised by nature. Then he thought of his flower. He got it out, rumpled and wilted, and it mightily increased his dismal felicity. He wondered if *she* would pity him if she knew! Would she cry, and wish that she had a right to put her arms around his neck and comfort him? Or would she turn coldly away like all the hollow world? This picture brought such an agony of pleasurable suffering that he worked it over and over again in his mind and set it up in new and varied lights till he wore it threadbare. At last he rose up sighing and departed in the darkness. About half past nine or ten o'clock he came along the deserted street to where the adored unknown lived; he paused a moment, no sound fell upon his listening ear; a candle was casting a dull glow upon the curtain of a second-story window. Was the sacred presence there? He climbed the fence, threaded his stealthy way through the plants, till he stood under that window; he looked up at it long, and with emotion; then he laid him down on the ground under it, disposing himself upon his back, with his hands clasped upon his breast, and holding his poor wilted flower. And thus he would die—out in the cold world with no shelter over his homeless head, no friendly hand to wipe the death-damps from his brow, no loving face to bend pityingly over him when the great agony came. And thus *she* would see him when she looked out upon the glad morning—and oh, would she drop one tear upon his poor lifeless form, would she heave one little sigh to see a bright young life so rudely blighted, so untimely cut down?

The window went up; a maid-servant's discordant voice profaned the holy calm, and a deluge of water drenched the prone martyr's remains!

The strangling hero sprang up with a relieving snort; there was a whiz as of a missile in the air, mingled with the murmur of a curse, a sound as of shivering glass followed, and a small vague form went over the fence and shot away in the gloom.

Not long after, as Tom, all undressed for bed, was surveying his drenched garments by the light of a tallow dip, Sid woke up; but if he had any dim idea of making 'references to allusions', he thought better of it, and held his peace—for there was danger in Tom's eye. Tom turned in without the added vexation of prayers, and Sid made mental note of the omission.

Chapter 4

THE SUN ROSE upon a tranquil world, and beamed down upon the peaceful village like a benediction. Breakfast over, Aunt Polly had family worship; it began with a prayer built from the ground up of solid courses of scriptural quotations welded together with a thin mortar of originality; and from the summit of this she delivered a grim chapter of the Mosaic Law, as from Sinai.

Then Tom girded up his loins, so to speak, and went to work to 'get his verses'. Sid had learned his lesson days before. Tom bent all his energies to the memorizing of five verses; and he chose part of the Sermon on the Mount, because he could find no verses that were shorter.

At the end of half an hour Tom had a vague general idea of his lesson, but no more, for his mind was traversing the whole field of human thought, and his hands were busy with distracting recreations. Mary took his book to hear him recite, and he tried to find his way through the fog.

'Blessed are the—a—a—'

'Poor—'

'Yes—poor; blessed are the poor—a—a—'

'In spirit—'

'In spirit; blessed are the poor in spirit, for they—they—'

'Theirs—'

'For theirs. Blessed are the poor in spirit, for theirs—is the kingdom of Heaven. Blessed are they that mourn, for they—they—'

'Sh—'

'For they—a—'

'S-H-A—'

'For they S-H—Oh, I don't know what it is!'

'Shall!'

'Oh, shall! for they shall—for they shall—a—a—shall mourn—a—a—blessed are they that shall—they that—a—they that shall mourn, for they shall—a—shall what? Why don't you tell me, Mary? What do you want to be so mean for?'

'Oh, Tom, you poor thick-headed thing, I'm not teasing you. I wouldn't do that. You must go and learn it again. Don't you be discouraged, Tom, you'll manage it—and if you do, I'll give you something ever so nice. There, now, that's a good boy.'

'All right! What is it, Mary? Tell me what it is.'

'Never you mind, Tom. You know if I say it's nice, it is nice.'

'You bet you that's so, Mary. All right, I'll tackle it again.'

And he did 'tackle it again'; and under the double pressure of curiosity and prospective gain, he did it with such spirit that he accomplished a shining success.

Mary gave him a brand-new 'Barlow' knife, worth twelve and a half cents; and the convulsion of delight that swept his system shook him to his foundations. True, the knife would not cut anything, but it was a 'sure-enough' Barlow, and there was inconceivable grandeur in that—though where the western boys ever got the idea that such a weapon could possibly be counterfeited to its injury is an imposing mystery, and will always remain so, perhaps. Tom contrived to scarify the cupboard with it and was arranging to begin on the bureau, when he was called off to dress for Sunday-school.

Mary gave him a tin basin of water and a piece of soap, and he went outside the door and set the basin on a little bench there; then he dipped the soap in the water and laid it down; turned up his sleeves; poured out the water on the ground gently, and then entered the kitchen, and began to wipe his face diligently on the towel behind the door. But Mary removed the towel and said:

'Now ain't you ashamed, Tom? You mustn't be so bad. Water won't hurt you.'

Tom was a trifle disconcerted. The basin was refilled, and this time he stood over it a little while, gathering resolution; took in a big breath and began. When he entered the kitchen presently, with both eyes shut, and groping for the towel with his hands, an honourable testimony of suds and water was dripping from his face. But when he emerged from the towel, he was not yet satisfactory; for the clean territory stopped short at his chin and his jaws like a mask; below and beyond this line there was a dark expanse of unirrigated soil that spread downward in front and backward around his neck. Mary took him in hand, and when she was done with him he was a man and a brother, without distinction of colour, and his saturated hair was neatly brushed, and its short curls wrought into a dainty and symmetrical general effect.

(He privately smoothed out the curls, with labour and difficulty, and plastered his hair close down to his head; for he held curls to be effeminate, and his own filled his life with bitterness.) Then Mary got out a suit of his clothing that had been used only on Sundays during two years—they were simply called his 'other clothes'—and so by that we know the size of his wardrobe. The girl 'put him to rights' after he had dressed himself; she buttoned his neat roundabout up to his chin, turned his vast shirt-collar down over his shoulders, brushed him off and crowned him with his speckled straw hat. He now looked exceedingly improved and uncomfortable; he was fully as uncomfortable as he looked; for there was a restraint about whole clothes and cleanliness that galled him. He hoped that Mary would forget his shoes, but the hope was blighted; she coated them thoroughly with tallow, as was the custom, and brought them out. He lost his temper and said he was always being made to do everything he didn't want to do. But Mary said, persuasively:

'Please, Tom—that's a good boy.'

So he got into his shoes, snarling. Mary was soon ready, and the three children set out for Sunday-school, a place that Tom hated with his whole heart; but Sid and Mary were fond of it.

Sabbath-school hours were from nine to half-past ten; and then church service. Two of the children always remained for the sermon voluntarily; and the other always remained too, for stronger reasons. The church's high-backed uncushioned pews would seat about three hundred persons; the edifice was but a small, plain affair, with a sort of pine-board tree-box on top of it for a steeple. At the door Tom dropped back a step and accosted a Sunday-dressed comrade:

'Say, Bill, got a yaller ticket?'

'Yes.'

'What'll you take for her?'

'What'll you give?'

'Piece of lickrish and a fish-hook.'

'Less see 'em.'

Tom exhibited. They were satisfactory, and the property changed hands. Then Tom traded a couple of white alleys for three red tickets, and some small trifle or other for a couple of blue ones. He waylaid other boys as they came, and went on buying tickets of various colours ten or fifteen minutes longer. He entered the church, now, with a swarm of clean and noisy boys and girls, proceeded to his seat and started a quarrel with the first boy that came handy. The teacher, a grave, elderly man, interfered; then turned his back a moment, and Tom pulled a boy's hair in the next bench, and was absorbed in his book when the boy turned around; stuck a pin in another boy, presently, in order to hear him say 'Ouch!' and got a new reprimand from his teacher. Tom's whole class were of a pattern—restless, noisy, and troublesome. When they came to recite their lessons, not one of them knew his verses perfectly, but had to be prompted all along. However, they worried through, and each got his reward in small blue tickets, each with a passage of Scripture on it; each blue ticket was pay for two verses of the recitation. Ten blue tickets equalled a red one, and could be exchanged for it; ten red tickets equalled a yellow one; for ten yellow tickets the Superintendent gave a very plainly bound Bible (worth forty cents in those easy times) to the pupil. How many of my readers would have the industry and the application to memorize two thousand verses, even for a Doré Bible? And yet Mary had acquired two Bibles in this way; it was the patient work of two years: and a boy of German parentage had won four or five. He once recited three thousand verses without stopping; but the strain upon his mental faculties was too great, and he was little better than an idiot from that day forth—a grievous misfortune for the school, for on great occasions before company the Superintendent (as Tom expressed it) had always made this boy come out and 'spread himself'. Only the older pupils managed to keep their tickets and stick to their tedious work long enough to get a Bible, and so the delivery of one of these prizes was a rare and noteworthy circumstance; the successful pupil was so great and conspicuous for that day that on the spot every scholar's breast was fired with a fresh ambition that often lasted a couple of weeks. It is possible that Tom's mental stomach had never really hungered for one of those prizes, but unquestionably his entire being had for many a day longed for the glory and the *éclat* that came with it.

In due course the Superintendent stood up in front of the pulpit, with a closed hymn-book in his hand and his forefinger inserted between its leaves, and commanded attention. When a Sunday-school superintendent makes his customary little speech, a hymn-book in the hand is as necessary as is the inevitable sheet of music in the hand of a singer who stands forward on the platform and sings a solo at a concert—though why is a mystery; for neither the hymn-book nor the sheet of music is ever referred to by the sufferer. This

Superintendent was a slim creature of thirty-five, with a sandy goatee, and short sandy hair; he wore a stiff standing-collar whose upper edge almost reached his ears, and whose sharp points curved forward abreast the corners of his mouth—a fence that compelled a straight look-out ahead, and a turning of the whole body when a side view was required. His chin was propped on a spreading cravat, which was as broad and as long as a bank-note, and had fringed ends; his boot toes were turned sharply up, in the fashion of the day, like sleigh-runners—an effect patiently and laboriously produced by the young men by sitting with their toes pressed against a wall for hours together. Mr Walters was very earnest of mien, and very sincere and honest at heart; and he held sacred things and places in such reverence, and so separated them from worldly matters, that unconsciously to himself his Sunday-school voice had acquired a peculiar intonation which was wholly absent on week-days. He began after this fashion:

'Now, children, I want you all to sit up just as straight and pretty as you can, and give me all your attention for a minute or two. There, that is it. That is the way good little boys and girls should do. I see one little girl who is looking out of the window—I am afraid she thinks I am out there somewhere—perhaps up in one of the trees making a speech to the little birds. [Applausive titter.] I want to tell you how good it makes me feel to see so many bright, clean little faces assembled in a place like this, learning to do right and be good.'

And so forth, and so on. It is not necessary to set down the rest of the oration. It was of a pattern which does not vary, and so it is familiar to us all.

The latter third of the speech was marred by the resumption of fights and other recreations among certain of the bad boys, and by fidgetings and whisperings that extended far and wide, washing even to the bases of isolated and incorruptible rocks like Sid and Mary. But now every sound ceased suddenly with the subsidence of Mr Walters's voice, and the conclusion of the speech was received with a burst of silent gratitude.

A good part of the whispering had been occasioned by an event which was more or less rare—the entrance of visitors; Lawyer Thatcher, accompanied by a very feeble and aged man, a fine, portly, middle-aged gentleman with iron-grey hair, and a dignified lady who was doubtless the latter's wife. The lady was leading a child. Tom had been restless and full of chafings and repinings, conscience-smitten, too—he could not meet Amy Lawrence's eye, he could not brook her loving gaze. But when he saw this small new-comer his soul was all ablaze with bliss in a moment. The next moment he was 'showing off' with all his might—cuffing boys, pulling hair, making faces, in a word, using every art that seemed likely to fascinate a girl, and win her applause. His exultation had but one alloy—the memory of his humiliation in this angel's garden; and that record in sand was fast washing out under the waves of happiness that were sweeping over it now. The visitors were given the highest seat of honour, and as soon as Mr Walters's speech was finished he introduced them to the school. The middle-aged man turned out to be a prodigious personage; no less a one than the county judge—altogether the most august creation these children had ever looked upon; and they wondered what kind of material he was made of; and they half wanted to hear him roar, and were half afraid he might, too. He was from Constantinople, twelve miles away—so he had travelled and seen the world—these very eyes had looked upon the County Court House, which was said to have a tin roof. The awe which these reflections inspired was attested by the impressive silence and the ranks of staring eyes. This was the great Judge Thatcher, brother of their own lawyer. Jeff Thatcher immediately went forward to be familiar with the great man and be envied by the school. It would have been music to his soul to hear the whisperings.

'Look at him, Jim! he's a going up there. Say, look! he's a going to shake hands with him; he *is* a shaking hands with him! By jinks, don't you wish you was Jeff?'

Mr Walters fell to 'showing off' with all sorts of official bustlings and activities, giving orders, delivering judgments, discharging directions here, there, everywhere that he could find a target. The librarian 'showed off', running hither and thither with his arms full of books and making a deal of the splutter and fuss that insect authority delights in. The young lady teachers 'showed off'—bending sweetly over pupils that were lately being boxed, lifting pretty warning fingers at bad little boys and patting good ones lovingly. The young gentlemen teachers 'showed off' with small scoldings and other little displays of authority and fine attention to discipline; and most of the teachers, of both sexes, found business up at the library by the pulpit; and it was business that frequently had to be done over again two or three times (with much seeming vexation). The little girls 'showed off' in various ways, and the little boys 'showed off' with such diligence that the air was thick with paper wads and the murmur of scufflings. And above it all the great man sat and beamed a majestic judicial smile upon all the house, and warmed himself in the sun of his own grandeur, for he was 'showing off' too. There was only one thing wanting to make Mr Walters's ecstasy complete, and that was a chance to deliver a Bible-prize and exhibit a prodigy. Several pupils had a few yellow tickets, but none had enough—he had been around among the star pupils inquiring. He would have given worlds, now, to have that German lad back again with a sound mind.

And now at this moment, when hope was dead, Tom Sawyer came forward with nine yellow tickets, nine red tickets, and ten blue ones, and demanded a Bible! This was a thunderbolt out of a clear sky. Walters was not expecting an application from this source for the next ten years. But there was no getting around it—here were the certified checks, and they were good for their face. Tom was therefore elevated to a place with the Judge and the other elect, and the great news was announced from headquarters. It was the most stunning surprise of the decade; and so profound was the sensation that it lifted the new hero up to the judicial one's altitude, and the school had two marvels to gaze upon in place of one. The boys were all eaten up with envy; but those that suffered the bitterest pangs were those who perceived too late that they themselves had contributed to this hated splendour by trading tickets to Tom for the wealth he had amassed in selling whitewashing privileges. These despised themselves, as being the dupes of a wily fraud, a guileful snake in the grass.

The prize was delivered to Tom with as much effusion as the Superintendent could pump up under the circumstances; but it lacked somewhat of the true gush, for the poor fellow's instinct taught him that there was a mystery here that could not well bear the light, perhaps; it was simply preposterous that *this* boy had warehoused two thousand sheaves of Scriptural wisdom on his premises—a dozen would strain his capacity, without a doubt. Amy Lawrence was proud and glad, and she tried to make Tom see it in her face; but he wouldn't look. She wondered; then she was just a grain troubled; next a dim suspicion came and went—came again; she watched; a furtive glance told her worlds—and then her heart broke, and she was jealous, and angry, and the tears came and she hated everybody; Tom most of all, she thought.

Tom was introduced to the Judge; but his tongue was tied, his breath would hardly come, his heart quaked—partly because of the awful greatness of the man, but mainly because he was *her* parent. He would have liked to fall down and worship him, if it were in the dark. The Judge put his hand on Tom's head and called him a fine little man, and asked him what his name was. The boy stammered, gasped, and got it out:

'Tom.'

'Oh, no, not Tom—it is—'

'Thomas.'

'Ah, that's it. I thought there was more to it, maybe. That's very well. But you've another one, I dare say, and you'll tell it to me, won't you?'

'Tell the gentleman your other name, Thomas,' said Walters, 'and say *sir*. You mustn't forget your manners.'

'Thomas Sawyer—sir.'

'That's it! that's a good boy. Fine boy. Fine, manly little fellow. Two thousand verses is a great many—very, very great many. And you never can be sorry for the trouble you took to learn them; for knowledge is worth more than anything there is in the world; it's what makes great men and good men; you'll be a great man and a good man yourself some day, Thomas, and then you'll look back and say, It's all owing to the precious Sunday-school privileges of my boyhood; it's all owing to my dear teachers that taught me to learn; it's all owing to the good Superintendent, who encouraged me and watched over me, and gave me a beautiful Bible, a splendid, elegant Bible, to keep and have it all for my own, always; it's all owing to right bringing up! That is what you will say, Thomas; and you wouldn't take any money for those two thousand verses, then—no, indeed you wouldn't. And now you wouldn't mind telling me and this lady some of the things you've learned— no, I know you wouldn't—for we are proud of little boys that learn. Now no doubt you know the names of all the twelve disciples. Won't you tell us the names of the first two that were appointed?'

Tom was tugging at a button and looking sheepish. He blushed, now, and his eyes fell. Mr Walters's heart sank within him. He said to himself, It is not possible that the boy can answer the simplest question— why *did* the Judge ask him? Yet he felt obliged to speak up and say:

'Answer the gentleman, Thomas—don't be afraid.'

Tom still hung fire.

'Now I know you'll tell *me*,' said the lady. 'The names of the first two disciples were—'

'DAVID AND GOLIATH!'

Let us draw the curtain of charity over the rest of the scene.

Chapter 5

ABOUT HALF PAST TEN the cracked bell of the small church began to ring, and presently the people began to gather for the morning sermon. The Sunday-school children distributed themselves about the house, and occupied pews with their parents, so as to be under supervision. Aunt Polly came, and Tom, and Sid and Mary sat with her, Tom being placed next the aisle, in order that he might be as far away from the open window and the seductive outside summer scenes as possible. The crowd filed up the aisle; the aged and needy postmaster, who had seen better days; the mayor and his wife—for they had a mayor there, among other unnecessaries; the justice of the peace; the widow Douglas, fair, smart, and forty, a generous, good-hearted soul and well-to-do, her hill mansion the only palace in the town, and the most hospitable and much the most lavish in the matter of festivities that St Petersburg could boast; the bent and venerable mayor and Mrs Ward; Lawyer Riverson, the new notable from a distance; next the belle of the village, followed by a troop of lawn-clad and ribbon-decked young heart-breakers; then all the young clerks in town in a body—for they had stood in the vestibule sucking their cane-heads, a circling wall of oiled and simpering admirers, till the last girl had run their gauntlet; and last of all came the model boy, Willie Mufferson, taking as heedful care of his mother as if she were cut glass. He always brought his mother to church, and was the pride of all the matrons. The boys all hated him, he was so good; and besides, he had been 'thrown up to them' so much. His white handkerchief was hanging out of his pocket behind, as usual on Sundays—accidentally. Tom had no handkerchief and he looked upon boys who had as snobs. The congregation being fully assembled now, the bell rang once more, to warn laggards and stragglers, and then a solemn hush fell upon the church, which was only broken by the tittering and whispering of the choir in the gallery. The choir always tittered and whispered all through service. There was once a church choir that was not ill-bred, but I have forgotten where it was, now. It was a great many years ago, and I can scarcely remember anything about it, but I think it was in some foreign country.

The minister gave out the hymn, and read it through with a relish, in a peculiar style which was much admired in that part of the country. His voice began on a medium key, and climbed steadily up till it reached a certain point, where it bore with strong emphasis upon the topmost word, and then plunged down as if from a spring-board:

Shall I be car-ri-ed toe the skies, on flow'ry beds

of ease.

Whilst others fight to win the prize, and sail thro' blood-

y seas?

He was regarded as a wonderful reader. At church 'sociables' he was always called upon to read poetry; and when he was through, the ladies would lift up their hands and let them fall helplessly in their laps, and 'wall' their eyes, and shake their heads, as much as to say, 'Words cannot express it; it is too beautiful, *too* beautiful for this mortal earth.'

After the hymn had been sung, the Rev Mr Sprague turned himself into a bulletin-board and read off 'notices' of meetings and societies and things till it seemed that the list would stretch out to the crack of doom—a queer custom which is still kept up in America, even in cities, away here in this age of abundant newspapers. Often the less there is to justify a traditional custom, the harder it is to get rid of it.

And now the minister prayed. A good, generous prayer it was, and went into details: it pleaded for the Church, and the little children of the Church; for the other churches of the village; for the village itself; for the county; for the State; for the State officers; for the United States; for the churches of the United States; for Congress; for the President; for the officers of the Government; for poor sailors, tossed by stormy seas; for the oppressed millions groaning under the heel of European monarchies and Oriental despotisms; for such as have the light and the good tidings, and yet have no eyes to see nor ears to hear withal; for the heathen in the far islands of the sea; and closed with a supplication that the words he was about to speak might find grace and favour, and be as seed sown in fertile ground, yielding in time a grateful harvest of good. Amen.

There was a rustling of dresses, and the standing congregation sat down. The boy whose history this book relates did not enjoy the prayer, he only endured it—if he even did that much. He was restive all through it; he kept tally of the details of the prayer, unconsciously—for he was not listening, but he knew the ground of old and the clergyman's regular route over it—and when a little trifle of new matter was interlarded, his ear detected it and his whole nature resented it; he considered additions unfair, and scoundrelly. In the midst of the prayer a fly had lit on the back of the pew in front of him, and tortured his spirit by calmly rubbing its hands together, embracing its head with its arms and polishing it so vigorously that it seemed to almost part company with the body, and the slender thread of a neck was exposed to view; scraping its wings with its hind legs and smoothing them to its body as if they had been coat-tails; going through its whole toilet as tranquilly as if it knew it was perfectly safe. As indeed it was; for as sorely as Tom's hands itched to grab for it they did not dare—he believed his soul would be instantly destroyed if he did such a thing while the prayer was going on. But with the closing sentence his hand began to curve and steal forward; and the instant the 'Amen' was out, the fly was a prisoner of war. His aunt detected the act, and made him let it go.

The minister gave out his text and droned along monotonously through an argument that was so prosy that many a head by-and-by began to nod—and yet it was an argument that dealt in limitless fire and brimstone, and thinned the predestined elect down to a company so small as to be hardly worth the saving. Tom counted the pages of the sermon; after church he always knew how many pages there had been, but he seldom knew anything else about the discourse. However, this time he was really interested for a little while. The minister made a grand and moving picture of the assembling together of the world's hosts at the millennium when the lion and the lamb should lie down together and a little child should lead them. But the pathos, the lesson, the moral of the great spectacle were lost upon the boy; he only thought of the conspicuousness of the principal character before the onlooking nations; his face lit up with the thought, and he said to himself that he wished he could be that child, if it was a tame lion.

Now he lapsed into suffering again, as the dry argument was resumed. Presently he bethought himself of a treasure he had, and got it out. It was a large black beetle with formidable jaws—a 'pinch-bug', he called it. It was in a percussion-cap box. The first thing the beetle did was to take him by the finger. A natural fillip followed, the beetle went floundering into the aisle, and lit on its back, and the hurt finger went into the boy's mouth. The beetle lay there working its helpless legs, unable to turn over. Tom eyed it, and longed for it, but it was safe out of his reach. Other people, uninterested in the sermon, found relief in the beetle, and they eyed it too.

Presently a vagrant poodle dog came idling along, sad at heart, lazy with the summer softness and the quiet, weary of captivity, sighing for change. He spied the beetle; the drooping tail lifted and wagged. He surveyed the prize; walked around it; smelt of it from a safe distance; walked around it again; grew bolder, and took a closer smell; then lifted his lips, and made a gingerly snatch at it, just missing it; made another, and another; began to enjoy the diversion; subsided to his stomach with the beetle between his paws, and continued his experiments; grew weary at last, and then indifferent and absent-minded. His head nodded, and little by little his chin descended and touched the enemy, who seized it. There was a sharp yelp, a flirt of the poodle's head and the beetle fell a couple of yards away, and lit on its back once more. The neighbouring spectators shook with a gentle inward joy, several faces went behind fans and handkerchiefs, and Tom was entirely happy. The dog looked foolish, and probably felt so; but there was resentment in his heart, too, and a craving for revenge. So he went to the beetle and began a wary attack on it again; jumping at it from every point of a circle, lighting with his forepaws within an inch of the creature, making even closer snatches at it with his teeth, and jerking his head till his ears flapped again. But he grew tired once more, after a while; tried to amuse himself with a fly, but found no relief; followed an ant around, with his nose close to the floor, and quickly wearied of that; yawned, sighed, forgot the beetle entirely, and sat down on it! Then there was a wild yelp of agony, and the poodle went sailing up the aisle; the yelps continued, and so did the dog; he crossed the house in front of the altar, he flew down the other aisle; he crossed before the doors; he clamored up the home-stretch; his anguish grew with his progress, till presently he was but a woolly comet moving in its orbit with the gleam and the speed of light. At last the frantic sufferer sheered from its course and sprang into its master's lap; he flung it out of the window, and the voice of distress quickly thinned away and died in the distance.

By this time the whole church was red-faced and suffocating with suppressed laughter, and the sermon had come to a dead standstill. The discourse was resumed presently, but it went lame and halting, all possibility of impressiveness being at an end; for even the gravest sentiments were constantly being received with a smothered burst of unholy mirth, under cover of some remote pew-back, as if the poor parson had said a rarely facetious thing. It was a genuine relief to the whole congregation when the ordeal was over and the benediction pronounced.

Tom Sawyer went home quite cheerful, thinking to himself that there was some satisfaction about divine service when there was a bit of variety in it. He had but one marring thought; he was willing that the dog should play with his pinch-bug, but he did not think it was upright in him to carry it off.

Chapter 6

Monday morning found Tom Sawyer miserable. Monday morning always found him so, because it began another week's slow suffering in school. He generally began that day with wishing he had had no intervening holiday, it made the going into captivity and fetters again so much more odious.

Tom lay thinking. Presently it occurred to him that he wished he was sick; then he could stay home from school. Here was a vague possibility. He canvassed his system. No ailment was found, and he investigated again. This time he thought he could detect colicky symptoms, and he began to encourage them with considerable hope. But they soon grew feeble, and presently died wholly away. He reflected further. Suddenly he discovered something. One of his upper front teeth was loose. This was lucky; he was about to begin to groan, as a 'starter', as he called it, when it occurred to him that if he came into court with that argument, his aunt would pull it out, and that would hurt. So he thought he would hold the tooth in reserve for the present, and seek further. Nothing offered for some little time, and then he remembered hearing the doctor tell about a certain thing that laid up a patient for two or three weeks and threatened to make him lose a finger. So the boy eagerly drew his sore toe from under the sheet and held it up for inspection. But now he did not know the necessary symptoms. However, it seemed well worth while to chance it, so he fell to groaning with considerable spirit.

But Sid slept on, unconscious.

Tom groaned louder, and fancied that he began to feel pain in the toe.

No result from Sid.

Tom was panting with his exertions by this time. He took a rest and then swelled himself up and fetched a succession of admirable groans.

Sid snored on.

Tom was aggravated. He said, 'Sid, Sid!' and shook him. This course worked well, and Tom began to groan again. Sid yawned, stretched, then brought himself up on his elbow with a snort, and began to stare at Tom. Tom went on groaning. Sid said:

'Tom! say, Tom!'

No response.

'Here, Tom! Tom! What is the matter, Tom?' And he shook him, and looked in his face anxiously.

Tom moaned out:

'Oh, don't, Sid. Don't joggle me.'

'Why, what's the matter, Tom? I must call Auntie.'

'No, never mind. It'll be over by and by, maybe. Don't call anybody.'

'But I must! Don't groan so, Tom, it's awful. How long you been this way?'

'Hours. Ouch! Oh, don't stir so, Sid. You'll kill me.'

'Tom, why didn't you wake me sooner? Oh, Tom, don't! It makes my flesh crawl to hear you. Tom, what is the matter?'

'I forgive you everything, Sid. [Groan.] Everything you've ever done to me. When I'm gone—'

'Oh, Tom, you ain't dying, are you? Don't, Tom. Oh, don't. Maybe—'

'I forgive everybody, Sid. [Groan.] Tell 'em so, Sid. And, Sid, you give my window-sash, and my cat with one eye to that new girl that's come to town, and tell her—'

But Sid had snatched his clothes and gone. Tom was suffering in reality now, so handsomely was his imagination working, and so his groans had gathered quite a genuine tone.

Sid flew downstairs and said:

'Oh, Aunt Polly, come! Tom's dying!'

'Dying!'

'Yes'm. Don't wait, come quick!'

'Rubbage! I don't believe it!'

But she fled upstairs nevertheless, with Sid and Mary at her heels. And her face grew white, too, and her lip trembled. When she reached the bedside she gasped out:

'You Tom! Tom, what's the matter with you?'

'Oh, Auntie, I'm—'

'What's the matter with you—what *is* the matter with you, child?'

'Oh, Auntie, my sore toe's mortified!'

The old lady sank down into a chair and laughed a little, then cried a little, then did both together. This restored her, and she said:

'Tom, what a turn you did give me. Now you shut up that nonsense and climb out of this.'

The groans ceased and the pain vanished from the toe. The boy felt a little foolish, and he said:

'Aunt Polly, it *seemed* mortified, and it hurt so I never minded my tooth at all.'

'Your tooth, indeed! What's the matter with your tooth?'

'One of them's loose, and it aches perfectly awful.'

'There, there now, don't begin that groaning again. Open your mouth. Well, your tooth *is* loose, but you're not going to die about that. Mary, get me a silk thread, and a chunk of fire out of the kitchen.'

Tom said:

'Oh, please, Auntie, don't pull it out, it don't hurt any more. I wish I may never stir if it does. Please don't, Auntie, I don't want to stay home from school.'

'Oh, you don't, don't you? So all this row was because you thought you'd get to stay home from school and go a fishing? Tom, Tom, I love you so, and you seem to try every way you can to break my old heart with your outrageousness.'

By this time the dental instruments were ready. The old lady made one end of the silk thread fast to Tom's tooth with a loop and tied the other to the bed-post. Then she seized the chunk of fire and suddenly thrust it almost into the boy's face. The tooth hung dangling by the bed-post, now.

But all trials bring their compensations. As Tom wended to school after breakfast, he was the envy of every boy he met because the gap in his upper row of teeth enabled him to expectorate in a new and admirable way. He gathered quite a following of lads interested in the exhibition; and one that had cut his finger and had been a centre of fascination and homage up to this time, now found himself suddenly without an adherent, and shorn of his glory. His heart was heavy, and he said with a disdain which he did not feel, that it wasn't anything to spit like Tom Sawyer; but another boy said 'Sour grapes!' and he wandered away a dismantled hero.

Shortly Tom came upon the juvenile pariah of the village, Huckleberry Finn, son of the town drunkard. Huckleberry was cordially hated and dreaded by all the mothers of the town because he was idle, and lawless, and vulgar, and bad—and because all their children admired him so, and delighted in his forbidden society, and wished they dared to be like him. Tom was like the rest of the respectable boys in that he envied Huckleberry his gaudy outcast condition, and was under strict orders not to play with him. So he played with him every time he got a chance. Huckleberry was always dressed in the cast-off clothes of full-grown men, and they were in perennial bloom and fluttering with rags. His hat was a vast ruin with a wide crescent lopped out of its brim; his coat, when he wore one, hung nearly to his heels, and had the rearward buttons far down the back; but one suspender supported his trousers; the seat of the trousers bagged low and contained nothing; the fringed legs dragged in the dirt when not rolled up. Huckleberry came and went at his own free will. He slept on door-steps in fine weather, and in empty hogsheads in wet; he did not have to go to school or to church, or call any being master, or obey anybody; he could go fishing or swimming when and where he chose, and stay as long as it suited him; nobody forbade him to fight; he could sit up as late as he pleased; he was always the first boy that went barefoot in the spring and the last to resume leather in the fall; he never had to wash, nor put on clean clothes; he could swear wonderfully. In a word, everything that goes to make life precious, that boy had. So thought every harassed, hampered, respectable boy in St Petersburg. Tom hailed the romantic outcast:

'Hello, Huckleberry!'

'Hello yourself, and see how you like it.'

'What's that you got?'

'Dead cat.'

'Lemme see him, Huck. My, he's pretty stiff. Where'd you get him?'

'Bought him off'n a boy.'

'What did you give?'

'I give a blue ticket and a bladder that I got at the slaughter-house.'

'Where'd you get the blue ticket?'

'Bought it off'n Ben Rogers two weeks ago for a hoop-stick.'

'Say—what is dead cats good for, Huck?'

'Good for? Cure warts with.'

'No! Is that so? I know something that's better.'

'I bet you don't. What is it?'

'Why, spunk-water.'

'Spunk-water! I wouldn't give a dern for spunk-water.'

'You wouldn't, wouldn't you? D'you ever try it?'

'No, I hain't. But Bob Tanner did.'

'Who told you so!'

'Why, he told Jeff Thatcher, and Jeff told Johnny Baker, and Johnny told Jim Hollis, and Jim told Ben Rogers, and Ben told a nigger, and the nigger told me. There now!'

'Well, what of it? They'll all lie. Leastways all but the nigger, I don't know *him*. But I never see a nigger that *wouldn't* lie. Shucks! Now you tell me how Bob Tanner done it, Huck.'

'Why, he took and dipped his hand in a rotten stump where the rain-water was.'

'In the daytime?'

'Certainly.'

'With his face to the stump?'

'Yes. Least I reckon so.'

'Did he *say* anything?'

'I don't reckon he did, I don't know.'

'Aha! Talk about trying to cure warts with spunk-water such a blame fool way as that! Why, that ain't a going to do any good. You got to go all by yourself to the middle of the woods, where you know there's a spunk-water stump, and just as it's midnight you back up against the stump and jam your hand in and say:

> Barley-corn, barley-corn, injun-meal shorts,
> Spunk-water, spunk-water, swaller these warts,

and then walk away quick, eleven steps, with your eyes shut, and then turn around three times and walk home without speaking to anybody. Because if you speak the charm's busted.'

'Well, that sounds like a good way; but that ain't the way Bob Tanner done.'

'No, sir, you can bet he didn't, becuz he's the wartiest boy in this town; and he wouldn't have a wart on him if he'd knowed how to work spunk-water. I've took off thousands of warts off of my hands that way, Huck. I play with frogs so much that I've always got considerable many warts. Sometimes I take 'em off with a bean.'

'Yes, bean's good. I've done that.'

'Have you? What's your way?'

'You take and split the bean, and cut the wart so as to get some blood, and then you put the blood on one piece of the bean, and take and dig a hole and bury it 'bout midnight at the cross-roads in the dark of the moon, and then you burn up the rest of the bean. You see that piece that's got the blood on it will keep drawing and drawing, trying to fetch the other piece to it, and so that helps the blood to draw the wart, and pretty soon off she comes.'

'Yes, that's it, Huck—that's it; though, when you're burying it, if you say, "Down bean, off wart; come no more to bother me!" it's better. That's the way Joe Harper does, and he's ben nearly to Coonville, and most everywhere. But say—how do you cure 'em with dead cats?'

'Why, you take your cat and go and get in the graveyard, 'long about midnight, where somebody that was wicked has been buried; and when it's midnight a devil will come, or maybe two or three, but you can't see 'em, you can only hear something like the wind, or maybe hear 'em talk; and when they're taking that feller away, you heave your cat after 'em and say, "Devil follow corpse, cat follow devil, warts follow cat. I'm done with ye!" That'll fetch any wart.'

'Sounds right. D'you ever try it, Huck?'

'No, but old Mother Hopkins told me.'

'Well, I reckon it's so, then, becuz they say she's a witch.'

'Say! Why, Tom, I know she is. She witched pap. Pap says so his own self. He come along one day, and he see she was a witching him, so he took up a rock, and if she hadn't dodged, he'd a got her. Well, that very night he rolled off'n a shed wher' he was a layin' drunk, and broke his arm.'

'Why, that's awful. How did he know she was a witching him?'

'Lord, pap can tell, easy. Pap says when they keep looking at you right stiddy, they're a witching you, specially if they mumble. Becuz when they mumble they're a saying the Lord's Prayer backards.'

'Say, Hucky, when you going to try the cat?'

'Tonight. I reckon they'll come after old Hoss Williams tonight.'

'But they buried him Saturday, Huck. Didn't they get him Saturday night?'

'Why, how you talk! How could their charms work till midnight? and then it's Sunday. Devils don't slosh around much of a Sunday, I don't reckon.'

'I never thought of that. That's so. Lemme go with you?'

'Of course—if you ain't afeard.'

'Afeard! 'Tain't likely. Will you meow?'

'Yes, and you meow back if you get a chance. Last time you kep'
me a meowing around till old Hays went to throwing rocks at me, and
says, "Dern that cat!" So I hove a brick through his window—but
don't you tell.'

'I won't. I couldn't meow that night becuz Auntie was watching
me; but I'll meow this time. Say, Huck, what's that?'

'Nothing but a tick.'

'Where'd you get him?'

'Out in the woods.'

'What'll you take for him?'

'I don't know. I don't want to sell him.'

'All right. It's a mighty small tick, anyway.'

'Oh, anybody can run a tick down that don't belong to them. I'm
satisfied with it. It's a good enough tick for me.'

'Sho, there's ticks a plenty. I could have a thousand of 'em if I
wanted to.'

'Well, why don't you? Becuz you know mighty well you can't. This
is a pretty early tick, I reckon. It's the first one I've seen this year.'

'Say, Huck, I'll give you my tooth for him.'

'Less see it.'

Tom got out a bit of paper and carefully unrolled it. Huckleberry
viewed it wistfully. The temptation was very strong. At last he said:

'Is it genuwyne?'

Tom lifted his lip and showed the vacancy.

'Well, all right,' said Huckleberry; 'it's a trade.'

Tom enclosed the tick in the percussion-cap box that had lately
been the pinch-bug's prison, and the boys separated, each feeling
wealthier than before.

When Tom reached the little isolated frame school-house, he
strode in briskly, with the manner of one who had come with all honest speed. He hung his hat on a peg, and flung himself into his seat
with businesslike alacrity. The master, throned on high in his great
splint-bottom armchair, was dozing, lulled by the frowsy hum of study.
The interruption roused him.

'Thomas Sawyer!'

Tom knew that when his name was pronounced in full, it meant
trouble.

'Sir!'

'Come up here. Now, sir, why are you late again, as usual?'

Tom was about to take refuge in a lie, when he saw two long tails of yellow hair hanging down a back that he recognized by the electric sympathy of love; and by that form was *the only vacant place* on the girls' side of the school-house. He instantly said:

'I STOPPED TO TALK WITH HUCKLEBERRY FINN!'

The master's pulse stood still, and he stared helplessly. The buzz of study ceased. The pupils wondered if this foolhardy boy had lost his mind. The master said:

'You—you did what?'

'Stopped to talk with Huckleberry Finn.'

There was no mistaking the words.

'Thomas Sawyer, this is the most astounding confession I have ever listened to; no mere ferule will answer for this offence. Take off your jacket.'

The master's arm performed until it was tired, and the stock of switches notably diminished. Then the order followed:

'Now, sir, go and sit with the *girls!* And let this be a warning to you.'

The titter that rippled around the room appeared to abash the boy, but in reality that result was caused rather more by his worshipful awe of his unknown idol and the dread pleasure that lay in his high good fortune. He sat down upon the end of the pine bench, and the girl hitched herself away from him with a toss of the head. Nudges and winks and whispers traversed the room, but Tom sat still, with his arms upon the long, low desk before him, and seemed to study his book. By and by attention ceased from him, and the accustomed school murmur rose upon the dull air once more. Presently the boy began to steal furtive glances at the girl. She observed it, 'made a mouth' at him, and gave him the back of her head for the space of a minute. When she cautiously faced around again, a peach lay before her. She thrust it away; Tom gently put it back; she thrust it away again, but with less animosity. Tom patiently returned it to its place; then she let it remain. Tom scrawled on his slate, 'Please take it—I got more.' The girl glanced at the words, but made no sign. Now the boy began to draw something on the slate, hiding his work with his left hand. For a time the girl refused to notice; but her human curiosity presently began to manifest itself by hardly perceptible signs. The boy worked on, apparently unconscious. The girl made a sort of non-committal attempt to see, but the boy did not betray that he was aware of it. At last she gave in, and hesitatingly whispered:

'Let me see it.'

Tom partly uncovered a dismal caricature of a house with two gable ends to it and a cork-screw of smoke issuing from the chimney. Then the girl's interest began to fasten itself upon the work, and she forgot everything else. When it was finished, she gazed a moment, then whispered:

'It's nice—make a man.'

The artist erected a man in the front yard, that resembled a derrick. He could have stepped over the house; but the girl was not hypercritical; she was satisfied with the monster, and whispered:

'It's a beautiful man—now make me coming along.'

Tom drew an hourglass, with a full moon and straw limbs to it, and armed the spreading fingers with a portentous fan. The girl said:

'It's ever so nice—I wish I could draw.'

'It's easy,' whispered Tom. 'I'll learn you.'

'Oh, will you? When?'

'At noon. Do you go home to dinner?'

'I'll stay if you will.'

'Good—that's a go. What's your name?'

'Becky Thatcher. What's yours? Oh, I know. It's Thomas Sawyer.'

'That's the name they lick me by. I'm Tom when I'm good. You call me Tom, will you?'

'Yes.'

Now Tom began to scrawl something on the slate, hiding the words from the girl. But she was not backward this time. She begged to see. Tom said:

'Oh, it ain't anything.'

'Yes it is.'

'No it ain't. You don't want to see.'

'Yes I do, indeed I do. Please let me.'

'You'll tell.'

'No I won't—deed and deed and double deed won't.'

'You won't tell anybody at all? Ever as long as you live?'

'No, I won't ever tell anybody. Now let me.'

'Oh, *you* don't want to see!'

'Now that you treat me so, I *will* see, Tom'—and she put her small hand on his, and a little scuffle ensued. Tom pretending to resist in earnest, but letting his hand slip by degrees till these words were revealed: '*I love you.*'

'Oh, you bad thing!' And she hit his hand a smart rap, but reddened and looked pleased nevertheless.

Just at this juncture the boy felt a slow fateful grip closing on his ear, and a steady lifting impulse. In that vise he was borne across the house and deposited in his own seat, under a peppering fire of giggles from the whole school. Then the master stood over him during a few awful moments, and finally moved away to his throne without saying a word. But although Tom's ear tingled, his heart was jubilant.

As the school quieted down, Tom made an honest effort to study, but the turmoil within him was too great. In turn he took his place in the reading class and made a botch of it, then in the geography class and turned lakes into mountains, mountains into rivers, and rivers into continents, till chaos was come again; then in the spelling class, and got 'turned down' by a succession of mere baby words till he brought up at the foot and yielded up the pewter medal which he had worn with ostentation for months.

Chapter 7

THE HARDER TOM TRIED to fasten his mind on his book, the more his ideas wandered. So at last, with a sigh and a yawn, he gave it up. It seemed to him that the noon recess would never come. The air was utterly dead. There was not a breath stirring. It was the sleepiest of sleepy days. The drowsing murmur of the five-and-twenty studying scholars soothed the soul like the spell that is in the murmur of bees. Away off in the flaming sunshine Cardiff Hill lifted its soft green sides through a shimmering veil of heat tinted with the purple of distance; a few birds floated on lazy wing high in the air; no other living thing was visible but some cows, and they were asleep.

Tom's heart ached to be free, or else to have something of interest to do to pass the dreary time. His hand wandered into his pocket, and his face lit up with a glow of gratitude that was prayer, though he did not know it. Then furtively the percussion-cap box came out. He released the tick, and put him on the long flat desk. The creature probably glowed with a gratitude that amounted to prayer, too, at this moment, but it was premature: for when he started thankfully to travel off, Tom turned him aside with a pin, and made him take a new direction.

Tom's bosom friend sat next him, suffering just as Tom had been, and now he was deeply and gratefully interested in this entertainment in an instant. This bosom friend was Joe Harper. The two boys were sworn friends all the week, and embattled enemies on Saturdays. Joe took a pin out of his lapel and began to assist in exercising the prisoner. The sport grew in interest momently. Soon Tom said that they were interfering with each other, and neither getting the fullest benefit of the tick. So he put Joe's slate on the desk and drew a line down the middle of it from top to bottom.

'Now,' said he, 'as long as he is on your side you can stir him up and I'll let him alone; but if you let him get away and get on my side, you're to leave him alone as long as I can keep him from crossing over.'

'All right, go ahead—start him up.'

The tick escaped from Tom, presently, and crossed the equator. Joe harassed him awhile, and then he got away and crossed back again. This change of base occurred often. While one boy was worrying the tick with absorbing interest, the other would look on with interest as strong, the two heads bowed together over the slate and the two souls dead to all things else. At last luck seemed to settle and abide with Joe. The tick tried this, that, and the other course, and got as excited and as anxious as the boys themselves, but time and again, just as he would have victory in his very grasp, so to speak, and Tom's fingers would be twitching to begin, Joe's pin would deftly head him off, and keep possession. At last Tom could stand it no longer. The temptation was too strong. So he reached out and lent a hand with his pin. Joe was angry in a moment. Said he:

'Tom, you let him alone.'

'I only just want to stir him up a little, Joe.'

'No, sir, it ain't fair; you just let him alone.'

'Blame it, I ain't going to stir him much.'

'Let him alone, I tell you!'

'I won't!'

'You shall—he's on my side of the line.'

'Look here, Joe Harper, whose is that tick?'

'I don't care whose tick he is—he's on my side of the line, and you shan't touch him.'

'Well, I'll just bet I will, though. He's my tick, and I'll do what I blame please with him, or die!'

A tremendous whack came down on Tom's shoulders, and its duplicate on Joe's; and for the space of two minutes the dust continued to fly from the two jackets and the whole school to enjoy it. The boys had been too absorbed to notice the hush that had stolen upon the school a while before when the master came tiptoeing down the room and stood over them. He had contemplated a good part of the performance before he contributed his bit of variety to it. When school broke up at noon, Tom flew to Becky Thatcher, and whispered in her ear.

'Put on your bonnet and let on you're going home; and when you get to the corner, give the rest of 'em the slip, and turn down through the lane and come back. I'll go the other way, and come it over 'em the same way.'

So the one went off with one group of scholars, and the other with another. In a little while the two met at the bottom of the lane, and when they reached the school they had it all to themselves. Then they sat together, with a slate before them, and Tom gave Becky the pencil and held her hand in his, guiding it, and so created another surprising house. When the interest in art began to wane, the two fell to talking. Tom was swimming in bliss. He said:

'Do you love rats?'

'No, I hate them!'

'Well, I do too—*live* ones. But I mean dead ones, to swing around your head with a string.'

'No, I don't care for rats much, anyway. What *I* like is chewing-gum!'

'Oh, I should say so! I wish I had some now!'

'Do you? I've got some. I'll let you chew it awhile, but you must give it back to me.'

That was agreeable, so they chewed it turn about, and dangled their legs against the bench in excess of contentment.

'Was you ever at a circus?' said Tom.

'Yes, and my pa's going to take me again some time, if I'm good.'

'I been to the circus three or four times—lots of times. Church ain't shucks to a circus. There's things going on at a circus all the time. I'm going to be a clown in a circus when I grow up.'

'Oh, are you! That will be nice. They're so lovely all spotted up.'

'Yes, that's so. And they get slathers of money—most a dollar a day, Ben Rogers says. Say, Becky, was you ever engaged?'

'What's that?'

'Why, engaged to be married.'

'No.'

'Would you like to?'

'I reckon so. I don't know. What is it like?'

'Like? Why it ain't like anything. You only just tell a boy you won't ever have anybody but him, ever ever *ever*, and then you kiss, and that's all. Anybody can do it.'

'Kiss? What do you kiss for?'

'Why, that, you know, is to—well, they always do that.'

'Everybody?'

'Why, yes, everybody that's in love with each other. Do you re-member what I wrote on the slate?'

'Ye—yes.'

'What was it?'

'I shan't tell you.'

'Shall I tell *you?*'

'Ye—yes—but some other time.'

'No, now.'

'No, not now—tomorrow.'

'Oh, no, *now*, please, Becky. I'll whisper it, I'll whisper it ever so easy.'

Becky hesitating, Tom took silence for consent, and passed his arm about her waist and whispered the tale ever so softly, with his mouth close to her ear. And then he added:

'Now you whisper it to me—just the same.'

She resisted, for a while, and then said:

'You turn your face away so you can't see, and then I will. But you mustn't ever tell anybody—*will* you, Tom? Now you won't—*will* you?'

'No, indeed, indeed I won't. Now, Becky.'

He turned his face away. She bent timidly around till her breath stirred his curls, and whispered, 'I love you!'

Then she sprang away and ran around and around the desks and benches, with Tom after her, and took refuge in a corner at last, with her little white apron to her face. Tom clasped her about her neck and pleaded.

'Now, Becky, it's all over—all over but the kiss. Don't you be afraid of that—it ain't anything at all. Please, Becky.'

And he tugged at the apron and the hands.

By-and-by she gave up and let her hands drop; her face, all glowing with the struggle, came up and submitted. Tom kissed the red lips and said:

'Now it's all done, Becky. And always after this, you know, you ain't ever to love anybody but me, and you ain't ever to marry anybody but me, never never and for ever. Will you?'

'No, I'll never love anybody but you, Tom, and I'll never marry anybody but you, and you ain't to ever marry anybody but me, either.'

'Certainly. Of course. That's *part* of it. And always, coming to school, or when we're going home, you're to walk with me, when there ain't anybody looking—and you choose me and I choose you at parties, because that's the way you do when you're engaged.'

'It's so nice. I never heard of it before.'

'Oh, it's ever so jolly! Why, me and Amy Lawrence—'

The big eyes told Tom his blunder, and he stopped, confused.
'Oh, Tom! Then I ain't the first you've ever been engaged to!'
The child began to cry. Tom said:
'Oh, don't cry, Becky, I don't care for her any more.'
'Yes you do, Tom—you know you do.'

Tom tried to put his arm about her neck, but she pushed him away and turned her face to the wall, and went on crying. Tom tried again, with soothing words in his mouth, and was repulsed again. Then his pride was up, and he strode away and went outside. He stood about, restless and uneasy, for a while, glancing at the door every now and then, hoping she would repent and come to find him. But she did not. Then he began to feel badly, and fear that he was in the wrong. It was a hard struggle with him to make new advances now, but he nerved himself to it and entered. She was still standing back there in the corner, sobbing with her face to the wall. Tom's heart smote him. He went to her and stood a moment, not knowing exactly how to proceed. Then he said hesitatingly:

'Becky, I—I don't care for anybody but you.'

No reply—but sobs.

'Becky,' pleadingly. 'Becky, won't you say something?'

More sobs.

Tom got out his chiefest jewel, a brass knob from the top of an andiron, and passed it around her so that she could see it, and said:

'Please, Becky, won't you take it?'

She struck it to the floor. Then Tom marched out of the house and over the hills and far away, to return to school no more that day. Presently Becky began to suspect. She ran to the door; he was not in sight; she flew around to the play-yard; he was not there. Then she called:

'Tom! Come back, Tom!'

She listened intently, but there was no answer. She had no companions but silence and loneliness. So she sat down to cry again and upbraid herself, and by this time the scholars began to gather again, and she had to hide her griefs and still her broken heart, and take up the cross of a long dreary aching afternoon with none among the strangers about her to exchange sorrows with.

Chapter 8

Tom DODGED HITHER AND THITHER through lanes until he was well out of the track of returning scholars, and then fell into a moody jog. He crossed a small 'branch' two or three times, because of a prevailing juvenile superstition that to cross water baffled pursuit. Half an hour later he was disappearing behind the Douglas mansion on the summit of Cardiff Hill, and the school-house was hardly distinguishable away off in the valley behind him. He entered a dense wood, picked his pathless way to the centre of it, and sat down on a mossy spot under a spreading oak. There was not even a zephyr stirring; the dead noonday heat had even stilled the songs of the birds; nature lay in a trance that was broken by no sound but the occasional far-off hammering of a woodpecker, and this seemed to render the pervading silence and sense of loneliness the more profound. The boy's soul was steeped in melancholy; his feelings were in happy accord with his surroundings. He sat long with his elbows on his knees and his chin in his hands, meditating. It seemed to him that life was but a trouble at best, and he more than half envied Jimmy Hodges, so lately released. It must be very peaceful, he thought, to lie and slumber and dream for ever and ever, with the wind whispering through the trees and caressing the grass and the flowers over the grave, and nothing to bother and grieve about, ever any more. If he only had a clean Sunday-school record he could be willing to go, and be done with it all. Now as to this girl. What had he done? Nothing. He had meant the best in the world and been treated like a dog—like a very dog. She would be sorry some day—maybe when it was too late. Ah, if he could only die *temporarily*!

But the elastic heart of youth cannot be compressed into one constrained shape long at a time. Tom presently began to drift insensibly back into the concerns of this life again. What if he turned his back, now, and disappeared mysteriously? What if he went away—ever so far away, into unknown countries beyond the seas—and never came back any more! How would she feel then? The idea of being a clown recurred to him now, only to fill him with disgust. For frivolity and jokes, and spotted tights, were an offence, when they intruded themselves upon a spirit that was exalted into the vague, august realm of the romantic. No, he would be a soldier, and return after long years, all war-worn and illustrious. No, better still, he would join the Indians and hunt buffaloes, and go on the war-path in the mountain ranges and the trackless great plains of the Far West, and away in the future come back a great chief, bristling with feathers, hideous with paint, and prance into Sunday-school, some drowsy summer morning, with a blood-curdling war-whoop, and sear the eyeballs of all his companions with unappeasable envy. But no, there was something grander even than this. He would be a pirate! That was it! *Now* his future lay plain before him, and glowing with unimaginable splendour. How his name would fill the world, and make people shudder! How gloriously he would go ploughing the dancing seas, in his long, low, black racer, the *Spirit of the Storm*, with his grisly flag flying at the fore! And, at the zenith of his fame, how he would suddenly appear at the old village and stalk into church all brown and weather-beaten, in his black velvet doublet and trunks, his great jack-boots, his crimson sash, his belt bristling with horse-pistols, his crime-rusted cutlass at his side, his slouch hat with waving plumes, his black flag unfurled with the skull and crossbones on it, and hear with swelling ecstasy the whisperings, 'It's Tom Sawyer the Pirate! the Black Avenger of the Spanish Main!'

Yes, it was settled; his career was determined. He would run away from home and enter upon it. He would start the very next morning. Therefore he must now begin to get ready. He would collect his resources together. He went to a rotten log near at hand, and began to dig under one end of it with his Barlow knife. He soon struck wood that sounded hollow. He put his hand there and uttered this incantation impressively:

'What hasn't come here, *come!* What's here, *stay* here!'

Then he scraped away the dirt, and exposed a pine shingle. He took it up and disclosed a shapely little treasure-house whose bottom and sides were of shingles. In it lay a marble. Tom's astonishment was boundless! He scratched his head with a perplexed air, and said:

'Well, that beats anything!'

Then he tossed the marble away pettishly, and stood cogitating. The truth was, that a superstition of his had failed here, which he and all his comrades had always looked upon as infallible. If you buried a

marble with certain necessary incantations, and left it alone a fortnight, and then opened the place with the incantation he had just
used, you would find that all the marbles you had ever lost had gathered themselves together there, meantime, no matter how widely
they had been separated. But now, this thing had actually and unquestionably failed. Tom's whole structure of faith was shaken to its
foundations. He had many a time heard of this thing succeeding, but
never of its failing before. It did not occur to him that he had tried it
several times before, himself, but could never find the hiding-place
afterwards. He puzzled over the matter some time, and finally decided
that some witch had interfered and broken the charm. He thought he
would satisfy himself on that point, so he searched around till he found
a small sandy spot with a little funnel-shaped depression in it. He laid
himself down and put his mouth close to this depression and called:

> Doodle-bug, doodle-bug, tell me what I want to know!
> Doodle-bug, doodle-bug, tell me what I want to know!

The sand began to work, and presently a small black bug appeared
for a second, and then darted under again in a fright.

'He dasn't tell! So it *was* a witch that done it. I just knowed it.'

He well knew the futility of trying to contend against witches, so
he gave up, discouraged. But it occurred to him that he might as well
have the marble he had just thrown away, and therefore he went and
made a patient search for it. But he could not find it. Now he went
back to his treasure-house, and carefully placed himself just as he had
been standing when he tossed the marble away; then he took another
marble from his pocket, and tossed it in the same way, saying:

'Brother, go find your brother!'

He watched where it stopped, and went there and looked. But it
must have fallen short or gone too far, so he tried twice more. The last
repetition was successful. The two marbles lay within a foot of each
other.

Just here the blast of a toy tin trumpet came faintly down the
green aisles of the forest. Tom flung off his jacket and trousers, turned
a suspender into a belt, raked away some brush behind the rotten log,
disclosing a rude bow and arrow, a lath sword, and a tin trumpet, and
in a moment had seized these things, and bounded away, barelegged,
with fluttering shirt. He presently halted under a great elm, blew an

answering blast, and then began to tip-toe and look warily out, this way and that. He said cautiously—to an imaginary company:

'Hold, my merry men! Keep hid till I blow.'

Now appeared Joe Harper, as airily clad and elaborately armed as Tom. Tom called:

'Hold! Who comes here into Sherwood Forest without my pass?'

'Guy of Guisborne wants no man's pass. Who art thou that—that—'

'Dares to hold such language,' said Tom, prompting, for they talked 'by the book', from memory.

'Who art thou that dares to hold such language?'

'I, indeed! I am Robin Hood, as thy caitiff carcase soon shall know.'

'Then art thou indeed that famous outlaw? Right gladly will I dispute with thee the passes of the merry wood. Have at thee!'

They took their lath swords, dumped their other traps on the ground, struck a fencing attitude, foot to foot, and began a grave, careful combat, 'two up and two down'. Presently Tom said:

'Now if you've got the hang, go it lively!'

So they 'went it lively', panting and perspiring with the work. By and by Tom shouted:

'Fall! fall! Why don't you fall?'

'I shan't! Why don't you fall yourself? You're getting the worst of it.'

'Why, that ain't anything. *I* can't fall; that ain't the way it is in the book. The book says, "Then with one back-handed stroke he slew poor Guy of Guisborne!" You're to turn around and let me hit you in the back.'

There was no getting around the authorities, so Joe turned, received the whack, and fell.

'Now,' said Joe, getting up, 'you got to let me kill you. That's fair.'

'Why, I can't do that. It ain't in the book.'

'Well, it's blamed mean. That's all.'

'Well, say, Joe, you can be Friar Tuck, or Much the Miller's son, and lam me with a quarter-staff; or I'll be the Sheriff of Nottingham, and you be Robin Hood a little while, and kill me.'

This was satisfactory, and so these adventures were carried out. Then Tom became Robin Hood again, and was allowed by the treacherous nun to bleed his strength away through his neglected wound. And at last Joe, representing a whole tribe of weeping outlaws, dragged him sadly forth, gave his bow into his feeble hands, and

Tom said, 'Where this arrow falls, there bury poor Robin Hood under the greenwood tree.' Then he shot the arrow, and fell back, and would have died; but he lit on a nettle, and sprang up too gaily for a corpse.

The boys dressed themselves, hid their accoutrements, and went off grieving that there were no outlaws any more, and wondering what modern civilization could claim to have done to compensate for their loss. They said they would rather be outlaws a year in Sherwood Forest than President of the United States for ever.

Chapter 9

AT HALF PAST NINE that night, Tom and Sid were sent to bed as usual. They said their prayers, and Sid was soon asleep. Tom lay awake and waited in restless impatience. When it seemed to him that it must be nearly daylight, he heard the clock strike ten! This was despair. He would have tossed and fidgeted, as his nerves demanded, but he was afraid he might wake Sid. So he lay still and stared up into the dark. Everything was dismally still. By-and-by, out of the stillness little scarcely preceptible noises began to emphasize themselves. The ticking of the clock began to bring itself into notice. Old beams began to crack mysteriously. The stairs creaked faintly. Evidently spirits were abroad. A measured, muffled snore issued from Aunt Polly's chamber. And now the tiresome chirping of a cricket that no human ingenuity could locate began. Next the ghastly ticking of a death-watch in the wall at the bed's head made Tom shudder—it meant that somebody's days were numbered. Then the howl of a far-off dog rose on the night air and was answered by a fainter howl from a remoter distance. Tom was in an agony. At last he was satisfied that time had ceased and eternity begun; he began to doze in spite of himself; the clock chimed eleven, but he did not hear it. And then there came, mingling with his half-formed dreams, a most melancholy caterwauling. The raising of a neighbouring window disturbed him. A cry of 'Scat! you devil!' and the crash of an empty bottle against the back of his aunt's wood-shed brought him wide awake, and a single minute later he was dressed and out of the window and creeping along the roof of the 'ell' on all fours. He 'meow'd' with caution once or twice as he went; then jumped to the roof of the wood-shed, and thence to the ground. Huckleberry Finn was there, with his dead cat. The boys moved off and disappeared in the gloom. At the end of half an hour they were wading through the tall grass of the graveyard.

It was a graveyard of the old-fashioned western kind. It was on a hill, about a mile and a half from the village. It had a crazy board fence around it, which leaned inward in places, and outward the rest of the time, but stood upright nowhere. Grass and weeds grew rank over the whole cemetery. All the old graves were sunken in. There was not a tombstone on the place; round-topped, worm-eaten boards staggered over the graves, leaning for support and finding none. 'Sacred to the memory of' so-and-so had been painted on them once, but it could no longer have been read, on the most of them, now, even if there had been light.

A faint wind moaned through the trees, and Tom feared it might be the spirits of the dead complaining at being disturbed. The boys talked little, and only under their breath, for the time and the place and the pervading solemnity and silence oppressed their spirits. They found the sharp new heap they were seeking, and ensconced themselves within the protection of three great elms that grew in a bunch within a few feet of the grave.

Then they waited in silence for what seemed a long time. The hooting of a distant owl was all the sound that troubled the dead stillness. Tom's reflection grew oppressive. He must force some talk. So he said in a whisper:

'Hucky, do you believe the dead people like it for us to be here?'
Huckleberry whispered:
'I wisht I knowed. It's awful solemn like, ain't it?'
'I bet it is.'

There was a considerable pause, while the boys canvassed this matter inwardly. Then Tom whispered:

'Say, Hucky—do you reckon Hoss Williams hears us talking?'
'O' course he does. Least his spirit does.'
Tom, after a pause:
'I wish I'd said *Mister* Williams. But I never meant any harm. Everybody calls him Hoss.'

'A body can't be too particular how they talk 'bout these yer dead people, Tom.'

This was a damper, and conversation died again. Presently Tom seized his comrade's arm and said:

'*Sh!*'
'What is it, Tom?' And the two clung together with beating hearts.

'*Sh!* There 'tis again! Didn't you hear it?'
'I—'
'There! Now you hear it!'

'Lord, Tom, they're coming! They're coming, sure. What'll we do?'

'I dono. Think they'll see us?'

'Oh, Tom, they can see in the dark, same as cats. I wish I hadn't come.'

'Oh, don't be afeard. I don't believe they'll bother us. We ain't doing any harm. If we keep perfectly still, maybe they won't notice us at all.'

'I'll try to, Tom, but Lord, I'm all of a shiver.'

'Listen!'

The boys bent their heads together and scarcely breathed. A muffled sound of voices floated up from the far end of the graveyard.

'Look! see there!' whispered Tom. 'What is it?'

'It's devil-fire. Oh, Tom, this is awful.'

Some vague figures approached through the gloom, swinging an old-fashioned tin lantern that freckled the ground with innumerable little spangles of light. Presently Huckleberry whispered with a shudder:

'It's the devils, sure enough. Three of 'em! Lordy, Tom, we're goners! Can you pray?'

'I'll try, but don't you be afeard. They ain't going to hurt us. "Now I lay me down to sleep, I—"'

'*Sh!*'

'What is it, Huck?'

'They're *humans!* One of 'em is, anyway. One of 'em's old Muff Potter's voice.'

'No—'tain't so, is it?'

'I bet I know it. Don't you stir nor budge. He ain't sharp enough to notice us. Drunk, the same as usual, likely—blamed old rip!'

'All right, I'll keep still. Now they're stuck. Can't find it. Here they come again. Now they're hot. Cold again. Hot again. Red-hot! They're pinted right, this time. Say, Huck, I know another o' them voices; it's Injun Joe.'

'That's so—that murderin' half-breed! I'd druther they was devils a dern sight. What kin they be up to?'

The whispers died wholly out now, for the three men had reached the grave, and stood within a few feet of the boys' hiding-place.

'Here it is,' said the third voice; and the owner of it held the lantern up and revealed the face of young Dr Robinson.

Potter and Injun Joe were carrying a hand-barrow with a rope and a couple of shovels on it. They cast down their load and began to open the grave. The doctor put the lantern at the head of the grave, and came and sat down with his back against one of the elm-trees. He was so close the boys could have touched him.

'Hurry, men!' he said in a low voice. 'The moon might come out at any moment.'

They growled a response and went on digging. For some time there was no noise but the grating sound of the spades discharging their freight of mould and gravel. It was very monotonous. Finally a spade struck upon the coffin with a dull, woody accent, and within another minute or two the men had hoisted it out on the ground. They prised off the lid with their shovels, got out the body and dumped it rudely on the ground. The moon drifted from behind the clouds and exposed the pallid face. The barrow was got ready and the corpse placed on it, covered with a blanket, and bound to its place with the rope. Potter took out a large spring-knife and cut off the dangling end of the rope, and then said:

'Now the cussed thing's ready, Sawbones, and you'll just out with another five, or here she stays.'

'That's the talk!' said Injun Joe.

'Look here; what does this mean?' said the doctor. 'You required your pay in advance and I've paid you.'

'Yes, and you done more than that,' said Injun Joe, approaching the doctor, who was now standing. 'Five years ago you drove me away from your father's kitchen one night when I come to ask for something to eat, and you said I warn't there for any good; and when I swore I'd get even with you if it took a hundred years, your father had me jailed for a vagrant. Did you think I'd forget? The Injun blood ain't in me for nothing. And now I've got you, and you got to *settle*, you know!'

He was threatening the doctor with his fist in his face by this time. The doctor struck out suddenly, and stretched the ruffian on the ground. Potter dropped his knife, and exclaimed:

'Here, now, don't you hit my pard!' and the next moment he had grappled with the doctor, and the two were struggling with might and main, trampling the grass, and tearing the ground with their heels. Injun Joe sprang to his feet, his eyes flaming with passion, snatched up Potter's knife, and went creeping, catlike, and stooping round and round about the combatants, seeking an opportunity. All at once the doctor flung himself free, seized the heavy headboard of Williams's grave and felled Potter to the earth with it; and in the same instant the half-breed saw his chance, and drove the knife to the hilt in the young man's breast. He reeled and fell partly upon Potter, flooding him with his blood, and in the same moment the clouds blotted out the dreadful spectacle, and the two frightened boys went speeding away in the dark.

Presently, when the moon emerged again Injun Joe was standing over the two forms, contemplating them. The doctor murmured inarticulately, gave a long gasp or two, and was still. The half-breed muttered:

'*That* score is settled, damn you.'

Then he robbed the body. After which he put the fatal knife in Potter's open right hand, and sat down on the dismantled coffin. Three—four—five minutes passed, and then Potter began to stir and moan. His hand closed upon the knife he raised it, glanced at it, and let it fall with a shudder. Then he sat up, pushing the body from him, and gazed at it and then around him confusedly. His eyes met Joe's.

'Lord, how is this, Joe?' he said.

'It's a dirty business,' said Joe, without moving. 'What did you do it for?'

'I! I never done it!'

'Look here! That kind of talk won't wash.'

Potter trembled and grew white.

'I thought I'd got sober. I'd no business to drink tonight. But it's in my head yet—worse'n when we started here. I'm all in a muddle; can't recollect anything of it hardly. Tell me, Joe—*honest*, now, old feller—did I do it, Joe? I never meant to; 'pon my soul and honour I never meant to, Joe. Tell me how it was, Joe. Oh, it's awful—and him so young and promising.'

'Why, you two was scuffling, and he fetched you one with the headboard, and you fell flat; and then up you come, all reeling and staggering like, and snatched the knife and jammed it into him just as he fetched you another awful clip, and here you've laid as dead as a wedge till now.'

'Oh, I didn't know what I was a doing. I wish I may die this minute if I did. It was all on accounts of the whiskey and the excitement, I reckon. I never used a weapon in my life before, Joe. I've fought, but never with weapons. They'll all say that, Joe, don't tell! Say you won't tell, Joe; that's a good feller. I always liked you, Joe, and stood up for you too. Don't you remember? You won't tell, will you, Joe?' And the poor creature dropped on his knees before the stolid murderer, and clasped his appealing hands.

'No, you've always been fair and square with me, Muff Potter, and I won't go back on you. There, now, that's as fair as a man can say.'

'Oh, Joe, you're an angel! I'll bless you for this the longest day I live.' And Potter began to cry.

'Come, now, that's enough of that. This ain't any time for blubbering. You be off yonder way, and I'll go this. Move, now, and don't leave any tracks behind you.'

Potter started on a trot that quickly increased to a run. The half-breed stood looking after him. He muttered:

'If he's as much stunned with the lick and fuddled with the rum as he had the look of being, he won't think of the knife till he's gone so far he'll be afraid to come back after it to such a place by himself—chicken-heart!'

Two or three minutes later the murdered man, the blanketed corpse, the lidless coffin, and the open grave, were under no inspection but the moon's. The stillness was complete again, too.

Chapter 10

THE TWO BOYS flew on and on, toward the village, speechless with horror. They glanced backward over their shoulders from time to time apprehensively, as if they feared they might be followed. Every stump that started up in their path seemed a man and an enemy, and made them catch their breath; and as they sped by some outlying cottages that lay near the village, the barking of the aroused watch-dogs seemed to give wings to their feet.

'If we can only get to the old tannery before we break down!' whispered Tom, in short catches between breaths. 'I can't stand it much longer.'

Huckleberry's hard pantings were his only reply, and the boys fixed their eyes on the goal of their hopes, and bent to their work to win it. They gained steadily on it, and at last, breast to breast, they burst through the open door, and fell, grateful and exhausted, in the sheltering shadows beyond. By and by their pulses slowed down, and Tom whispered:

'Huckleberry, what do you reckon'll come of this?'

'If Dr Robinson dies, I reckon hanging'll come of it.'

'Do you, though?'

'Why, I know it, Tom.'

Tom thought awhile; then he said:

'Who'll tell? We?'

'What are you talking about? S'pose something happened and Injun Joe didn't hang, why he'd kill us some time or other, just as dead sure as we're a laying here.'

'That's just what I was thinking to myself, Huck.'

'If anybody tells, let Muff Potter do it, if he's fool enough. He's generally drunk enough.'

Tom said nothing—went on thinking. Presently he whispered:

'Huck, Muff Potter don't know it. How can he tell?'

'What's the reason he don't know it?'

'Because he'd just got that whack when Injun Joe done it. D'you reckon he could see anything? D'you reckon he knowed anything?'

'By hokey, that's so, Tom!'

'And besides, look-a-here—maybe that whack done for him!'

'No, 'taint likely, Tom. He had liquor in him; I could see that; and besides, he always has. Well, when Pap's full, you might take and belt him over the head with a church and you couldn't phase him. He says so his own self. So it's the same with Muff Potter, of course. But if a man was dead sober, I reckon, maybe that whack might fetch him; I dono.'

After another reflective silence, Tom said:

'Hucky, you sure you can keep mum?'

'Tom, we got to keep mum. You know that. That Injun devil wouldn't make any more of drownding us than a couple of cats, if we was to squeak 'bout this and they didn't hang him. Now look-a-here, Tom, less take and swear to one another—that's what we got to do—swear to keep mum.'

'I'm agreed, Huck. It's the best thing. Would you just hold hands and swear that we—'

'Oh, no, that wouldn't do for this. That's good enough for little rubbishy common things—specially with gals, cuz they go back on you any way, and blab if they get in a huff—but there orter be writing 'bout a big thing like this. And blood.'

Tom's whole being applauded this idea. It was deep, and dark, and awful; the hour, the circumstances, the surroundings, were in keeping with it. He picked up a clean pine shingle that lay in the moonlight, took a little fragment of 'red keel' out of his pocket, got the moon on his work, and painfully scrawled these lines, emphasizing each slow down-stroke by clamping his tongue between his teeth, and letting up the pressure on the up-strokes.

"Huck Finn and Tom Sawyer
swears they will keep mum
about This and They Wish They
may Drop down dead in Their
Tracks if They ever Tell and Rot."

Huckleberry was filled with admiration of Tom's facility in writing, and the sublimity of his language. He at once took a pin from his lapel and was going to prick his flesh, but Tom said:

'Hold on! Don't do that. A pin's brass. It might have verdigrease on it.'

'What's verdigrease?'

'It's poison. That's what it is. You just swaller some of it once—you'll see.'

So Tom unwound the thread from one of his needles, and each boy pricked the ball of his thumb and squeezed out a drop of blood.

In time, after many squeezes, Tom managed to sign his initials, using the ball of his little finger for a pen. Then he showed Huckleberry how to make an H and an F, and the oath was complete. They buried the shingle close to the wall, with some dismal ceremonies and incantations, and the fetters that bound their tongues were considered to be locked and the key thrown away.

A figure crept stealthily through a break in the other end of the ruined building now, but they did not notice it.

'Tom,' whispered Huckleberry, 'does this keep us from ever telling—always?'

'Of course it does. It don't make any difference what happens, we got to keep mum. We'd drop down dead—don't you know that?'

'Yes, I reckon that's so.'

They continued to whisper for some little time. Presently a dog set up a long, lugubrious howl just outside—within ten feet of them. The boys clasped each other suddenly, in an agony of fright.

'Which of us does he mean?' gasped Huckleberry.

'I dono—peep through the crack. Quick!'

'No, you, Tom!'

'I can't—I can't do it, Huck!'

'Please, Tom. There 'tis again!'

'Oh, Lordy, I'm thankful!' whispered Tom. 'I know his voice. It's Bull Harbison.'[1]

'Oh, that's good—I tell you, Tom, I was most scared to death; I'd a bet anything it was a stray dog.'

The dog howled again. The boys' hearts sank once more.

---

1. If Mr. Harbison owned a slave named Bull, Tom would have spoken of him as 'Harbison's Bull'; but a son or a dog of that name was 'Bull Harbison'.

'Oh, my! that ain't no Bull Harbison!' whispered Huckleberry. 'Do, Tom!'

Tom, quaking with fear, yielded, and put his eye to the crack. His whisper was hardly audible when he said:

'Oh, Huck, it's A STRAY DOG!'

'Quick, Tom, quick! Who does he mean?'

'Huck, he must mean us both—we're right together.'

'Oh, Tom, I reckon we're goners. I reckon there ain't no mistake 'bout where I'll go to. I been so wicked.'

'Dad fetch it! This comes of playing hookey and doing everything a feller's told *not* to do. I might a been good, like Sid, if I'd tried—but no, I wouldn't, of course. But if ever I get off this time, I lay I'll just *waller* in Sunday-schools!'

And Tom began to snuffle a little.

'*You* bad!' and Huckleberry began to snuffle, too. 'Confound it, Tom Sawyer, you're just old pie, 'longside o' what I am. Oh, *Lordy*, Lordy, Lordy, I wisht I only had half your chance.'

Tom choked off and whispered:

'Look, Hucky, look! He's got his *back* to us!'

Hucky looked with joy in his heart.

'Well he has, by jingoes! Did he before?'

'Yes, he did. But I, like a fool, never thought. Oh, this is bully, you know. *Now*, who can he mean?'

The howling stopped. Tom pricked up his ears.

'*Sh!* What's that?' he whispered.

'Sounds like—like hogs grunting. No—it's somebody snoring, Tom.'

'That *is* it? Where 'bouts is it, Huck?'

'I b'leeve it's down at t'other end. Sounds so, anyway. Pap used to sleep there sometimes, 'long with the hogs, but, laws bless you, he just lifts things when he snores. Besides, I reckon he ain't ever coming back to this town any more.'

The spirit of adventure rose in the boys' souls once more. 'Hucky, do you das't to go if I lead?'

'I don't like to, much, Tom. S'pose it's Injun Joe!'

Tom quailed. But presently the temptation rose up strong again and the boys agreed to try, with the understanding that they would take to their heels if the snoring stopped. So they went tip-toeing stealthily down, the one behind the other. When they had got to within five steps of the snorer, Tom stepped on a stick, and it broke with a sharp snap. The man moaned, writhed a little, and his face came into the moonlight. It was Muff Potter. The boys' hearts had stood still, and their bodies too, when the man moved, but their fears passed away now. They tip-toed out, through the broken weather-boarding, and stopped at a little distance to exchange a parting word. That long, lugubrious howl rose on the night air again! They turned and saw the strange dog standing within a few feet of where Potter was lying, and facing Potter with his nose pointing heavenward.

'Oh, geeminy, it's *him!*' exclaimed both boys in a breath.

'Say, Tom, they say a stray dog come howling around Johnny Miller's house, 'bout midnight, as much as two weeks ago; and a whippowill come in and lit on the banisters and sung, the very same evening; and there ain't anybody dead there yet.'

'Well, I know that. And suppose there ain't. Didn't Gracie Miller fall in the kitchen fire and burn herself terrible the very next Saturday?'

'Yes, but she ain't *dead*. And what's more, she's getting better too.'

'All right; you wait and see. She's a goner, just as dead sure as Muff Potter's a goner. That's what the niggers say, and they know all about these kind of things, Huck.'

Then they separated, cogitating.

When Tom crept in at his bedroom window, the night was almost spent. He undressed with excessive caution, and fell asleep congratulating himself that nobody knew of his escapade. He was not aware that the gently snoring Sid was awake, and had been so for an hour.

When Tom awoke, Sid was dressed and gone. There was a late look in the light, a late sense in the atmosphere. He was startled. Why had he not been called—persecuted till he was up as usual? The thought filled him with bodings. Within five minutes he was dressed and downstairs, feeling sore and drowsy. The family were still at table, but they had finished breakfast. There was no voice of rebuke; but there were averted eyes; there was a silence and an air of solemnity that struck a chill to the culprit's heart. He sat down and tried to seem gay, but it was up-hill work; it roused no smile, no response, and he lapsed into silence and let his heart sink down to the depths.

After breakfast his aunt took him aside, and Tom almost brightened in the hope that he was going to be flogged; but it was not so. His aunt wept over him and asked him how he could go and break her old heart so; and finally told him to go on, and ruin himself, and bring her grey hairs with sorrow to the grave, for it was no use for her to try any more. This was worse than a thousand whippings, and Tom's heart was sorer now than his body. He cried, he pleaded for forgiveness, promised to reform over and over again, and then received his dismissal, feeling that he had won but an imperfect forgiveness and established but a feeble confidence.

He left the presence too miserable to even feel revengeful towards Sid; and so the latter's prompt retreat through the back gate was unnecessary. He moped to school gloomy and sad, and took his flogging along with Joe Harper for playing hookey the day before, with the air of one whose heart was busy with heavier woes and wholly dead to trifles. Then he betook himself to his seat, rested his elbows on his desk and his jaws in his hands, and stared at the wall with the stony stare of suffering that has reached the limit and can no further go. His elbow was pressing against some hard substance. After a long time he slowly and sadly changed his position, and took up this object with a sigh. It was in a paper. He unrolled it. A long, lingering, colossal sigh followed, and his heart broke. It was his brass andiron knob!

This final feather broke the camel's back.

Chapter 11

Close upon the hour of noon the whole village was suddenly electrified with the ghastly news. No need of the as yet undreamed-of telegraph; the tale flew from man to man, from group to group, from house to house with little less than telegraphic speed. Of course the schoolmaster gave holiday for that afternoon; the town would have thought strangely of him if he had not. A gory knife had been found close to the murdered man, and it had been recognized by somebody as belonging to Muff Potter—so the story ran. And it was said that a belated citizen had come upon Potter washing himself in the 'branch' about one or two o'clock in the morning, and that Potter had at once sneaked off—suspicious circumstances, especially the washing, which was not a habit with Potter. It was also said that the town had been ransacked for this 'murderer' (the public are not slow in the matter of sifting evidence and arriving at a verdict), but that he could not be found. Horsemen had departed down all the roads in every direction, and the Sheriff was confident that he would be captured before night.

All the town was drifting towards the graveyard. Tom's heartbreak vanished, and he joined the procession, not because he would not a thousand times rather go anywhere else, but because an awful, unaccountable fascination drew him on. Arrived at the dreadful place, he wormed his small body through the crowd and saw the dismal spectacle. It seemed to him an age since he was there before. Somebody pinched his arm. He turned, and his eyes met Huckleberry's. Then both looked elsewhere at once, and wondered if anybody had noticed anything in their mutual glance. But everybody was talking, and intent upon the grisly spectacle before them.

'Poor fellow!' 'Poor young fellow!' 'This ought to be a lesson to grave-robbers!' 'Muff Potter'll hang for this if they catch him!' This was the drift of remark, and the minister said, 'It was a judgement; His hand is here.'

Now Tom shivered from head to heel; for his eye fell upon the stolid face of Injun Joe. At this moment the crowd began to sway and struggle, and voices shouted, 'It's him! it's him! he's coming himself!'

'Who? who?' from twenty voices.

'Muff Potter!'

'Hallo, he's stopped! Look out, he's turning! Don't let him get away!'

People in the branches of the trees over Tom's head said he wasn't trying to get away—he only looked doubtful and perplexed.

'Infernal impudence!' said a bystander; 'wanted to come and take a quiet look at his work—didn't expect any company.'

The crowd fell apart now, and the Sheriff came through, ostentatiously leading Potter by the arm. The poor fellow's face was haggard, and his eyes showed the fear that was upon him. When he stood before the murdered man, he shook as with a palsy, and he put his face in his hands and burst into tears.

'I didn't do it, friends,' he sobbed; ''pon my word and honour I never done it.'

'Who's accused you?' shouted a voice.

This shot seemed to carry home. Potter lifted his face and looked around him with a pathetic hopelessness in his eyes. He saw Injun Joe, and exclaimed:

'Oh, Injun Joe, you promised me you'd never—'

'Is that your knife?' and it was thrust before him by the Sheriff.

Potter would have fallen if they had not caught him and eased him to the ground. Then he said:

'Something told me 't if I didn't come back and get—' He shuddered; then waved his nerveless hand with a vanquished gesture and said, 'Tell 'em, Joe, tell 'em—it ain't any use any more.'

Then Huckleberry and Tom stood dumb and staring, and heard the stony-hearted liar reel off his serene statement, they expecting every moment that the clear sky would deliver God's lightnings upon his head, and wondering to see how long the stroke was delayed. And when he had finished and still stood alive and whole, their wavering impulse to break their oath and save the poor betrayed prisoner's life faded and vanished away, for plainly this miscreant had sold himself to Satan, and it would be fatal to meddle with the property of such a power as that.

'Why didn't you leave? What did you want to come here for?' somebody said.

'I couldn't help it—I couldn't help it,' Potter moaned. 'I wanted to run away, but I couldn't seem to come anywhere but here.' And he fell to sobbing again.

Injun Joe repeated his statement, just as calmly, a few minutes afterwards on the inquest, under oath; and the boys, seeing that the lightnings were still withheld, were confirmed in their belief that Joe had sold himself to the devil. He was now become, to them, the most balefully interesting object they had ever looked upon, and they could not take their fascinated eyes from his face. They inwardly resolved to watch him, nights, when opportunity should offer, in the hope of getting a glimpse of his dread master.

Injun Joe helped to raise the body of the murdered man, and put it in a wagon for removal; and it was whispered through the shuddering crowd that the wound bled a little! The boys thought that this happy circumstance would turn suspicion in the right direction; but they were disappointed, for more than one villager remarked:

'It was within three feet of Muff Potter when it done it.'

Tom's fearful secret and gnawing conscience disturbed his sleep for as much as a week after this; and at breakfast one morning Sid said:

'Tom, you pitch around and talk in your sleep so much that you keep me awake about half the time.'

Tom blanched and dropped his eyes.

'It's a bad sign,' said Aunt Polly, gravely. 'What you got on your mind, Tom?'

'Nothing. Nothing 't I know of.' But the boy's hand shook so that he spilled his coffee.

'And you do talk such stuff,' Sid said. 'Last night you said, 'It's blood, it's blood, that's what it is!' You said that over and over. And you said, 'Don't torment me so—I'll tell!' Tell what? What is it you'll tell?'

Everything was swimming before Tom. There is no telling what might have happened now, but luckily the concern passed out of Aunt Polly's face, and she came to Tom's relief without knowing it. She said:

'Sho! It's that dreadful murder. I dream about it most every night myself. Sometimes I dream it's me that done it.'

Mary said she had been affected much the same way. Sid seemed satisfied. Tom got out of the presence as quickly as he plausibly could, and after that he complained of toothache for a week, and tied up his jaws every night. He never knew that Sid lay nightly watching, and frequently slipped the bandage free, and then leaned on his elbow listening a good while at a time, and afterwards slipped the bandage back to its place again. Tom's distress of mind wore off gradually, and the toothache grew irksome and was discarded. If Sid really managed to make anything out of Tom's disjointed mutterings, he kept it to himself. It seemed to Tom that his schoolmates never would get done holding inquests on dead cats, and thus keeping his trouble present to his mind. Sid noticed that Tom never was coroner at one of these inquiries, though it had been his habit to take the lead in all new enterprises; he noticed, too, that Tom never acted as a witness—and that was strange; and Sid did not overlook the fact that Tom even showed a marked aversion to these inquests, and always avoided them when he could. Sid marvelled, but said nothing. However, even inquests went out of vogue at last, and ceased to torture Tom's conscience.

Every day or two during this time of sorrow, Tom watched his opportunity and went to the little grated jail window and smuggled such small comforts through to the 'murderer' as he could get hold of. The jail was a trifling little brick den that stood in a marsh at the edge of the village, and no guards were afforded for it; indeed, it was seldom occupied. These offerings greatly helped to ease Tom's conscience. The villagers had a strong desire to tar-and-feather Injun Joe and ride him on a rail for body-snatching, but so formidable was his character that nobody could be found who was willing to take the lead in the matter, so it was dropped. He had been careful to begin both of his inquest-statements with the fight, without confessing the grave-robbery that preceded it; therefore it was deemed wisest not to try the case in the courts at present.

Chapter 12

ONE OF THE REASONS why Tom's mind had drifted away from its secret troubles was that it had found a new and weighty matter to interest itself about. Becky Thatcher had stopped coming to school. Tom had struggled with his pride a few days, and tried to 'whistle her down the wind', but failed. He began to find himself hanging around her father's house, nights, and feeling very miserable. She was sick. What if she should die! There was distraction in the thought. He no longer took an interest in war, nor even in piracy. The charm of life was gone, there was nothing but dreariness left. He put his hoop away, and his bat; there was no joy in them any more. His aunt was concerned; she began to try all manner of medicines on him. She was one of those people who are infatuated with patent medicines and all new-fangled methods of producing health or mending it. She was an inveterate experimenter in these things. When something fresh in this line came out she was in a fever right away to try it; not on herself, for she was never ailing; but on anybody else that came handy. She was a subscriber for all the 'Health' periodicals and phrenological frauds; and the solemn ignorance they were inflated with was breath to her nostrils. All the rot they contained about ventilation, and how to go to bed, and how to get up, and what to eat, and what to drink, and how much exercise to take, and what frame of mind to keep oneself in, and what sort of clothing to wear, was all gospel to her, and she never observed that her health journals of the current month customarily upset everything they had recommended the month before. She was as simple-hearted and honest as the day was long, and so she was an easy victim. She gathered together her quack periodicals and her quack medicines, and, thus armed with death, went about on her pale horse, metaphorically speaking, with 'hell following after'. But she never suspected that she was not an angel of healing and the balm of Gilead in disguise to the suffering neighbours.

The water treatment was new, now, and Tom's low condition was a windfall to her. She had him out at daylight every morning, stood him up in the wood-shed and drowned him with a deluge of cold water; then she scrubbed him down with a towel like a file, and so brought him to; then she rolled him up in a wet sheet and put him away under blankets till she sweated his soul clean and 'the yellow stains of it came through his pores', as Tom said.

Yet notwithstanding all this the boy grew more and more melancholy and pale and dejected. She added hot baths, sitz baths, and plunges. The boy remained as dismal as a hearse. She began to assist the water with a slim oatmeal diet and blister plasters. She calculated his capacity as she would a jug's, and filled him up every day with quack cure-alls.

Tom had become indifferent to persecution by this time. This phase filled the old lady's heart with consternation. This indifference must be broken up at any cost. Now she heard of Pain-killer for the first time. She ordered a lot at once. She tasted it and was filled with gratitude. It was simply fire in a liquid form. She dropped the water treatment and everything else, and pinned her faith to Pain-killer. She gave Tom a teaspoonful and watched with the deepest anxiety for the result. Her troubles were instantly at rest, her soul at peace again; for the 'indifference' was broken up. The boy could not have shown a wilder, heartier interest if she had built a fire under him.

Tom felt that it was time to wake up; this sort of life might be romantic enough in his blighted condition, but it was getting to have too little sentiment and too much distracting variety about it. So he thought over various plans for relief, and finally hit upon that of professing to be fond of Pain-killer. He asked for it so often that he became a nuisance, and his aunt ended by telling him to help himself and quit bothering her. If it had been Sid she would have had no misgivings to alloy her delight; but since it was Tom she watched the bottle clandestinely. She found that the medicine did really diminish, but it did not occur to her that the boy was mending the health of a crack in the sitting-room floor with it.

One day Tom was in the act of dosing the crack when his aunt's yellow cat came along, purring, eyeing the tea-spoon avariciously, and begging for a taste. Tom said:

'Don't ask for it unless you want it, Peter.'

But Peter signified that he did want it.

'You better make sure.'

Peter was sure.

'Now you've asked for it, and I'll give it to you, because there ain't anything mean about *me*; but if you find you don't like it you mustn't blame anybody but your own self.'

Peter was agreeable, so Tom pried his mouth open and poured down the Pain-killer. Peter sprang a couple of yards in the air, and then delivered a war-whoop and set off round and round the room, banging against furniture, upsetting flower-pots, and making general havoc. Next he rose on his hind feet and pranced around, in a frenzy of enjoyment, with his head over his shoulder and his voice proclaiming his unappeasable happiness. Then he went tearing around the house again, spreading chaos and destruction in his path. Aunt Polly entered in time to see him throw a few double summersets, deliver a final mighty hurrah, and sail through the open window, carrying the rest of the flower-pots with him. The old lady stood petrified with astonishment, peering over her glasses; Tom lay on the floor, expiring with laughter.

'Tom, what on earth ails that cat?'

'I don't know, Aunt,' gasped the boy.

'Why, I never seen anything like it. What *did* make him act so?'

' 'Deed I don't know, Aunt Polly; cats always act so when they're having a good time.'

'They do, do they?' There was something in the tone that made Tom apprehensive.

'Yes'm. That is, I believe they do.'

'You *do*?'

'Yes'm.'

The old lady was bending down, Tom watching with interest emphasized by anxiety. Too late he divined her 'drift.' The handle of the tell-tale teaspoon was visible under the bed-valance. Aunt Polly took it, held it up. Tom winced, and dropped his eyes. Aunt Polly raised him by the usual handle—his ear—and cracked his head soundly with her thimble.

'Now, sir, what did you want to treat that poor dumb beast so for?'

'I done it out of pity for him—because he hadn't any aunt.'

'Hadn't any aunt!—you numskull. What has that got to do with it?'

'Heaps. Because if he'd a had one she'd a burnt him out herself! She'd a roasted his bowels out of him 'thout any more feeling than if he was a human!'

Aunt Polly felt a sudden pang of remorse. This was putting the thing in a new light; what was cruelty to a cat *might* be cruelty to a boy too. She began to soften: she felt sorry. Her eyes watered a little, and she put her hand on Tom's head and said gently:

'I was meaning for the best, Tom. And, Tom, it *did* do you good.'

Tom looked up in her face with just a perceptible twinkle peeping through his gravity:

'I know you was meaning for the best, Aunty, and so was I with Peter. It done *him* good, too. I never see him get around so nice—'

'Oh, go 'long with you, Tom, before you aggravate me again. And you try and see if you can't be a good boy for once, and you needn't take any more medicine.'

Tom reached school ahead of time. It was noticed that this strange thing had been occurring every day latterly. And now, as usual of late, he hung about the gate of the school-yard instead of playing with his comrades. He was sick, he said; and he looked it. He tried to seem to be looking everywhere but whither he really was looking—down the road. Presently Jeff Thatcher hove in sight, and Tom's face lighted; he gazed a moment, and then turned sorrowfully away. When Jeff Thatcher arrived, Tom accosted him, and 'led up' warily to opportunities for remark about Becky, but the giddy lad never could see the bait. Tom watched and watched, hoping whenever a frisking frock came in sight, and hating the owner of it as soon as he saw she was not the right one. At last frocks ceased to appear, and he dropped hopelessly into the dumps; he entered the empty school-house and sat down to suffer. Then one more frock passed in at the gate, and Tom's heart gave a great bound. The next instant he was out, and 'going on' like an Indian; yelling, laughing, chasing boys, jumping over the fence at risk of life and limb, throwing handsprings, standing on his head—doing all the heroic things he could conceive of, and keeping a furtive eye out, all the while, to see if Becky Thatcher was noticing. But she seemed to be unconscious of it all; she never looked. Could it be possible that she was not aware that he was there? He carried his exploits to her immediate vicinity; came war-whooping around, snatched a boy's cap, hurled it to the roof of the school-house, broke through a group of boys, tumbling them in every direction, and fell sprawling himself under Becky's nose, almost upsetting her—and she turned, with her nose in the air, and he heard her say, 'Mf! some people think they're mighty smart—always showing off!'

Tom's cheeks burned. He gathered himself up and sneaked off, crushed and crestfallen.

Chapter 13

Tom's mind was made up now. He was gloomy and desperate. He was a forsaken, friendless boy, he said; nobody loved him; when they found out what they had driven him to, perhaps they would be sorry; he had tried to do right and get along, but they would not let him; since nothing would do them but to be rid of him, let it be so; and let them blame him for the consequences—why shouldn't they? what right had the friendless to complain? Yes, they had forced him to it at last: he would lead a life of crime. There was no choice. By this time he was far down Meadow Lane, and the bell for school to 'take up' tinkled faintly upon his ear. He sobbed, now, to think he should never, never hear that old familiar sound any more—it was very hard, but it was forced on him; since he was driven out into the cold world, he must submit—but he forgave them. Then the sobs came thick and fast.

Just at this point he met his soul's sworn comrade, Joe Harper—hard-eyed, and with evidently a great and dismal purpose in his heart. Plainly here were 'two souls with but a single thought'. Tom, wiping his eyes with his sleeve, began to blubber out something about a resolution to escape from hard usage and lack of sympathy at home by roaming abroad into the great world, never to return; and ended by hoping that Joe would not forget him.

But it transpired that this was a request which Joe had just been going to make of Tom, and had come to hunt him up for that purpose. His mother had whipped him for drinking some cream which he had never tasted and knew nothing about; it was plain that she was tired of him and wished him to go; if she felt that way, there was nothing for him to do but succumb; he hoped she would be happy, and never regret having driven her poor boy out into the unfeeling world to suffer and die.

As the two boys walked sorrowing along, they made a new compact to stand by each other and be brothers, and never separate till death relieved them of their troubles. Then they began to lay their plans. Joe was for being a hermit, and living on crusts in a remote cave, and dying, sometime, of cold, and want, and grief; but, after listening to Tom, he conceded that there were some conspicuous advantages about a life of crime, and so he consented to be a pirate.

Three miles below St Petersburg, at a point where the Mississippi River was a trifle over a mile wide, there was a long, narrow, wooded island, with a shallow bar at the head of it, and this offered well as a rendezvous. It was not inhabited; it lay far over towards the farther shore, abreast a dense and almost wholly unpeopled forest. So Jackson's Island was chosen. Who were to be the subjects of their piracies was a matter that did not occur to them. Then they hunted up Huckleberry Finn, and he joined them promptly, for all careers were one to him; he was indifferent. They presently separated, to meet at a lonely spot on the river bank two miles above the village, at the favourite hour, which was midnight. There was a small log raft there which they meant to capture. Each would bring hooks and lines, and such provisions as he could steal in the most dark and mysterious way—as became outlaws; and before the afternoon was done, they had all managed to enjoy the sweet glory of spreading the fact that pretty soon the town would 'hear something'. All who got this vague hint were cautioned to 'be mum and wait'.

About midnight Tom arrived with a boiled ham and a few trifles, and stopped in a dense undergrowth on a small bluff overlooking the meeting-place. It was starlight, and very still. The mighty river lay like an ocean at rest. Tom listened a moment, but no sound disturbed the quiet. Then he gave a low, distinct whistle. It was answered from under the bluff. Tom whistled twice more; these signals were answered in the same way. Then a guarded voice said:

'Who goes there?'

'Tom Sawyer, the Black Avenger of the Spanish Main. Name your names.'

'Huck Finn the Red-handed, and Joe Harper the Terror of the Seas.' Tom had furnished these titles, from his favourite literature.

''Tis well. Give the countersign.'

Two hoarse whispers delivered the same awful word simultaneously to the brooding night:

'BLOOD!'

Then Tom tumbled his ham over the bluff and let himself down after it, tearing both skin and clothes to some extent in the effort.

There was an easy, comfortable path along the shore under the bluff, but it lacked the advantages of difficulty and danger so valued by a pirate.

The Terror of the Seas had brought a side of bacon, and had about worn himself out with getting it there. Finn the Red-handed had stolen a skillet, and a quantity of half-cured leaf tobacco, and had also brought a few corn-cobs to make pipes with. But none of the pirates smoked or 'chewed' but himself. The Black Avenger of the Spanish Main said it would never do to start without some fire. That was a wise thought; matches were hardly known there in that day. They saw a fire smouldering upon a great raft a hundred yards above, and they went stealthily thither and helped themselves to a chunk. They made an imposing adventure of it, saying 'hist' every now and then and suddenly halting with finger on lip; moving with hands on imaginary dagger-hilts; and giving orders in dismal whispers that if 'the foe' stirred to 'let him have it to the hilt', because 'dead men tell no tales'. They knew well enough that the raftmen were all down at the village laying in stores or having a spree, but still that was no excuse for their conducting this thing in an unpiratical way.

They shoved off presently, Tom in command, Huck at the left oar and Joe at the forward. Tom stood amidships, gloomy-browed and with folded arms, and gave his orders in a low, stern whisper.

'Luff, and bring her to the wind!'

'Aye-aye, sir!'

'Steady, steady-y-y-y!'

'Steady it is, sir!'

'Let her go off a point!'

'Point it is, sir!'

As the boys steadily and monotonously drove the raft towards mid-stream, it was no doubt understood that these orders were given only for 'style', and were not intended to mean anything in particular.

'What sail's she carrying?'

'Courses, tops'ls, and flying-jib, sir!'

'Send the r'yals up! Lay out aloft there, half a dozen of ye, foretomast-stuns'l! Lively, now!'

'Aye-aye, sir!'

'Shake out that mainto-galans'l! Sheets and braces! *Now*, my hearties!'

'Aye-aye, sir!'

'Hellum-a-lee—hard a-port! Stand by to meet her when she comes! Port, port! *Now*, men! With a will! Stead-y-y-y!'

'Steady it is, sir!'

The raft drew beyond the middle of the river; the boys pointed her head right and then lay on their oars. The river was not high, so there was not more than a two or three mile current. Hardly a word was said during the next three-quarters of an hour. Now the raft was passing before the distant town. Two or three glimmering lights showed where it lay, peacefully sleeping, beyond the vague vast sweep of star-gemmed water, unconscious of the tremendous event that was happening. The Black Avenger stood still with folded arms, 'looking his last' upon the scene of his former joys and his later sufferings, and wishing 'she' could see him, now abroad on the wild sea, facing peril and death with dauntless heart, going to his doom with a grim smile on his lips. It was but a small strain on his imagination to remove Jackson's Island beyond eye-shot of the village, and so he 'looked his last' with a broken and satisfied heart. The other pirates were looking their last, too; and they all looked so long that they came near letting the current drift them out of the range of the island. But they discovered the danger in time, and made shift to avert it. About two o'clock in the morning the raft grounded on the bar two hundred yards above the head of the island, and they waded back and forth until they had landed their freight. Part of the little raft's belongings consisted of an old sail, and this they spread over a nook in the bushes for a tent to shelter their provisions; but they themselves would sleep in the open air in good weather, as became outlaws.

They built a fire against the side of a great log twenty or thirty steps within the sombre depths of the forest, and then cooked some bacon in the frying-pan for supper, and used up half of the corn 'pone' stock they had brought. It seemed glorious sport to be feasting in that wild free way in the virgin forest of an unexplored and uninhabited island, far from the haunts of men, and they said they never would return to civilization. The climbing fire lit up their faces and threw its ruddy glare upon the pillared tree-trunks of their forest temple, and upon the varnished foliage and festooning vines. When the last crisp slice of bacon was gone, and the last allowance of corn pone devoured, the boys stretched themselves out on the grass, filled with contentment. They could have found a cooler place, but they would not deny themselves such a romantic feature as the roasting camp-fire.

'*Ain't* it jolly?' said Joe.

'It's *nuts*,' said Tom.

'What would the boys say if they could see us?'

'Say? Well, they'd just die to be here—hey, Hucky?'

'I reckon so,' said Huckleberry; 'anyways *I'm* suited. I don't want nothing better'n this. I don't ever get enough to eat gen'ally—and here they can't come and kick at a feller and bullyrag him so.'

'It's just the life for me,' said Tom. 'You don't have to get up, mornings, and you don't have to go to school, and wash, and all that blame foolishness. You see a pirate don't have to do *anything*, Joe, when he's ashore, but a hermit *he* has to be praying considerable, and then he don't have any fun, any way, all by himself that way.'

'Oh yes, that's so,' said Joe, 'but I hadn't thought much about it, you know. I'd a good deal ruther be a pirate now that I've tried it.'

'You see,' said Tom, 'people don't go much on hermits, now-a-days, like they used to in old times, but a pirate's always respected. And a hermit's got to sleep on the hardest place he can find, and put sackcloth and ashes on his head, and stand out in the rain, and—'

'What does he put sackcloth and ashes on his head for?' inquired Huck.

'*I* dunno. But they've *got* to do it. Hermits always do. You'd have to do that if you was a hermit.'

'Dern'd if I would,' said Huck.

'Well, what would you do?'

'I dunno. But I wouldn't do that.'

'Why, Huck, you'd *have* to. How'd you get around it?'

'Why, I just wouldn't stand it. I'd run away.'

'Run away! Well, you *would* be a nice old slouch of a hermit. You'd be a disgrace.'

The Red-handed made no response, being better employed. He had finished gouging out a cob, and now he fitted a weed stem to it, loaded it with tobacco, and was pressing a coal to the charge and blowing a cloud of fragrant smoke; he was in the full bloom of luxurious contentment. The other pirates envied him this majestic vice, and secretly resolved to acquire it shortly. Presently Huck said:

'What does pirates have to do?'

Tom said:

'Oh, they have just a bully time—take ships, and burn them, and get the money and bury it in awful places in their island where there's ghosts and things to watch it, and kill everybody in the ships—make 'em walk a plank.'

'And they carry the women to the island,' said Joe; 'they don't kill the women.'

'No,' assented Tom, 'they don't kill the women—they're too noble. And the women's always beautiful, too.'

'And don't they wear the bulliest clothes! Oh, no! All gold and silver and di'monds,' said Joe with enthusiasm.

'Who?' said Huck.

'Why, the pirates.'

Huck scanned his own clothing forlornly.

'I reckon I ain't dressed fitten for a pirate,' said he, with a regretful pathos in his voice; 'but I ain't got none but these.'

But the other boys told him the fine clothes would come fast enough after they should have begun their adventures. They made him understand that his poor rags would do to begin with, though it was customary for wealthy pirates to start with a proper wardrobe.

Gradually their talk died out and drowsiness began to steal upon the eyelids of the little waifs. The pipe dropped from the fingers of the Red-handed, and he slept the sleep of the conscience-free and the weary. The Terror of the Seas and the Black Avenger of the Spanish Main had more difficulty in getting to sleep. They said their prayers inwardly, and lying down, since there was nobody there with authority to make them kneel and recite aloud in truth, they had a mind not to say them at all, but they were afraid to proceed to such lengths as that, lest they might call down a sudden and special thunder-bolt from heaven. Then at once they reached and hovered upon the imminent verge of sleep—but an intruder came now that would not 'down'. It was conscience. They began to feel a vague fear that they had been doing wrong to run away; and next they thought of the stolen meat, and then the real torture came. They tried to argue it away by reminding conscience that they had purloined sweetmeats and apples scores of times; but conscience was not to be appeased by such thin plausibilities. It seemed to them, in the end, that there was no getting around the stubborn fact that taking sweetmeats was only 'hooking' while taking bacon and ham and such valuables was plain, simple stealing—and there was a command against that in the

Bible. So they inwardly resolved that so long as they remained in the business, their piracies should not again be sullied with the crime of stealing. Then conscience granted a truce, and these curiously inconsistent pirates fell peacefully to sleep.

Chapter 14

WHEN TOM AWOKE in the morning, he wondered where he was. He sat up and rubbed his eyes and looked around; then he comprehended. It was the cool grey dawn, and there was a delicious sense of repose and peace in the deep pervading calm and silence of the woods. Not a leaf stirred; not a sound obtruded upon great Nature's meditation. Beaded dewdrops stood upon the leaves and grasses. A white layer of ashes covered the fire, and a thin blue breath of smoke rose straight into the air. Joe and Huck still slept. Now, far away in the woods, a bird called; another answered; presently the hammering of a woodpecker was heard. Gradually the cool dim grey of the morning whitened, and as gradually sounds multiplied and life manifested itself. The marvel of Nature shaking off sleep and going to work unfolded itself to the musing boy. A little green worm came crawling over a dewy leaf, lifting two-thirds of his body into the air from time to time, 'sniffing around', then proceeding again, for he was measuring, Tom said; and when the worm approached him of its own accord, he sat as still as a stone, with his hopes rising and falling by turns as the creature still came towards him or seemed inclined to go elsewhere; and when at last it considered a painful moment with its curved body in the air and then came decisively down upon Tom's leg and began a journey over him, his whole heart was glad—for that meant that he was going to have a new suit of clothes—without the shadow of a doubt, a gaudy piratical uniform. Now a procession of ants appeared, from nowhere in particular, and went about their labours; one struggled manfully by with a dead spider five times as big as itself in its arms, and lugged it straight up a tree-trunk. A brown spotted lady-bug climbed the dizzy heights of a grass-blade, and Tom bent down close to it and said:

> Lady-bug, lady-bug, fly away home,
> Your house is on fire, your children's alone;

and she took wing and went off to see about it—which did not surprise the boy, for he knew of old that this insect was credulous about conflagrations, and he had practised upon its simplicity more than once. A tumblebug came next, heaving sturdily at its ball, and Tom touched the creature, to see it shut its legs against its body and pretend to be dead. The birds were fairly rioting by this time. A cat-bird, the northern mocker, lit in a tree over Tom's head, and trilled out her imitations of her neighbours in a rapture of enjoyment; then a shrill jay swept down, a flash of blue flame, and stopped on a twig almost within the boy's reach, cocked his head to one side and eyed the strangers with a consuming curiosity; a grey squirrel and a big fellow of the 'fox' kind came scurrying along, sitting up at intervals to inspect and chatter at the boys, for the wild things had probably never seen a human being before, and scarcely knew whether to be afraid or not. All Nature was wide awake and stirring now, long lances of sunlight pierced down through the dense foliage far and near, and a few butterflies came fluttering upon the scene.

Tom stirred up the other pirates and they all clattered away with a shout, and in a minute or two were stripped and chasing after and tumbling over each other in the shallow limpid water of the white sand-bar. They felt no longing for the little village sleeping in the distance beyond the majestic waste of water. A vagrant current or a slight rise in the river had carried off their raft, but this only gratified them, since its going was something like burning the bridge between them and civilization.

They came back to camp wonderfully refreshed, glad-hearted, and ravenous; and they soon had the camp-fire blazing up again. Huck found a spring of clear cold water close by, and the boys made cups of broad oak or hickory leaves, and felt that water, sweetened with such a wild-wood charm as that, would be a good enough substitute for coffee. While Joe was slicing bacon for breakfast, Tom and Huck asked him to hold on a minute; they stepped to a promising nook in the river bank and threw in their lines; almost immediately they had reward. Joe had not had time to get impatient before they were back again with some handsome bass, a couple of sun-perch, and a small catfish—provisions enough for quite a family. They fried the fish with the bacon and were astonished; for no fish had ever seemed so delicious before. They did not know that the quicker a freshwater fish is on the fire after he is caught the better he is; and they reflected little upon what a sauce open-air sleeping, open-air exercise, bathing, and a large ingredient of hunger make, too.

They lay around in the shade after breakfast, while Huck had a smoke, and then went off through the woods on an exploring expedition. They tramped gaily along, over decaying logs, through tangled underbrush, among solemn monarchs of the forest, hung from their crowns to the ground with a drooping regalia of grape-vines. Now and then they came upon snug nooks carpeted with grass and jeweled with flowers.

They found plenty of things to be delighted with, but nothing to be astonished at. They discovered that the island was about three miles long and a quarter of a mile wide, and that the shore it lay closest to was only separated from it by a narrow channel hardly two hundred yards wide. They took a swim about every hour, so it was close upon the middle of the afternoon when they got back to camp. They were too hungry to stop to fish, but they fared sumptuously upon cold ham, and then threw themselves down in the shade to talk. But the talk soon began to drag, and then died. The stillness, the solemnity, that brooded in the woods, and the sense of loneliness, began to tell upon the spirits of the boys. They fell to thinking. A sort of undefined longing crept upon them. This took dim shape presently—it was budding homesickness. Even Finn the Red-handed was dreaming of his door-steps and empty hogsheads. But they were all ashamed of their weakness, and none was brave enough to speak his thought.

For some time, now, the boys had been dully conscious of a peculiar sound in the distance, just as one sometimes is of the ticking of a clock which he takes no distinct note of. But now this mysterious sound became more pronounced, and forced a recognition. The boys started, glanced at each other, and then each assumed a listening attitude. There was a long silence, profound and unbroken; then a deep, sullen boom came floating down out of the distance.

'What is it!' exclaimed Joe, under his breath.

'I wonder,' said Tom in a whisper.

'Tain't thunder,' said Huckleberry, in an awed tone, 'becuz thunder—'

'Hark!' said Tom; 'listen—don't talk.'

They waited a time that seemed an age, and then the same muffled boom troubled the solemn hush.

'Let's go and see.'

They sprang to their feet and hurried to the shore towards the town. They parted the bushes on the bank and peered out over the water. The little steam ferry-boat was about a mile below the village, drifting with the current. Her broad deck seemed crowded with people. There were a great many skiffs rowing about or floating with the stream in the neighbourhood of the ferry-boat, but the boys could not determine what the men in them were doing. Presently a great jet of white smoke burst from the ferry-boat's side, and as it expanded and rose in a lazy cloud, that same dull throb of sound was borne to the listeners again.

'I know now!' exclaimed Tom; 'somebody's drownded!'

'That's it,' said Huck; 'they done that last summer when Bill Turner got drownded; they shoot a cannon over the water, and that makes him come up to the top. Yes, and they take loaves of bread and put quicksilver in 'em and set 'em afloat, and wherever there's anybody that's drownded, they'll float right there and stop.'

'Yes, I've heard about that,' said Joe. 'I wonder what makes the bread do that.'

'Oh, it ain't the bread so much,' said Tom; 'I reckon it's mostly what they *say* over it before they start it out.'

'But they don't say anything over it,' said Huck. 'I've seen 'em, and they don't.'

'Well, that's funny,' said Tom. 'But maybe they say it to themselves. Of *course* they do. Anybody might know that.'

The other boys agreed that there was reason in what Tom said, because an ignorant lump of bread, uninstructed by an incantation, could not be expected to act very intelligently when set upon an errand of such gravity.

'By jings, I wish I was over there now,' said Joe.

'I do too,' said Huck. 'I'd give heaps to know who it is.'

The boys still listened and watched. Presently a revealing thought flashed through Tom's mind, and he exclaimed:

'Boys, I know who's drownded; it's us!'

They felt like heroes in an instant. Here was a gorgeous triumph; they were missed; they were mourned; hearts were breaking on their account; tears were being shed; accusing memories of unkindnesses to these poor lost lads were rising up, and unavailing regrets and remorse were being indulged; and, best of all, the departed were the talk of the whole town, and the envy of all the boys, as far as this dazzling notoriety was concerned. This was fine. It was worth while to be a pirate, after all.

As twilight drew on, the ferry-boat went back to her accustomed business and the skiffs disappeared. The pirates returned to camp. They were jubilant with vanity over their new grandeur and the illustrious trouble they were making. They caught fish, cooked supper, and ate it, and then fell to guessing at what the village was thinking and saying about them; and the pictures they drew of the public distress on their account were gratifying to look upon from their point of view. But when the shadows of night closed them in, they gradually ceased to talk, and sat gazing into the fire, with their minds evidently wandering elsewhere. The excitement was gone, now, and Tom and Joe could not keep back thoughts of certain persons at home who were not enjoying this fine frolic as much as they were. Misgivings came; they grew troubled and unhappy; a sigh or two escaped unawares. By-and-by Joe timidly ventured upon a roundabout 'feeler' as to how the others might look upon a return to civilization—not right now, but—

Tom withered him with derision. Huck, being uncommitted as yet, joined in with Tom, and the waverer quickly 'explained', and was glad to get out of the scrape with as little taint of chickenhearted homesickness clinging to his garments as he could. Mutiny was effectually laid to rest for the moment.

As the night deepened, Huck began to nod, and presently to snore; Joe followed next. Tom lay upon his elbow motionless for some time, watching the two intently. At last he got up cautiously on his knees, and went searching among the grass and the flickering reflections flung by the camp-fire. He picked up and inspected several large semi-cylinders of the thin white bark of a sycamore, and finally chose two which seemed to suit him. Then he knelt by the fire and painfully wrote something upon each of these with his 'red keel'; one he rolled up and put in his jacket-pocket, and the other he put in Joe's hat and removed it to a little distance from the owner. And he also put into the hat certain school-boy treasures of almost inestimable value, among them a lump of chalk, an indiarubber ball, three fishhooks, and one of that kind of marbles known as a 'sure 'nough crystal.' Then he tip-toed his way cautiously among the trees till he felt that he was out of hearing, and straightway broke into a keen run in the direction of the sand-bar.

Chapter 15

A FEW MINUTES LATER Tom was in the shoal water of the bar, wading toward the Illinois shore. Before the depth reached his middle he was half-way over: the current would permit no more wading now, so he struck out confidently to swim the remaining hundred yards. He swam quartering up stream, but still was swept downward rather faster than he had expected. However, he reached the shore finally, and drifted along till he found a low place and drew himself out. He put his hand on his jacket pocket, found his piece of bark safe, and then struck through the woods, following the shore with streaming garments. Shortly before ten o'clock he came out into an open place opposite the village, and saw the ferry-boat lying in the shadow of the trees and the high bank. Everything was quiet under the blinking stars. He crept down the bank, watching with all his eyes, slipped into the water, swam three or four strokes, and climbed into the skiff that did 'yawl' duty at the boat's stern. He laid himself down under the thwarts and waited, panting. Presently the cracked bell tapped, and a voice gave the order to 'cast off'. A minute or two later the skiff's head was standing high up against the boat's swell, and the voyage was begun. Tom felt happy in his success, for he knew it was the boat's last trip for the night. At the end of a long twelve or fifteen minutes the wheels stopped, and Tom slipped overboard and swam ashore in the dusk, landing fifty yards down stream, out of danger of possible stragglers. He flew along unfrequented alleys, and shortly found himself at his aunt's back fence. He climbed over, approached the 'ell' and looked in at the sitting-room window, for a light was burning there. There sat Aunt Polly, Sid, Mary, and Joe Harper's mother, grouped together, talking. They were by the bed, and the bed was between them and the door. Tom went to the door and began to softly lift the latch; then he pressed gently and the door yielded a crack; he continued pushing cautiously, and quaking every time it creaked, till he judged he might squeeze through on his knees; so he put his head through and began, warily.

'What makes the candle blow so?' said Aunt Polly. Tom hurried up. 'Why, that door's open, I believe. Why, of course it is. No end of strange things now. Go along and shut it, Sid.'

Tom disappeared under the bed just in time. He lay and 'breathed' himself for a time, and then crept to where he could almost touch his aunt's foot.

'But as I was saying,' said Aunt Polly, 'he warn't *bad*, so to say— only mische*e*vous. Only just giddy, and harum-scarum, you know. He warn't any more responsible than a colt. *He* never meant any harm, and he was the best-hearted boy that ever was'—and she began to cry.

'It was just so with my Joe—always full of his devilment, and up to every kind of mischief, but he was just as unselfish and kind as he could be—and laws bless me, to think I went and whipped him for taking that cream, never once recollecting that I throwed it out myself because it was sour, and I never to see him again in this world, never, never, never, poor abused boy!' And Mrs Harper sobbed as if her heart would break.

'I hope Tom's better off where he is,' said Sid, 'but if he'd been better in some ways—'

'*Sid!*' Tom felt the glare of the old lady's eye, though he could not see it. 'Not a word against my Tom, now that he's gone! God'll take care of *him*—never you trouble *your*self, sir. Oh, Mrs Harper, I don't know how to give him up, I don't know how to give him up! He was such a comfort to me, although he tormented my old heart out of me, 'most.'

'The Lord giveth, and the Lord taketh away. Blessed be the name of the Lord! But it's *so* hard. Oh, it's so hard—only last Saturday my Joe bursted a shooting-cracker right under my nose, and I knocked him sprawling. Little did I know then, how soon—oh, if it was to do over again I'd hug him and bless him for it.'

'Yes, yes, yes, I know just how you feel, Mrs Harper, I know just exactly how you feel. No longer ago than yesterday noon, my Tom took and filled the cat full of Pain-killer, and I did think the cretur would tear the house down. And, God forgive me, I cracked Tom's head with my thimble, poor boy, poor dead boy. But he's out of all his troubles now. And the last words I ever heard him say was to reproach—'

But this memory was too much for the old lady, and she broke entirely down. Tom was snuffling now himself—and more in pity of himself than anybody else. He could hear Mary crying, and putting in a kindly word for him from time to time. He began to have a nobler opinion of himself than ever before. Still he was sufficiently touched by his aunt's grief to long to rush out from under the bed and overwhelm her with joy—and the theatrical gorgeousness of the thing appealed strongly to his nature, too, but he resisted and lay still. He went on listening, and gathered by odds and ends that it was conjectured at first that the boys had got drowned while taking a swim; then the small raft had been missed; next, certain boys said the missing lads had promised that the village should 'hear something' soon; and the wise-heads had 'put this and that together', and decided that the lads had gone off on that raft, and would turn up at the next town below presently; but towards noon the raft had been found, lodged against the Missouri shore some five or six miles below the village, and then hope perished; they must be drowned, else hunger would have driven them home by nightfall if not sooner. It was believed that the search for the bodies had been a fruitless effort merely because the drowning must have occurred in mid-channel, since the boys, being good swimmers, would otherwise have escaped to shore. This was Wednesday night. If the bodies continued missing until Sunday, all hope would be given over, and the funerals would be preached on that morning. Tom shuddered.

Mrs Harper gave a sobbing good night and turned to go. Then with a mutual impulse the two bereaved women flung themselves into each other's arms and had a good consoling cry, and then parted. Aunt Polly was tender far beyond her wont in her good night to Sid and Mary. Sid snuffled a bit, and Mary went off crying with all her heart.

Aunt Polly knelt down and prayed for Tom so touchingly, so appealingly, and with such measureless love in her words and her old trembling voice, that he was weltering in tears again long before she was through.

He had to keep still long after she went to bed, for she kept making broken-hearted ejaculations from time to time, tossing unrestfully, and turning over. But at last she was still, only moaning a little in her sleep. Now the boy stole out, rose gradually by the bedside, shaded the candle-light with his hand, and stood regarding her. His heart was full of pity for her. He took out his sycamore scroll and placed it by the candle. But something occurred to him, and he lingered considering. His face lighted with a happy solution of his thought; he put the bark hastily in his pocket, then he bent over and kissed the faded lips, and straightway made his stealthy exit, latching the door behind him.

He threaded his way back to the ferry landing, found nobody at large there, and walked boldly on board the boat, for he knew she was tenantless except that there was a watchman, who always turned in and slept like a graven image. He untied the skiff at the stern, slipped into it, and was soon rowing cautiously up stream. When he had pulled a mile above the village, he started quartering across, and bent himself stoutly to his work. He hit the landing on the other side neatly, for this was a familiar bit of work to him. He was moved to capture the skiff, arguing that it might be considered a ship and there-fore legitimate prey for a pirate; but he knew a thorough search would be made for it, and that might end in revelations. So he stepped ashore and entered the woods. He sat down and took a long rest, tor-turing himself meanwhile to keep awake, and then started warily down the home stretch. The night was far spent. It was broad daylight before he found himself fairly abreast the island bar. He rested again until the sun was well up and gilding the great river with its splen-dour, and then he plunged into the stream. A little later he paused, dripping, upon the threshold of the camp, and heard Joe say:

'No, Tom's true-blue, Huck, and he'll come back. He won't desert. He knows that would be a disgrace to a pirate, and Tom's too proud for that sort of thing. He's up to something or other. Now, I wonder what?'

'Well, the things is ours anyway, ain't they?'

'Pretty near, but not yet, Huck. The writing says they are if he ain't back to breakfast.'

'Which he is!' exclaimed Tom, with fine dramatic effect, stepping grandly into camp.

A sumptuous breakfast of bacon and fish was shortly provided, and as the boys set to work upon it Tom recounted (and adorned) his ad-ventures. They were a vain and boastful company of heroes when the tale was done. Then Tom hid himself away in a shady nook to sleep till noon, and the other pirates got ready to fish and explore.

Chapter 16

Aﬆer dinner all the gang turned out to hunt for turtle eggs on the bar. They went about poking sticks into the sand, and when they found a soft place they went down on their knees and dug with their hands. Sometimes they would take fifty or sixty eggs out of one hole. They were perfectly round, white things, a trifle smaller than an English walnut. They had a famous fried-egg feast that night, and another on Friday morning. After breakfast they went whooping and prancing out on the bar, and chased each other round and round, shedding clothes as they went, until they were naked, and then continued the frolic far away up the shoal water of the bar, against the stiff current, which latter tripped their legs from under them from time to time, and greatly increased the fun. And now and then they stooped in a group and splashed water in each other's faces with their palms, gradually approaching each other with averted faces, to avoid the strangling sprays, and finally gripping and struggling till the best man ducked his neighbour, and then they all went under in a tangle of white legs and arms, and came up blowing, sputtering, laughing, and gasping for breath at one and the same time.

When they were well exhausted, they would run out and sprawl on the dry, hot sand, and lie there and cover themselves up with it, and by-and-by break for the water again and go through the original performance once more. Finally it occurred to them that their naked skin represented flesh-coloured 'tights' very fairly; so they drew a ring in the sand and had a circus—with three clowns in it, for none would yield this proudest post to his neighbour.

Next they got their marbles, and played 'knucks' and 'ring-taw' and 'keeps', till that amusement grew stale. Then Joe and Huck had another swim, but Tom would not venture, because he found that in kicking off his trousers he had kicked his string of rattlesnake rattles off his ankle, and he wondered how he had escaped cramp so long without the protection of this mysterious charm. He did not venture again until he had found it, and by that time the other boys were tired and ready to rest. They gradually wandered apart, dropped into the 'dumps', and fell to gazing longingly across the wide river to where the village lay drowsing in the sun. Tom found himself writing '*Becky*' in the sand with his big toe; he scratched it out and was angry with himself for his weakness. But he wrote it again, nevertheless; he could not help it. He erased it once more, and then took himself out of temptation by driving the other boys together, and then joining them.

But Joe's spirits had gone down almost beyond resurrection. He was so homesick that he could hardly endure the misery of it. The tears lay very near the surface. Huck was melancholy too. Tom was downhearted, but tried hard not to show it. He had a secret which he was not ready to tell yet, but if this mutinous depression was not broken up soon, he would have to bring it out. He said with a great show of cheerfulness:

'I bet there's been pirates on this island before, boys. We'll explore it again. They've hid treasures here somewhere. How'd you feel to light on a rotten chest full of gold and silver—hey?'

But it roused only faint enthusiasm, which faded out with no reply. Tom tried one or two other seductions; but they failed too. It was discouraging work. Joe sat poking up the sand with a stick, and looking very gloomy. Finally he said:

'Oh boys, let's give it up. I want to go home. It's so lonesome.'

'Oh, no, Joe, you'll feel better by-and-by,' said Tom. 'Just think of the fishing that's here.'

'I don't care for the fishing. I want to go home.'

'But, Joe, there ain't such another swimming-place anywhere.'

'Swimming's no good. I don't seem to care for it, somehow, when there ain't anybody to say I shan't go in. I mean to go home.'

'Oh, shucks! baby! You want to see your mother, I reckon.'

'Yes, I *do* want to see my mother, and you would too, if you had one. I ain't any more baby than you are.' And Joe snuffled a little.

'Well, we'll let the cry-baby go home to his mother, won't we, Huck? Poor thing—does it want to see its mother? And so it shall. *You* like it here, don't you, Huck? We'll stay, won't we?'

Huck said, 'Y-e-s—' without any heart in it.

'I'll never speak to you again as long as I live,' said Joe, rising. 'There now!' And he moved moodily away and began to dress himself.

'Who cares?' said Tom. 'Nobody wants you to. Go 'long home and get laughed at. Oh, you're a nice pirate. Huck and me ain't cry-babies. We'll stay, won't we, Huck? Let him go if he wants to. I reckon we can get along without him, per'aps.'

But Tom was uneasy nevertheless, and was alarmed to see Joe go sullenly on with his dressing. And then it was discomforting to see Huck eying Joe's preparations so wistfully, and keeping up such an ominous silence. Presently, without a parting word, Joe began to wade off towards the Illinois shore. Tom's heart began to sink. He glanced at Huck. Huck could not bear the look, and dropped his eyes. Then he said:

'I want to go too, Tom. It was getting so lonesome anyway, and now it'll be worse. Let's go too, Tom.'

'I won't; you can all go if you want to. I mean to stay.'

'Tom, I better go.'

'Well, go 'long—who's hindering you?'

Huck began to pick up his scattered clothes. He said:

'Tom, I wisht you'd come too. Now, you think it over. We'll wait for you when we get to shore.'

'Well, you'll wait a blame long time, that's all.'

Huck started sorrowfully away, and Tom stood looking after him, with a strong desire tugging at his heart to yield his pride and go along too. He hoped the boys would stop, but they still waded slowly on. It suddenly dawned on Tom that it was become very lonely and still. He made one final struggle with his pride, and then darted after his comrades, yelling:

'Wait! wait! I want to tell you something!'

They presently stopped and turned around. When he got to where they were, he began unfolding his secret, and they listened moodily till at last they saw the 'point' he was driving at, and then they set up a war-whoop of applause and said it was 'splendid!' and said if he had told them that at first, they wouldn't have started away. He made a plausible excuse; but his real reason had been the fear that not even the secret would keep them with him any very great length of time, and so he had meant to hold it in reserve as a last seduction.

The lads came gaily back and went at their sports again with a will, chattering all the time about Tom's stupendous plan and admiring the genius of it. After a dainty egg and fish dinner, Tom said he wanted to learn to smoke now. Joe caught at the idea and said he would like to try too. So Huck made pipes and filled them. These novices had never smoked anything before but cigars made of grape-vine, and they 'bit' the tongue, and were not considered manly, anyway.

Now they stretched themselves out on their elbows and began to puff charily, and with slender confidence. The smoke had an unpleasant taste, and they gagged a little, but Tom said:

'Why, it's just as easy! If I'd a knowed *this* was all, I'd a learnt long ago.'

'So would I,' said Joe. 'It's just nothing.'

'Why, many a time I've looked at people smoking and thought, Well, I wish I could do that; but I never thought I could,' said Tom. 'That's just the way with me, ain't it, Huck? You've heard me talk just that way haven't you, Huck? I'll leave it to Huck if I haven't.'

'Yes, heaps of times,' said Huck.

'Well, I have too,' said Tom; 'oh, hundreds of times. Once down there by the slaughter-house. Don't you remember, Huck? Bob Tanner was there, and Johnny Miller, and Jeff Thatcher, when I said it. Don't you remember, Huck, 'bout me saying that?'

'Yes, that's so,' said Huck. 'That was the day after I lost a white alley—no, 'twas the day before!'

'There, I told you so,' said Tom. 'Huck recollects it.'

'I believe I could smoke this pipe all day,' said Joe. '*I* don't feel sick.'

'Neither do I,' said Tom. '*I* could smoke it all day, but I bet you Jeff Thatcher couldn't.'

'Jeff Thatcher! Why, he'd keel over just with two draws. Just let him try it once; *he'd* see!'

'I bet he would, and Johnny Miller—I wish I could see Johnny Miller tackle it once.'

'Oh, don't *I*?' said Joe. 'Why, I bet you Johnny Miller couldn't any more do this than nothing. Just one little snifter would fetch *him*.'

''Deed it would, Joe. Say—I wish the boys could see us now.'

'So do I!'

'Say, boys, don't say anything about it, and some time when they're around, I'll come up to you and say, "Joe, got a pipe? I want a smoke!" And you'll say, kind of careless like, as if it warn't anything, you'll say, "Yes, I got my *old* pipe, and another one, but my tobacker ain't very good." And I'll say, "Oh, that's all right, if it's *strong* enough." And then you'll out with the pipes, and we'll light up just as ca'm, and then just see 'em look!'

'By jings, that'll be gay, Tom; I wish it was *now!*'

'So do I! And when we tell 'em we learned when we was off pirating, won't they wish they'd been along?'

'Oh, I reckon not! I'll just *bet* they will!'

So the talk ran on; but presently it began to flag a trifle, and grow disjointed. The silences widened; the expectoration marvellously increased. Every pore inside the boys' cheeks became a spouting fountain; they could scarcely bail out the cellars under their tongues fast enough to prevent an inundation; little overflowings down their throats occurred in spite of all they could do, and sudden retchings followed every time. Both boys were looking very pale and miserable now. Joe's pipe dropped from his nerveless fingers. Tom's followed. Both fountains were going furiously, and both pumps bailing with might and main. Joe said feebly:

'I've lost my knife. I reckon I better go and find it.'

Tom said, with quivering lips and halting utterance:

'I'll help you. You go over that way and I'll hunt around by the spring. No, you needn't come, Huck—we can find it.'

So Huck sat down again, and waited an hour. Then he found it lonesome, and went to find his comrades. They were wide apart in the woods, both very pale, both fast asleep. But something informed him that if they had had any trouble they had got rid of it.

They were not talkative at supper that night; they had a humble look; and when Huck prepared his pipe after the meal, and was going to prepare theirs, they said no, they were not feeling very well— something they ate at dinner had disagreed with them.

Chapter 17

Aʙᴏᴜᴛ ᴍɪᴅɴɪɢʜᴛ Jᴏᴇ ᴀᴡᴏᴋᴇ, and called the boys. There was a brooding oppressiveness in the air that seemed to bode something. The boys huddled themselves together, and sought the friendly companionship of the fire, though the dull dead heat of the breathless atmosphere was stifling. They sat still, intent and waiting. Beyond the light of the fire, everything was swallowed up in the blackness of darkness. Presently there came a quivering glow that vaguely revealed the foliage for a moment and then vanished. By and by another came, a little stronger. Then another. Then a faint moan came sighing through the branches of the forest, and the boys felt a fleeting breath upon their cheeks, and shuddered with the fancy that the Spirit of the Night had gone by. There was a pause. Now a weird flash turned night into day, and showed every little grass-blade separate and distinct, that grew about their feet. And it showed three white startled faces, too. A deep peal of thunder went rolling and tumbling down the heavens, and lost itself in sullen rumblings in the distance. A sweep of chilly air passed by, rustling all the leaves and snowing the flaky ashes broadcast about the fire. Another fierce glare lit up the forest, and an instant crash followed that seemed to rend the tree-tops right over the boys' heads. They clung together in terror, in the thick gloom that followed. A few big rain-drops fell pattering upon the leaves.

'Quick, boys, go for the tent!' exclaimed Tom.

They sprang away, stumbling over roots and among vines in the dark, no two plunging in the same direction. A furious blast roared through the trees, making everything sing as it went. One blinding flash after another came, and peal on peal of deafening thunder. And now a drenching rain poured down, and the rising hurricane drove it in sheets along the ground. The boys cried out to each other, but the roaring wind and the booming thunder-blasts drowned their voices utterly. However, one by one they straggled in at last, and took shelter under the tent, cold, scared, and streaming with water; but to have company in misery seemed something to be grateful for. They could not talk, the old sail flapped so furiously, even if the other noises would have allowed them. The tempest rose higher and higher, and presently the sail tore loose from its fastenings, and went winging away on the blast. The boys seized each others' hands, and fled, with many tumblings and bruises, to the shelter of a great oak that stood upon the river bank. Now the battle was at its highest. Under the ceaseless conflagrations of lightnings that flamed in the skies, every-thing below stood out in clean-cut and shadowless distinctness; the bending trees, the billowy river white with foam, the driving spray of spume-flakes, the dim outlines of the high bluffs on the other side, glimpsed through the drifting cloud-rack and the slanting veil of rain. Every little while some giant tree yielded the fight and fell crashing through the younger growth; and the unflagging thunder-peals came now in ear-splitting explosive bursts, keen and sharp, and unspeak-ably appalling. The storm culminated in one matchless effort that seemed likely to tear the island to pieces, burn it up, drown it to the tree-tops, blow it away and deafen every creature in it, all at one and the same moment. It was a wild night for homeless young heads to be out in.

But at last the battle was done, and the forces retired, with weaker and weaker threatenings and grumblings, and peace resumed her sway. The boys went back to camp a good deal awed; but they found there was still something to be thankful for, because the great sycamore, the shelter of their beds, was a ruin, now, blasted by the lightnings, and they were not under it when the catastrophe happened.

Everything in camp was drenched, the camp-fire as well; for they were but heedless lads, like their generation, and had made no provi-sion against rain. Here was matter for dismay, for they were soaked through and chilled. They were eloquent in their distress: but they presently discovered that the fire had eaten so far up under the great log it had been built against (where it curved upward and separated itself from the ground), that a handbreadth or so of it had escaped wetting; so they patiently wrought until, with shreds and bark gath-ered from the under sides of sheltered logs, they coaxed the fire to burn again. Then they piled on great dead boughs till they had a roaring furnace and were glad-hearted once more. They dried their boiled ham and had a feast, and after that they sat by the fire and expanded and glorified their midnight adventure until morning, for there was not a dry spot to sleep on anywhere around.

As the sun began to steal in upon the boys, drowsiness came over them and they went out on the sand-bar and lay down to sleep. They got scorched out by-and-by, and drearily set about getting breakfast. After the meal they felt rusty, and stiff-jointed, and a little homesick once more. Tom saw the signs, and fell to cheering up the pirates as well as he could. But they cared nothing for marbles, or circus, or swimming, or anything. He reminded them of the imposing secret, and raised a ray of cheer. While it lasted he got them interested in a new device. This was to knock off being pirates for a while, and be Indians for a change. They were attracted by this idea; so it was not long before they were stripped, and striped from head to heel with black mud, like so many zebras, all of them chiefs, of course, and then they went tearing through the woods to attack an English settlement.

By-and-by they separated into three hostile tribes, and darted upon each other from ambush with dreadful war-whoops, and killed and scalped each other by thousands. It was a gory day. Consequently it was a satisfactory one.

They assembled in camp towards supper-time, hungry and happy; but now a difficulty arose—hostile Indians could not break the bread of hospitality together without first making peace, and this was a simple impossibility without smoking a pipe of peace. There was no other process that ever they had heard of. Two of the savages almost wished they had remained pirates. However, there was no other way, so with such show of cheerfulness as they could muster they called for the pipe and took their whiff, as it passed, in due form.

And behold, they were glad they had gone into savagery, for they had gained something; they found that they could now smoke a little without having to go and hunt for a lost knife; they did not get sick enough to be seriously uncomfortable. They were not likely to fool away this high promise for lack of effort. No, they practised cautiously after supper with right fair success, and so they spent a jubilant evening. They were prouder and happier in their new acquirement than they would have been in the scalping and skinning of the Six Nations. We will leave them to smoke and chatter and brag, since we have no further use for them at present.

Chapter 18

BUT THERE WAS NO HILARITY in the little town that tranquil Saturday afternoon. The Harpers and Aunt Polly's family, were being put into mourning with great grief and many tears. An unusual quiet possessed the village, although it was ordinarily quiet enough in all conscience. The villagers conducted their concerns with an abstracted air, and talked little; but they sighed often. The Saturday holiday seemed a burden to the children. They had no heart in their sports, and gradually gave them up.

In the afternoon Becky Thatcher found herself moping about the deserted school-house yard, and feeling very melancholy. But she found nothing there to comfort her. She soliloquized:

'Oh, if I only had his brass andiron knob again! But I haven't got anything now to remember him by,' and she choked back a little sob.

Presently she stopped, and said to herself:

'It was right here. Oh, if it was to do over again, I wouldn't say that—I wouldn't say it for the whole world. But he's gone now; I'll never, never, never see him any more.'

This thought broke her down, and she wandered away with the tears rolling down her cheeks. Then quite a group of boys and girls—playmates of Tom's and Joe's—came by, and stood looking over the paling fence and talking in reverent tones of how Tom did so-and-so the last time they saw him, and how Joe said this and that small trifle (pregnant with awful prophecy, as they could easily see now!)—and each speaker pointed out the exact spot where the lost lads stood at the time, and then added something like, 'and I was a standing just so—just as I am now, and as if you was him—I was as close as that—and he smiled, just this way—and then something seemed to go all over me, like—awful, you know—and I never thought what it meant, of course, but I can see now!'

Then there was a dispute about who saw the dead boys last in life, and many claimed that dismal distinction, and offered evidences more or less tampered with by the witness; and when it was ultimately decided who did see the departed last, and exchanged the last words with them, the lucky parties took upon themselves a sort of sacred importance, and were gaped at and envied by all the rest. One poor chap who had no other grandeur to offer, said, with tolerably manifest pride in the remembrance:

'Well, Tom Sawyer he licked me once.'

But that bid for glory was a failure. Most of the boys could say that, and so that cheapened the distinction too much. The group loitered away, still recalling memories of the lost heroes in awed voices.

When the Sunday-school hour was finished the next morning, the bell began to toll, instead of ringing in the usual way. It was a very still Sabbath, and the mournful sound seemed in keeping with the musing hush that lay upon nature. The villagers began to gather, loitering a moment in the vestibule to converse in whispers about the sad event. But there was no whispering in the house; only the funereal rustling of dresses, as the women gathered to their seats, disturbed the silence there. None could remember when the little church had been so full before. There was finally a waiting pause, an expectant dumbness, and then Aunt Polly entered, followed by Sid and Mary, and then by the Harper family, all in deep black, and the whole congregation, the old minister as well, rose reverently and stood, until the mourners were seated in the front pew. There was another communing silence, broken at intervals by muffled sobs, and then the minister spread his hands abroad and prayed. A moving hymn was sung, and the text followed: 'I am the resurrection and the life.'

As the service proceeded, the clergyman drew such pictures of the graces, the winning ways, and the rare promise of the lost lads, that every soul there, thinking he recognized these pictures, felt a pang in remembering that he had persistently blinded himself to them always before, and had as persistently seen only faults and flaws in the poor boys. The minister related many a touching incident in the lives of the departed, too, which illustrated their sweet, generous natures, and the people could easily see, now, how noble and beautiful those episodes were, and remembered with grief that at the time they occurred they had seemed rank rascalities, well deserving the cowhide. The congregation became more and more moved as the pathetic tale went on, till at last the whole company broke down and joined the weeping mourners in a chorus of anguished sobs, the preacher himself giving way to his feelings, and crying in the pulpit.

There was a rustle in the gallery, which nobody noticed; a moment later the church door creaked; the minister raised his streaming eyes above his handkerchief, and stood transfixed! First one and then another pair of eyes followed the minister's, and then, almost with one impulse, the congregation rose and stared while the three dead boys came marching up the aisle, Tom in the lead, Joe next, and Huck, a ruin of drooping rags, sneaking sheepishly in the rear. They had been hid in the unused gallery, listening to their own funeral sermon!

Aunt Polly, Mary, and the Harpers threw themselves upon their restored ones, smothered them with kisses and poured out thanksgivings, while poor Huck stood abashed and uncomfortable, not knowing exactly what to do or where to hide from so many unwelcoming eyes. He wavered, and started to slink away, but Tom seized him and said:

'Aunt Polly, it ain't fair. Somebody's got to be glad to see Huck.'

'And so they shall! I'm glad to see him, poor motherless thing!' And the loving attentions Aunt Polly lavished upon him were the one thing capable of making him more uncomfortable than he was before.

Suddenly the minister shouted at the top of his voice:

' "Praise God from whom all blessings flow"—SING!—and put your hearts in it!'

And they did. Old Hundred swelled up with a triumphant burst, and while it shook the rafters Tom Sawyer the Pirate looked around upon the envying juveniles about him, and confessed in his heart that this was the proudest moment of his life.

As the 'sold' congregation trooped out, they said they would almost be willing to be made ridiculous again to hear Old Hundred sung like that once more.

Tom got more cuffs and kisses that day—according to Aunt Polly's varying moods—than he had earned before in a year; and he hardly knew which expressed the most gratefulness to God and affection for himself.

Chapter 19

THAT WAS TOM'S GREAT SECRET—the scheme to return home with his brother pirates and attend their own funerals. They had paddled over to the Missouri shore on a log, at dusk on Saturday, landing five or six miles below the village; they had slept in the woods at the edge of the town till nearly daylight, and had then crept through back lanes and alleys and finished their sleep in the gallery of the church among a chaos of invalid benches.

At breakfast, Monday morning, Aunt Polly and Mary were very loving to Tom, and very attentive to his wants. There was an unusual amount of talk. In the course of it Aunt Polly said:

'Well, I don't say it wasn't a fine joke, Tom, to keep everybody suffering 'most a week so you boys had a good time, but it is a pity you could be so hard-hearted as to let me suffer so. If you could come over on a log to go to your funeral, you could have come over and give me a hint some way that you warn't dead, but only run off.'

'Yes, you could have done that, Tom,' said Mary; 'and I believe you would if you had thought of it.'

'Would you, Tom?' said Aunt Polly, her face lighting wistfully. 'Say, now, would you, if you'd thought of it?'

'I—well, I don't know. 'Twould a spoiled everything.'

'Tom, I hoped you loved me that much,' said Aunt Polly, with a grieved tone that discomforted the boy. 'It would have been something if you'd cared enough to think of it, even if you didn't do it.'

'Now, Auntie, that ain't any harm,' pleaded Mary; 'it's only Tom's giddy way—he is always in such a rush that he never thinks of anything.'

'More's the pity. Sid would have thought. And Sid would have come and done it, too. Tom, you'll look back, some day, when it's too late, and wish you'd cared a little more for me when it would have cost you so little.'

'Now, Auntie, you know I do care for you,' said Tom.

'I'd know it better if you acted more like it.'

'I wish now I'd thought,' said Tom, with a repentant tone; 'but I dreamt about you, anyway. That's something, ain't it?'

'It ain't much—a cat does that much—but it's better than nothing. What did you dream?'

'Why, Wednesday night I dreamt that you was sitting over there by the bed, and Sid was sitting by the wood-box, and Mary next to him.'

'Well, so we did. So we always do. I'm glad your dreams could take even that much trouble about us.'

'And I dreamt that Joe Harper's mother was here.'

'Why, she was here! Did you dream any more?'

'Oh, lots. But it's so dim now.'

'Well, try to recollect—can't you?'

'Somehow it seems to me that the wind—the wind blowed the—the—'

'Try harder, Tom! The wind did blow something, come!'

Tom pressed his fingers on his forehead an anxious minute, and then said:

'I've got it now! I've got it now! It blowed the candle!'

'Mercy on us! Go on, Tom, go on!'

'And it seems to me that you said, "Why, I believe that that door—"'

'Go on, Tom!'

'Just let me study a moment—just a moment. Oh, yes—you said you believed the door was open.'

'As I'm sitting here, I did! Didn't I, Mary? Go on!'

'And then—and then—well, I won't be certain, but it seems like as if you made Sid go and—and—'

'Well? Well? What did I make him do, Tom? What did I make him do?'

'You made him—you—Oh, you made him shut it!'

'Well, for the land's sake! I never heard the beat of that in all my days! Don't tell me there ain't anything in dreams any more. Sereny Harper shall know of this before I'm an hour older. I'd like to see her get around this with her rubbage about superstition. Go on, Tom!'

'Oh, it's all getting just as bright as day, now. Next you said I warn't bad, only mischeevous and harum-scarum, and not any more responsible than—than—I think it was a colt, or something.'

'And so it was! Well! Goodness gracious! Go on, Tom!'

'And then you began to cry.'

'So I did. So I did. Not the first time, neither. And then—'

'Then Mrs Harper she began to cry, and said Joe was just the same, and she wished she hadn't whipped him for taking cream when she'd throwed it out her ownself—'

'Tom! The sperrit was upon you! You was a prophesying—that's what you was doing! Land alive!—go on, Tom!'

'Then Sid he said—he said—'

'I don't think I said anything,' said Sid.

'Yes, you did, Sid,' said Mary.

'Shut your heads and let Tom go on! What did he say, Tom?'

'He said—I think he said he hoped I was better off where I was gone to, but if I'd been better sometimes—'

'There, d'you hear that! It was his very words!'

'And you shut him up sharp.'

'I lay I did! There must a been an angel there. There was an angel there, somewheres!'

'And Mrs Harper told about Joe scaring her with a fire-cracker, and you told about Peter and the Pain-killer—'

'Just as true as I live!'

'And then there was a whole lot of talk 'bout dragging the river for us, and 'bout having the funeral Sunday, and then you and old Mrs Harper hugged and cried, and she went.'

'It happened just so! It happened just so, as sure as I'm a sitting in these very tracks. Tom, you couldn't told it more like if you'd a seen it! And then what? Go on, Tom.'

'Then I thought you prayed for me—and I could see you and hear every word you said. And you went to bed, and I was so sorry that I took and wrote on a piece of sycamore bark, "We ain't dead—we are only off being pirates", and put it on the table by the candle; and then you looked so good, laying there asleep, that I thought I went and leaned over and kissed you on the lips.'

'Did you, Tom, did you! I just forgive you everything for that!' And she seized the boy in a crushing embrace that made him feel like the guiltiest of villains.

'It was very kind, even though it was only a—dream,' Sid soliloquized just audibly.

'Shut up, Sid! A body does just the same in a dream as he'd do if he was awake. Here's a big Milum apple I've been saving for you, Tom, if you was ever found again—now go 'long to school. I'm thankful to the good God and Father of us all I've got you back, that's long-suffering and merciful to them that believe on Him and keep His word, though goodness knows I'm unworthy of it, but if only the worthy ones got His blessings and had His hand to help them over the rough places, there's few enough would smile here or ever enter into His rest when the long night comes. Go 'long, Sid, Mary, Tom—take yourselves off—you've hendered me long enough.'

The children left for school, and the old lady to call on Mrs Harper and vanquish her realism with Tom's marvellous dream. Sid had better judgement than to utter the thought that was in his mind as he left the house. It was this:

'Pretty thin—as long a dream as that, without any mistakes in it!'

What a hero Tom was become now! He did not go skipping and prancing, but moved with a dignified swagger, as became a pirate who felt that the public eye was on him. And indeed it was; he tried not to seem to see the looks or hear the remarks as he passed along, but they were food and drink to him. Smaller boys than himself flocked at his heels, as proud to be seen with him and tolerated by him as if he had been the drummer at the head of a procession, or the elephant leading a menagerie into town. Boys of his own size pretended not to know he had been away at all, but they were consuming with envy, nevertheless. They would have given anything to have that swarthy, sun-tanned skin of his, and his glittering notoriety; and Tom would not have parted with either for a circus.

At school the children made so much of him and Joe, and delivered such eloquent admiration from their eyes, that the two heroes were not long in becoming insufferably 'stuck-up.' They began to tell their adventures to hungry listeners—but they only began; it was not a thing likely to have an end, with imaginations like theirs to furnish material. And finally, when they got out their pipes and went serenely puffing around, the very summit of glory was reached.

Tom decided that he could be independent of Becky Thatcher now. Glory was sufficient. He would live for glory. Now that he was distinguished, maybe she would be wanting to 'make up.' Well, let her—she should see that he could be as indifferent as some other people. Presently she arrived. Tom pretended not to see her. He moved away and joined a group of boys and girls and began to talk. Soon he observed that she was tripping gaily back and forth with flushed face and dancing eyes, pretending to be busy chasing schoolmates, and screaming with laughter when she made a capture, but he noticed that she always made her captures in his vicinity, and that she seemed to cast a conscious eye in his direction at such times, too. It gratified all the vicious vanity that was in him; and so, instead of winning him, it only 'set him up' the more and made him the more diligent to avoid betraying that he knew she was about. Presently, she gave over skylarking, and moved irresolutely about, sighing once or twice and glancing furtively and wistfully towards Tom. Then she observed that now Tom was talking more particularly to Amy Lawrence than to anyone else. She felt a sharp pang and grew disturbed and uneasy at once. She tried to go away, but her feet were treacherous, and carried her to the group instead. She said to a girl almost at Tom's elbow—with sham vivacity:

'Why, Mary Austin! you bad girl, why didn't you come to Sunday-school?'

'I did come—didn't you see me?'

'Why, no! Did you? Where did you sit?'

'I was in Miss Peter's class, where I always go. I saw you.'

'Did you? Why, it's funny I didn't see you. I wanted to tell you about the picnic.'

'Oh, that's jolly. Who's going to give it?'

'My ma's going to let me have one.'

'Oh, goody; I hope she'll let me come.'

'Well, she will. The picnic's for me. She'll let anybody come that I want, and I want you.'

'That's ever so nice. When is it going to be?'

'By-and-by. Maybe about vacation.'

'Oh, won't it be fun! You going to have all the girls and boys?'

'Yes, every one that's friends to me—or wants to be,' and she glanced ever so furtively at Tom, but he talked right along to Amy Lawrence about the terrible storm on the island, and how the lightning tore the great sycamore tree 'all to flinders' while he was 'standing within three feet of it.'

'Oh, may I come?' said Gracie Miller.

'Yes.'

'And me?' said Sally Rogers.

'Yes.'

'And me too?' said Susy Harper. 'And Joe?'

'Yes.'

And so on, with clapping of joyful hands till all the group had begged for invitations but Tom and Amy. Then Tom turned coolly away, still talking, and took Amy with him. Becky's lips trembled and the tears came to her eyes; she hid these signs with a forced gaiety and went on chattering, but the life had gone out of the picnic, now, and out of everything else; she got away as soon as she could and hid herself, and had what her sex call 'a good cry.' Then she sat moody, with wounded pride, till the bell rang. She roused up, now, with a vindictive cast in her eye, and gave her plaited tails a shake, and said she knew what she'd do.

At recess Tom continued his flirtation with Amy with jubilant self-satisfaction. And he kept drifting about to find Becky and lacerate her with the performance. At last he spied her, but there was a sudden falling of his mercury. She was sitting cosily on a little bench behind the school-house, looking at a picture-book with Alfred Temple; and so absorbed were they, and their heads so close together over the book, that they did not seem to be conscious of anything in the world beside. Jealousy ran red-hot through Tom's veins. He began to hate himself for throwing away the chance Becky had offered for a reconciliation. He called himself a fool, and all the hard names he could think of. He wanted to cry with vexation. Amy chatted happily along, as they walked, for her heart was singing, but Tom's tongue had lost its function. He did not hear what Amy was saying, and whenever she paused expectantly, he could only stammer an awkward assent, which was as often misplaced as otherwise. He kept drifting to the rear of the school-house again and again, to sear his eyeballs with the hateful spectacle there. He could not help it. And it maddened him to see, as he thought he saw, that Becky Thatcher never once suspected that he was even in the land of the living. But she did see, nevertheless; and she knew she was winning her fight, too, and was glad to see him suffer as she had suffered. Amy's happy prattle became intolerable. Tom hinted at things he had to attend to; things that must be done; and time was fleeting. But in vain—the girl chirped on. Tom thought, 'Oh, hang her, ain't I ever going to get rid of her?' At last he must be attending to those things; she said artlessly that she would be 'around' when school let out. And he hastened away, hating her for it.

'Any other boy!' Tom thought, grating his teeth. 'Any boy in the whole town but that Saint Louis smarty, that thinks he dresses so fine and is aristocracy! Oh, all right. I licked you the first time you ever saw this town, mister, and I'll lick you again! You just wait till I catch you out! I'll just take and—'

And he went through the motions of thrashing an imaginary boy—pummelling the air, and kicking and gouging.

'Oh, you do, do you? you holler 'nough, do you? Now, then, let that learn you!'

And so the imaginary flogging was finished to his satisfaction.

Tom fled home at noon. His conscience could not endure any more of Amy's grateful happiness, and his jealousy could bear no more of the other distress. Becky resumed her picture-inspections with Alfred, but as the minutes dragged along and no Tom came to suffer, her triumph began to cloud and she lost interest; gravity and absent-mindedness followed, and then melancholy; two or three times she pricked up her ear at a footstep, but it was a false hope; no Tom came. At last she grew entirely miserable, and wished she hadn't carried it so far. When poor Alfred, seeing that he was losing her he did not know how, kept exclaiming: 'Oh, here's a jolly one! look at this!' she lost patience at last and said, 'Oh, don't bother me! I don't care for them!' and burst into tears, and got up and walked away.

Alfred dropped alongside and was going to try to comfort her, but she said:

'Go away and leave me alone, can't you! I hate you!'

So the boy halted, wondering what he could have done—for she had said she would look at pictures all through the nooning—and she walked on, crying. Then Alfred went musing into the deserted school-house. He was humiliated and angry. He easily guessed his way to the truth—the girl had simply made a convenience of him to vent her spite on Tom Sawyer. He was far from hating Tom the less when this thought occurred to him. He wished there was some way to get that boy into trouble without much risk to himself. Tom's spelling-book fell under his eye. Here was his opportunity. He gratefully opened to the lesson for the afternoon, and poured ink upon the page. Becky, glancing in at a window behind him at the moment, saw the act and moved on without discovering herself. She started homeward, now, intending to find Tom and tell him: Tom would be thankful and their troubles would be healed. Before she was half-way home, however, she had changed her mind. The thought of Tom's treatment of her when she was talking about her picnic came scorching back, and filled her with shame. She resolved to let him get whipped on the damaged spelling-book's account, and to hate him for ever into the bargain.

Chapter 20

Tom ARRIVED AT HOME in a dreary mood, and the first thing his aunt said to him showed him that he had brought his sorrows to an unpromising market:

'Tom, I've a notion to skin you alive.'

'Auntie, what have I done?'

'Well, you've done enough. Here I go over to Sereny Harper like an old softy, expecting I'm going to make her believe all that rubbage about that dream, when, lo and behold you, she'd found out from Joe that you was over here and heard all the talk we had that night. Tom, I don't know what is to become of a boy that will act like that. It makes me feel so bad to think you could let me go to Sereny Harper, and make such a fool of myself, and never say a word.'

This was a new aspect of the thing. His smartness of the morning had seemed to Tom a good joke before, and very ingenious. It merely looked mean and shabby now. He hung his head and could not think of anything to say for a moment; then he said:

'Auntie, I wish I hadn't done it—but I didn't think.'

'Oh, child, you never think. You never think of anything but your own selfishness. You could think to come all the way over here from Jackson's Island in the night to laugh at our troubles, and you could think to fool me with a lie about a dream: but you couldn't ever think to pity us and save us from sorrow.'

'Auntie, I know now it was mean, but I didn't mean to be mean; I didn't, honest. And besides, I didn't come over here to laugh at you that night.'

'What did you come for, then?'

'It was to tell you not to be uneasy about us, because we hadn't got drowned.'

'Tom, Tom, I would be the thankfullest soul in this world if I could believe you ever had as good a thought as that, but you know you never did—and I know it, Tom.'

'Indeed and 'deed I did, Auntie—I wish I may never stir if I didn't.'

'Oh, Tom, don't lie—don't do it. It only makes things a hundred times worse.'

'It ain't a lie, Auntie; it's the truth. I wanted to keep you from grieving—that was all that made me come.'

'I'd give the whole world to believe that—it would cover up a power of sins, Tom. I'd 'most be glad you'd run off and acted so bad. But it ain't reasonable; because why didn't you tell me, child?'

'Why, you see, Auntie, when you got to talking about the funeral, I just got all full of the idea of our coming and hiding in the church, and I couldn't, somehow, bear to spoil it. So I just put the bark back in my pocket and kept mum.'

'What bark?'

'The bark I had wrote on to tell you we'd gone pirating. I wish now, you'd waked up when I kissed you—I do, honest.'

The hard lines in his aunt's face relaxed, and sudden tenderness dawned in her eyes.

'*Did* you kiss me, Tom?'

'Why, yes, I did.'

'Are you sure you did, Tom?'

'Why, yes, I did, Auntie—certain sure.'

'What did you kiss me for, Tom?'

'Because I loved you so, and you laid there moaning, and I was so sorry.'

The words sounded like truth. The old lady could not hide a tremor in her voice when she said:

'Kiss me again, Tom!—and be off with you to school, now, and don't bother me any more.'

The moment he was gone, she ran to a closet and got out the ruin of a jacket which Tom had gone pirating in. Then she stopped with it in her hand, and said to herself:

'No, I don't dare. Poor boy, I reckon he's lied about it—but it's a blessed, blessed lie, there's such comfort come in it. I hope the Lord—I *know* the Lord will forgive him because it was such good-heartedness in him to tell it. But I don't want to find out it's a lie. I won't look.'

She put the jacket away, and stood by musing a minute. Twice she put out her hand to take the garment again, and twice she refrained. Once more she ventured, and this time she fortified herself with the thought: 'It's a good lie—it's a good lie—I won't let it grieve me.' So she sought the jacket pocket. A moment later she was reading Tom's piece of bark through flowing tears and saying:

'I could forgive the boy, now, if he'd committed a million sins!'

Chapter 21

THERE WAS SOMETHING about Aunt Polly's manner when she kissed Tom, that swept away his low spirits and made him light-hearted and happy again. He started to school, and had the luck of coming upon Becky Thatcher at the head of Meadow Lane. His mood always determined his manner. Without a moment's hesitation he ran to her and said:

'I acted mighty mean today, Becky, and I'm so sorry. I won't ever, ever do that way again as long as ever I live—please make up, won't you?'

The girl stopped and looked him scornfully in the face:

'I'll thank you to keep yourself *to* yourself, Mr Thomas Sawyer. I'll never speak to you again.'

She tossed her head and passed on. Tom was so stunned that he had not even presence of mind enough to say 'Who cares, Miss Smarty?' until the right time to say it had gone by. So he said nothing. But he was in a fine rage, nevertheless. He moped into the school-yard wishing she were a boy, and imagining how he would trounce her if she were. He presently encountered her and delivered a stinging re-mark as he passed. She hurled one in return, and the angry breach was complete. It seemed to Becky, in her hot resentment, that she could hardly wait for school to 'take in,' she was so impatient to see Tom flogged for the injured spelling-book. If she had had any linger-ing notion of exposing Alfred Temple, Tom's offensive fling had driven it entirely away.

Poor girl, she did not know how fast she was nearing trouble her-self. The master, Mr Dobbins, had reached middle age with an unsat-isfied ambition. The darling of his desires was to be a doctor, but poverty had decreed that he should be nothing higher than a village schoolmaster. Every day he took a mysterious book out of his desk, and absorbed himself in it at times when no classes were reciting. He kept that book under lock and key. There was not an urchin in school but was perishing to have a glimpse of it, but the chance never came.

Every boy and girl had a theory about the nature of that book; but no two theories were alike, and there was no way of getting at the facts in the case. Now as Becky was passing by the desk, which stood near the door, she noticed that the key was in the lock! It was a precious moment. She glanced around; found herself alone, and the next instant she had the book in her hands. The title-page—Professor somebody's *Anatomy*—carried no information to her mind; so she began to turn the leaves. She came at once upon a handsomely engraved and coloured frontispiece—a human figure. At that moment a shadow fell on the page, and Tom Sawyer stepped in at the door and caught a glimpse of the picture. Becky snatched at the book to close it, and had the hard luck to tear the pictured page half down the middle. She thrust the volume into the desk, turned the key, and burst out crying with shame and vexation:

'Tom Sawyer, you are just as mean as you can be, to sneak up on a person and look at what they're looking at.'

'How could *I* know you was looking at anything?'

'You ought to be ashamed of yourself, Tom Sawyer; you know you're going to tell on me, and, oh, what shall I do, what shall I do? I'll be whipped, and I never was whipped in school.'

Then she stamped her little foot and said:

'*Be* so mean if you want to! *I* know something that's going to happen. You just wait, and you'll see! Hateful, hateful, hateful!'—and she flung out of the house with a new explosion of crying.

Tom stood still, rather flustered by this onslaught. Presently he said to himself:

'What a curious kind of a fool a girl is. Never been licked in school! Shucks, what's a licking! That's just like a girl—they're so thin-skinned and chicken-hearted. Well, of course *I* ain't going to tell old Dobbins on this little fool, because there's other ways of getting even on her that ain't so mean; but what of it? Old Dobbins will ask who it was tore his book. Nobody'll answer. Then he'll do just the way he always does—ask first one and then t'other, and when he comes to the right girl he'll know it, without any telling. Girls' faces always tell on them. They ain't got any backbone. She'll get licked. Well, it's a kind of a tight place for Becky Thatcher, because there ain't any way out of it.' Tom conned the thing a moment longer, and then added: 'All right, though; she'd like to see me in just such a fix—let her sweat it out!'

Tom joined the mob of skylarking scholars outside. In a few moments the master arrived and school 'took in'. Tom did not feel a strong interest in his studies. Every time he stole a glance at the girls' side of the room, Becky's face troubled him. Considering all things, he did not want to pity her, and yet it was all he could do to help it. He could get up no exultation that was really worth the name. Presently the spelling-book discovery was made, and Tom's mind was entirely full of his own matters for a while after that. Becky roused up from her lethargy of distress, and showed good interest in the proceedings. She did not expect that Tom could get out of his trouble by denying that he spilt the ink on the book himself; and she was right. The denial only seemed to make the thing worse for Tom. Becky supposed she would be glad of that, and she tried to believe she was glad of it, but she found she was not certain. When the worst came to the worst, she had an impulse to get up and tell on Alfred Temple, but she made an effort and forced herself to keep still, because, said she to herself, 'he'll tell about me tearing the picture, sure. I wouldn't say a word, not to save his life!'

Tom took his whipping and went back to his seat not at all broken-hearted, for he thought it was possible that he had unknowingly upset the ink on the spelling-book himself, in some skylarking bout—he had denied it for form's sake and because it was custom, and had stuck to the denial from principle.

A whole hour drifted by; the master sat nodding in his throne, the air was drowsy with the hum of study. By-and-by Mr Dobbins straightened himself up, yawned, then unlocked his desk, and reached for his book, but seemed undecided whether to take it out or leave it. Most of the pupils glanced up languidly, but there were two among them that watched his movements with intent eyes. Mr Dobbins fingered his book absently for a while, then took it out, and settled himself in his chair to read.

Tom shot a glance at Becky. He had seen a hunted and helpless rabbit look as she did, with a gun levelled at its head. Instantly he forgot his quarrel with her. Quick, something must be done! done in a flash, too! But the very imminence of the emergency paralyzed his invention. Good! he had an inspiration! He would run and snatch the book, spring through the door and fly! but his resolution shook for one little instant, and the chance was lost—the master opened the volume. If Tom only had the wasted opportunity back again! Too late; there was no help for Becky now, he said. The next moment the master faced the school. Every eye sank under his gaze; there was that in it which smote even the innocent with fear. There was silence while one might count ten; the master was gathering his wrath. Then he spoke:

'Who tore this book?'

There was not a sound. One could have heard a pin drop. The stillness continued; the master searched face after face for signs of guilt.

'Benjamin Rogers, did you tear this book?'

A denial. Another pause.

'Joseph Harper, did you?'

Another denial. Tom's uneasiness grew more and more intense under the slow torture of these proceedings. The master scanned the ranks of boys, considered a while, then turned to the girls:

'Amy Lawrence?'

A shake of the head.

'Gracie Miller?'

The same sign.

'Susan Harper, did you do this?'

Another negative. The next girl was Becky Thatcher. Tom was trembling from head to foot with excitement, and a sense of the hopelessness of the situation.

'Rebecca Thatcher'—(Tom glanced at her face; it was white with terror)—'did you tear—no, look me in the face'—(her hands rose in appeal)—'did you tear this book?'

A thought shot like lightning through Tom's brain. He sprang to his feet and shouted:

'I done it!'

The school stared in perplexity at this incredible folly. Tom stood a moment to gather his dismembered faculties; and when he stepped forward to go to his punishment, the surprise, the gratitude, the adoration that shone upon him out of poor Becky's eyes seemed pay enough for a hundred floggings. Inspired by the splendour of his own act, he took without an outcry the most merciless flogging that even Mr Dobbins had ever administered; and also received with indifference the added cruelty of a command to remain two hours after school should be dismissed—for he knew who would wait for him outside till his captivity was done, and not count the tedious time as loss either.

Tom went to bed that night planning vengeance against Alfred Temple; for with shame and repentance Becky had told him all, not forgetting her own treachery; but even the longing for vengeance had to give way soon to pleasanter musings, and he fell asleep at last with Becky's latest words lingering dreamily in his ear:

'Tom, how *could* you be so noble!'

Chapter 22

VACATION WAS APPROACHING. The schoolmaster, always severe, grew severer and more exacting than ever, for he wanted the school to make a good showing on 'Examination' day. His rod and his ferule were seldom idle now—at least among the smaller pupils. Only the biggest boys, and young ladies of eighteen and twenty, escaped lashing. Mr Dobbins's lashings were very vigorous ones too; for although he carried, under his wig, a perfectly bald and shiny head, he had only reached middle age and there was no sign of feebleness in his muscle. As the great day approached, all the tyranny that was in him came to the surface; he seemed to take a vindictive pleasure in punishing the least shortcomings. The consequence was that the smallest boys spent their days in terror and suffering and their nights in plotting revenge. They threw away no opportunity to do the master a mischief. But he kept ahead all the time. The retribution that followed every vengeful success was so sweeping and majestic that the boys always retired from the field badly worsted. At last they conspired together and hit upon a plan that promised a dazzling victory. They swore in the sign-painter's boy, told him the scheme, and asked his help. He had his own reasons for being delighted, for the master boarded in his father's family and had given the boy ample cause to hate him. The master's wife would go on a visit to the country in a few days, and there would be nothing to interfere with the plan; the master always prepared himself for great occasions by getting pretty well fuddled, and the sign-painter's boy said that when the dominie had reached the proper condition on 'Examination' evening he could 'manage the thing' while he napped on his chair; then he would have him awakened at the right time and hurried away to school.

In the fullness of time the interesting occasion arrived. At eight in the evening the school-house was brilliantly lighted and adorned with wreaths and festoons of foliage and flowers. The master sat throned in his great chair upon a raised platform, with his blackboard behind him. He was looking tolerably mellow. Three rows of benches on each side and six rows in front of him were occupied by the dignitaries of the town and by the parents of the pupils. To his left, back of the rows of citizens, was a spacious temporary platform upon which were seated the scholars who were to take part in the exercises of the evening; rows of small boys, washed and dressed to an intolerable state of discomfort; rows of gawky big boys; snow-banks of girls and young ladies clad in lawn and muslin, and conspicuously conscious of their bare arms, their grandmothers' ancient trinkets, their bits of pink and blue ribbon, and the flowers in their hair. All the rest of the house was filled with non-participating scholars.

The exercises began. A very little boy stood up and sheepishly recited, 'You'd scarce expect one of my age, to speak in public on the stage,' etc., accompanying himself with the painfully exact and spasmodic gestures which a machine might have used—supposing the machine to be a trifle out of order. But he got through safely, though cruelly scared, and got a fine round of applause when he made his manufactured bow and retired.

A little shamefaced girl lisped, 'Mary had a little lamb,' etc., performed a compassion-inspiring curtsey, got her meed of applause, and sat down flushed and happy.

Tom Sawyer stepped forward with conceited confidence, and soared into the unquenchable and indestructible 'Give me liberty or give me death' speech, with fine fury and frantic gesticulation, and broke down in the middle of it. A ghastly stage-fright seized him, his legs quaked under him and he was like to choke. True, he had the manifest sympathy of the house—but he had the house's silence too, which was even worse than its sympathy. The master frowned, and this completed the disaster. Tom struggled a while and then retired, utterly defeated. There was a weak attempt at applause, but it died early.

'The Boy Stood on the Burning Deck' followed; also 'The Assyrian Came Down', and other declamatory gems. Then there were reading exercises, and a spelling fight. The meagre Latin class recited with honour. The prime feature of the evening was in order, now— original 'compositions' by the young ladies. Each in her turn stepped forward to the edge of the platform, cleared her throat, held up her manuscript (tied with dainty ribbon), and proceeded to read, with laboured attention to 'expression' and punctuation. The themes were the same that had been illuminated upon similar occasions by their mothers before them, their grandmothers, and doubtless all their ancestors in the female line clear back to the Crusades. 'Friendship' was one; 'Memories of Other Days'; 'Religion in History'; 'Dream Land'; 'The Adventures of Culture'; 'Forms of Political Government Compared and Contrasted'; 'Melancholy'; 'Filial Love'; 'Heart Longings', etc., etc.

A prevalent feature in these compositions was a nursed and petted melancholy; another was a wasteful and opulent gush of 'fine language'; another was a tendency to lug in by the ears particularly prized words and phrases until they were worn entirely out; and a peculiarity that conspicuously marked and marred them was the inveterate and intolerable sermon that wagged its crippled tail at the end of each and every one of them. No matter what the subject might be, a brainracking effort was made to squirm it into some aspect or other that the moral and religious mind could contemplate with edification. The glaring insincerity of these sermons was not sufficient to compass banishment of the fashion from the schools, and it is not sufficient today; it never will be sufficient while the world stands, perhaps. There is no school in all our land where the young ladies do not feel obliged to close their compositions with a sermon; and you will find that the sermon of the most frivolous and the least religious girl in the school is always the longest and the most relentlessly pious. But enough of this. Homely truth is unpalatable. Let us return to the 'Examination'. The first composition that was read was one entitled 'Is this, then, Life?' Perhaps the reader can endure an extract from it:

'In the common walks of life, with what delightful emotions does the youthful mind look forward to some anticipated scene of festivity! Imagination is busy sketching rose-tinted pictures of joy. In fancy, the voluptuous votary of fashion sees herself amid the festive throng, "the observed of all observers". Her graceful form, arrayed in snowy robes, is whirling through the mazes of the joyous dance; her eye is brightest, her step is lightest in the gay assembly. In such delicious fancies time quickly glides by, and the welcome hour arrives for her entrance into the Elysian world, of which she has had such bright dreams. How fairylike does everything appear to her enchanted vision! Each new scene is more charming than the last. But after a while she finds that beneath this goodly exterior, all is vanity; the flattery which once charmed her soul, now grates harshly upon her ear; the ballroom has lost its charms; and with wasted health and embittered heart, she turns away with the conviction that earthly pleasures cannot satisfy the longings of the soul!'

And so forth and so on. There was a buzz of gratification from time to time during the reading, accompanied by whispered ejaculations of 'How sweet!' 'How eloquent!' 'So true!' etc., and after the thing had closed with a peculiarly afflicting sermon, the applause was enthusiastic.

Then arose a slim, melancholy girl, whose face had the 'interesting' paleness that comes of pills and indigestion, and read a 'poem'. Two stanzas of it will do.

> A MISSOURI MAIDEN'S FAREWELL TO ALABAMA
> Alabama, good-bye! I love thee well!
> But yet for a while do I leave thee now!
> Sad, yes, sad thoughts of thee my heart doth swell,
> And burning recollections throng my brow!
> For I have wandered through thy flowery woods;
> Have roamed and read near Tallapoosa's stream;
> Have listened to Talassee's warring floods,
> And wooed on Coosa's side Aurora's beam.
>
> Yet shame I not to bear an o'er-full heart,
> Nor blush to turn behind my tearful eyes;
> 'Tis from no stranger land I now must part,
> 'Tis to no strangers left I yield these sighs.
> Welcome and home were mine within this State
> Whose vales I leave, whose spires fade fast from me;
> And cold must be mine eyes, and heart, and *tête*,
> When, clear Alabama! they turn cold on thee!

There were very few there who knew what 'tête' meant but the poem was very satisfactory nevertheless.

Next appeared a dark-complexioned, black-eyed, black-haired young lady, who paused an impressive moment, assumed a tragic expression, and began to read in a measured, solemn tone:

A VISION

Dark and tempestuous was the night. Around the throne on high not a single star quivered; but the deep intonations of the heavy thunder constantly vibrated upon the ear; whilst the terrific lightning revelled in angry mood through the cloudy chambers of heaven, seeming to scorn the power exerted over its terror by the illustrious Franklin! Even the boisterous winds unanimously came forth from their mystic homes, and blustered about as if to enhance by their aid the wildness of the scene. At such a time, so dark, so dreary, for human sympathy my very spirit sighed; but instead thereof,

> My dearest friend, my counsellor, my comforter and guide,
> My joy is grief, my second bliss in joy, came to my side.

She moved like one of those bright beings pictured in the sunny walks of fancy's Eden by the romantic and young, a queen of beauty unadorned save by her own transcendent loveliness. So soft was her step, it failed to make even a sound, and but for the magical thrill imparted by her genial touch, as other unobtrusive beauties she would have glided away unperceived—unsought. A strange sadness rested upon her features, like icy tears upon the robe of December, as she pointed to the contending elements without, and bade me contemplate the two beings presented.

This nightmare occupied some ten pages of manuscript, and wound up with a sermon so destructive of all hope to non-Presbyterians that it took the first prize. This composition was considered to be the very finest effort of the evening. The mayor of the village, in delivering the prize to the author of it, made a warm speech, in which he said that it was by far the most 'eloquent thing he had ever listened to, and that Daniel Webster himself might well be proud of it.'

It may be remarked in passing, that the number of compositions in which the word 'beauteous' was over-fondled, and human experience referred to as 'life's page', was up to the usual average.

Now the master, mellow almost to the verge of geniality, put his chair aside, turned his back to the audience, and began to draw a map of America on the blackboard, to exercise the geography class upon. But he made a sad business of it with his unsteady hand, and a smothered titter rippled over the house. He knew what the matter was, and set himself to right it. He sponged out lines and remade them; but he only distorted them more than ever, and the tittering was more pronounced. He threw his entire attention upon his work, now, as if determined not to be put down by the mirth. He felt that all eyes were fastened upon him; he imagined he was succeeding, and yet the tittering continued; it even manifestly increased. And well it might. There was a garret above, pierced with a scuttle over his head; and down through this scuttle came a cat suspended around the haunches by a string; she had a rag tied about her head and jaws to keep her from mewing; she slowly descended, she curved upward and clawed at the string, she swung downward and clawed at the intangible air. The tittering rose higher and higher, the cat was within six inches of the absorbed teacher's head; down, down, a little lower, and she grabbed his wig with her desperate claws, clung to it, and was snatched up into the garret in an instant with her trophy still in her possession! And how the light did blaze abroad from the master's bald pate, for the sign-painter's boy had *gilded* it!

That broke up the meeting. The boys were avenged. Vacation was come.

Note.– The pretended 'compositions' quoted above are taken without alteration from a volume entitled *Prose and Poetry by a Western Lady,* but they are exactly and precisely after the school-girl pattern, and hence are much happier than any mere imitations could be.

Chapter 23

Tom joined the new order of Cadets of Temperance, being attracted by the showy character of their 'regalia'. He promised to abstain from smoking, chewing, and profanity as long as he remained a member. Now he found out a new thing—namely, that to promise not to do a thing is the surest way in the world to make a body want to go and do that very thing. Tom soon found himself tormented with a desire to drink, and swear; the desire grew to be so intense that nothing but the hope of a chance to display himself in his red sash kept him from withdrawing from the order. Fourth of July was coming: but he soon gave that up—gave it up before he had worn his shackles over forty-eight hours, and fixed his hopes upon old Judge Frazer, justice of the peace, who was apparently on his deathbed, and would have a big public funeral, since he was so high an official. During three days Tom was deeply concerned about the Judge's condition, and hungry for news of it. Sometimes his hopes ran high, so high that he would venture to get out his regalia and practise before the looking-glass. But the Judge had a most discouraging way of fluctuating. At last he was pronounced upon the mend, and then convalescent. Tom was disgusted; and felt a sense of injury, too. He handed in his resignation at once, and that night the Judge suffered a relapse and died. Tom resolved that he would never trust a man like that again. The funeral was a fine thing. The Cadets paraded in a style calculated to kill the late member with envy.

Tom was a free boy again, however; there was something in that. He could drink and swear now, but found to his surprise that he did not want to. The simple fact that he could took the desire away, and the charm of it.

Tom presently wondered to find that his coveted vacation was beginning to hang a little heavily on his hands.

He attempted a diary, but nothing happened during three days, and so he abandoned it.

The first of all the Negro minstrel shows came to town, and made a sensation. Tom and Joe Harper got up a band of performers, and were happy for two days.

Even the Glorious Fourth was in some sense a failure, for it rained hard; there was no procession in consequence, and the greatest man in the world (as Tom supposed), Mr Benton, an actual United States Senator, proved an overwhelming disappointment, for he was not twenty-five feet high, nor even anywhere in the neighbourhood of it.

A circus came. The boys played circus for three days afterwards in tents made of rag carpeting—admission, three pins for boys, two for girls—and then circusing was abandoned.

A phrenologist and a mesmerizer came—and went again and left the village duller and drearier than ever.

There were some boys' and girls' parties, but they were so few and so delightful that they only made the aching voids between ache the harder.

Becky Thatcher was gone to her Constantinople home to stay with her parents during vacation—so there was no bright side to life anywhere.

The dreadful secret of the murder was a chronic misery. It was a very cancer for permanency and pain.

Then came the measles.

During two long weeks Tom lay a prisoner, dead to the world and its happenings. He was very ill, he was interested in nothing. When he got upon his feet at last and moved feebly down town, a melancholy change had come over everything and every creature. There had been a 'revival', and everybody had 'got religion'; not only the adults, but even the boys and girls. Tom went about, hoping against hope for the sight of one blessed sinful face, but disappointment crossed him everywhere. He found Joe Harper studying a Testament, and turned sadly away from the depressing spectacle. He sought Ben Rogers, and found him visiting the poor with a basket of tracts. He hunted up Jim Hollis, who called his attention to the precious blessing of his late measles as a warning. Every boy he encountered added another ton to his depression; and when, in desperation, he flew for refuge at last to the bosom of Huckleberry Finn and was received with a scriptural quotation, his heart broke, and he crept home and to bed, realizing that he alone of all the town was lost, for ever and for ever.

And that night there came on a terrific storm, with driving rain, awful claps of thunder and blinding sheets of lightning. He covered his head with the bedclothes and waited in a horror of suspense for his doom; for he had not the shadow of a doubt that all this hubbub

was about him. He believed he had taxed the forbearance of the pow-
ers above to the extremity of endurance, and that this was the result.
It might have seemed to him a waste of pomp and ammunition to kill
a bug with a battery of artillery, but there seemed nothing incongru-
ous about the getting up of such an expensive thunderstorm as this to
knock the turf from under an insect like himself.

By-and-by the tempest spent itself and died without accomplish-
ing its object. The boy's first impulse was to be grateful and reform.
His second was to wait—for there might not be any more storms.

The next day the doctors were back; Tom had relapsed. The three
weeks he spent on his back this time seemed an entire age. When he
got abroad at last he was hardly grateful that he had been spared, remembering how lonely was his estate, how companionless and forlorn
he was. He drifted listlessly down the street and found Jim Hollis act-
ing as judge in a juvenile court that was trying a cat for murder, in the
presence of her victim, a bird. He found Joe Harper and Huck Finn
up an alley eating a stolen melon. Poor fellows, they, like Tom, had
suffered a relapse.

Chapter 24

At last the sleepy atmosphere was stirred, and vigorously. The murder trial came on in the court. It became the absorbing topic of village talk immediately. Tom could not get away from it. Every reference to the murder sent a shudder to his heart, for his troubled conscience and fears almost persuaded him that these remarks were put forth in his hearing as 'feelers'; he did not see how he could be suspected of knowing anything about the murder, but still he could not be comfortable in the midst of this gossip. It kept him in a cold shiver all the time. He took Huck to a lonely place to have a talk with him. It would be some relief to unseal his tongue for a little while, to divide his burden of distress with another sufferer. Moreover, he wanted to assure himself that Huck had remained discreet.

'Huck, have you ever told anybody about that?'

''Bout what?'

'You know what.'

'Oh, 'course I haven't.'

'Never a word?'

'Never a solitary word, so help me. What makes you ask?'

'Well, I was afeard.'

'Why, Tom Sawyer, we wouldn't be alive two days if that got found out. *You* know that.'

Tom felt more comfortable. After a pause:

'Huck, they couldn't anybody get you to tell, could they?'

'Get me to tell? Why, if I wanted that half-breed devil to drownd me they could get me to tell. They ain't no different way.'

'Well, that's all right then. I reckon we're safe as long as we keep mum. But let's swear again, anyway. It's more surer!'

'I'm agreed.'

So they swore again with dread solemnities.

'What is the talk around, Huck? I've heard a power of it.'

'Talk? Well, it's just Muff Potter, Muff Potter, Muff Potter all the time. It keeps me in a sweat, constant, so's I want to hide som'ers.'

'That's just the same way they go on round me. I reckon he's a goner. Don't you feel sorry for him sometimes?'

'Most always—most always. He ain't no account; but then he ain't ever done anything to hurt anybody. Just fishes a little to get money to get drunk on—and loafs around considerable; but, Lord, we all do that—leastways most of us—preachers and such like. But he's kind of good—he gives me half a fish, once, when there wasn't enough for two; and lots of times he's kind of stood by me when I was out of luck.'

'Well, he's mended kites for me, Huck, and knitted hooks on to my line. I wish we could get him out of there.'

'My! we couldn't get him out, Tom. And besides, 'twouldn't do any good; they'd ketch him again.'

'Yes—so they would. But I hate to hear 'em abuse him so like the dickens when he never done—that.'

'I do too, Tom. Lord, I hear 'em say he's the bloodiest-looking villain in this country, and they wonder he wasn't ever hung before.'

'Yes; they talk like that all the time. I've heard 'em say that if he was to get free they'd lynch him.'

'And they'd do it, too.'

The boys had a long talk, but it brought them little comfort. As the twilight drew on, they found themselves hanging about the neighbourhood of the little isolated jail, perhaps with an undefined hope that something would happen that might clear away their difficulties. But nothing happened; there seemed to be no angels or fairies interested in this luckless captive.

The boys did as they had often done before—went to the cell grating and gave Potter some tobacco and matches. He was on the ground floor, and there were no guards.

His gratitude for their gifts had always smote their consciences before—it cut deeper than ever, this time. They felt cowardly and treacherous to the last degree when Potter said:

'You've ben mighty good to me, boys—better'n anybody else in this town. And I don't forget it, I don't. Often I says to myself, says I, "I used to mend all the boys' kites and things, and show 'em where the good fishin' places was, and befriend 'em when I could, and now they've all forgot old Muff wen he's in trouble, but Tom don't, and Huck don't—*they* don't forget him," says I, "and I don't forget *them!*" Well, boys, I done an awful thing—drunk and crazy at the time, that's the only way I account for it, and now I got to swing for it, and it's right. Right, and *best*, too, I reckon; hope so, anyway. Well, we won't talk about that. I don't want to make *you* feel bad; you've befriended me. But what I want to say is, don't *you* ever get drunk, then you won't ever get here. Stand a litter furder west; so, that's it; it's a prime comfort to see faces that's friendly when a body's in such a muck of trouble, and there don't none come here but yourn. Good friendly faces—good friendly faces. Get up on one another's backs, and let me touch 'em. That's it. Shake hands—yourn'll come through the bars, but mine's too big. Little hands, and weak—but they've helped Muff Potter a power, and they'd help him more if they could.'

Tom went home miserable, and his dreams that night were full of horrors. The next day and the day after, he hung about the court-room, drawn by an almost irresistible impulse to go in, but forcing himself to stay out. Huck was having the same experience. They studiously avoided each other. Each wandered away from time to time, but the same dismal fascination always brought them back presently. Tom kept his ears open when idlers sauntered out of the court-room, but invariably heard distressing news; the toils were closing more and more relentlessly around poor Potter. At the end of the second day the village talk was to the effect that Injun Joe's evidence stood firm and unshaken, and that there was not the slightest question as to what the jury's verdict would be.

Tom was out late that night, and came to bed through the window. He was in a tremendous state of excitement. It was hours before he got to sleep. All the village flocked to the court-house the next morning, for this was to be the great day. Both sexes were about equally represented in the packed audience. After a long wait the jury filed in and took their places; shortly afterwards, Potter, pale and haggard, timid and hopeless, was brought in with chains upon him, and seated where all the curious eyes could stare at him; no less conspicuous was Injun Joe, stolid as ever. There was another pause, and then the judge arrived, and the sheriff proclaimed the opening of the court. The usual whisperings among the lawyers and gathering together of papers followed. These details and accompanying delays worked up an atmosphere of preparation that was as impressive as it was fascinating.

Now a witness was called who testified that he found Muff Potter washing in the brook at an early hour of the morning that the murder was discovered, and that he immediately sneaked away. After some further questioning, counsel for the prosecution said:

'Take the witness.'

The prisoner raised his eyes for a moment, but dropped them again when his own counsel said:

'I have no questions to ask him.'

The next witness proved the finding of the knife near the corpse. Counsel for the prosecution said:

'Take the witness.'

'I have no questions to ask him,' Potter's lawyer replied.

A third witness swore he had often seen the knife in Potter's possession.

'Take the witness.'

Counsel for Potter declined to question him.

The faces of the audience began to betray annoyance. Did this attorney mean to throw away his client's life without an effort?

Several witnesses deposed concerning Potter's guilty behavior when brought to the scene of the murder. They were allowed to leave the stand without being cross-questioned.

Every detail of the damaging circumstances that occurred in the graveyard upon that morning which all present remembered so well was brought out by credible witnesses, but none of them were cross-examined by Potter's lawyer. The perplexity and dissatisfaction of the house expressed itself in murmurs and provoked a reproof from the bench. Counsel for the prosecution now said:

'By the oaths of citizens whose simple word is above suspicion, we have fastened this awful crime beyond all possibility of question upon the unhappy prisoner at the bar. We rest our case here.'

A groan escaped from poor Potter, and he put his face in his hands, and rocked his body softly to and fro, while a painful silence reigned in the court-room. Many men were moved, and many women's compassion testified itself in tears. Counsel for the defence rose and said:

'Your Honour, in our remarks at the opening of this trial, we foreshadowed our purpose to prove that our client did this fearful deed while under the influence of a blind and irresponsible delirium produced by drink. We have changed our mind; we shall not offer that plea. [Then to the clerk.] Call Thomas Sawyer.'

A puzzled amazement awoke in every face in the house, not even excepting Potter's. Every eye fastened itself with wondering interest upon Tom as he rose and took his place upon the stand.

The boy looked wild enough, for he was badly scared. The oath was administered.

'Thomas Sawyer, where were you on the seventeenth of June, about the hour of midnight?'

Tom glanced at Injun Joe's iron face, and his tongue failed him. The audience listened breathless, but the words refused to come. After a few moments, however, the boy got a little of his strength back, and managed to put enough of it into his voice to make part of the house hear:

'In the graveyard!'

'A little bit louder, please. Don't be afraid. You were—'

'In the graveyard.'

A contemptuous smile flitted across Injun Joe's face.

'Were you anywhere near Horse Williams's grave?'

'Yes, sir.'

'Speak up just a trifle louder. How near were you?'

'Near as I am to you.'

'Were you hidden or not?'

'I was hid.'

'Where?'

'Behind the elms that's on the edge of the grave.'

Injun Joe gave a barely perceptible start.

'Anyone with you?'

'Yes, sir. I went there with—'

'Wait—wait a moment. Never mind mentioning your companion's name. We will produce him at the proper time. Did you carry anything there with you?'

Tom hesitated and looked confused.

'Speak out, my boy—don't be diffident. The truth is always respectable. What did you take there?'

'Only a—a—dead cat.'

There was a ripple of mirth, which the court checked.

'We will produce the skeleton of that cat. Now my boy, tell us everything that occurred—tell it in your own way—don't skip anything, and don't be afraid.'

Tom began—hesitatingly at first, but, as he warmed to his subject, his words flowed more and more easily; in a little while every sound ceased but his own voice; every eye fixed itself upon him; with parted lips and bated breath the audience hung upon his words, taking no note of time, rapt in the ghastly fascinations of the tale. The strain upon pent emotion reached its climax when the boy said, 'And as the doctor fetched the board around and Muff Potter fell, Injun Joe jumped with the knife and—'

Crash! Quick as lightning, the half-breed sprang for a window, tore his way through all opposers, and was gone!

Chapter 25

Tom was a glittering hero once more—the pet of the old, the envy of the young. His name even went into immortal print, for the village paper magnified him. There were some that believed he would be President yet, if he escaped hanging.

As usual, the fickle unreasoning world took Muff Potter to its bosom, and fondled him as lavishly as it had abused him before. But that sort of conduct is to the world's credit; therefore it is not well to find fault with it.

Tom's days were days of splendour and exultation to him, but his nights were seasons of horror. Injun Joe infested all his dreams, and always with doom in his eye. Hardly any temptation could persuade the boy to stir abroad after nightfall. Poor Huck was in the same state of wretchedness and terror, for Tom had told the whole story to the lawyer the night before the great day of the trial, and Huck was sore afraid that his share in the business might leak out yet, notwithstanding Injun Joe's flight had saved him the suffering of testifying in court. The poor fellow had got the attorney to promise secrecy, but what of that? Since Tom's harassed conscience had managed to drive him to the lawyer's house by night and wring a dread tale from lips that had been sealed with the dismalest and most formidable of oaths, Huck's confidence in the human race was well-nigh obliterated. Daily Muff Potter's gratitude made Tom glad he had spoken; but nightly he wished he had sealed up his tongue. Half the time Tom was afraid Injun Joe would never be captured; the other half he was afraid he would be. He felt sure he never could draw a safe breath again until that man was dead and he had seen the corpse.

Rewards had been offered, the country had been scoured, but no Injun Joe was found. One of those omniscient and awe-inspiring marvels, a detective, came up from St Louis, moused around, shook his head, looked wise, and made that sort of astounding success which members of that craft usually achieve. That is to say, he 'found a clue'. But you can't hang a 'clue' for murder, and so after that detective had got through and gone home, Tom felt just as insecure as he was before.

The slow days drifted on, and each left behind it a slightly lightened weight of apprehension.

Chapter 26

THERE COMES A TIME in every rightly constructed boy's life when he has a raging desire to go somewhere and dig for hidden treasure. This desire suddenly came upon Tom one day. He sallied out to find Joe Harper, but failed of success. Next he sought Ben Rogers; he had gone fishing. Presently he stumbled upon Huck Finn the Red-handed. Huck would answer. Tom took him to a private place, and opened the matter to him confidentially. Huck was willing. Huck was always willing to take a hand in any enterprise that offered entertainment and required no capital, for he had a troublesome superabundance of that sort of time which is *not* money.

'Where'll we dig?' said Huck.

'Oh, most anywhere.'

'Why, is it hid all around?'

'No, indeed it ain't. It's hid in mighty particular places, Huck—sometimes on islands, sometimes in rotten chests under the end of a limb of an old dead tree, just where the shadow falls at midnight; but mostly under the floor in ha'nted houses.'

'Who hides it?'

'Why, robbers, of course—who'd you reckon? Sunday-school sup'rintendents?'

'I don't know. If it was mine I wouldn't hide it; I'd spend it and have a good time.'

'So would I; but robbers don't do that way, they always hide it and leave it there.'

'Don't they come after it any more?'

'No, they think they will, but they generally forget the marks, or else they die. Anyway it lays there a long time and gets rusty; and by-and-by somebody finds an old yellow paper that tells how to find the marks—a paper that's got to be ciphered over about a week because it's mostly signs and hy'roglyphics.'

'Hyro—which?'

'Hy'roglyphics—pictures and things, you know, that don't seem to mean anything.'

'Have you got one of them papers, Tom?'

'No.'

'Well, then, how you going to find the marks?'

'I don't want any marks. They always bury it under a ha'nted house, or on an island, or under a dead tree that's got one limb sticking out. Well, we've tried Jackson's Island a little, and we can try it again sometime; and there's the old ha'nted house up the Still-House branch, and there's lots of dead-limb trees—dead loads of 'em.'

'Is it under all of them?'

'How you talk! No!'

'Then how you going to know which one to go for?'

'Go for all of 'em.'

'Why, Tom, it'll take all summer.'

'Well, what of that? Suppose you find a brass pot with a hundred dollars in it, all rusty and gay, or a rotten chest full of di'monds. How's that?'

Huck's eyes glowed.

'That's bully, plenty bully enough for me. Just you gimme the hundred dollars, and I don't want no di'monds.'

'All right. But I bet you *I* ain't going to throw off on di'monds. Some of 'em's worth twenty dollars apiece. There ain't any, hardly, but's worth six bits or a dollar.'

'No! Is that so?'

'Cert'nly—anybody'll tell you so. Hain't you ever seen one, Huck?'

'Not as I remember.'

'Oh, kings have slathers of them.'

'Well, I don' know no kings, Tom.'

'I reckon you don't. But if you was to go to Europe you'd see a raft of 'em hopping around.'

'Do they hop?'

'Hop?—your granny! No!'

'Well, what did you say they did for?'

'Shucks! I only meant you'd *see* 'em—not hopping, of course— what do they want to hop for? But I mean you'd just see 'em—scattered around, you know, in a kind of a general way. Like that old humpbacked Richard.'

'Richard! What's his other name?'

'He didn't have any other name. Kings don't have any but a given name.'

'No?'

'But they don't.'

'Well, if they like it, Tom, all right; but I don't want to be a king and have only just a given name, like a nigger. But say—where you going to dig first?'

'Well, I don't know. S'pose we tackle that old dead limb tree on the hill t'other side of Still-House branch?'

'I'm agreed.'

So they got a crippled pick and a shovel, and set out on their three-mile tramp. They arrived hot and panting, and threw themselves down in the shade of a neighbouring elm to rest and have a smoke.

'I like this,' said Tom.

'So do I.'

'Say, Huck, if we find a treasure here, what you going to do with your share?'

'Well, I'll have a pie and a glass of soda every day, and I'll go to every circus that comes along. I'll bet I'll have a gay time.'

'Well, ain't you going to save any of it?'

'Save it? What for?'

'Why, so as to have something to live on by-and-by.'

'Oh, that ain't any use. Pap would come back to thish yer town some day and get his claws on it if I didn't hurry up, and I tell you he'd clean it out pretty quick. What you going to do with yourn, Tom?'

'I'm going to buy a new drum, and a sure-'nough sword, and a red necktie, and a bull-pup, and get married.'

'Married!'

'That's it.'

'Tom, you—why, you ain't in your right mind.'

'Wait—you'll see.'

'Well, that's the foolishest thing you could do, Tom. Look at Pap and my mother. Fight! why they used to fight all the time. I remember, mighty well.'

'That ain't anything. The girl I'm going to marry won't fight.'

'Tom, I reckon they're all alike. They'll all comb a body. Now you better think about this a while. I tell you you better. What's the name of the gal?'

'It ain't a gal at all—it's a girl.'

'It's all the same, I reckon; some says gal, some says girl—both's right, like enough. Anyway, what's her name, Tom?'

'I'll tell you some time—not now.'

'All right—that'll do. Only if you get married I'll be more lonesomer than ever.'

'No, you won't, you'll come and live with me. Now stir out of this, and we'll go to digging.'

They worked and sweated for half an hour. No result. They toiled another half hour. Still no result. Huck said:

'Do they always bury it as deep as this?'

'Sometimes—not always. Not generally. I reckon we haven't got the right place.'

So they chose a new spot and began again. The labour dragged a little, but still they made progress. They pegged away in silence for some time. Finally Huck leaned on his shovel, swabbed the beaded drops from his brow with his sleeve, and said:

'Where you going to dig next, after we get this one?'

'I reckon maybe we'll tackle the old tree that's over yonder on Cardiff Hill, back of the widow's.'

'I reckon that'll be a good one. But won't the widow take it away from us, Tom? It's on her land.'

'She take it away! Maybe she'd like to try it once. Whoever finds one of these hid treasures, it belongs to him. It don't make any difference whose land it's on.'

That was satisfactory. The work went on. By-and-by Huck said:

'Blame it, we must be in the wrong place again. What do you think?'

'It is mighty curious, Huck. I don't understand it. Sometimes witches interfere. I reckon maybe that's what's the trouble now.'

'Shucks! witches ain't got no power in the daytime.'

'Well, that's so. I didn't think of that. Oh, I know what the matter is! What a blamed lot of fools we are! You got to find out where the shadow of the limb falls at midnight, and that's where you dig!'

'Then confound it, we've fooled away all this work for nothing. Now hang it all, we got to come back in the night. It's an awful long way. Can you get out?'

'I bet I will. We've got to do it tonight, too, because if somebody sees these holes they'll know in a minute what's here and they'll go for it.'

'Well, I'll come around and meow tonight.'

'All right. Let's hide the tools in the bushes.'

The boys were there that night about the appointed time. They sat in the shadow waiting. It was a lonely place, and an hour made solemn by old traditions. Spirits whispered in the rustling leaves, ghosts lurked in the murky nooks, the deep baying of a hound floated up out of the distance, an owl answered with his sepulchral note. The boys were subdued by these solemnities, and talked little. By-and-by they judged that twelve had come; they marked where the shadow fell and began to dig. Their hopes commenced to rise. Their interest grew stronger, and their industry kept pace with it. The hole deepened and still deepened, but every time their hearts jumped to hear the pick strike upon something, they only suffered a new disappointment. It was only a stone or a chunk. At last Tom said:

'It ain't any use, Huck, we're wrong again.'

'Well, but we can't be wrong. We spotted the shadder to a dot.'

'I know it, but then there's another thing.'

'What's that?'

'Why, we only guessed at the time. Like enough it was too late or too early.'

Huck dropped his shovel.

'That's it,' said he. 'That's the very trouble. We got to give this one up. We can't ever tell the right time, and besides, this kind of thing's too awful, here this time of night with witches and ghosts a-fluttering around so. I feel as if something's behind me all the time; and I'm afeard to turn around, becuz maybe there's others in front a waiting for a chance. I been creeping all over ever since I got here.'

'Well, I've been pretty much so too, Huck. They 'most always put in a dead man when they bury a treasure under a tree, to look out for it.'

'Lordy!'

'Yes, they do. I've always heard that.'

'Tom, I don't like to fool around much where there's dead people. A body's bound to get into trouble with 'em, sure.'

'I don't like to stir 'em up, either, Huck. S'pose this one here was to stick his skull out and say something!'

'Don't, Tom! It's awful.'

'Well, it just is, Huck. I don't feel comfortable a bit.'

'Say, Tom, let's give this place up, and try somewheres else.'

'All right, I reckon we better.'

'What'll it be?'

Tom considered awhile, and then said:

'The ha'nted house. That's it.'

'Blame it. I don't like ha'nted houses, Tom. Why, they're a dern sight worse'n dead people. Dead people might talk maybe, but they don't come sliding around in a shroud when you ain't noticing, and peep over your shoulder all of a sudden and grit their teeth the way a ghost does. I couldn't stand such a thing as that, Tom—nobody could.'

'Yes; but, Huck, ghosts don't travel around only at night—they won't hinder us from digging there in the daytime.'

'Well, that's so. But you know mighty well people don't go about that ha'nted house in the day nor the night.'

'Well, that's mostly because they don't like to go where a man's been murdered, anyway. But nothing's ever been seen around that house in the night—just some blue lights slipping by the window— no regular ghosts.'

'Well, where you see one of them blue lights flickering around, Tom, you can bet there's a ghost mighty close behind it. It stands to reason. Becuz you know that they don't anybody but ghosts use 'em.'

'Yes, that's so. But anyway they don't come around in the daytime, so what's the use of our being afeard?'

'Well, all right. We'll tackle the ha'nted house if you say so; but I reckon it's taking chances.'

They had started down the hill by this time. There in the middle of the moonlit valley below them stood the 'haunted' house, utterly isolated, its fences gone long ago, rank weeds smothering the very door-step, the chimney crumbled to ruin, the window-sashes vacant, a corner of the roof caved in. The boys gazed awhile, half expecting to see a blue light flit past a window; then talking in a low tone, as befitted the time and the circumstances, they struck far off to the right, to give the haunted house a wide berth, and took their way homeward through the woods that adorned the rearward side of Cardiff Hill.

Chapter 27

ABOUT NOON THE NEXT DAY the boys arrived at the dead tree; they had come for their tools. Tom was impatient to go to the haunted house; Huck was measurably so, also, but suddenly said:

'Looky here, Tom, do you know what day it is?'

Tom mentally ran over the days of the week, and then quickly lifted his eyes with a startled look in them:

'My! I never once thought of it, Huck!'

'Well, I didn't, neither, but all at once it popped on to me that it was Friday.'

'Blame it; a body can't be too careful, Huck. We might a got into an awful scrape, tackling such a thing on a Friday.'

'Might! Better say we would! There's some lucky days, maybe, but Friday ain't.'

'Any fool knows that. I don't reckon you was the first that found it out, Huck.'

'Well, I never said I was, did I? And Friday ain't all, neither. I had a rotten bad dream last night—dreamt about rats.'

'No! Sure sign of trouble. Did they fight?'

'No.'

'Well, that's good, Huck. When they don't fight, it's only a sign that there's trouble around, you know. All we got to do is to look mighty sharp and keep out of it. We'll drop this thing for today, and play. Do you know Robin Hood, Huck?'

'No. Who's Robin Hood?'

'Why, he was one of the greatest men that was ever in England— and the best. He was a robber.'

'Cracky, I wisht I was. Who did he rob?'

'Only sheriffs and bishops and rich people and kings, and such like. But he never bothered the poor. He loved 'em. He always divided up with 'em perfectly square.'

'Well, he must a ben a brick.'

'I bet you he was, Huck. Oh, he was the noblest man that ever was. They ain't any such men now, I can tell you. He could lick any man in England with one hand tied behind him; and he could take his yew bow and plug a ten cent piece every time, a mile and a half.'

'What's a *yew* bow?'

'I don't know. It's some kind of a bow, of course. And if he hit that dime only on the edge he could set down and cry—and curse. But we'll play Robin Hood—it's noble fun. I'll learn you.'

'I'm agreed.'

So they played Robin Hood all the afternoon, now and then casting a yearning eye down upon the haunted house and passing a remark about the morrow's prospects and possibilities there. As the sun began to sink into the west, they took their way homeward athwart the long shadows of the trees and soon were buried from sight in the forests of Cardiff Hill.

On Saturday, shortly after noon, the boys were at the dead tree again. They had a smoke and a chat in the shade, and then dug a little in their last hole, not with great hope, but merely because Tom said there were so many cases where people had given up a treasure after getting down within six inches of it, and then somebody else had come along and turned it up with a single thrust of a shovel. The thing failed this time, however, so the boys shouldered their tools and went away, feeling that they had not trifled with fortune, but had fulfilled all the requirements that belong to the business of treasure-hunting.

When they reached the haunted house, there was something so weird and grisly about the dead silence that reigned there under the baking sun, and something so depressing about the loneliness and desolation of the place, that they were afraid, for a moment, to venture in. Then they crept to the door and took a trembling peep. They saw a weed-grown, floorless room, unplastered, an ancient fire-place, vacant windows, a ruinous staircase; and here, there, and everywhere, hung ragged and abandoned cobwebs. They presently entered softly, with quickened pulses, talking in whispers, ears alert to catch the slightest sound, and muscles tense and ready for instant retreat.

In a little while familiarity modified their fears, and they gave the place a critical and interested examination, rather admiring their own boldness, and wondering at it, too. Next they wanted to look upstairs. This was something like cutting off retreat, but they got to

daring each other, and of course there could be but one result—they
threw their tools into a corner and made the ascent. Up there were
the same signs of decay. In one corner they found a closet that promised mystery, but the promise was a fraud—there was nothing in it.
Their courage was up now, and well in hand. They were about to go
down and begin work when—

'*Sht!*' said Tom.

'What is it?' whispered Huck, blanching with fright.

'*Sh!* There! Hear it?'

'Yes! Oh, my! Let's run!'

'Keep still! Don't you budge! They're coming right towards the
door.'

The boys stretched themselves upon the floor with their eyes to
knot-holes in the planking, and lay waiting in a misery of fear.

'They've stopped—No—coming—Here they are. Don't whisper
another word, Huck. My goodness, I wish I was out of this!'

Two men entered. Each boy said to himself:

'There's the old deaf and dumb Spaniard that's been about town
once or twice lately—never saw t'other man before.'

'T'other' was a ragged, unkempt creature, with nothing very pleasant in his face. The Spaniard was wrapped in a *serape*; he had bushy
white whiskers, long white hair flowed from under his sombrero, and
he wore green goggles. When they came in, 't'other' was talking in a
low voice; they sat down on the ground, facing the door, with their
backs to the wall, and the speaker continued his remarks. His manner
became less guarded and his words more distinct as he proceeded.

'No,' said he, 'I've thought it all over, and I don't like it. It's
dangerous.'

'Dangerous!' grunted the 'deaf and dumb' Spaniard, to the vast
surprise of the boys. 'Milksop!'

This voice made the boys gasp and quake. It was Injun Joe's!
There was silence for some time. Then Joe said:

'What's any more dangerous than that job up yonder—but nothing's come of it.'

'That's different. Away up the river so, and not another house
about. 'Twon't ever be known that we tried, anyway, long as we didn't
succeed.'

'Well, what's more dangerous than coming here in the daytime?—
anybody would suspicion us that saw us.'

'I know that. But there wasn't any other place as handy after that fool of a job. I want to quit this shanty. I wanted to yesterday, only it warn't any use trying to stir out of here with those infernal boys playing over there on the hill right in full view.'

'Those infernal boys' quaked again under the inspiration of this remark, and thought how lucky it was that they had remembered it was Friday and concluded to wait a day. They wished in their hearts they had waited a year. The two men got out some food and made a luncheon. After a long and thoughtful silence, Injun Joe said:

'Look here, lad, you go back up the river where you belong. Wait there till you hear from me. I'll take the chances on dropping into this town just once more, for a look. We'll do that "dangerous" job after I've spied around a little and think things look well for it. Then for Texas! We'll leg it together!'

This was satisfactory. Both men presently fell to yawning, and Injun Joe said:

'I'm dead for sleep! It's your turn to watch.'

He curled down in the weeds and soon began to snore. His comrade stirred him once or twice, and he became quiet. Presently the watcher began to nod; his head drooped lower and lower; both men began to snore now.

The boys drew a long, grateful breath. Tom whispered:

'Now's our chance—come!'

Huck said: 'I can't—I'd die if they was to wake.'

Tom urged—Huck held back. At last Tom rose slowly and softly, and started alone. But the first step he made wrung such a hideous creak from the crazy floor that he sank down almost dead with fright. He never made a second attempt. The boys lay there counting the dragging moments till it seemed to them that time must be done and eternity growing grey; and then they were grateful to note that at last the sun was setting.

Now one snore ceased. Injun Joe sat up, stared around—smiled grimly upon his comrade, whose head was drooping upon his knees— stirred him up with his foot and said:

'Here! You're a watchman, ain't you! All right, though—nothing's happened.'

'My! have I been asleep?'

'Oh, partly, partly. Nearly time for us to be moving, pard. What'll we do with what little swag we've got left?'

'I don't know—leave it here as we've always done, I reckon. No use to take it away till we start south. Six hundred and fifty in silver's something to carry.'

'Well—all right—it won't matter to come here again.'

'No—but I'd say come in the night as we used to do—it's better.'

'Yes, but look here; it may be a good while before I get the right chance at that job; accidents might happen, 'tain't in such a very good place; we'll just regularly bury it—and bury it deep.'

'Good idea,' said the comrade, who walked across the room, knelt down, raised one of the rearward hearth-stones and took out a bag that jingled pleasantly. He subtracted from it twenty or thirty dollars for himself and as much for Injun Joe, and passed the bag to the latter, who was on his knees in the corner, now, digging with his bowie-knife.

The boys forgot all their fears, all their miseries in an instant. With gloating eyes they watched every movement. Luck!—the splendour of it was beyond all imagination! Six hundred dollars was money enough to make half a dozen boys rich! Here was treasure-hunting under the happiest auspices—there would not be any bothersome uncertainty as to where to dig. They nudged each other every moment—eloquent nudges and easily understood, for they simply meant, 'Oh, but ain't you glad now we're here!'

Joe's knife struck upon something.

'Hello!' said he.

'What is it?' said his comrade.

'Half-rotten plank—no, it's a box, I believe. Here bear a hand, and we'll see what it's here for. Never mind. I've broke a hole.'

He reached his hand in and drew it out.

'Man, it's money!'

The two men examined the handful of coins. They were gold. The boys above were as excited as themselves, and as delighted.

Joe's comrade said:

'We'll make quick work of this. There's an old rusty pick over amongst the weeds in the corner, the other side of the fire-place—I saw it a minute ago.'

He ran and brought the boys' pick and shovel. Injun Joe took the pick, looked it over critically, shook his head, muttered something to himself, and then began to use it.

The box was soon unearthed. It was not very large; it was

iron-bound and had been very strong before the slow years had injured it. The men contemplated the treasure awhile in blissful silence.

'Pard, there's thousands of dollars here,' said Injun Joe.

''Twas always said that Murrel's gang used to be around here one summer,' the stranger observed.

'I know it,' said Injun Joe; 'and this looks like it, I should say.'

'Now you won't need to do that job.'

The half-breed frowned. Said he:

'You don't know me. Least you don't know all about that thing. 'Tain't robbery altogether—it's revenge!' and a wicked light flamed in his eyes. 'I'll need your help in it. When it's finished—then Texas. Go home to your Nance and your kids, and stand by till you hear from me.'

'Well, if you say so. What'll we do with this—bury it again?'

'Yes. [Ravishing delight overhead.] No! by the great Sacham, no! [Profound distress overhead.] I'd nearly forgot. That pick had fresh earth on it! [The boys were sick with terror in a moment.] What business has a pick and a shovel here? What business with fresh earth on them? Who brought them here—and where are they gone? Have you heard anybody?—seen anybody? What! bury it again and leave them to come and see the ground disturbed? Not exactly—not exactly. We'll take it to my den.'

'Why, of course! Might have thought of that before. You mean number one?'

'No—number two—under the cross. The other place is bad—too common.'

'All right. It's nearly dark enough to start.'

Injun Joe got up and went about from window to window, cautiously peeping out. Presently he said:

'Who could have brought those tools here? Do you reckon they can be upstairs?'

The boys' breath forsook them. Injun Joe put his hand on his knife, halted a moment, undecided, and then turned towards the stairway. The boys thought of the closet, but their strength was gone. The steps came creaking up the stairs—the intolerable distress of the situation woke the stricken resolution of the lads—they were about to spring for the closet, when there was a crash of rotten timbers, and Injun Joe landed on the ground amid the *débris* of the ruined stairway. He gathered himself up cursing, and his comrade said:

'Now what's the use of all that? If it's anybody, and they're up there, let them stay there—who cares? If they want to jump down, now, and get into trouble, who objects? It will be dark in fifteen minutes—and then let them follow us if they want to; I'm willing. In my opinion, whoever hove those things in here caught a sight of us, and took us for ghosts or devils or something. I'll bet they're running yet.'

Joe grumbled awhile; then he agreed with his friend that what daylight was left ought to be economized in getting things ready for leaving. Shortly afterwards they slipped out of the house in the deepening twilight, and moved towards the river with their precious box.

Tom and Huck rose up, weak but vastly relieved, and stared after them through the chinks between the logs of the house. Follow? Not they—they were content to reach ground again without broken necks, and take the townward track over the hill. They did not talk much, they were too much absorbed in hating themselves—hating the ill-luck that made them take the spade and the pick there. But for that, Injun Joe never would have suspected. He would have hidden the silver with the gold to wait there till his 'revenge' was satisfied, and then he would have had the misfortune to find that money turn up missing. Bitter, bitter luck that the tools were ever brought there! They resolved to keep a lookout for that Spaniard when he should come to town spying out for chances to do his revengeful job, and follow him to 'number two', wherever that might be. Then a ghastly thought occurred to Tom:

'Revenge? What if he means *us*, Huck!'

'Oh, don't,' said Huck, nearly fainting.

They talked it all over, and as they entered town they agreed to believe that he might possibly mean somebody else—at least that he might at least mean nobody but Tom, since only Tom had testified.

Very, very small comfort it was to Tom to be alone in danger! Company would be a palpable improvement, he thought.

Chapter 28

THE ADVENTURE OF THE DAY mightily tormented Tom's dreams that night. Four times he had his hands on that rich treasure, and four times it wasted to nothingness in his fingers as sleep forsook him, and wakefulness brought back the hard reality of his misfortune. As he lay in the early morning recalling the incidents of his great adventure he noticed that they seemed curiously subdued and far away, somewhat as if they had happened in another world, or in a time long gone by. Then it occurred to him that the great adventure itself must be a dream! There was one very strong argument in favour of this idea, namely, that the quantity of coin he had seen was too vast to be real. He had never seen as much as fifty dollars in one mass before, and he was like all boys of his age and station in life, in that he imagined that all references to 'hundreds' and 'thousands' were mere fanciful forms of speech, and that no such sums existed in the world. He never had supposed for a moment that so large a sum as a hundred dollars was to be found in actual money in anybody's possession. If his notions of hidden treasure had been analysed, they would have been found to consist of a handful of real dimes, and a bushel of vague, splendid, un-graspable ones.

But the incidents of his adventure grew sensibly sharper and clearer under the attrition of thinking them over, and so he presently found himself leaning to the impression that the thing might not have been a dream after all. This uncertainty must be swept away. He would snatch a hurried breakfast, and go and find Huck.

Huck was sitting on the gunwale of a flat boat, listlessly dangling his feet in the water, and looking very melancholy. Tom concluded to let Huck lead up to the subject. If he did not do it, then the adventure would be proved to have been only a dream.

'Hello, Huck!'

'Hello, yourself.'

Silence for a minute.

'Tom, if we'd a left the blame tools at the dead tree we'd a got the money. Oh, ain't it awful!'

''Tain't a dream, then, 'tain't a dream! Somehow I 'most wish it was. Dog'd if I don't.'

'What ain't a dream?'

'Oh, that thing yesterday. I ben half thinking it was.'

'Dream! If them stairs hadn't broke down you'd a seen how much dream it was! I've had dreams enough all night, with that patch-eyed Spanish devil going for me all through 'em, rot him!'

'No, not rot him. Find him! Track the money!'

'Tom, we'll never find him. A feller don't only have one chance for such a pile, and that one's lost. I'd feel mighty shaky if I was to see him, anyway.'

'Well, so'd I; but I'd like to see him anyway, and track him out—to his number two.'

'Number two; yes, that's it. I ben thinking 'bout that. But I can't make nothing out of it. What do you reckon it is?'

'I dono. It's too deep. Say, Huck—maybe it's the number of a house!'

'Goody!—No, Tom, that ain't it. If it is, it ain't in this one-horse town. They ain't no numbers here.'

'Well, that's so. Lemme think a minute. Here—it's the number of a room—in a tavern, you know!'

'Oh, that's the trick! They ain't only two taverns. We can find out quick.'

'You stay here, Huck, till I come.'

Tom was off at once. He did not care to have Huck's company in public places. He was gone half an hour. He found that in the best tavern number two had long been occupied by a young lawyer, and was still so occupied. In the less ostentatious house number two was a mystery. The tavern-keeper's young son said it was kept locked all the time, and he never saw anybody go into it or come out of it except at night; he did not know any particular reason for this state of things; had had some little curiosity, but it was rather feeble; had made the most of the mystery by entertaining himself with the idea that that room was 'ha'nted'; had noticed that there was a light in there the night before.

'That's what I've found out, Huck. I reckon that's the very number two we're after.'

'I reckon it is, Tom. Now what you going to do?'

'Lemme think.'

Tom thought a long time. Then he said:

'I'll tell you. The back door of that number two is the door that comes out into that little close alley between the tavern and the old rattle-trap of a brick-store. Now you get hold of all the door keys you can find and I'll nip all of Auntie's, and the first dark night we'll go there and try 'em. And mind you keep a look out for Injun Joe, because he said he was going to drop into town and spy around once more for a chance to get his revenge. If you see him, you just follow him; and if he don't go to that number two, that ain't the place.'

'Lordy, I don't want to foller him by myself!'

'Why, it'll be night, sure. He mightn't ever see you—and if he did, maybe he'd never think anything.'

'Well, if it's pretty dark I reckon I'll track him. I dono—I dono. I'll try.'

'You bet I'll follow him if it's dark, Huck! Why, he might a found out he couldn't get his revenge, and be going right after that money.'

'It's so, Tom, it's so. I'll foller him; I will, by jingoes.'

'Now you're talking! Don't you ever weaken, Huck, and I won't.'

Chapter 29

THAT NIGHT TOM AND HUCK were ready for their adventure. They hung about the neighbourhood of the tavern until after nine, one watching the alley at a distance and the other the tavern door. Nobody entered the alley or left it; nobody resembling the Spaniard entered or left the tavern door. The night promised to be a fair one; so Tom went home with the understanding that if a considerable degree of darkness came on, Huck was to come and 'meow', whereupon he would slip out and try the keys. But the night remained clear, and Huck closed his watch and retired to bed in an empty sugar hogshead about twelve.

Tuesday the boys had the same ill-luck. Also Wednesday. But Thursday night promised better. Tom slipped out in good season with his aunt's old tin lantern, and a large towel to blindfold it with. He hid the lantern in Huck's sugar hogshead and the watch began. An hour before midnight the tavern closed up, and its lights (the only ones thereabouts) were put out. No Spaniard had been seen. Nobody had entered or left the alley. Everything was auspicious. The blackness of darkness reigned, the perfect stillness was interrupted only by occasional mutterings of distant thunder.

Tom got his lantern, lit it in the hogshead, wrapped it closely in the towel, and the two adventurers crept in the gloom towards the tavern. Huck stood sentry and Tom felt his way into the alley. Then there was a season of waiting anxiety that weighed upon Huck's spirits like a mountain. He began to wish he could see a flash from the lantern—it would frighten him, but it would at least tell him that Tom was alive yet.

It seemed hours since Tom had disappeared. Surely he must have fainted; maybe he was dead; maybe his heart had burst under terror and excitement. In his uneasiness Huck found himself drawing closer and closer to the alley, fearing all sorts of dreadful things, and momentarily expecting some catastrophe to happen that would take away his breath. There was not much to take away, for he seemed only able to inhale it by thimblefuls, and his heart would soon wear itself out, the way it was beating. Suddenly there was a flash of light, and Tom came tearing by him:

'Run!' said he; 'run for your life!'

He needn't have repeated it; once was enough; Huck was making thirty or forty miles an hour before the repetition was uttered. The boys never stopped till they reached the shed of a deserted slaughter-house at the lower end of the village. Just as they got within its shelter the storm burst and the rain poured down. As soon as Tom got his breath he said:

'Huck, it was awful! I tried two of the keys, just as soft as I could; but they seemed to make such a power of racket that I couldn't hardly get my breath, I was so scared. They wouldn't turn in the lock either. Well, without noticing what I was doing, I took hold of the knob, and open comes the door! It wasn't locked! I hopped in and shook off the towel, and, *great Caesar's ghost!*'

'What!—what'd you see, Tom?'

'Huck, I most stepped on to Injun Joe's hand!'

'No!'

'Yes! He was laying there, sound asleep on the floor, with his old patch on his eye and his arms spread out.'

'Lordy, what did you do? Did he wake up?'

'No, never budged. Drunk, I reckon. I just grabbed that towel and started!'

'I'd never a thought of the towel, I bet!'

'Well, I would. My aunt would make me mighty sick if I lost it.'

'Say, Tom, did you see that box?'

'Huck, I didn't wait to look around. I didn't see the box, I didn't see the cross. I didn't see anything but a bottle and a tin cup on the floor by Injun Joe! Yes, and I saw two barrels and lots more bottles in the room. Don't you see, now, what's the matter with that ha'nted room?'

'How?'

'Why, it's ha'nted with whiskey! Maybe all the Temperance Taverns have got a ha'nted room, hey, Huck?'

'Well, I reckon maybe that's so. Who'd a thought such a thing? But say, Tom, now's a mighty good time to get that box, if Injun Joe's drunk.'

'It is that! You try it!'

Huck shuddered.

'Well, no—I reckon not.'

'And I reckon not, Huck. Only one bottle alongside of Injun Joe ain't enough. If there'd been three he'd be drunk enough and I'd do it.'

There was a long pause for reflection, and then Tom said:

'Looky here, Huck, less not try that thing any more till we know Injun Joe's not in there. It's too scary. Now if we watch every night, we'll be dead sure to see him go out some time or other, then we'll snatch that box quicker'n lightning.'

'Well, I'm agreed. I'll watch the whole night long, and I'll do it every night, too, if you'll do the other part of the job.'

'All right, I will. All you got to do is to trot up Hooper Street a block and meow—and if I'm asleep, you throw some gravel at the window and that'll fetch me.'

'Agreed, and good as wheat!'

'Now, Huck, the storm's over, and I'll go home. It'll begin to be daylight in a couple of hours. You go back and watch that long, will you?'

'I said I would, Tom, and I will. I'll ha'nt that tavern every night for a year. I'll sleep all day and I'll stand watch all night.'

'That's all right. Now where you going to sleep?'

'In Ben Rogers' hayloft. He lets me, and so does his pap's nigger man, Uncle Jake. I tote water for Uncle Jake whenever he wants me to, and any time I ask him he gives me a little something to eat if he can spare it. That's a mighty good nigger, Tom. He likes me, becuz I don't ever act as if I was above him. Sometimes I've set right down and eat with him. But you needn't tell that. A body's got to do things when he's awful hungry he wouldn't want to do as a steady thing.'

'Well, if I don't want you in the daytime, Huck, I'll let you sleep. I won't come bothering around. Any time you see something's up in the night, just skip right around and meow.'

Chapter 30

THE FIRST THING TOM HEARD on Friday morning was a glad piece
of news—Judge Thatcher's family had come back to town the night
before. Both Injun Joe and the treasure sank into secondary importance for a moment, and Becky took the chief place in the boy's interest. He saw her and they had an exhausting good time playing 'hi-spy'
and 'gully-keeper' with a crowd of their schoolmates. The day was
completed and crowned in a peculiarly satisfactory way: Becky teased
her mother to appoint the next day for the long-promised and long-
delayed picnic, and she consented. The child's delight was boundless,
and Tom's not more moderate. The invitations were sent out before
sunset, and straightway the young folks of the village were thrown
into a fever of preparation and pleasurable anticipation. Tom's excitement enabled him to keep awake until a pretty late hour, and he had
good hopes of hearing Huck's 'meow' and of having his treasure to as-
tonish Becky and the picnickers with, next day; but he was disappointed. No signal came that night.

Morning came eventually, and by ten or eleven o'clock a giddy
and rollicking company were gathered at Judge Thatcher's, and everything was ready for a start. It was not the custom for elderly people to
mar the picnics with their presence. The children were considered
safe enough under the wings of a few young ladies of eighteen and a
few young gentlemen of twenty-three or thereabouts. The old steam
ferry-boat was chartered for the occasion: presently the gay throng
filed up the main street laden with provision baskets. Sid was sick and
had to miss the fun; Mary remained at home to entertain him. The
last thing Mrs Thatcher said to Becky was:

'You'll not get back till late. Perhaps you'd better stay all night
with some of the girls that live near the ferry landing, child!'

'Then I'll stay with Susy Harper, mamma.'

'Very well. And mind and behave yourself, and don't be any trouble.'

Presently, as they tripped along, Tom said to Becky:

'Say—I'll tell you what we'll do. 'Stead of going to Joe Harper's,
we'll climb right up the hill and stop at the Widow Douglas's. She'll

have ice-cream! She has it most every day—dead loads of it. And she'll be awful glad to have us.'

'Oh, that will be fun!'

Then Becky reflected a moment, and said:

'But what will mamma say?'

'How'll she ever know?'

The girl turned the idea over in her mind, and said reluctantly:

'I reckon it's wrong—but—'

'But—shucks! Your mother won't know, and so what's the harm? All she wants is that you'll be safe; and I bet you she'd a said go there if she'd a thought of it. I know she would!'

The Widow Douglas's splendid hospitality was a tempting bait. It and Tom's persuasions presently carried the day. So it was decided to say nothing to anybody about the night's programme.

Presently it occurred to Tom that maybe Huck might come this very night and give the signal. The thought took a deal of the spirit out of his anticipations. Still he could not bear to give up the fun at Widow Douglas's. And why should he give it up, he reasoned—the signal did not come the night before, so why should it be any more likely to come tonight? The sure fun of the evening outweighed the uncertain treasure; and, boy-like, he determined to yield to the stronger inclination and not allow himself to think of the box of money another time that day.

Three miles below town the ferry-boat stopped at the mouth of a woody hollow and tied up. The crowd swarmed ashore, and soon the forest distances and craggy heights echoed far and near with shoutings and laughter. All the different ways of getting hot and tired were gone through with, and by-and-by the rovers straggled back to camp fortified with responsible appetites, and then the destruction of the good things began. After the feast there was a refreshing season of rest and chat in the shade of spreading oaks. By-and-by somebody shouted:

'Who's ready for the cave?'

Everybody was. Bundles of candles were produced, and straightway there was a general scamper up the hill. The mouth of the cave was up the hill-side, an opening shaped like the letter A. Its massive oaken door stood unbarred. Within was a small chamber, chilly as an ice-house, and walled by Nature with solid lime-stone that was dewy with a cold sweat. It was romantic and mysterious to stand here in the deep gloom and look out upon the green valley shining in the sun. But the impressiveness of the situation quickly wore off, and the romping began again. The moment a candle was lighted, there was a general rush upon the owner of it; a struggle and a gallant defence followed, but the candle was soon knocked down or blown out, and then there was a glad clamour of laughter and a new chase. But all things have an end. By-and-by the procession went filing down the steep descent of the main avenue, the flickering rank of lights dimly revealing the lofty walls of rock almost to their point of junction sixty feet overhead. This main avenue was not more than eight or ten feet wide. Every few steps other lofty and still narrower crevices branched from it on either hand, for McDougal's cave was but a vast labyrinth of crooked aisles that ran into each other and out again and led nowhere. It was said that one might wander days and nights together through its intricate tangle of rifts and chasms, and never find the end of the cave; and that he might go down and down, and still down into the earth, and it was just the same—labyrinth underneath labyrinth, and no end to any of them. No man 'knew' the cave. That was an impossible thing. Most of the young men knew a portion of it, and it was not customary to venture much beyond this known portion. Tom Sawyer knew as much of the cave as anyone.

The procession moved along the main avenue some three-quarters of a mile, and then groups and couples began to slip aside into branch avenues, fly along the dismal corridors, and take each other by surprise at points where the corridors joined again. Parties were able to elude each other for the space of half an hour without going beyond the 'known' ground.

By-and-by, one group after another came straggling back to the mouth of the cave, panting, hilarious, smeared from head to foot with tallow drippings, daubed with clay, and entirely delighted with the success of the day. Then they were astonished to find that they had been taking no note of time, and that night was about at hand. The clanging bell had been calling for half an hour. However, this sort of close to the day's adventures was romantic and therefore satisfactory. When the ferry-boat with her wild freight pushed into the stream, nobody cared sixpence for the wasted time but the captain of the craft.

Huck was already upon his watch when the ferry-boat's lights went glinting past the wharf. He heard no noise on board, for the young people were as subdued and still as people usually are who are nearly tired to death. He wondered what boat it was, and why she did not stop at the wharf—and then he dropped her out of his mind and put his attention upon his business. The night was growing cloudy and dark. Ten o'clock came, and the noise of vehicles ceased, scattered lights began to wink out, all straggling foot-passengers disappeared, the village betook itself to its slumbers and left the small watcher alone with the silence and the ghosts. Eleven o'clock came, and the tavern lights were put out; darkness everywhere, now. Huck waited what seemed a weary long time, but nothing happened. His faith was weakening. Was there any use? Was there really any use? Why not give it up and turn in?

A noise fell upon his ear. He was all attention in an instant. The alley door closed softly. He sprang to the corner of the brick-store. The next moment two men brushed by him, and one seemed to have something under his arm. It must be that box! So they were going to remove the treasure. Why call Tom now? It would be absurd—the men would get away with the box and never be found again. No, he would stick to their wake and follow them; he would trust to the darkness for security from discovery. So communing with himself, Huck stepped out and glided along behind the men, cat-like, with bare feet, allowing them to keep just far enough ahead not to be invisible.

They moved up the river street three blocks, then turned to the left up a cross street. They went straight ahead, then, until they came to the path that led up Cardiff Hill; this they took. They passed by the old Welshman's house, half way up the hill, without hesitating, and still climbed upward. Good, thought Huck, they will bury it in the old quarry. But they never stopped at the quarry. They passed on, up the summit. They plunged into the narrow path between the tall sumach bushes, and were at once hidden in the gloom. Huck closed up and shortened his distance, now, for they would never be able to see him. He trotted along a while; then slackened his pace, fearing he was gaining too fast; moved on a piece, then stopped altogether; listened; no sound; none, save that he seemed to hear the beating of his own heart. The hooting of an owl came from over the hill—ominous sound! But no footsteps. Heavens, was everything lost! He was about to spring with winged feet, when a man cleared his throat not four feet from him! Huck's heart shot into his throat, but he swallowed it again; and then he stood there shaking as if a dozen agues had taken charge of him at once, and so weak that he thought he must surely fall to the ground. He knew where he was. He knew he was within five steps of the stile leading into Widow Douglas's grounds. 'Very well,' he thought, 'let them bury it there; it won't be hard to find.'

Now there was a low voice—a very low voice—Injun Joe's:

'Damn her, maybe she's got company—there's lights, late as it is.'

'I can't see any.'

This was that stranger's voice—the stranger of the haunted house. A deadly chill went to Huck's heart—this, then, was the 'revenge' job! His thought was to fly. Then he remembered that the Widow Douglas had been kind to him more than once, and maybe these men were going to murder her. He wished he dared venture to warn her; but he knew he didn't dare—they might come and catch him. He thought all this and more in the moment that elapsed between the stranger's remark and Injun Joe's next—which was:

'Because the bush is in your way. Now—this way—now you see, don't you?'

'Yes. Well, there is company there, I reckon. Better give it up.'

'Give it up, and I just leaving this country for ever! Give it up, and maybe never have another chance. I tell you again, as I've told you before, I don't care for her swag—you may have it. But her husband was rough on me—many times he was rough on me—and mainly he was the justice of the peace that jugged me for a vagrant. And that ain't all! It ain't the millionth part of it! He had me horsewhipped!— horsewhipped in front of the jail, like a nigger!—with all the town looking on! Horsewhipped!—do you understand? He took advantage of me and died. But I'll take it out of her.'

'Oh, don't kill her! Don't do that!'

'Kill? Who said anything about killing? I would kill him if he was here; but not her. When you want to get revenge on a woman you don't kill her—bosh! you go for her looks. You slit her nostrils—you notch her ears like a sow's!'

'By God, that's—'

'Keep your opinion to yourself! It will be safest for you. I'll tie her to the bed. If she bleeds to death, is that my fault? I'll not cry if she does. My friend, you'll help me in this thing—for my sake—that's why you're here—I mightn't be able alone. If you flinch, I'll kill you! Do you understand that? And if I have to kill you, I'll kill her—and then I reckon nobody'll ever know much about who done this business.'

'Well, if it's got to be done, let's get at it. The quicker the better—I'm all in a shiver.'

'Do it now?—and company there? Look here—I'll get suspicious of you, first thing, you know. No—we'll wait till the lights are out—there's no hurry.'

Huck felt that a silence was going to ensue—a thing still more awful than any amount of murderous talk; so he held his breath and stepped gingerly back; planted his foot carefully and firmly, after balancing, one-legged, in a precarious way and almost toppling over, first on one side and then on the other. He took another step back with the same elaboration and the same risks; then another and another, and a twig snapped under his foot! His breath stopped and he listened. There was no sound—the stillness was perfect. His gratitude was measureless. Now he turned in his tracks between the walls of sumach bushes—turned himself as carefully as if he were a ship—and then stepped quickly but cautiously along. When he emerged at the quarry he felt secure, so he picked up his nimble heels and flew. Down, down he sped till he reached the Welshman's. He banged at the door, and presently the heads of the old man and his two stalwart sons were thrust from windows.

'What's the row there? Who's banging? What do you want?'

'Let me in—quick! I'll tell everything.'

'Why, who are you?'

'Huckleberry Finn—quick, let me in!'

'Huckleberry Finn, indeed! It ain't a name to open many doors, I judge! But let him in, lads, and let's see what's the trouble?'

'Please don't ever tell I told you,' were Huck's first words when he got in. 'Please don't—I'd be killed sure—but the widow's been good friends to me sometimes, and I want to tell—I will tell if you'll promise you won't ever say it was me.'

'By George, he has got something to tell, or he wouldn't act so!' exclaimed the old man. 'Out with it, and nobody here'll ever tell, lad.'

Three minutes later the old man and his sons, well armed, were up the hill, and just entering the sumach path on tiptoe, their weapons in their hands. Huck accompanied them no farther. He hid behind a great boulder and fell to listening. There was a lagging, anxious silence, and then all of a sudden there was an explosion of firearms and a cry. Huck waited for no particulars. He sprang away and sped down the hill as fast as his legs could carry him.

Chapter 31

As THE EARLIEST SUSPICION of dawn appeared on Sunday morning, Huck came groping up the hill and rapped gently at the old Welsh-man's door. The inmates were asleep, but it was a sleep that was set on a hair-trigger, on account of the exciting episode of the night. A call came from a window:

'Who's there?'

Huck's scared voice answered in a low tone:

'Please let me in! It's only Huck Finn!'

'It's a name that can open this door night or day, lad!—and welcome!'

These were strange words to the vagabond boy's ears, and the pleasantest he had ever heard. He could not recollect that the closing word had ever been applied in his case before.

The door was quickly unlocked and he entered. Huck was given a seat, and the old man and his brace of tall sons speedily dressed themselves.

'Now, my boy, I hope you're good and hungry, because breakfast will be ready as soon as the sun's up, and we'll have a piping hot one, too—make yourself easy about that. I and the boys hoped you'd turn up and stop here last night.'

'I was awful scared,' said Huck, 'and I run. I took out when the pistols went off, and I didn't stop for three mile. I've come now becuz I wanted to know about it, you know; and I come before daylight becuz I didn't want to run across them devils, even if they was dead.'

'Well, poor chap, you do look as if you'd had a hard night of it—but there's a bed here for you when you've had your breakfast. No, they ain't dead, lad—we are sorry enough for that. You see, we knew right where to put our hands on them, by your description; so we crept along on tip-toe till we got within fifteen feet of them—dark as a cellar that sumach path was—and just then I found I was going to sneeze. It was the meanest kind of luck! I tried to keep it back, but no use—'twas bound to come, and it did come! I was in the lead, with my pistol raised, and when the sneeze started those scoundrels a rustling to get out of the path, I sang out 'Fire, boys!' and blazed away at the place where the rustling was. So did the boys. But they were off in a jiffy, those villains, and we after them, down through the woods. I judge we never touched them. They fired a shot apiece as they started, but their bullets whizzed by and didn't do us any harm. As soon as we lost the sound of their feet we quit chasing, and went down and stirred up the constables. They got a posse together, and went off to guard the river bank and as soon as it is light the sheriff and a gang are going to beat up the woods. My boys will be with them presently. I wish we had some sort of description of those rascals—'twould help a good deal. But you couldn't see what they were like in the dark, lad, I suppose?'

'Oh, yes, I saw them down town, and follered them.'

'Splendid! Describe them—describe them, my boy!'

'One's the old deaf and dumb Spaniard that's been around here once or twice, and t'other's a mean-looking, ragged—'

'That's enough, lad, we know the men! Happened on them in the woods back of the widow's one day, and they slunk away. Off with you, boys, and tell the sheriff—get your breakfast tomorrow morning!'

The Welshman's sons departed at once. As they were leaving the room Huck sprang up and exclaimed:

'Oh, please don't tell anybody it was me that blowed on them! Oh, please!'

'All right if you say it, Huck, but you ought to have the credit of what you did.'

'Oh, no, no! Please don't tell!'

When the young men were gone, the old Welshman said:

'They won't tell—and I won't. But why don't you want it known?'

Huck would not explain further than to say that he already knew too much about one of those men, and would not have the man know that he knew anything against him for the whole world—he would be killed for knowing it, sure.

The old man promised secrecy once more, and said:

'How did you come to follow these fellows, lad? Were they looking suspicious?'

Huck was silent, while he framed a duly cautious reply. Then he said:

'Well, you see, I'm a kind of a hard lot—least everybody says so, and I don't see nothing agin it—and sometimes I can't sleep much, on accounts of thinking about it, and sort of trying to strike out a new way of doing. That was the way of it last night. I couldn't sleep, and so I came along up street 'bout midnight a turning it all over, and when I got to that old shackly brick-store by the Temperance Tavern, I backed up agin the wall to have another think. Well, just then along comes these two chaps slipping along close by me, with something under their arm, and I reckoned they'd stole it. One was a smoking, and t'other one wanted a light; so they stopped right before me, and the cigars lit up their faces, and I see that the big one was the deaf and dumb Spaniard, by his white whiskers and the patch on his eye, and t'other one was a rusty, ragged-looking devil.'

'Could you see the rags by the light of the cigars?'

This staggered Huck for a moment. Then he said:

'Well, I don't know, but somehow it seems as if I did.'

'Then they went on, and you—'

'Follered 'em—yes. That was it. I wanted to see what was up—they sneaked along so. I dogged 'em to the widder's stile, and stood in the dark, and heard the ragged one beg for the widder, and the Spaniard swear he'd spile her looks, just as I told you and your two—'

'What! the deaf and dumb man said all that?'

Huck had made another terrible mistake! He was trying his best to keep the old man from getting the faintest hint of who the Spaniard might be, and yet his tongue seemed determined to get him into trouble in spite of all he could do. He made several efforts to creep out of his scrape, but the old man's eye was upon him, and he made blunder after blunder. Presently the Welshman said:

'My boy, don't be afraid of me. I wouldn't hurt a hair of your head for all the world. No—I'd protect you—I'd protect you. This Spaniard is not deaf and dumb; you've let that slip without intending it; you can't cover that up now. You know something about that Spaniard that you want to keep dark. Now trust me—tell me what it is, and trust me—I won't betray you.'

Huck looked into the old man's honest eyes a moment, then bent over and whispered in his ear:

"'Tain't a Spaniard—it's Injun Joe!'

The Welshman almost jumped out of his chair. In a moment he said:

'It's all plain enough now. When you talked about notching ears and slitting noses, I judged that that was your own embellishment, because white men don't take that sort of revenge. But an Injun! That's a different matter, altogether.'

During breakfast the talk went on, and in the course of it the old man said that the last thing which he and his sons had done, before going to bed, was to get a lantern and examine the stile and its vicinity for marks of blood. They found none, but captured a bulky bundle of—

'Of WHAT?'

If the words had been lightning, they could not have leaped with a more stunning suddenness from Huck's blanched lips. His eyes were staring wide, now, and his breath suspended—waiting for the answer. The Welshman started—stared in return—three seconds—five seconds—ten—then replied:

'Of burglar's tools. Why, what's the matter with you?'

Huck sank back, panting gently, but deeply, unutterably grateful. The Welshman eyed him gravely, curiously—and presently said:

'Yes, burglar's tools. That appears to relieve you a good deal. But what did give you that turn? What were you expecting we'd found?'

Huck was in a close place; the inquiring eye was upon him—he would have given anything for material for a plausible answer. Nothing suggested itself; the inquiring eye was boring deeper and deeper—a senseless reply offered—there was no time to weigh it, so at a venture he uttered it, feebly:

'Sunday-school books, maybe.'

Poor Huck was too distressed to smile, but the old man laughed loud and joyously, shook up the details of his anatomy from head to foot, and ended by saying that such a laugh was money in a man's pocket, because it cut down the doctor's bills like everything. Then he added:

'Poor old chap, you're white and jaded; you ain't well a bit. No wonder you're a little flighty and off your balance. But you'll come out of it. Rest and sleep will fetch you all right, I hope.'

Huck was irritated to think he had been such a goose and betrayed such a suspicious excitement, for he had dropped the idea that the parcel brought from the tavern was the treasure as soon as he had heard the talk at the widow's stile. He had only thought it was not the treasure, however; he had not known that it wasn't; and so the suggestion of a captured bundle was too much for his self-possession. But on the whole he felt glad the little episode had happened, for now he knew beyond all question that that bundle was not *the* bundle, and so his mind was at rest and exceedingly comfortable. In fact everything seemed to be drifting just in the right direction, now; the treasure must be still in number two, the men would be captured and jailed that day, and he and Tom could seize the gold that night without any trouble or any fear of interruption.

Just as breakfast was completed there was a knock at the door. Huck jumped for a hiding-place, for he had no mind to be connected even remotely with the late event. The Welshman admitted several ladies and gentlemen, among them the Widow Douglas, and noticed that groups of citizens were climbing up the hill to stare at the stile. So the news had spread.

The Welshman had to tell the story of the night to the visitors. The widow's gratitude for her preservation was outspoken.

'Don't say a word about it, madam. There's another that you're more beholden to than you are to me and my boys maybe, but he don't allow me to tell his name. We wouldn't have been there but for him.'

Of course this excited a curiosity so vast that it almost belittled the main matter; but the Welshman allowed it to eat into the vitals of his visitors, and through them be transmitted to the whole town, for he refused to part with his secret. When all else had been learned the widow said:

'I went to sleep reading in bed, and slept straight through all that noise. Why didn't you come and wake me?'

'We judged it wasn't worth while. Those fellows weren't likely to come again; they hadn't any tools left to work with, and what was the use of waking you up and scaring you to death? My three negro men stood guard at your house all the rest of the night. They've just come back.'

More visitors came, and the story had to be told and retold for a couple of hours more.

There was no Sabbath-school during day-school vacation, but everybody was early at church. The stirring event was well canvassed. News came that not a sign of the two villains had been yet discovered. When the sermon was finished Judge Thatcher's wife dropped alongside of Mrs Harper as she moved down the aisle with the crowd, and said:

'Is my Becky going to sleep all day? I just expected she would be tired to death.'

'Your Becky?'

'Yes,' with a startled look. 'Didn't she stay with you last night?'

'Why, no.'

Mrs Thatcher turned pale, and sank into a pew just as Aunt Polly, talking briskly with a friend, passed by. Aunt Polly said:

'Good morning, Mrs Thatcher. Good morning, Mrs Harper. I've got a boy that's turned up missing. I reckon my Tom stayed at your house last night—one of you. And now he's afraid to come to church. I've got to settle with him.'

Mrs Thatcher shook her head feebly and turned paler than ever.

'He didn't stay with us,' said Mrs Harper, beginning to look uneasy. A marked anxiety came into Aunt Polly's face.

'Joe Harper, have you seen my Tom this morning?'

'No'm.'

'When did you see him last?'

Joe tried to remember, but was not sure he could say. The people had stopped moving out of church. Whispers passed along, and a boding uneasiness took possession of every countenance. Children were anxiously questioned, and young teachers. They all said they had not noticed whether Tom and Becky were on board the ferry-boat on the homeward trip; it was dark; no one thought of inquiring if anyone was missing. One young man finally blurted out his fear that they were still in the cave! Mrs Thatcher swooned away; Aunt Polly fell to crying and wringing her hands.

The alarm swept from lip to lip, from group to group, from street to street; and within five minutes the bells were wildly clanging, and the whole town was up! The Cardiff Hill episode sank into instant insignificance, the burglars were forgotten, horses were saddled, skiffs were manned, the ferry-boat ordered out, and before the horror was half an hour old two hundred men were pouring down high-road and river towards the cave.

All the long afternoon the village seemed empty and dead. Many women visited Aunt Polly and Mrs Thatcher, and tried to comfort them. They cried with them, too, and that was still better than words.

All the tedious night the town waited for news; but when the morning dawned at last, all the word that came was 'Send more candles, and send food.' Mrs Thatcher was almost crazed, and Aunt Polly also. Judge Thatcher sent messages of hope and encouragement from the cave, but they conveyed no real cheer.

The old Welshman came home towards daylight, spattered with

candle-grease, smeared with clay, and almost worn out. He found Huck still in the bed that had been provided for him, and delirious with fever. The physicians were all at the cave, so the Widow Douglas came and took charge of the patient. She said she would do her best by him, because, whether he was good, bad, or indifferent, he was the Lord's and nothing that was the Lord's was a thing to be neglected. The Welshman said Huck had good spots in him, and the widow said:

'You can depend on it. That's the Lord's mark. He don't leave it off. He never does. Puts it somewhere on every creature that comes from His hands.'

Early in the forenoon parties of jaded men began to straggle into the village, but the strongest of the citizens continued searching. All the news that could be gained was that remotenesses of the cavern were being ransacked that had never been visited before; that every corner and crevice was going to be thoroughly searched; that wherever one wandered through the maze of passages, lights were to be seen flitting hither and thither in the distance, and shoutings and pistol-shots sent their hollow reverberations to the ear down the sombre aisles. In one place, far from the section usually traversed by tourists, the names 'BECKY' and 'TOM' had been found traced upon the rocky wall with candle smoke, and near at hand a grease-soiled bit of ribbon. Mrs Thatcher recognized the ribbon and cried over it. She said it was the last relic she should ever have of her child; and that no other memorial of her could ever be so precious, because this one parted latest from the living body before the awful death came. Some said that now and then in the cave a far-away speck of light would glimmer, and then a glorious shout would burst forth and a score of men go trooping down the echoing aisle—and then a sickening disappointment always followed; the children were not there; it was only a searcher's light.

Three dreadful days and nights dragged their tedious hours along, and the village sank into a hopeless stupor. No one had heart for anything. The accidental discovery, just made, that the proprietor of the Temperance Tavern kept liquor on his premises, scarcely fluttered the public pulse, tremendous as the fact was. In a lucid interval, Huck feebly led up to the subject of taverns and finally asked, dimly dreading the worst, if anything had been discovered at the Temperance Tavern since he had been ill.

'Yes,' said the widow.

Huck started up in bed, wild-eyed:

'What? What was it?'

'Liquor!—and the place has been shut up. Lie down, child—what a turn you did give me!'

'Only tell me one thing—only just one—please! Was it Tom Sawyer that found it?'

The widow burst into tears.

'Hush, hush, child, hush! I've told you before, you must *not* talk. You are very, very sick!'

Then nothing but liquor had been found; there would have been a great pow-wow if it had been the gold. So the treasure was gone for ever—gone for ever. But what could she be crying about? Curious that she should cry.

These thoughts worked their dim way through Huck's mind, and under the weariness they gave him he fell asleep. The widow said to herself:

'There—he's asleep, poor wreck. Tom Sawyer find it! Pity but somebody could find Tom Sawyer! Ah, there ain't many left, now, that's got hope enough, or strength enough either, to go on searching.'

Chapter 32

Now to return to Tom and Becky's share in the picnic. They tripped along the murky aisles with the rest of the company, visiting the familiar wonders of the cave—wonders dubbed with rather overdescriptive names, such as 'The Drawing-room', 'The Cathedral', 'Aladdin's Palace', and so on. Presently the hide-and-seek frolicking began, and Tom and Becky engaged in it with zeal until the exertion began to grow a trifle wearisome; then they wandered down a sinuous avenue, holding their candles aloft and reading the tangled web-work of names, dates, post-office addresses, and mottoes with which the rocky walls had been frescoed (in candle smoke). Still drifting along and talking, they scarcely noticed that they were now in a part of the cave whose walls were not frescoed. They smoked their own names under an overhanging shelf and moved on. Presently they came to a place where a little stream of water, trickling over a ledge and carrying a limestone sediment with it, had, in the slow-dragging ages, formed a laced and ruffled Niagara in gleaming and imperishable stone. Tom squeezed his small body behind it in order to illuminate it for Becky's gratification. He found that it curtained a sort of steep natural stair-way which was enclosed between narrow walls, and at once the ambition to be a discoverer seized him. Becky responded to his call, and they made a smoke mark for future guidance and started upon their quest. They wound this way and that, far down into the secret depths of the cave, made another mark, and branched off in search of novelties to tell the upper world about. In one place they found a spacious cavern, from whose ceiling depended a multitude of shining stalactites of the length and circumference of a man's leg; they walked all about it, wondering and admiring, and presently left it by one of the numerous passages that opened into it. This shortly brought them to a bewitching spring, whose basin was encrusted with a frostwork of glittering crystals; it was in the midst of a cavern whose walls were supported by many fantastic pillars which had been formed by the joining of great stalactites and stalagmites together, the result of the ceaseless water-drip of centuries. Under the roof vast knots of bats had packed themselves together, thousands in a bunch; the lights disturbed the creatures, and they came flocking down by hundreds, squeaking and darting furiously at the candles. Tom knew their ways, and the danger of this sort of conduct. He seized Becky's hand and hurried her into the first corridor that offered; and none too soon, for a bat struck Becky's light out with its wing while she was passing out of the cavern. The bats chased the children a good distance; but the fugitives plunged into every new passage that offered, and at last got rid of the perilous things. Tom found a subterranean lake, shortly, which stretched its dim length away until its shape was lost in the shadows. He wanted to explore its borders, but concluded that it would be best to sit down and rest a while first. Now for the first time the deep stillness of the place laid a clammy hand upon the spirits of the children. Becky said:

'Why, I didn't notice, but it seems ever so long since I heard any of the others.'

'Come to think, Becky, we are away down below them, and I don't know how far away north, or south, or east, or whichever it is. We couldn't hear them here.'

Becky grew apprehensive.

'I wonder how long we've been down here, Tom. We better start back.'

'Yes, I reckon we better. P'raps we better.'

'Can you find the way, Tom? It's all a mixed-up crookedness to me.'

'I reckon I could find it, but then the bats. If they put both our candles out it will be an awful fix. Let's try some other way, so as not to go through there.'

'Well, but I hope we won't get lost. It would be so awful!' and the girl shuddered at the thought of the dreadful possibilities.

They started through a corridor, and traversed it in silence a long way, glancing at each new opening, to see if there was anything familiar about the look of it; but they were all strange. Every time Tom made an examination, Becky would watch his face for an encouraging sign, and he would say cheerily:

'Oh, it's all right. This ain't the one, but we'll come to it right away!' But he felt less and less hopeful with each failure, and presently began to turn off into diverging avenues at sheer random, in the desperate hope of finding the one that was wanted. He still said it was

'All right,' but there was such a leaden dread at his heart, that the words had lost their ring, and sounded just as if he had said, 'All is lost!' Becky clung to his side in an anguish of fear, and tried hard to keep back the tears, but they would come. At last she said:

'Oh, Tom, never mind the bats; let's go back that way! We seem to get worse and worse off all the time.'

Tom stopped.

'Listen!' said he.

Profound silence; silence so deep that even their breathings were conspicuous in the hush. Tom shouted. The call went echoing down the empty aisles, and died out in the distance in a faint sound that resembled a ripple of mocking laughter.

'Oh, don't do it again, Tom, it is too horrid,' said Becky.

'It is horrid, but I better, Becky; they *might* hear us, you know,' and he shouted again.

The 'might' was even a chillier horror than the ghostly laughter, it so confessed a perishing hope. The children stood still and listened; but there was no result. Tom turned upon the back track at once, and hurried his steps. It was but a little while before a certain indecision in his manner revealed another fearful fact to Becky; he could not find his way back!

'Oh, Tom, you didn't make any marks!'

'Becky, I was such a fool! such a fool! I never thought we might want to come back! No, I can't find the way. It's all mixed up.'

'Tom, Tom, we're lost! we're lost! We never, never can get out of this awful place! Oh, why did we ever leave the others?'

She sank to the ground, and burst into such a frenzy of crying that Tom was appalled with the idea that she might die, or lose her reason. He sat down by her and put his arms around her; she buried her face in his bosom, she clung to him, she poured out her terrors, her unavailing regrets, and the far echoes turned them all to jeering laughter. Tom begged her to pluck up hope again, and she said she could not. He fell to blaming and abusing himself for getting her into this miserable situation; this had a better effect. She said she would try to hope again, she would get up and follow wherever he might lead, if only he would not talk like that any more. For he was no more to blame than she, she said.

So they moved on again—aimlessly—simply at random—all they could do was to move, keep moving. For a little while hope made a show of reviving—not with any reason to back it, but only because it is its nature to revive when the spring has not been taken out of it by age and familiarity with failure.

By-and-by Tom took Becky's candle and blew it out. This economy meant so much. Words were not needed. Becky understood, and her hope died again. She knew that Tom had a whole candle and three or four pieces in his pocket—yet he must economize.

By-and-by fatigue began to assert its claims; the children tried to pay attention, for it was dreadful to think of sitting down when time was grown to be so precious; moving, in some direction, in any direction, was at least progress and might bear fruit; but to sit down was to invite death and shorten its pursuit.

At last Becky's frail limbs refused to carry her farther. She sat down. Tom rested with her, and they talked of home, and the friends there, and the comfortable beds, and above all, the light! Becky cried, and Tom tried to think of some way of comforting her, but all his encouragements were grown threadbare with use, and sounded like sarcasms. Fatigue bore so heavily upon Becky that she drowsed off to sleep. Tom was grateful. He sat looking into her drawn face and saw it grow smooth and natural under the influence of pleasant dreams; and by-and-by a smile dawned and rested there. The peaceful face reflected somewhat of peace and healing into his own spirit, and his thoughts wandered away to bygone times and dreamy memories. While he was deep in his musings, Becky woke up with a breezy little laugh: but it was stricken dead upon her lips, and a groan followed it.

'Oh, how *could* I sleep! I wish I never, never had waked! No, no, I don't, Tom! Don't look so! I won't say it again.'

'I'm glad you slept, Becky; you'll feel rested, now, and we'll find the way out.'

'We can try, Tom; but I've seen such a beautiful country in my dream. I reckon we are going there.'

'Maybe not, maybe not. Cheer up, Becky, and let's go on trying.'

They rose up and wandered along, hand in hand and hopeless. They tried to estimate how long they had been in the cave, but all they knew was that it seemed days and weeks, and yet it was plain that this could not be, for their candles were not gone yet.

A long time after this—they could not tell how long—Tom said they must go softly and listen for dripping water—they must find a spring. They found one presently, and Tom said it was time to rest again. Both were cruelly tired, yet Becky said she thought she could go a little farther. She was surprised to hear Tom dissent. She could not understand it. They sat down, and Tom fastened his candle to the wall in front of them with some clay. Thought was soon busy; nothing was said for some time. Then Becky broke the silence:

'Tom, I am so hungry!'

Tom took something out of his pocket.

'Do you remember this?' said he.

Becky almost smiled.

'It's our wedding-cake, Tom.'

'Yes—I wish it was as big as a barrel, for it's all we've got.'

'I saved it from the picnic for us to dream on, Tom, the way grown-up people do with wedding-cake—but it'll be our—'

She dropped the sentence where it was. Tom divided the cake, and Becky ate with good appetite, while Tom nibbled at his moiety. There was abundance of cold water to finish the feast with. By-and-by Becky suggested that they move on again. Tom was silent a moment. Then he said:

'Becky, can you bear it if I tell you something?'

Becky's face paled, but she said she thought she could.

'Well, then, Becky, we must stay here, where there's water to drink. That little piece is our last candle!'

Becky gave loose to tears and wailings. Tom did what he could to comfort her, but with little effect. At length Becky said:

'Tom!'

'Well, Becky?'

'They'll miss us and hunt for us!'

'Yes, they will! Certainly they will!'

'Maybe they're hunting for us now, Tom?'

'Why, I reckon maybe they are! I hope they are.'

'When would they miss us, Tom?'

'When they get back to the boat, I reckon.'

'Tom, it might be dark, then—would they notice we hadn't come?'

'I don't know. But anyway, your mother would miss you as soon as they got home.'

A frightened look in Becky's face brought Tom to his senses, and he saw that he had made a blunder. Becky was not to have gone home that night! The children became silent and thoughtful. In a moment a new burst of grief from Becky showed Tom that the thing in his mind had struck hers also—that the Sabbath morning might be half spent before Mrs Thatcher discovered that Becky was not at Mrs Harper's. The children fastened their eyes upon their bit of candle and watched it melt slowly and pitilessly away; saw the half inch of wick stand alone at last; saw the feeble flame rise and fall, rise and fall, climb the thin column of smoke, linger at its top a moment, and then—the horror of utter darkness reigned.

How long afterwards it was that Becky came to a slow conscious- ness that she was crying in Tom's arms, neither could tell. All that they knew was that after what seemed a mighty stretch of time, both awoke out of a dead stupor of sleep, and resumed their miseries once more. Tom said it might be Sunday now—maybe Monday. He tried to get Becky to talk, but her sorrows were too oppressive, all her hopes were gone. Tom said that they must have been missed long ago, and no doubt the search was going on. He would shout, and maybe some- one would come. He tried it; but in the darkness the distant echoes sounded so hideously that he tried it no more.

The hours wasted away, and hunger came to torment the captives again. A portion of Tom's half of the cake was left; they divided and ate it. But they seemed hungrier than before. The poor morsel of food only whetted desire.

By-and-by Tom said:

'Sh! Did you hear that?'

Both held their breath and listened. There was a sound like the faintest, far-off shout. Instantly Tom answered it, and leading Becky by the hand, started groping down the corridor in its direction. Presently he listened again; again the sound was heard, and appar- ently a little nearer.

'It's them!' said Tom; 'they're coming! Come along, Becky—we're all right now!'

The joy of the prisoners was almost overwhelming. Their speed was slow, however, because pitfalls were somewhat common, and had to be guarded against. They shortly came to one, and had to stop. It might be three feet deep, it might be a hundred—there was no pass- ing it, at any rate. Tom got down on his breast, and reached as far down as he could. No bottom. They must stay there and wait until the searchers came. They listened; evidently the distant shoutings were growing more distant! A moment or two more, and they had gone altogether. The heart-sinking misery of it! Tom whooped until he was hoarse, but it was of no use. He talked hopefully to Becky; but an age of anxious waiting passed and no sound came again.

The children groped their way back to the spring. The weary time dragged on; they slept again, and awoke famished and woe-stricken. Tom believed it must be Tuesday by this time.

Now an idea struck him. There were some side-passages near at hand. It would be better to explore some of these than bear the weight of the heavy time in idleness. He took a kite-line from his pocket, tied it to a projection, and he and Becky started, Tom in the lead, unwinding the line as he groped along. At the end of twenty steps the corridor ended in a 'jumping-off place'. Tom got down on his knees and felt below, and then as far around the corner as he could reach with his hands conveniently; he made an effort to stretch yet a little further to the right, and at that moment, not twenty yards away, a human hand, holding a candle, appeared from behind a rock! Tom lifted up a glorious shout, and instantly that hand was followed by the body it belonged to—Injun Joe's! Tom was paralysed; he could not move. He was vastly gratified the next moment to see the 'Spaniard' take to his heels and get himself out of sight. Tom wondered that Joe had not recognized his voice and come over and killed him for testifying in court. But the echoes must have disguised the voice. Without doubt that was it, he reasoned. Tom's fright weakened every muscle in his body. He said to himself that if he had strength enough to get back to the spring he would stay there, and nothing should tempt him to run the risk of meeting Injun Joe again. He was careful to keep from Becky what it was he had seen. He told her he had only shouted 'for luck'.

But hunger and wretchedness rise superior to fears in the long run. Another tedious wait at the spring, and another long sleep brought changes. The children awoke, tortured with a raging hunger. Tom believed that it must be Wednesday or Thursday, or even Friday or Saturday, now, and that the search had been given over. He proposed to explore another passage. He felt willing to risk Injun Joe and all other terrors. But Becky was very weak. She had sunk into a dreary apathy, and would not be roused. She said she would wait, now, where she was, and die—it would not be long. She told Tom to go with the kite-line and explore if he chose; but she implored him to come back every little while and speak to her; and she made him promise that when the awful time came, he would stay by her and hold her hand until all was over. Tom kissed her, with a choking sensation in his throat, and made a show of being confident of finding the searchers or an escape from the cave; then he took the kite-line in his hand and went groping down one of the passages on his hands and knees, distressed with hunger and sick with bodings of coming doom.

Chapter 33

TUESDAY AFTERNOON CAME, and waned to the twilight. The village of St Petersburg still mourned. The lost children had not been found. Public prayers had been offered up for them, and many and many a private prayer that had the petitioner's whole heart in it; but still no good news came from the cave. The majority of the searchers had given up the quest and gone back to their daily avocations, saying that it was plain the children could never be found. Mrs Thatcher was very ill, and a great part of the time delirious. People said it was heartbreaking to hear her call her child, and raise her head and listen a whole minute at a time, then lay it wearily down again with a moan. Aunt Polly had drooped into a settled melancholy, and her grey hair had grown almost white. The village went to its rest on Tuesday night, sad and forlorn.

Away in the middle of the night a wild peal burst from the village bells, and in a moment the streets were swarming with frantic half-clad people, who shouted, 'Turn out! turn out! they're found! they're found!' Tin pans and horns were added to the din, the population massed itself and moved towards the river, met the children coming in an open carriage drawn by shouting citizens, thronged around it, joined its homeward march, and swept magnificently up the main street roaring huzza after huzza!

The village was illuminated; nobody went to bed again; it was the greatest night the little town had ever seen. During the first half-hour a procession of villagers filed through Judge Thatcher's house, seized the saved ones and kissed them, squeezed Mrs Thatcher's hand, tried to speak but couldn't, and drifted out raining tears all over the place.

Aunt Polly's happiness was complete, and Mrs Thatcher's nearly so. It would be complete, however, as soon as the messenger despatched with the great news to the cave should get the word to her husband.

Tom lay upon a sofa with an eager auditory about him, and told the history of the wonderful adventure, putting in many striking additions to adorn it withal; and closed with a description of how he left

Becky and went on an exploring expedition; how he followed two avenues as far as his kite-line would reach; how he followed a third to the fullest stretch of the kite-line, and was about to turn back when he glimpsed a far-off speck that looked like daylight; dropped the line and groped towards it, pushed his head and shoulders through a small hole and saw the broad Mississippi rolling by! And if it had only happened to be night he would not have seen that speck of daylight, and would not have explored that passage any more! He told how he went back for Becky and broke the good news, and she told him not to fret her with such stuff, for she was tired, and knew she was going to die, and wanted to. He described how he laboured with her and convinced her, and how she almost died for joy when she had groped to where she actually saw the blue speck of daylight; how he pushed his way out of the hole and then helped her out; how they sat there and cried for gladness; how some men came along in a skiff, and Tom hailed them and told them their situation and their famished condition; how the men didn't believe the wild tale at first, 'because,' said they, 'you are five miles down the river below the valley the cave is in'; then took them aboard, rowed to a house, gave them supper, made them rest till two or three hours after dark, and then brought them home.

Before day-dawn Judge Thatcher and the handful of searchers with him were tracked out in the cave by the twine clues they had strung behind them, and informed of the great news.

Three days and nights of toil and hunger in the cave were not to be shaken off at once, as Tom and Becky soon discovered. They were bedridden all of Wednesday and Thursday, and seemed to grow more and more tired and worn all the time. Tom got about a little on Thursday, was down town Friday, and nearly as whole as ever Saturday; but Becky did not leave her room until Sunday, and then she looked as if she had passed through a wasting illness.

Tom learned of Huck's sickness, and went to see him on Friday, but could not be admitted to the bedroom; neither could he on Saturday or Sunday. He was admitted daily after that, but was warned to keep still about his adventure and introduce no exciting topic. The Widow Douglas stayed by to see that he obeyed. At home Tom learned of the Cardiff Hill event; also that the ragged man's body had eventually been found in the river near the ferry landing; he had been drowned while trying to escape, perhaps.

About a fortnight after Tom's rescue from the cave he started off to visit Huck, who had grown plenty strong enough, now, to hear exciting talk, and Tom had some that would interest him, he thought. Judge Thatcher's house was on Tom's way, and he stopped to see Becky. The Judge and some friends set Tom to talking, and someone asked him ironically if he wouldn't like to go to the cave again. Tom said yes, he thought he wouldn't mind it.

The Judge said:

'Well, there are others just like you, Tom, I've not the least doubt. But we have taken care of that. Nobody will get lost in that cave any more.'

'Why?'

'Because I had its big door sheathed with boiler iron two weeks ago, and triple-locked; and I've got the keys.'

Tom turned as white as a sheet.

'What's the matter, boy? Here, run, somebody! Fetch a glass of water!'

The water was brought and thrown into Tom's face.

'Ah, now you're all right. What was the matter with you, Tom?'

'Oh, Judge, Injun Joe's in the cave!'

Chapter 34

Within a few minutes the news had spread, and a dozen skiff-loads of men were on their way to McDougal's cave, and the ferry-boat, well filled with passengers, soon followed. Tom Sawyer was in the skiff that bore Judge Thatcher. When the cave door was un-locked, a sorrowful sight presented itself in the dim twilight of the place. Injun Joe lay stretched upon the ground, dead, with his face close to the crack of the door, as if his longing eyes had been fixed to the latest moment upon the light and the cheer of the free world out-side. Tom was touched, for he knew by his own experience how this wretch had suffered. His pity was moved, but nevertheless he felt an abounding sense of relief and security, now, which revealed to him in a degree which he had not fully appreciated before, how vast a weight of dread had been lying upon him since the day he lifted his voice against this bloody-minded outcast.

Injun Joe's bowie-knife lay close by, its blade broken in two. The great foundation-beam of the door had been chipped and hacked through with tedious labour; useless labour, too, it was, for the native rock formed a sill outside it, and upon that stubborn material the knife had wrought no effect; the only damage done was to the knife itself. But if there had been no stony obstruction there, labour would have been useless still, for if the beam had been wholly cut away Injun Joe could not have squeezed his body under the door, and he knew it. So he had only hacked that place in order to be doing something—in order to pass the weary time—in order to employ his tortured faculties. Ordinarily one could find half a dozen bits of candle stuck around in the crevices of this vestibule, left by tourists; but there were none, now. The prisoner had searched them out and eaten them. He had also con-trived to catch a few bats, and these, also, he had eaten, leaving only their claws. The poor unfortunate had starved to death. In one place near at hand, a stalagmite had been slowly growing up from the ground for ages, built by the water-drip from a stalactite overhead. The cap-tive had broken off the stalagmite, and upon the stump had placed a stone wherein he had scooped a shallow hollow to catch the precious drop that fell once in every twenty minutes with the dreary regularity of a clock-tick—a dessert-spoonful once in four-and-twenty hours. That drop was falling when the Pyramids were new; when Troy fell; when the foundations of Rome were laid; when Christ was crucified; when the Conqueror created the British Empire; when Columbus sailed; when the massacre at Lexington was 'news'. It is falling now; it will still be falling when all these things shall have sunk down the afternoon of history and the twilight of tradition, and been swallowed up in the thick night of oblivion. Has everything a purpose and a mission? Did this drop fall patiently during five thousand years to be ready for this flitting human insect's need, and has it another important object to accomplish ten thousand years to come? No matter. It is many and many a year since the hapless half-breed scooped out the stone to catch the priceless drops, but to this day the tourist stares longest at that pathetic stone and that slow-dropping water when he comes to see the wonders of McDougal's cave. Injun Joe's cup stands first in the list of the cavern's marvels; even 'Aladdin's Palace' cannot rival it.

Injun Joe was buried near the mouth of the cave; and people flocked there in boats and wagons from the town and from all the farms and hamlets for seven miles around; they brought their children, and all sorts of provisions, and confessed that they had had almost as satisfactory a time at the funeral as they could have had at the hanging.

This funeral stopped the further growth of one thing—the petition to the Governor for Injun Joe's pardon. The petition had been largely signed; many tearful and eloquent meetings had been held, and a committee of sappy women been appointed to go in deep mourning and wail around the Governor, and implore him to be a merciful ass, and trample his duty underfoot. Injun Joe was believed to have killed five citizens of the village, but what of that? If he had been Satan himself, there would have been plenty of weaklings ready to scribble their names to a pardon-petition, and drip a tear on it from their permanently impaired and leaky waterworks.

The morning after the funeral Tom took Huck to a private place to have an important talk. Huck had learned all about Tom's adventure from the Welshman and the Widow Douglas by this time, but Tom said he reckoned there was one thing they had not told him; that thing was what he wanted to talk about now. Huck's face saddened. He said:

'I know what it is. You got into number two, and never found any-thing but whiskey. Nobody told me it was you, but I just knowed it must a ben you, soon as I heard 'bout that whiskey business; and I knowed you hadn't got the money becuz you'd a got at me some way or other, and told me, even if you was mum to everybody else. Tom, something's always told me we'd never get hold of that swag.'

'Why, Huck, I never told on that tavern-keeper. You know his tav-ern was all right the Saturday I went to the picnic. Don't you remem-ber you was to watch there that night?'

'Oh, yes! Why, it seems 'bout a year ago. It was that very night that I follered Injun Joe to the widder's.'

'You followed him?'

'Yes—but you keep mum. I reckon Injun Joe's left friends behind him. I don't want 'em souring on me, and doing me mean tricks. If it hadn't been for me he'd be down in Texas now, all right.'

Then Huck told his entire adventure in confidence to Tom, who had only heard of the Welshman's part of it before.

'Well,' said Huck, presently, coming back to the main question, 'whoever nipped the whiskey in number two nipped the money too, I reckon—anyways it's a goner for us, Tom.'

'Huck, that money wasn't ever in number two!'

'What!' Huck searched his comrade's face keenly. 'Tom, have you got on the track of that money again?'

'Huck, it's in the cave!'

Huck's eyes blazed.

'Say it again, Tom!'

'The money's in the cave!'

'Tom—honest injun, now—is it fun or earnest?'

'Earnest, Huck—just as earnest as ever I was in my life. Will you go in there with me and help get it out?'

'I bet I will! I will if it's where we can blaze our way to it and not get lost.'

'Huck, we can do that without the least little bit of trouble in the world.'

'Good as wheat! What makes you think the money's—'

'Huck, you just wait till we get in there. If we don't find it, I'll agree to give you my drum and everything I've got in the world. I will, by jings.'

'All right—it's a whiz. When do you say?'

'Right now, if you say it. Are you strong enough?'

'Is it far in the cave? I ben on my pins a little three or four days, now, but I can't walk more'n a mile, Tom—least I don't think I could.'

'It's about five miles into there the way anybody but me would go, Huck, but there's a mighty short cut that they don't anybody but me know about. Huck, I'll take you right to it in a skiff. I'll float the skiff down there, and I'll pull it back again, all by myself. You needn't ever turn your hand over.'

'Less start right off, Tom.'

'All right. We want some bread and meat, and our pipes, and a little bag or two, and two or three kite-strings, and some of those new-fangled things they call lucifer-matches. I tell you many's the time I wished I had some when I was in there before.'

A trifle after noon the boys borrowed a small skiff from a citizen who was absent, and got under way at once. When they were several miles below 'Cave Hollow', Tom said:

'Now you see this bluff here looks all alike all the way down from the cave hollow—no houses, no woodyards, bushes all alike. But do you see that white place up yonder where there's been a land-slide? Well, that's one of my marks. We'll get ashore now.'

They landed.

'Now, Huck, where we're a standing you could touch that hole I got out of with a fishing-pole. See if you can find it.'

Huck searched all the place about, and found nothing. Tom proudly marched into a thick clump of sumach bushes and said:

'Here you are! Look at it, Huck; it's the snuggest hole in this country. You just keep mum about it. All along I've been wanting to be a robber, but I knew I'd got to have a thing like this, and where to run across it was the bother. We've got it now, and we'll keep it quiet, only we'll let Joe Harper and Ben Rogers in—because of course there's got to be a gang, or else there wouldn't be any style about it. Tom Sawyer's Gang—it sounds splendid, don't it, Huck?'

'Well, it just does, Tom. And who'll we rob?'

'Oh, most anybody. Waylay people—that's mostly the way.'

'And kill them?'

'No—not always. Hide them in the cave till they raise a ransom!'

'What's a ransom?'

'Money. You make them raise all they can off'n their friends, and after you've kept them a year, if it ain't raised then you kill them.

That's the general way. Only you don't kill the women. You shut up the women, but you don't kill them. They're always beautiful and rich, and awfully scared. You take their watches and things, but you always take your hat off and talk polite. They ain't anybody as polite as robbers—you'll see that in any book. Well, the women get to loving you, and after they've been in the cave a week or two weeks they stop crying, and after that you couldn't get them to leave. If you drove them out, they'd turn right around and come back. It's so in all the books.'

'Why, it's real bully, Tom. I b'lieve it's better'n to be a pirate.'

'Yes, it's better in some ways, because it's close to home, and circuses, and all that.'

By this time everything was ready and the boys entered the hole, Tom in the lead. They toiled their way to the farther end of the tunnel, then made their spliced kite-strings fast and moved on. A few steps brought them to the spring, and Tom felt a shudder quiver all through him. He showed Huck the fragment of candle-wick perched on a lump of clay against the wall, and described how he and Becky had watched the flame struggle and expire.

The boys began to quiet down to whispers, now, for the stillness and gloom of the place oppressed their spirits. They went on, and presently entered and followed Tom's other corridor until they reached the 'jumping-off place'. The candles revealed the fact that it was not really a precipice, but only a steep clay hill, twenty or thirty feet high. Tom whispered:

'Now I'll show you something, Huck.'

He held his candle aloft and said:

'Look as far around the corner as you can. Do you see that? There—on the big rock over yonder—done with candle smoke.'

'Tom, it's a *cross*!'

'Now where's your number two? "*Under the cross*", hey? Right yonder's where I saw Injun Joe poke up his candle, Huck!'

Huck stared at the mystic sign a while, and then said with a shaky voice:

'Tom, less git out of here!'

'What! and leave the treasure?'

'Yes—leave it. Injun Joe's ghost is round about there, certain.'

'No it ain't, Huck, no it ain't. It would ha'nt the place where he died—away out at the mouth of the cave—five mile from here.'

'No, Tom, it wouldn't. It would hang round the money. I know the ways of ghosts, and so do you.'

Tom began to fear that Huck was right. Misgivings gathered in his mind. But presently an idea occurred to him

'Looky here, Huck, what fools we're making of ourselves! Injun Joe's ghost ain't a going to come around where there's a cross!'

The point was well taken. It had its effect.

'Tom, I didn't think of that. But that's so. It's luck for us, that cross is. I reckon we'll climb down there and have a hunt for that box.'

Tom went first, cutting rude steps in the clay hill as he descended. Huck followed. Four avenues opened out of the small cavern which the great rock stood in. The boys examined three of them with no re-sult. They found a small recess in the one nearest the base of the rock, with a pallet of blankets spread down in it; also an old suspender, some bacon rind, and the well-gnawed bones of two or three fowls. But there was no money-box. The lads searched and re-searched this place, but in vain. Tom said:

'He said *under* the cross. Well, this comes nearest to being under the cross. It can't be under the rock itself, because that sets solid on the ground.'

They searched everywhere once more, and then sat down discour-aged. Huck could suggest nothing. By-and-by Tom said:

'Looky here, Huck; there's foot-prints and some candle-grease on the clay about one side of this rock, but not on the other sides. Now, what's that for? I bet you the money *is* under the rock. I'm going to dig in the clay.'

'That ain't no bad notion, Tom!' said Huck, with animation.

Tom's 'real Barlow' was out at once, and he had not dug four inches before he struck wood.

'Hey, Huck! you hear that?'

Huck began to dig and scratch now. Some boards were soon un-covered and removed. They had concealed a natural chasm which led under the rock. Tom got into this and held his candle as far under the rock as he could, but said he could not see to the end of the rift. He proposed to explore. He stooped and passed under; the narrow way descended gradually. He followed its winding course, first to the right, then to the left, Huck at his heels. Tom turned a short curve by-and-by, and exclaimed:

'My goodness, Huck, looky here!'

It was the treasure-box, sure enough, occupying a snug little cavern, along with an empty powder-keg, a couple of guns in leather cases, two or three pairs of old moccasins, a leather belt, and some other rubbish well soaked with the water drip.

'Got it at last!' said Huck, ploughing among the tarnished coins with his hand. 'My, but we're rich, Tom!'

'Huck, I always reckoned we'd get it. It's just too good to believe, but we *have* got it, sure! Say, let's not fool around here, let's snake it out. Lemme see if I can lift the box.'

It weighed about fifty pounds. Tom could lift it after an awkward fashion, but could not carry it conveniently.

'I thought so,' he said; 'they carried it like it was heavy that day at the ha'nted house—I noticed that. I reckon I was right to think of fetching the little bags along.'

The money was soon in the bags, and the boys took it up to the cross rock.

'Now let's fetch the guns and things,' said Huck.

'No, Huck, leave them there. They're just the tricks to have when we go to robbing. We'll keep them there all the time, and we'll hold our orgies there, too. It's an awful snug place for orgies.'

'What's orgies?'

'I dunno. But robbers always have orgies, and of course we've got to have them too. Come along, Huck, we've been in here a long time. It's getting late, I reckon. I'm hungry, too. We'll eat and smoke when we get to the skiff.'

They presently emerged into the clump of sumach bushes, looked warily out, found the coast clear, and were soon lunching and smoking in the skiff. As the sun dipped towards the horizon they pushed out and got under way. Tom skimmed up the shore through the long twilight, chatting cheerily with Huck, and landed shortly after dark.

'Now, Huck,' said Tom, 'we'll hide the money in the loft of the widow's wood-shed, and I'll come up in the morning and we'll count and divide, and then we'll hunt up a place out in the woods for it where it will be safe. Just you lay quiet here and watch the stuff till I run and hook Benny Taylor's little wagon. I won't be gone a minute.'

He disappeared, and presently returned with the wagon, put the two small sacks into it, threw some old rags on top of them, and started off, dragging his cargo behind him. When the boys reached the Welshman's house they stopped to rest. Just as they were about to move on the Welshman stepped out and said:

'Hallo, who's that?'

'Huck and Tom Sawyer.'

'Good! Come along with me, boys, you are keeping everybody waiting. Here, hurry up, trot ahead; I'll haul the wagon for you. Why, it's not as light as it might be. Got bricks in it, or old metal?'

'Old metal,' said Tom.

'I judged so; the boys in this town will take more trouble and fool away more time hunting up six bits' worth of old iron to sell to the foundry, than they would to make twice the money at regular work. But that's human nature. Hurry along, hurry along!'

The boys wanted to know what the hurry was about.

'Never mind; you'll see when we get to the Widow Douglas's.'

Huck said with some apprehension, for he was long used to being falsely accused:

'Mr Jones, we haven't been doing nothing.'

The Welshman laughed.

'Well, I don't know, Huck, my boy. I don't know about that. Ain't you and the widow good friends?'

'Yes. Well, she's ben a good friend to me, anyways.'

'All right, then. What do you want to be afraid for?'

This question was not entirely answered in Huck's slow mind before he found himself pushed, along with Tom, into Mrs Douglas's drawing-room. Mr Jones left the wagon near the door and followed.

The place was grandly lighted, and everybody that was of any consequence in the village was there. The Thatchers were there, the Harpers, the Rogerses, Aunt Polly, Sid, Mary, the minister, the editor, and a great many more, and all dressed in their best. The widow received the boys as heartily as any one could well receive two such looking beings. They were covered with clay and candle-grease. Aunt Polly blushed crimson with humiliation, and frowned and shook her head at Tom. Nobody suffered half as much as the two boys did, however. Mr Jones said:

'Tom wasn't at home, yet, so I gave him up; but I stumbled on him and Huck right at my door, and so I just brought them along in a hurry.'

'And you did just right,' said the widow. 'Come with me, boys.'

She took them to a bedchamber and said:

'Now wash and dress yourselves. Here are two new suits of clothes—shirts, socks, everything complete. They're Huck's—no, no thanks, Huck—Mr Jones bought one and I the other. But they'll fit both of you. Get into them. We'll wait—come down when you are slicked up enough.'

Then she left.

Chapter 35

HUCK SAID:

'Tom, we can slope if we can find a rope. The window ain't high from the ground.'

'Shucks! what do you want to slope for?'

'Well, I ain't used to that kind of a crowd. I can't stand it. I ain't going down there, Tom.'

'Oh, bother! It ain't anything. I don't mind it a bit. I'll take care of you.'

Sid appeared.

'Tom,' said he, 'Auntie has been waiting for you all the afternoon. Mary got your Sunday clothes ready, and everybody's been fretting about you. Say, ain't this grease and clay on your clothes?'

'Now, Mr Siddy, you just 'tend to your own business. What's all this blow-out about, anyway?'

'It's one of the widow's parties that she's always having. This time it's for the Welshman and his sons, on account of that scrape they helped her out of the other night. And say—I can tell you something, if you want to know.'

'Well, what?'

'Why, old Mr Jones is going to try to spring something on the people here tonight, but I overheard him tell Auntie today about it, as a secret, but I reckon it's not much of a secret now. Everybody knows— the widow, too, for all she tries to let on she don't. Oh, Mr Jones was bound Huck should be here—couldn't get along with his grand secret without Huck, you know!'

'Secret about what, Sid?'

'About Huck tracking the robbers to the widow's. I reckon Mr Jones was going to make a grand time over his surprise, but I bet you it will drop pretty flat.'

Sid chuckled in a very contented and satisfied way.

'Sid, was it you that told?'

'Oh, never mind who it was. Somebody told, that's enough.'

'Sid, there's only one person in this town mean enough to do that, and that's you. If you had been in Huck's place you'd a sneaked down the hill and never told anybody on the robbers. You can't do any but mean things, and you can't bear to see anybody praised for doing good ones. There—no thanks, as the widow says.' And Tom cuffed Sid's ears and helped him to the door with several kicks. 'Now go and tell Auntie if you dare, and tomorrow you'll catch it!'

Some minutes later the widow's guests were at the supper table, and a dozen children were propped up at little side tables in the same room, after the fashion of that country and that day. At the proper time Mr Jones made his little speech, in which he thanked the widow for the honour she was doing himself and his sons, but said that there was another person whose modesty—

And so forth and so on. He sprang his secret about Huck's share in the adventure in the finest dramatic manner he was master of, but the surprise it occasioned was largely counterfeit, and not as clamorous and effusive as it might have been under happier circumstances. However, the widow made a pretty fair show of astonishment, and heaped so many compliments and so much gratitude upon Huck, that he almost forgot the nearly intolerable discomfort of his new clothes in the entirely intolerable discomfort of being set up as a target for everybody's gaze and everybody's laudations.

The widow said she meant to give Huck a home under her roof and have him educated; and that when she could spare the money she would start him in business in a modest way. Tom's chance was come. He said:

'Huck don't need it. Huck's rich!'

Nothing but a heavy strain upon the good manners of the company kept back the due and proper complimentary laugh at this pleasant joke. But the silence was a little awkward. Tom broke it.

'Huck's got money. Maybe you don't believe it, but he's got lots of it. Oh, you needn't smile; I reckon I can show you. You just wait a minute.'

Tom ran out of doors. The company looked at each other with a perplexed interest, and inquiringly at Huck, who was tongue-tied.

'Sid, what ails Tom?' said Aunt Polly. 'He—well, there ain't ever any making of that boy out. I never—'

Tom entered, struggling with the weight of his sacks, and Aunt Polly did not finish her sentence. Tom poured the mass of yellow coin upon the table and said:

'There—what did I tell you? Half of it's Huck's, and half of it's mine!'

The spectacle took the general breath away. All gazed, nobody spoke for a moment. Then there was a unanimous call for an explanation. Tom said he could furnish it, and he did. The tale was long, but brimful of interest. There was scarcely an interruption from anyone to break the charm of its flow. When he had finished, Mr Jones said:

'I thought I had fixed up a little surprise for this occasion, but it don't amount to anything now. This one makes it sing mighty small, I'm willing to allow.'

The money was counted. The sum amounted to a little over twelve thousand dollars. It was more than anyone present had ever seen at one time before, though several persons were there who were worth considerably more than that in property.

Chapter 36

THE READER MAY REST SATISFIED that Tom's and Huck's windfall made a mighty stir in the poor little village of St Petersburg. So vast a sum, all in actual cash, seemed next to incredible. It was talked about, gloated over, glorified, until the reason of many of the citizens tottered under the strain of the unhealthy excitement. Every 'haunted' house in St Petersburg and the neighbouring villages was dissected, plank by plank, and its foundations dug up and ransacked for hidden treasures—and not by boys, but men—pretty grave, unromantic men, too, some of them. Wherever Tom and Huck appeared they were courted, admired, stared at. The boys were not able to remember that their remarks had possessed weight before; but now their sayings were treasured and repeated; everything they did seemed somehow to be regarded as remarkable; they had evidently lost the power of doing and saying commonplace things; moreover, their past history was raked up and discovered to bear marks of conspicuous originality. The village paper published biographical sketches of the boys.

The Widow Douglas put Huck's money out at six per cent and Judge Thatcher did the same with Tom's at Aunt Polly's request. Each lad had an income now that was simply prodigious—a dollar for every weekday in the year and half of the Sundays. It was just what the minister got—no, it was what he was promised—he generally couldn't collect it. A dollar and a quarter a week would board, lodge, and school a boy in those old simple days—and clothe him and wash him, too, for that matter.

Judge Thatcher had conceived a great opinion of Tom. He said that no commonplace boy would ever have got his daughter out of the cave. When Becky told her father, in strict confidence, how Tom had taken her whipping at school, the Judge was visibly moved; and when she pleaded grace for the mighty lie which Tom had told in order to shift that whipping from her shoulders to his own, the Judge said with a fine outburst that it was a noble, a generous, a magnanimous lie—a lie that was worthy to hold up its head and march down through history breast to breast with George Washington's lauded Truth about the hatchet! Becky thought her father had never looked so tall and so superb as when he walked the floor and stamped his foot and said that. She went straight off and told Tom about it.

Judge Thatcher hoped to see Tom a great lawyer or a great soldier some day. He said he meant to look to it that Tom should be admitted to the National Military Academy, and afterwards trained in the best law-school in the country, in order that he might be ready for either career, or both.

Huck Finn's wealth, and the fact that he was now under the Widow Douglas's protection, introduced him into society—no, dragged him into it, hurled him into it—and his sufferings were almost more than he could bear. The widow's servants kept him clean and neat, combed and brushed, and they bedded him nightly in unsympathetic sheets that had not one little spot or stain which he could press to his heart and know for a friend. He had to eat with knife and fork; he had to use napkin, cup, and plate; he had to learn his book; he had to go to church; he had to talk so properly that speech was become insipid in his mouth; whithersoever he turned, the bars and shackles of civilization shut him in and bound him hand and foot.

He bravely bore his miseries three weeks, and then one day turned up missing. For forty-eight hours the widow hunted for him everywhere in great distress. The public were profoundly concerned; they searched high and low, they dragged the river for his body. Early the third morning Tom Sawyer wisely went poking among some old empty hogsheads down behind the abandoned slaughterhouse, and in one of them he found the refugee. Huck had slept there; he had just breakfasted upon some stolen odds and ends of food, and was lying off, now, in comfort with his pipe. He was unkempt, uncombed, and clad in the same old ruin of rags that had made him picturesque in the days when he was free and happy. Tom routed him out, told him the trouble he had been causing, and urged him to go home. Huck's face lost its tranquil content and took a melancholy cast. He said:

'Don't talk about it, Tom. I've tried it, and it don't work; it don't work, Tom. It ain't for me; I ain't used to it. The widder's good to me, and friendly; but I can't stand them ways. She makes me git up just at the same time every morning; she makes me wash, they comb me all to thunder; she won't let me sleep in the woodshed; I got to wear them blamed clothes that just smothers me, Tom; they don't seem to any air git through 'em, somehow; and they're so rotten nice that I can't set down, or lay down, nor roll around anywheres; I ain't slid on a cellar door for—well, it 'pears to be years; I got to go to church, and sweat and sweat—I hate them ornery sermons! I can't ketch a fly in there, I can't chaw, I got to wear shoes all Sunday. The widder eats by a bell; she goes to bed by a bell; she gits up by a bell—everything's so awful reg'lar a body can't stand it.'

'Well, everybody does that way, Huck.'

'Tom, it don't make no difference. I ain't everybody and I can't stand it. It's awful to be tied up so. And grub comes too easy—I don't take no interest in vittles that way. I got to ask to go a fishing; I got to ask to go in a swimming—dern'd if I hain't got to ask to do everything. Well, I'd got to talk so nice it wasn't no comfort; I'd got to go up in the attic and rip out a while every day to git a taste in my mouth, or I'd a died, Tom. The widder wouldn't let me smoke, she wouldn't let me yell, she wouldn't let me gape, nor stretch, nor scratch before folks.' Then with a spasm of special irritation and injury: 'And dad fetch it, she prayed all the time! I never see such a woman! I had to shove, Tom, I just had to. And besides, that school's going to open, and I'd a had to go to it; well, I wouldn't stand that, Tom. Looky here, Tom, being rich ain't what it's cracked up to be. It's just worry and worry, and sweat and sweat, and a wishing you was dead all the time. Now these clothes suits me and this bar'l suits me, and I ain't ever going to shake 'em any more. Tom, I wouldn't ever got into all this trouble if it hadn't a ben for that money; now you just take my sheer of it along with yourn, and gimme a ten-center sometimes—not many times, becuz I don't give a dern for a thing 'thout it's tollable hard to git—and you go and beg off for me with the widder.'

'Oh, Huck, you know I can't do that. 'Tain't fair; and besides, if you'll try this thing just a while longer you'll come to like it.'

'Like it! Yes—the way I'd like a hot stove if I was to set on it long enough. No Tom, I won't be rich, and I won't live in them cussed smothery houses. I like the woods, and the river, and hogsheads, and I'll stick to 'em too. Blame it all! just as we'd got guns, and a cave, and all just fixed to rob, here this dern foolishness has got to come up and spile it all!'

Tom saw his opportunity:

'Looky here, Huck, being rich ain't going to keep me back from turning robber.'

'No! Oh, good licks, are you in real dead-wood earnest, Tom?'

'Just as dead earnest as I'm a sitting here. But, Huck, we can't let you into the gang if you ain't respectable, you know.'

Huck's joy was quenched.

'Can't let me in, Tom? Didn't you let me go for a pirate?'

'Yes, but that's different. A robber is more high-toned than what a pirate is—as a general thing. In most countries they're awful high up in the nobility—dukes and such.'

'Now, Tom, hain't you always ben friendly to me? You wouldn't shet me out, would you, Tom? You wouldn't do that, now, would you, Tom?'

'Huck, I wouldn't want to and I don't want to, but what would people say? Why, they'd say, "Mph! Tom Sawyer's Gang! pretty low characters in it!" They'd mean you, Huck. You wouldn't like that, and I wouldn't.'

Huck was silent for some time, engaged in a mental struggle. Finally he said:

'Well, I'll go back to the widder for a month and tackle it and see if I can come to stand it, if you'll let me b'long to the gang, Tom.'

'All right, Huck, it's a whiz! Come along, old chap, and I'll ask the widow to let up on you a little, Huck.'

'Will you, Tom, now will you? That's good. If she'll let up on some of the roughest things, I'll smoke private and cuss private, and crowd through or bust. When you going to start the gang and turn robbers?'

'Oh, right off. We'll get the boys together and have the initiation tonight, maybe.'

'Have the which?'

'Have the initiation.'

'What's that?'

'It's to swear to stand by one another, and never tell the gang's secrets, even if you're chopped all to flinders, and kill anybody and all his family that hurts one of the gang.'

'That's gay—that's mighty gay, Tom, I tell you.'

'Well, I bet it is. And all that swearing's got to be done at midnight, in the lonesomest, awfulest place you can find—a ha'nted house is the best, but they're all ripped up, now.'

'Well, midnight's good, anyway, Tom.'

'Yes, so it is. And you've got to swear on a coffin, and sign it with blood.'

'Now that's something like! Why, it's a million times bullier than pirating. I'll stick to the widder till I rot, Tom; and if I git to be a reg'lar ripper of a robber, and everybody talking 'bout it, I reckon she'll be proud she snaked me in out of the wet.'

Conclusion

So ENDETH THIS CHRONICLE. It being strictly a history of a boy, it must stop here; the story could not go much further without becoming the history of a man. When one writes a novel about grown people, he knows exactly where to stop—that is, with a marriage; but when he writes of juveniles, he must stop where he best can.

Most of the characters that perform in this book still live, and are prosperous and happy. Some day it may seem worth while to take up the story of the younger ones again, and see what sort of men and women they turned out to be; therefore it will be wisest not to reveal any of that part of their lives at present.

Related Readings

Mark Twain	Boy's Manuscript	short story	197
Deborah Morris	A Rescue from an Underground Mine!	true life adventure	214
John D. Evans	Getting the Bugs Out of *Tom Sawyer*: An Entomologist's View of a Classic	natural science essay	240
John Ciardi	Sometimes I Feel This Way	poem	247
Susan Neiburg Terkel	from *Ethics*	essay	249

Mark Twain

Boy's Manuscript

Based on his own childhood experiences, Mark Twain's "Boy's Manuscript" was an inspiration for The Adventures of Tom Sawyer.

[two manuscript pages (about 300 words) missing]

me that put the apple there. I don't know how long I waited, but it was very long. I didn't mind it, because I was fixing up what I was going to say, and so it was delicious. First I thought I would call her Dear Amy, though I was a little afraid; but soon I got used to it and it was beautiful. Then I changed it to Sweet Amy—which was better— and then I changed it again, to Darling Amy—which was bliss. When I got it all fixed at last, I was going to say, "Darling Amy, if you found an apple on the doorstep, which I think you did find one there, it was *me* that done it, and I hope you'll think of me sometimes, if you can— only a little"—and I said that over ever so many times and got it all by heart so I could say it right off without ever thinking at all. And directly I saw a blue ribbon and a white frock[1]—my heart began to beat again and my head began to swim and I began to choke—it got worse and worse the closer she came—and so, just in time I jumped behind the lumber and she went by. I only had the strength to sing out "APPLES!" and then I shinned it through the lumber yard and hid. How I did wish she knew my voice! And then I got chicken-hearted and all in a tremble for fear she *did* know it. But I got easy after a while, when I came to remember that she didn't know *me*, and so per- haps she wouldn't know my voice either. When I said my prayers at night, I prayed for her. And I prayed the good God not to let the apple make her sick, and to bless her every way for the sake of Christ the Lord. And then I tried to go to sleep but I was troubled about

---

1. **frock** dress

Jimmy Riley, though she don't know him, and I said the first chance I got I would lick him again. Which I will.

   Tuesday.—I played hookey yesterday morning, and stayed around about her street pretending I wasn't doing it for anything, but I was looking out sideways at her window all the time, because I was sure I knew which one it was—and when people came along I turned away and sneaked off a piece when they looked at me, because I was dead sure from the way they looked that they knew what I was up to—but I watched out, and when they had got far away I went back again. Once I saw part of a dress flutter in that window, and O, how I felt! I was so happy as long as it was in sight—and so awful miserable when it went away—and so happy again when it came back. I could have staid there a year. Once I was watching it so close I didn't notice, and kept getting further and further out in the street, till a man hollered "Hi!" and nearly ran over me with his wagon. I wished he had, because then I would have been crippled and they would have carried me into her house all bloody and busted up, and she would have cried, and I would have been per-fectly happy, because I would have had to stay there till I got well, which I wish I never *would* get well. But by and bye it turned out that that was the . . . chambermaid[2] fluttering her dress at the window, and then I felt so down-hearted I wished I had never found it out. But I know which is her window now, because she came to it all of a sudden, and I thought my heart, was going to burst with happiness—but I turned my back and pretended I didn't know she was there, and I went to shouting at some boys (there wasn't any in sight,) and "showing off" all I could. But when I sort of glanced around to see if she was taking notice of me she was gone—and then I wished I had-n't been such a fool, and had looked at her when I had a chance. Maybe she thought I was cold towards her? It made me feel awful to think of it. Our torchlight procession came off last night. There was nearly eleven of us, and we had a lantern. It was splendid. It was John Wagner's uncle's lantern. I walked right alongside of John Wagner all the evening. Once he let me carry the lantern myself a little piece. Not when we were going by *her* house, but if she was where she could see us she could see easy enough that I knowed the boy that had the lantern. It was the best torchlight procession the boys ever got up—all

---

2. chambermaid maid

the boys said so. I only wish I could find out what she thinks of it. I got them to go by her house four times. They didn't want to go, because it is in a back street, but I hired them with marbles. I had twenty-two commas and a white alley when I started out, but I went home dead broke. Suppose I grieved any? No. I said I didn't mind any expense when her happiness was concerned. I shouted all the time we were going by her house, and ordered the procession around lively, and so I don't make any doubt but she thinks I was the captain of it—that is, if she knows me and my voice. I expect she does. I've got acquainted with her brother Tom, and I expect he tells her about me. I'm always hanging around him, and giving him things, and following him home and waiting outside the gate for him. I gave him a fish-hook yesterday; and last night I showed him my sore toe where I stumped it—and today I let him take my tooth that was pulled out New-Year's to show to his mother. I hope *she* seen it. I was a-playing for that, anyway. How awful it is to meet her father and mother! They seem like kings and queens to me. And her brother Tom—I can hardly understand how it can be—but he can hug her and kiss her whenever he wants to. I wish I was her brother. But it can't be, I don't reckon.

Wednesday.—I don't take any pleasure, nights, now, but carrying on with the boys out in the street before her house, and talking loud and shouting, so she can hear me and know I'm there. And after school I go by about three times, all in a flutter and afraid to hardly glance over, and always letting on that I am in an awful hurry—going after the doctor or something. But about the fourth time I only get in sight of the house, and then I weaken—because I am afraid the people in the houses along will know what I am about. I am all the time wishing that a wild bull or an Injun would get after her so I could save her, but somehow it don't happen so. It happens so in the books, but it don't seem to happen so to me. After I go to bed, I think all the time of big boys insulting her and me a-licking them. Here lately, sometimes I feel ever so happy, and then again, and dreadful often, too, I feel mighty bad. *Then* I don't take any interest in anything. I don't care for apples, I don't care for molasses candy, swinging on the gate don't do me no good, and even sliding on the cellar door don't seem like it used to did. I just go around hankering[3] after something I

---

3. **hankering** craving

don't know what. I've put away my kite. I don't care for kites now. I saw the cat pull the tail off of it without a pang. I don't seem to want to go in a-swimming, even when Ma don't allow me to. I don't try to catch flies any more. I don't take any interest in flies. Even when they light right where I could nab them easy, I don't pay any attention to them. And I don't take any interest in property. To-day I took everything out of my pockets, and looked at them—and the very things I thought the most of I don't think the least about now. There was a ball, and a top, and a piece of chalk, and two fish hooks, and a buckskin string, and a long piece of twine, and two slate pencils, and a sure-enough china, and three white alleys, and a spool cannon, and a wooden soldier with his leg broke, and a real Barlow, and a hunk of maple sugar, and a jewsharp,[4] and a dead frog, and a jaybird's egg, and a door knob, and a glass thing that's broke off of the top of a decanter[5] (I traded two fish-hooks and a tin injun for it,) and a penny, and a potato-gun, and two grasshoppers which their legs was pulled off, and a spectacle glass, and a picture of Adam and Eve without a rag. I took them all up stairs and put them away. And I know I shall never care anything about property any more. I had all that trouble accumulating a fortune, and now I am not as happy as I was when I was poor. Joe Baldwin's cat is dead, and they are expecting me to go to the funeral, but I shall not go. I don't take any interest in funerals any more. I don't wish to do anything but just go off by myself and think of *her*. I wish I was dead—that is what I wish I was. Then maybe she would be sorry.

Friday.—My mother don't understand it. And I can't tell her. She worries about me, and asks me if I'm sick, and where it hurts me—and I have to say that I ain't sick and nothing don't hurt me, but she says she knows better, because it's the measles. So she gave me ipecac,[6] and calomel,[7] and all that sort of stuff and made me awful sick. And I had to go to bed, and she gave me a mug of hot sage tea and a mug of hot saffron tea, and covered me up with blankets and said that that would sweat me and bring it to the surface. I suffered. But I couldn't tell her. Then she said I had bile. And so she gave me some warm salt

---

4. **jewsharp** small musical instrument
5. **decanter** bottle with a stopper
6. **ipecac** medicine that causes vomiting
7. **calomel** medicinal powder used as a laxative

water and I heaved up everything that was in me. But she wasn't satisfied. She said there wasn't any bile in that. So she gave me two blue mass pills, and after that a tumbler of Epsom salts[8] to work them off—which it did work them off. I felt that what was left of me was dying, but still I couldn't tell. The measles wouldn't come to the surface and so it wasn't measles; there wasn't any bile, and so it wasn't bile. Then she said she was stumped—but there was *some thing* the matter, and so there was nothing to do but tackle it in a sort of a *general* way. I was too weak and miserable to care much. And so she put bottles of hot water to my feet, and socks full of hot ashes on my breast, and a poultice[9] on my head. But they didn't work, and so she gave me some rhubarb to regulate my bowels, and put a mustard plaster on my back. But at last she said she was satisfied it wasn't a cold on the chest. It must be general stagnation[10] of the blood, and then I knew what was coming. But I couldn't tell, and so, with *her* name on my lips I delivered myself up and went through the water treatment—douche,[11] sitz,[12] wet-sheet and shower-bath (awful,)—and came out all weak, and sick, and played out. Does *she*—ah, no, she knows nothing of it. And all the time that I lay suffering, I did so want to hear somebody only mention her name—and I hated them because they thought of everything else to please me but that. And when at last somebody *did* mention it my face and my eyes lit up so that my mother clasped her hands and said: "Thanks, O thanks, the pills are operating!"

Saturday Night.—This was a blessed day. Mrs. Johnson came to call and as she passed through the hall I saw—O, I like to jumped out of bed!—I saw the flash of a little red dress, and I knew who was in it. Mrs. Johnson is her aunt. And when they came in with Ma to see me I was perfectly happy. I was perfectly happy but I was afraid to look at her except when she was not looking at me. Ma said I had been very sick, but was looking ever so much better now. Mrs. Johnson said it was a dangerous time, because children got hold of so much fruit. Now she said Amy found an apple [I started,] on the doorstep [Oh!] last Sunday, [Oh, geeminy, the very, very one!] and ate it all up, [Bless

---

8. **Epsom salts** a crystalline compound used as a laxative
9. **poultice** bandage
10. **stagnation** standing still
11. **douche** jet of water or other liquid directed into or onto a body part for cleansing or medicinal purposes
12. **sitz** short for *sitz bath;* a therapeutic warm-water bath in whch one immerses one's hips and thighs

her heart!] and it gave her the colic.[13] [Dern that apple!] And so *she* had been sick, too, poor dear, and it was her Billy that did it—though she couldn't know that, of course. I wanted to take her in my arms and tell her all about it and ask her to forgive me, but I was afraid to even speak to her. But she had suffered for my sake, and I was happy. By and bye she came near the bed and looked at me with her big blue eyes, and never flinched. It gave me some spunk. Then she said:

"What's your name?—Eddie, or Joe?"

I said, "It ain't neither—it's Billy."

"Billy what?"

"Billy Rogers."

"Has your sister got a doll?"

"I ain't got any sister."

"It ain't a pretty name I don't think—much."

"Which?"

"Why Billy Rogers—Rogers ain't, but Billy is. Did you ever see two cats fighting?—*I* have."

"Well I reckon I have. I've *made* 'em fight. More'n a thousand times. I've fit 'em over close-lines, and in boxes, and under barrels—every way. But the most fun is to tie fire-crackers to their tails and see 'em scatter for home. Your name's Amy, ain't it?—and you're eight years old, ain't you?"

"Yes, I'll be *nine*, ten months and a half from now, and I've got two dolls, and one of 'em can cry and the other's got its head broke and all the sawdust is out of its legs—it don't make no difference, though—I've give all its dresses to the other. Is this the first time you ever been sick?"

"*No!* I've had the scarlet fever and the mumps, and the hoop'n cough, and ever so many things. H'mph! *I* don't consider it anything to be sick."

"My mother don't, either. She's been sick maybe a thousand times—and once, would you believe it, they thought she was going to die."

"They *always* think *I'm* going to die. The doctors always gives me up and has the family crying and snuffling round here. But I only think it's bully."

"Bully is naughty, my mother says, and she don't 'low Tom to say it. Who do you go to school to?"

---

13. **colic** sudden attack of severe pain in the abdomen

"Peg-leg Bliven. That's what the boys calls him, cause he's got a cork leg."

"Goody! I'm going to him, too."

"Oh, *that's* bul—. I like that. When?"

"To-morrow. Will you play with me?"

"You bet!"

Then Mrs. Johnson called her and she said "Good-bye, Billy"— she called me Billy—and then she went away and left me *so* happy. And she gave me a chunk of molasses candy, and I put it next my heart, and it got warm and stuck, and it won't come off, and I can't get my shirt off, but I don't mind it. I'm only glad. But won't I be out of this and at school Monday? I should *think* so.

Thursday.—They've been plaguing us. We've been playing to-gether three days, and to-day I asked her if she would be my little wife and she said she would, and just then Jim Riley and Bob Sawyer jumped up from behind the fence where they'd been listening, and begun to holler at the other scholars and told them all about it. So she went away crying, and I felt bad enough to cry myself. I licked Jim Riley, and Bob Sawyer licked me, and Jo Bryant licked Sawyer, and Peg-leg licked all of us. But nothing could make me happy. I was too dreadful miserable on account of seeing her cry.

Friday.—She didn't come to school this morning, and I felt awful. I couldn't study, I couldn't do anything. I got a black mark because I couldn't tell if a man had five apples and divided them equally among himself and gave the rest away, how much it was— or something like that. I didn't know how many parts of speech there was, and I didn't care. I was head of the spelling class and I spellt baker with two k's and got turned down foot. I got lathered[14] for drawing a picture of her on the slate, though it looked more like women's hoops with a hatchet on top than it looked like her. But I didn't care for sufferings. Bill Williams bent a pin and I set down on it, but I never even squirmed. Jake Warner hit me with a spit-ball, but I never took any notice of it. The world was all dark to me. The first hour that morning was awful. Something told me she wouldn't be there. I don't know what, but *something* told me. And

---

14. **lathered** beaten

my heart sunk away down when I looked among all the girls and didn't find her. No matter what was going on, that first hour, I was watching the door. I wouldn't hear the teacher sometimes, and then I got scolded. I kept on hoping and hoping—and starting, a little, every time the door opened—till it was no use—she wasn't coming. And when she came in the afternoon, it was all bright again. But she passed by me and never even looked at me. I felt so bad. I tried to catch her eye, but I couldn't. She always looked the other way. At last she set up close to Jimmy Riley and whispered to him a long, long time—five minutes, I should think. I wished that I could die right in my tracks. And I said to myself I would lick Jim Riley till he couldn't stand. Presently she looked at me—for the first time—but she didn't smile. She laid something as far as she could toward the end of the bench and motioned that it was for me. Soon as the teacher turned I rushed there and got it. It was wrote on a piece of copy-book, and so the first line wasn't hers. This is the letter:

"*Time and Tide wait for no Man.*

"mister william rogers i do not love you dont come about me any more i will not speak to you"

I cried all the afternoon, nearly, and I hated her. She passed by me two or three times, but I never noticed her. At recess I licked three of the boys and put my arms round May Warner's neck, and *she* saw me do it, too, and she didn't play with anybody at all. Once she came near me and said very low, "*Billy, I—I'm sorry.*" But I went away and wouldn't look at her. But pretty soon I was sorry myself. I was scared, then. I jumped up and ran, but school was just taking in and she was already gone to her seat. I thought what a fool I was; and I wished it was to do over again, I wouldn't go away. She had said she was sorry—*and I wouldn't notice her.* I wished the house would fall on me. I felt so mean for treating her so when she wanted to be friendly. How I did wish I could catch her eye!—I would look a look that she would understand. But she never, never looked at me. She sat with her head down, looking sad, poor thing. She never spoke but once during the afternoon, and then it was to that hateful Jim Riley. *I* will pay him for this conduct.

Saturday.—Going home from school Friday evening, she went with the girls all around her, and though I walked on the outside, and talked loud, and ran ahead sometimes, and cavorted[15] around, and said all sorts of funny things that made the other girls laugh, *she* wouldn't laugh, and wouldn't take any notice of me at all. At her gate I was close enough to her to touch her, and she knew it, but she wouldn't look around, but just went straight in and straight to the door, without ever turning. And Oh, how I felt! I said the world was a mean, sad place, and had nothing for me to love or care for in it—and life, life was only misery. It was then that it first came into my head to take my life. I don't know why I wanted to do that, except that I thought it would make her feel sorry. I liked that, but then she could only feel sorry a little while, because she would forget it, but I would be dead for always. I did not like that. If she would be sorry as long as I would be dead, it would be different. But anyway, I felt so dreadful that I said at last that it was better to die than to live. So I wrote a letter like this:

"*Darling Amy*

"I take my pen in hand to inform you that I am in good health and hope these few lines will find you injoying the same god's blessing I love you. I cannot live and see you hate me and talk to that Jim riley which I will lick every time I ketch him and have done so already I do not wish to live any more as we must part. I will pisen myself when I am done writing this and that is the last you will ever see of your poor Billy forever. I enclose my tooth which was pulled out newyears, keep it always to remember me by, I wish it was larger. Your dyeing BILLY ROGERS."

I directed it to her and took it and put it under her father's door. Then I looked up at her window a long time, and prayed that she might be forgiven for what I was going to do—and then cried and kissed the ground where she used to step out at the door, and took a pinch of the dirt and put it next my heart where the candy was, and started away to die. But I had forgotten to get any poison. Something else had to be done. I went down to the river, but it would not do, for I remembered that there was no place there but was over my head. I went home and thought I would jump off of the kitchen, but every time, just I had clumb nearly to the eaves[16] I slipped and fell, and it was plain to be seen that it was dangerous—so I gave up that plan. I thought of hanging, and started up stairs, because I knew where there

---

15. **cavorted** ran and jumped playfully
16. **eaves** lower edge of a sloping roof

was a new bed-cord, but I recollected my father telling me if he ever caught me meddling with that bed-cord he would thrash me in an inch of my life—and so I had to give *that* up. So there was nothing for it but poison. I found a bottle in the closet, labeled laudanum[17] on one side and castor oil on the other. I didn't know which it was, but I drank it all. I think it was oil. I was dreadful sick all night, and not constipated, my mother says, and this morning I had lost all interest in things, and didn't care whether I lived or died. But Oh, by nine o'-clock *she* was here, and came right in—how my heart did beat and my face flush when I saw her dress go by the window!—she came right in and came right up to the bed, before Ma, and kissed me, and the tears were in her eyes, and she said, "Oh, Billy, how *could* you be so naughty!—and Bingo is going to die, too, because another dog's bit him behind and all over, and Oh, I shan't have *anybody* to love!"—and she cried and cried. But I told her I was not going to die and *I* would love her, always—and then her face brightened up, and she laughed and clapped her hands and said now as Ma was gone out, we'd talk all about it. So I kissed her and she kissed me, and she promised to be my little wife and love me forever and never love anybody else; and I promised just the same to her. And then I asked her if she had any plans, and she said No, she hadn't thought of that—no doubt I could plan everything. I said I could, and it would be my place, being the husband, to always plan and direct, and look out for her, and protect her all the time. She said that was right. But I said she could make suggestions—she *ought* to say what kind of a house she would rather live in. So she said she would prefer to have a little cosy cottage, with vines running over the windows and a four-story brick attached where she could receive company and give parties—that was all. And we talked a long time about what profession I had better follow. I wished to be a pirate, but she said that would be horrid. I said there was nothing horrid about it—it was grand. She said pirates killed people. I said of course they did—what would you have a pirate do?—it's in his line. She said, But just think of the blood! I said I loved blood and carnage. She shuddered. She said, well, perhaps it was best, and she hoped I would be great. Great! I said, where was there ever a pirate that *wasn't* great? Look at Capt. Kydd—look at Morgan—look at Gibbs—look at the noble Lafitte—look at the Black Avenger of the Spanish Main!—

---

17. **laudanum** medicinal solution of opium in alcohol

names that 'll never die. That pleased her, and so she said, let it be so. And then we talked about what *she* should do. She wanted to keep a milliner[18] shop, because then she could have all the fine clothes she wanted; and on Sundays, when the shop was closed, she would be a teacher in Sunday-school. And she said I could help her teach her class Sundays when I was in port. So it was all fixed that as soon as ever we grow up we'll be married, and I am to be a pirate and she's to keep a milliner shop. Oh it is splendid. I wish we were grown up now. Time does drag along so! But won't it be glorious! I will be away a long time cruising, and then some Sunday morning I'll step into Sunday School with my long black hair, and my slouch hat with a plume in it, and my long sword and high boots and splendid belt and red satin doublet and breeches, and my black flag with scull and cross-bones on it, and all the children will say, "Look—look—that's Rogers the pirate!" Oh, I wish time would move along faster.

Tuesday.—I was disgraced in school before her yesterday. These long summer days are awful. I *couldn't* study. I couldn't think of anything but being free and far away on the bounding billow. I hate school, anyway. It is so dull. I sat looking out of the window and listening to the buzz, buzz, buzzing of the scholars learning their lessons, till I was drowsy and did want to be out of that place so much. I could see idle boys playing on the hill-side, and catching butterflies whose fathers ain't able to send them to school, and I wondered what *I* had done that God should pick me out more than any other boy and give me a father able to send me to school. But *I* never could have any luck. There wasn't anything I could do to pass off the time. I caught some flies, but I got tired of that. I couldn't see Amy, because they've moved her seat. I got mad looking out of the window at those boys. By and bye, my chum, Bill Bowen, he bought a louse from Archy Thompson—he's got millions of them—bought him for a white alley and put him on the slate in front of him on the desk and begun to stir him up with a pin. He made him travel a while in one direction, and then he headed him off and made him go some other way. It was glorious fun. I wanted one, but I hadn't any white alley. Bill kept him a-moving—this way—that way— every way—and I did wish I could get a chance at him myself, and

---

18. **milliner** one who designs and sells hats

I begged for it. Well, Bill made a mark down the middle of the slate, and he says,

"Now when he is on my side, *I'll* stir him up—and I'll try to keep him from getting over the line, but if he *does* get over it, then *you* can stir him up as long as he's over there."

So he kept stirring him up, and two or three times he was so near getting over the line that I was in a perfect fever; but Bill always headed him off again. But at last he got on the line and all Bill could do he couldn't turn him—he made a dead set to come over, and presently over he *did* come, head over heels, upside down, a-reaching for things and a-clawing the air with all his hands! I snatched a pin out of my jacket and begun to waltz him around, and I made him git up and git—it was splendid fun—but at last, I kept him on my side so long that Bill couldn't stand it any longer, he was so excited, and he reached out to stir him up himself. I told him to let him alone, and behave himself. He said he wouldn't. I said

"You've got to—he's on my side, now, and you haven't got any right to punch him."

He said, "I haven't, haven't I? By George he's *my* louse—I bought him for a white alley, and I'll do just as I blame please with him!"

And then I felt somebody nip me by the ear, and I saw a hand nip Bill by the ear. It was Peg-leg the schoolmaster. He had sneaked up behind, just in his natural mean way, and seen it all and heard it all, and we had been so taken up with our circus that we hadn't noticed that the buzzing was all still and the scholars watching Peg-leg and us. He took us up to his throne by the ears and thrashed us good, and Amy saw it all. I felt so mean that I sneaked away from school without speaking to her, and at night when I said my prayers I prayed that I might be taken away from school and kept at home until I was old enough to be a pirate.[19]

Tuesday Week.—For six whole days she has been gone to the country. The first three days, I played hookey all the time, and got licked for it as much as a dozen times. But I didn't care. I was desperate. I didn't care for anything. Last Saturday was the day for the battle between our school and Hog Davis's school (that is the boys's name for their teacher). I'm captain of a company of the littlest boys in our

---

19. Every detail of the above incident is strictly true, as I have excellent reason to remember.—[M.T.]

school. I came on the ground without any paper hat and without any wooden sword, and with my jacket on my arm. The Colonel said I was a fool—said I had kept both armies waiting for me a half an hour, and now to come looking like that—and I better not let the General see me. I said him and the General both could lump it if they didn't like it. Then he put me under arrest—under arrest of that Jim Riley—and I just licked Jim Riley and got out of arrest—and then I waltzed into Hog Davis's infant department and the way I made the fur fly was awful. I wished Amy could see me then. We drove the whole army over the hill and down by the slaughter house and lathered them good, and then they surrendered till next Saturday. I was made a lieutenant-colonel for desperate conduct in the field and now I am almost the youngest lieutenant-colonel we've got. I reckon I ain't no slouch. We've got thirty-two officers and fourteen men in our army, and we can take that Hog Davis crowd and do for them any time, even if they *have* got two more men than we have, and eleven more officers. But nobody knew what made me fight so—nobody but two or three, I guess. They never thought of Amy. Going home, Wart Hopkins overtook me (that's his nickname—because he's all over warts). He'd been out to the cross-roads burying a bean that he'd bloodied with a wart to make them go away and he was going home, now. I was in business with him once, and we had fell out. We had a circus and both of us wanted to be clown, and he wouldn't give up. He was always contrary that way. And he wanted to do the zam, and I wanted to do the zam (which the zam means the zampillerostation), and there it was again. He knocked a barrel from under me when I was a-standing on my head one night, and once when we were playing Jack the Giant-Killer I tripped his stilts up and pretty near broke him in two. We charged two pins admission for big boys and one pin for little ones—and when we came to divide up he wanted to shove off all the pins on me that hadn't any heads on. That was the kind of boy he was—always mean. He always tied the little boys' clothes when they went in a-swimming. . . . He would sneak around and nip marbles with his toes and carry them off when the boys were playing knucks, or anything like that; and when he was playing himself he always poked or he always hunched. He always throwed his nutshells under some small boy's bench in school and let him get lammed.[20] He

---

20. **lammed** beaten

used to put shoemaker's wax in the teacher's seat and then play hookey and let some other fellow catch it. I hated Wart Hopkins. But now he was in the same fix as myself, and I did want somebody to talk to *so* bad, who was in that fix. He loved Susan Hawkins and she was gone to the country too. I could see he was suffering, and he could see I was. I wanted to talk, and he wanted to talk, though we hadn't spoken for a long, long time. Both of us was full. So he said let bygones be bygones—let's make up and be good friends, because we'd ought to be, fixed as we were. I just overflowed, and took him around the neck and went to crying, and he took me around the neck and went to crying, and we were perfectly happy because we were so miserable together. And I said I would always love him and Susan, and he said he would always love me and Amy—beautiful, beautiful Amy, he called her, which made me feel good and proud; but not quite so beautiful as Susan, he said, and I said it was a lie and he said I was another and a fighting one and darsn't take it up; and I hit him and he hit me back, and then we had a fight and rolled down a gulley[21] into the mud and gouged and bit and hit and scratched, and neither of us was whipped; and then we got out and commenced it all over again and he put a chip on his shoulder and dared me to knock it off and I did, and so we had it again, and then he went home and I went home, and Ma asked me how I got my clothes all tore off and was so ragged and bloody and bruised up, and I told her I fell down, and then she black-snaked me and I was all right. And the very next day I got a letter from Amy! Mrs. Johnson brought it to me. It said:

"mister william rogers dear billy I have took on so I am all Wore out a crying becos i Want to see you so bad the cat has got kittens but it Dont make me happy i Want to see you all the Hens lays eggs excep the old Rooster and mother and me Went to church Sunday and had hooklebeary pie for Dinner i think of you Always and love you no more from your amy at present

AMY."

I read it over and over and over again, and kissed it, and studied out new meanings in it, and carried it to bed with me and read it again first thing in the morning. And I did feel so delicious I wanted to lay there and think of her hours and hours and never get up. But they made me. The first chance I got I wrote to her, and this is it:

---

21. **gulley** ditch

"Darling Amy

"I have had lots of fights and I love you all the same. I have changed my dog which his name was Bull and now his name is Amy. I think its splendid and so does he I reckon because he always comes when I call him *Amy* though he'd come anyhow ruther than be walloped, which I *would* wallop him if he didn't. I send you my picture. The things on the lower side are the legs, the head is on the other end, the horable thing which its got in its hand is you though not so pretty by a long sight. I didn't mean to put only one eye in your face but there wasnt room. I have been thinking sometimes I'll be a pirate and sometimes I'll keep grocery on account of candy And I would like ever so much to be a brigadire General or a deck hand on a steamboat because they have fun you know and go everywheres. But a fellow cant be everything I dont reckon. I have traded off my sunday school book and Ma's hatchet for a pup and I reckon I'm going to ketch it, maybe. Its a good pup though. It nipped a chicken yesterday and goes around raising cain all the time. I love you to destruction Amy and I can't live if you dont come back. I had the branch dammed up beautiful for water-mills, but I dont care for water mills when you are away so I traded the dam to Jo Whipple for a squirt gun though if you was here I wouldnt give a dam for a squirt gun because we could have water mills. So no more from your own true love.

> My pen is bad my ink is pale
> Roses is red the violets blue
> But my love for you shall never change.
>
> William T. Rogers.

"P.S. I learnt that poetry from Sarah Mackleroy—its beautiful."

Tuesday Fortnight.—I'm thankful that I'm free. I've come to myself. I'll never love another girl again. There's no dependence in them. If I was going to hunt up a wife I would just go in amongst a crowd of girls and say

> "Eggs, cheese, butter, bread,
> Stick, stock, stone—DEAD!"

and take the one it lit on just the same as if I was choosing up for fox or baste or three-cornered cat or hide'n'whoop or anything like that. I'd get along just as well as by selecting them out and falling in love with them the way I did with—with—I can't write her name, for the tears *will* come. But she has treated me Shameful. The first thing she did when she got back from the country was to begin to object to me being a pirate—because some of her kin is down on pirates I reckon—though *she* said it was because I would be away from home so much. A likely story, indeed—if she knowed anything about pirates she'd know that they go and come just whenever they please, which other people can't. Well I'll be a pirate now, in spite of all the girls in the world. And next she didn't want me to be a deck hand on a steamboat, or else it was a judge she didn't want me to be, because one of them wasn't respectable, she didn't know which—some more bosh from relations I reckon. And then she said she didn't want to keep a milliner shop, she wanted to clerk in a toy-shop, and have an open barouche[22] and she'd like me to sell peanuts and papers on the railroad so she could ride without it costing anything.

"What!" I said, "and not be a pirate at all?"

She said yes. I was disgusted. I told her so. Then she cried, and said I didn't love her, and wouldn't do anything to please her, and wanted to break her heart and have some other girl when she was dead, and then I cried, too, and told her I *did* love her, and nobody but her, and I'd do anything she wanted me to and I was sorry, Oh, so sorry. But she shook her head, and pouted—and I begged again, and she turned her back—and I went on pleading and she wouldn't answer—only pouted—and at last when I was getting mad, she slammed the jews-harp, and the tin locomotive and the spool cannon and everything I'd given her, on the floor, and flourished out mad and crying like sin, and said I was a mean, good-for-nothing thing and I might go and *be* a pirate and welcome!—*she* never wanted to see me any more! And I was mad and crying, too, and I said By George I *would* be a pirate, and an awful bloody one, too, or my name warn't Bill Rogers!

And so it's all over between us. But now that it is all over, I feel mighty, mighty bad. The whole school knowed we were engaged, and they think it strange to see us flirting with other boys and girls, but we can't help that. I flirt with other girls, but I don't care anything about them. And I see her lip quiver sometimes and the tears come in her eyes when she looks my way when she's flirting with some other boy—and then I do *want* to rush there and grab her in my arms and be friends again!

---

22. **barouche** large carriage

Saturday.—I am happy again, and forever, this time. I've seen her! I've seen the girl that is my doom. I shall die if I cannot get her. The first time I looked at her I fell in love with her. She looked at me twice in church yesterday, and Oh how I felt! She was with her mother and her brother. When they came out of church I followed them, and twice she looked back and smiled, and I would have smiled too, but there was a tall young man by my side and I was afraid he would notice. At last she dropped a leaf of a flower—rose geranium Ma calls it—and I could see by the way she looked that she meant it for me, and when I stopped to pick it up the tall young man stooped too. I got it, but I felt awful sheepish, and I think he did, too, because he blushed. He asked me for it, and I had to give it to him, though I'd rather given him my bleeding heart, but I pinched off just a little piece and kept it, and shall keep it forever. Oh, she is *so* lovely! And she loves me. I know it. I could see it, easy. Her name's Laura Miller. She's nineteen years old, Christmas. I never, never, never will part with *this* one! NEVER.

Deborah Morris

A Rescue from an Underground Mine!

In this true-life story, a ten-year-old Boy Scout is trapped inside a cave, much like Tom Sawyer and Becky Thatcher were in The Adventures of Tom Sawyer.

On the Road

Gross, Adam! Put it back in your mouth!" The chorus of boyish groans from the back of the yellow van was too loud for the two adults in the front to ignore.

"Adam!" said Ron Van Sleeuwen, Adam's father, who was driving. "Don't be a troublemaker!" Mr. Dennis, in the passenger seat, just smiled and shook his head.

Sitting in the farthest back seat, Adam grinned and popped a bloated, neon-green wad of gum back into his mouth. "There, happy now?" he asked the other boys around him. Except for Josh, they all laughed.

"Hey, Josh, you okay?" Adam asked, noticing for the first time how quiet his friend had been for the last thirty minutes, ever since the road had turned bumpy. "You want a piece of my candy or anything?"

Josh groaned. "No, thanks. I don't feel very good." At the last gas station, when most of the boys had loaded up on candy, he had stayed in the van. Now he clutched his stomach and leaned sideways against the window, trying to get more comfortable. His face looked a little green.

"Mr. Dennis!" Adam called. "I think Josh is carsick!"

Mr. Dennis looked back. "Why don't you guys make some room for him to lie down? Maybe he can sleep the rest of the way." Adam and Terry scooted over, and Josh gratefully curled into a ball on the seat. He didn't wake up until the van lurched[1] to a stop about thirty minutes later.

He sat up dazedly, noticing that they had pulled off the side of the road. Towering all around them were the Oquirrh Mountains, rugged slopes broken with craggy[2] rock outcroppings and thick stretches of forest. Behind them, the rest of the cars carrying Troop 845 had also stopped.

"Where are we?" he asked groggily as some of the other boys jumped out of the van. "Are we already at the mine?"

"We've still got a couple of miles to go," Mr. Dennis explained. "We just stopped so some of the boys can earn their camping merit badges by hiking the rest of the way."

Josh perked up. "Can I go with them? I'd rather walk than ride any more."

Mr. Dennis shrugged. "I guess so. Are you sure you feel up to it?"

"I'm okay. Besides, Terry and Adam are both going. We can stick together."

The boys who got out waited until all the cars and vans passed them going up the steep, winding road and then started up after them. It was hard walking, and several of the older Scouts were soon out of breath. Josh, thin and wiry, had no trouble keeping up with the group.

As they got closer to the level area marking the entrance to the Hidden Treasure Mine, they started noticing old mine shafts dotting the surrounding slopes. Some were dug sideways into the hillside; others went straight down. In the canyon below, they spotted what was left of the once-booming mining town of Jacob City.

"It must have been neat to live here when the mine was still open," said Josh. "Instead of a paycheck, I guess you'd just bring home a sack of gold each week!"

The sun was dipping low in the sky as they reached the campsite. Some of the boys who had ridden the rest of the way were

---

1. **lurched** rolled suddenly
2. **craggy** rugged

already setting up their tents while others scavenged the rocky hillside for firewood. Josh found his dad and sat down to rest for a minute.

"How was your walk?" Mr. Dennis asked. "Are you feeling any better?"

"I think so. What are we having for dinner?"

"Beef stew. I'm getting ready to start it now. Why don't you just take it easy for a while?" Josh nodded and wandered off in the direction of a group of boys.

Thirty minutes later, as the sun disappeared behind the mountains, the hillside slowly came alive with bobbing flashlights and the flickering, red-orange glow of campfires. Some of the boys were playing flashlight tag while waiting for dinner. Their laughter and shouts echoed clearly in the still night air as they tried to pinion[3] each other in the beams of their flashlights. Josh, still a little queasy, decided just to watch.

Finally, Mr. Weaver and some of the other Scout leaders shouted, "Food!" causing an instant stampede toward the camp. Josh accepted a bowl of beef stew and sat down cross-legged next to the fire to eat it.

"Mm-mm!" he said, scooping a warm mouthful of beef and boiled potatoes into his mouth. "This is great!"

Mr. Dennis smiled. "Everything always tastes better outdoors, doesn't it? I wonder why that is?"

"Probably because you're starving to death before you get it," Josh mumbled, his mouth full. Mr. Dennis laughed and nudged him playfully with his foot.

Josh was finishing up a second bowl when he noticed a group of boys gathering over by the mine entrance. He went over to find out what was happening.

"We're going inside to explore!" Adam Van Sleeuwen told him excitedly. "Mr. Weaver says it doesn't matter whether it's day or night outside, because inside the mine it's dark all the time. You want to come?"

Josh ran back to his dad. "A bunch of guys are going inside the mine. Can I go with them?"

Mr. Dennis looked doubtful. "I don't know. I need to clean up this mess from dinner. How many leaders are going?"

---

3. **pinion** catch

"A bunch of them. Mr. Weaver and Mr. Powell, I think. Terry Nelson's going in. Please, can I go?"

Mr. Dennis glanced over at the group outside the mine. Scoutmaster Kevin Weaver was standing there in front of the boys, raising his voice slightly to carry over their excited chatter.

"Each of you will need a flashlight," he was saying. "You'll have to stay together and keep your adult leader in sight at all times. There are a lot of dangerous pits in there, so you'll need to shine your light at your feet. Okay?"

There was a unanimous chorus of agreement from the boys. Mr. Weaver knelt and then lowered himself through the three-foot opening into the mine. The other boys followed one at a time. "Dad?" Josh said urgently. "Can I go please?"

Mr. Dennis sighed. "All right, all right. But listen—you pay attention to what Mr. Weaver said, you hear me? I'll be along in just a few minutes."

"Okay!" Josh said. "Thanks!"

After grabbing his dad's flashlight and a handful of licorice bits for dessert, Josh raced over to the mine entrance where the last few boys were just climbing down. He was the last one in line to lower himself through the narrow opening leading down into the cool, underground darkness of the Hidden Treasure Mine.

He was surprised when his cleats hit the dusty floor of the mine shaft with a muffled *thud*. He immediately swung his flashlight around, curious.

The other Scouts were already heading off, single-file, down the main tunnel, their wildly bobbing flashlights casting eerie shadows on the tunnel walls. Their voices also sounded oddly muffled. The air smelled musty and damp and was surprisingly chilly. Josh was glad he was wearing his blue and gray parka.

He took several quick steps in the direction of the group before remembering Mr. Weaver's warning about pits. He pointed the flashlight down at his feet as he hurried to catch up. They were following some kind of underground railroad track—probably what the old ore carts rolled along. He smiled at the picture of carts heaped with gold and silver. Maybe if he looked close enough he'd spot a chunk they'd dropped.

Hidden Treasure. What a great name for a mine!

Down into Hidden Treasure

Still lagging behind the others, Josh darted the beam of his flashlight back and forth over the floor and up the walls. They looked as if they'd been cut through solid rock. He didn't see any gold, but he did spot several interesting pieces of junk—rusted railroad spikes, chunks of rotting wood.

Stopping to examine a twisted piece of iron, he was startled, when he looked up again, to discover that the others had moved out of sight around a bend. He was surprised at how silent—and dark—the shaft had suddenly become. He quickly ran to catch up.

A few minutes later they reached an open chamber, and Mr. Weaver had everybody gather around him.

"Before we go any deeper," he said, "I want to remind you guys about how important it is to stay together. I know it's a lot of fun to fool around down here—" he looked over at a couple of boys who were shining their flashlights on their faces and grinning at each other, "but the fact is, it can be dangerous."

He paused. "Let's do something. Everybody turn off your flashlights for a minute." One by one the flashlights were clicked off amidst a ripple of laughter. Finally, the tunnel was left in total blackness. After a moment the murmur of voices also died away, leaving a heavy silence broken only by a hollow dripping sound and a few nervous whispers. In the darkness, the damp, chilly air seemed even colder.

Mr. Weaver's voice broke the silence. "Can you imagine," he said, "being stuck in here without a flashlight? You'd never find your way out. Now you can see why it's so important to stay together." He clicked his flashlight back on, and with a sigh of relief the boys did the same.

Josh was glad when they started forward again. They peered into a few side tunnels and looked at some scribbles on the walls, but after a few minutes Josh decided to go back up the tunnel and meet his dad.

He slowly worked his way along the old rail tracks until he was almost to the entrance again. Where was his dad? He had said he was coming in just a minute.

Josh heard voices and footsteps in the tunnel ahead and then could see lights bouncing off the walls. As he watched, several shadowy figures stepped around a bend and aimed their flashlights straight at him. Squinting into the glare, he called out, "Dad, is that you?"

"Josh?" a hollow voice answered in reply. When the light moved away from his face, Josh saw four figures: Cary, Tyler, and Danny, all older Scouts, and his dad. Mr. Dennis didn't have a flashlight, since Josh had taken his.

"Hi, son!" Mr. Dennis greeted him with a smile. "You coming or going?"

"Neither. I just came back to wait for you."

"Where's everybody else?"

Josh pointed. "They're all back there."

"Great! Let's get going and see if we can catch up with them." He paused. "Josh, can I hold your flashlight for Danny? His batteries are dead, and I don't have one."

Danny, a visually impaired Scout, wasn't finding the experience of shuffling over uneven ground in a dark tunnel a pleasant one. "Sure," Josh said, handing over the flashlight. Mr. Dennis held it up as they started forward again.

Soon they spotted the flickering lights of the first group in the tunnel just ahead. Danny, however, was still having a hard time seeing.

"Mr. Dennis, can I please go back?" he asked. "This really isn't much fun for me. Everything's just a big blur."

"No problem," Mr. Dennis said. "Just hang on a minute and let me tell the others."

Josh was a few steps ahead, with Cary and Tyler; in front of them the large group was in clear sight. "Hey, guys!" Mr. Dennis shouted. "I'm taking Danny back out, so you need to hurry and catch up with the others. Josh, you want to come with us?"

Josh paused and looked back. "Do I have to?"

Mr. Dennis shrugged. "No, I don't guess so. But I'll need your flashlight to get Danny back out of here."

"That's okay. Cary and Tyler both have lights."

Mr. Dennis nodded and then turned to lead Danny back the way they'd come. Josh turned in the other direction to go with Cary and Tyler. He was surprised to see how far ahead their bobbing lights had gotten.

"Hey!" he exclaimed. He started after them, but without his flashlight he couldn't go very fast. He'd only taken a few steps in their direction when their lights totally disappeared. He stopped, unable to see.

Guess I'll have to go with Dad and Danny after all, he thought. But when he turned around, there was nothing but darkness in that direction, too.

He frowned and then yelled, "Dad?"

He held his breath and listened, hoping to hear faint voices or footsteps, but all he heard was a distant dripping sound. He stood for a moment in indecision, feeling the eerie blackness closing in around him like some kind of clammy blanket.

It was just like when Mr. Weaver made them all turn out their flashlights—only this time, it was for real.

"Wasn't that neat when we all turned out our flashlights? It was like being on another planet."

"Feels warmer out here. I was freezing in there!"

Mr. Dennis smiled as, one by one, the boys popped back up out of the mine entrance, chattering and laughing. Some made a beeline to the campfire to get a second helping of stew while others scampered up the rocky hillside for another round of flashlight tag. Mr. Dennis kept glancing over at the entrance, watching for Josh.

He wasn't concerned until Mr. Weaver and his group climbed up out of the shaft. Josh wasn't with them.

"Kevin!" Mr. Dennis called to the Scoutmaster. "How many boys are still down there?"

"Not many. Rick's with some of the older boys scouting around that one dead-end shaft, but that's about it."

"I guess Josh went with them?" he asked.

"Josh? I don't think so. Didn't he come out with you?"

"No, he went with Cary and Tyler to join your group."

"Mr. Weaver started to say something but stopped. "He might've come out with one of the other groups," he said, glancing at all the Scouts milling around. "It's hard to keep track of them as fast as they move. Let's ask around to see if anybody's seen him."

Several younger Scouts had been sitting near the mine entrance. "Did any of you see Joshua Dennis come out?" asked Mr. Weaver. "His dad is looking for him."

The boys shook their heads. Mr. Weaver turned back to Mr. Dennis. "I'll bet he's running around out here somewhere. Let's go find Cary and Tyler; maybe he's still with them."

When they found the two older Scouts, though, they shook their heads in bewilderment.

"He didn't go with us," Cary told Mr. Dennis. "Remember? We met him when we were first going in, but then he went back out with you and Danny."

"No, he didn't," Mr. Dennis's voice sounded strained. "I asked him if he wanted to, and he said no. I sent him back with you guys."

Cary and Tyler looked at each other. "We never saw him after that," Tyler said. "We were going pretty fast, trying to catch up with Mr. Weaver's group. Maybe Josh couldn't keep up. Still," he added, "he shouldn't have had any trouble finding us as long as he stayed in the main tunnel. Even though it twists around a lot it's not really that complicated."

Mr. Dennis's face was suddenly grim. "I took his flashlight. Well, *my* flashlight, but I had to take it. Danny's was dead. Josh didn't have another one with him."

His words brought a shocked silence to the small group.

"Well, let's have another quick look around out here before we jump to any conclusions," Mr. Weaver said. "You boys go check the tents; Josh was feeling sick earlier, so maybe he just crawled into a sleeping bag and dozed off. Terry and I will scout around and see if he's off playing tag or something."

He turned back to Mr. Dennis and placed a hand on his shoulder. "I'm sure he's fine. But if he's not out here, we'll get together a search crew to go in the mine and find him. Okay?"

"Okay," Mr. Dennis said carefully. He pushed away the thought of Josh alone in the inky blackness, wandering blindly near mine shafts and other dangers. *Please, God,* he prayed. *Don't let anything happen to my son.*

Getting no answer from his father, Josh stood frozen in the misty darkness, his heart pounding. What should he do?

"Dad!" he screamed again. His voice sounded strange, like it was being swallowed up by the darkness. "Dad, come back!" After a moment, though, he calmed down. He couldn't be far from the mine entrance; he could find his way back by following the rail tracks. All he had to do was figure out which way was out.

It was weird, he thought as he groped[4] in the direction where he thought the wall should be, how really dark it was. It wasn't like the darkness outside where you could see shadowy shapes or reflections, or like closing your eyes in a bright room and you could still sort of

---

4. **groped** felt about

sense light. This must be what it was like to be blind. He didn't blame Danny for not wanting to hang around down here.

After fumbling around, his hand touched cold rock. "Found it!" he exclaimed. "Now, which way should I go?"

Placing both hands on the wall, he closed his eyes and tried to picture the tunnel where he'd stopped. It was confusing, but left felt more "right" to him. He decided to go that way.

He started off slowly, trailing his right hand along the rough wall while extending his other hand out in front of him to keep from running into anything. He shuffled his feet on the dusty floor, remembering what Mr. Weaver had said about deep pits. He'd feel pretty stupid falling down in some hole!

He walked for several minutes in what seemed like a straight line, stopping every now and then to grope his way over to the rail tracks to make sure he was still following them. Several times he splashed without warning into puddles, yelping as the icy water soaked his socks and cleats. He paused to zip up his parka before continuing on.

Soon he realized that the tunnel seemed to be angling slightly upward—and that a faint, cool breeze was stirring. *I must be getting near the entrance!* he thought. *This must be that downslope we were on when we first came in.*

But after going a little farther he began to wonder. Shouldn't he have reached the entrance by now? He couldn't have missed it; he'd been peering up through the darkness every few steps, watching for the three-foot opening. Besides, the slope was much steeper now than he remembered it coming in.

It probably just seems steeper because I'm going up instead of down, he told himself. *I'll see the entrance any second.*

But the uneven slope finally grew so steep that he had to use his hands. When he slipped on the gravel, he slid backwards.

"Ow!" Josh exclaimed, rubbing his scraped knee. He sank down on the cold floor, disgusted. His hands were muddy, his jeans wet halfway up to his knee, and he was shivering. He was getting hungry again, and thought longingly of the warm campfire and leftover stew waiting just outside—if he just knew where "outside" was!

After a minute he sighed and stood up again, but he'd only taken a few steps when he banged his head, hard, on something in the darkness. He reached up to find that the tunnel ceiling was much lower than it should have been. Groping his way over toward the opposite wall, he felt for the rail tracks. They weren't there anymore. He slowly sank back down onto the floor, hugging his knees for warmth.

He had taken a wrong turn in the dark. He was lost.

The Search Begins

Outside the mine, Mr. Dennis anxiously paced back and forth. He'd already checked the tents and asked dozens of boys, including Terry Nelson, if they'd seen Josh since they'd come back out of the mine. None of them had.

"He's still in there," Mr. Dennis told Mr. Weaver. His voice broke, and he swallowed hard. "I'm going in to find him."

"I'll go with you," Mr. Weaver said, "But look, Josh might still turn up out here somewhere. I've sent a group of the boys to recheck all the tents and look in all the cars. Everybody knows now that he's missing. It's not time yet to panic."

A moment later, flashlights in hand, Mr. Dennis and the Scoutmaster dropped back down through the opening into the mine. Swinging the lights back and forth, they started down the main tunnel, shouting, "Jo-o-sh!"

Josh spent another ten or fifteen minutes walking and crawling in circles trying to figure where he was, but finally gave up. He sat huddled and shivering, leaning against the cold rock wall, wondering what to do next.

Should he backtrack? He thought about that, imagining the dark journey back down the winding tunnel with no landmarks to guide him. What if he took another wrong turn? He'd be in even worse trouble.

Then he remembered something he should have thought of earlier. Every time his family went camping or to amusement parks, his mom always said, "If you get separated, just stay put. Don't move around, or it'll be that much harder for us to find you."

Guess I should've just sat down and waited when Dad went off, he thought belatedly. Now, however, he decided to take his mom's advice. He'd "stay put" and wait for his dad to find him.

"Did Josh ever turn up out here?"

The anxiety in Mr. Dennis's voice was apparent. He and the Scoutmaster had just wriggled their way back up out of the mine shaft entrance and were glancing around at the crowd of boys.

Mr. Van Sleeuwen shook his head. "Afraid not. And I think we've done a pretty good search of the area. You didn't see any sign of him in there?"

"No, none at all," said Mr. Dennis. "We went all the way back down the main tunnel and shouted into most of the side tunnels." His voice was unsteady. "If Josh fell into one of those shafts, I'll never forgive myself. This is all my fault."

Mr. Van Sleeuwen put a hand on his shoulder. "Take it easy, Terry. Let's get a search party and go through the mine. He's got to be there somewhere. We'll find him."

Within minutes, eight Scout leaders were gathered, flashlights in hand, at the entrance. Darryl Thomas, an experienced spelunker, or cave explorer, had his rappelling[5] gear along in case they needed to climb down any of the vertical shafts.

"Okay, listen up!" Mr. Weaver said. "Let's work in small teams and check out every single tunnel we were in today. These tunnels muffle sound so you're going to have to yell loud. We'll all meet back at the dead end of the main tunnel."

One by one, the men dropped down through the hole and fanned out. Mr. Dennis and Mr. Weaver started down the main tunnel together, following the same path they'd taken a few hours earlier.

"Jo-o-sh!" Mr. Dennis shouted. "Joshua! Can you hear me?"

"Joshua Dennis!" Mr. Weaver shouted. "Yell if you can hear us!"

Their voices bounced back at them, sounding strangely hollow. But although they stopped and listened closely for a reply, the only sounds they heard were the distant echoes of the other searchers. They moved on, shining their flashlights into every tiny crack, every shadowy corner, praying that they'd see Josh.

About halfway down the main shaft they were joined by Rick Powell and Darryl Thomas. "Any luck yet?" Mr. Powell asked.

"No," Mr. Dennis said. "We went right past the spot where I turned around to take Danny out, but there's no sign of him. It doesn't make sense! He knows to just sit down and wait if he gets separated. That's what worries me the most. Something must have happened to him!"

"Don't jump to conclusions," Mr. Thomas said. "People often get lost in caves, but they usually turn up."

---

5. **rappelling** descending a steep slope using a rope for support

They continued down the main shaft, calling Josh every few minutes. The dusty floor, crisscrossed with footprints pointing both directions, gave no clue to where one small boy might have gone. Several searchers emerged from side tunnels and joined their group.

"Look." Mr. Weaver's flashlight suddenly stopped, trained on a broken board lying on the mine floor—one of several that had been laid down to cover the opening of a deep shaft. "Was that broken when we came through here earlier?"

"I don't think so," said Mr. Powell. He walked over and knelt down to examine the board. "Looks like a fresh break." He shifted his flashlight to shine it down into the shaft. "It's pretty deep. I can't see the bottom."

He looked up, as all the men slowly turned to look over at Mr. Dennis. His face was hidden by the darkness, but his voice revealed his fear as he spoke.

"You think Josh fell in there?"

No one contradicted him. He pushed his way past the others to kneel by the shaft. "Josh!" he screamed. "Joshua, are you in there?" Although the men strained to hear any faint reply, the shaft remained silent.

"Look," Mr. Powell said. "Why don't I rappel down and check it out, just to make sure? Darryl brought along his gear.""

A moment later, strapped into the rappelling harness, Mr. Powell began to lower himself foot by foot into the narrow shaft, supported by a rope held by the other men. Mr. Dennis waited, praying silently that his son's body wouldn't be at the bottom.

"Nothing here!" Mr. Powell's voice drifted up, muted, from the shaft. "Go ahead and pull me back up!"

Mr. Dennis let out his breath, almost dizzy with relief. The Scoutmaster walked over and said firmly, "We'll find him. He's probably safe and sound, sitting down here somewhere waiting for us."

Josh was, at that moment, doing exactly that. Chewing a piece of the licorice he'd found in his pocket, he was trying to pass the time until his dad returned. It was so cold that the candy was tough and hard, but it was better than nothing. In the chilled air his stomach was quivering, and his nose felt like ice.

Suddenly he sat up straight. Were those voices? He turned his head back and forth, trying to figure out which way the sound was coming from, but the solid rock walls made it confusing. The sounds were so faint and faraway that he couldn't make out the words, but they were definitely voices.

"Hey!" he yelled. "Hey, you guys, over here!"

He listened, but there was no answering call. "He-e-y! It's Josh Dennis! I'm over here!"

Instead of getting closer, the voices now seemed to be moving farther away. "Hey, come back!" he shouted. "You're going the wrong way!"

But soon the muffled silence of the underground tunnel was once again unbroken. Josh slumped back against the wall and gnawed off another piece of licorice, disappointed. Next time, he told himself, they'd hear him.

Next time.

"What were you guys thinking, taking a bunch of kids into an abandoned mine like that? Didn't you see the 'No Trespassing' signs?"

The sheriff's deputy sounded angry. It was just after midnight; after searching for more than three hours, Mr. Dennis and Mr. Thomas had finally driven into the nearby town of Tooele to ask for help.

"No, we didn't," Mr. Dennis said shortly. "Look, why don't you save the lectures for later? My son's in trouble, and he needs help—now!"

The deputy sighed. "Okay, okay. I'll call the sheriff and send a couple of men back up there with you to check out the situation."

Soon a police cruiser arrived with two deputies. After making a quick exploration of the major tunnels, the men reported that it seemed to be a genuine emergency.

Sheriff Don Proctor was notified. He called in the official search and rescue team.

The Search Continues

By nine o'clock Saturday morning, the peaceful hillside outside the mine was milling with dozens of searchers, police, and Boy Scouts. Earlier that morning the Salt Lake County Search and Rescue had also joined the search, but despite hours of combing the dark underground passages, no sign of Joshua Dennis had been found. The situation was growing more serious by the minute.

Mr. Dennis was, by now, frantic with worry. "I should call Janeen and let her know," he told Mr. Weaver, "but I just keep hoping Josh will turn up. It wouldn't be so bad for her if it was already all over and I could tell her he was okay."

"Well, I don't see the harm in waiting a little longer," Mr. Weaver said. "The sheriff finally got a map of the mine from the owners, and he says there are tunnels marked on there that we didn't even know about. Josh might have wandered into one of them."

Mr. Weaver didn't add what he was thinking: that the map, in some ways, made it all seem much worse. Instead of being the "simple" mine shaft they'd all imagined, the Hidden Treasure was actually a confusing maze of twisting passages that sprawled over six different levels. There were also countless vertical shafts, some over a thousand feet deep. To add to the problem, the map itself was old and faded, almost impossible to read. It would be a miracle if they could find, much less explore, all the tunnels it noted, some of them hidden by rock slides.

As news of the lost boy leaked out into the community, a crowd of volunteers began to gather, wanting in some way to help with the search. But Sheriff Proctor gave strict orders that only official rescue crews be allowed through the roadblock.

"We've got trained teams on the job," he told his deputies. "We don't need anybody else up here to get lost or hurt. Keep the sight-seers out."

Late Saturday afternoon, a chemical foreman named John Skinner returned home from vacation to learn about Josh's disap-pearance. He immediately drove to the sheriff's department to offer his help. His grandfather had been the superintendent of the Hidden Treasure years before, and he had grown up playing in and around the mine.

To his surprise he, too, was turned away.

"But I know that mine like the back of my hand!" he insisted, smoothing his mustache nervously with one hand. "There are lots of places in there you'd never notice if you didn't know where to look."

"Sorry, sir. Those are the sheriff's orders."

Mr. Skinner finally gave up and went back home. *I hope they find him soon*, he thought. *With all the hidden shafts and old cases of dynamite still scattered around in there, I'd hate to be in there without a light.*

It was almost five o'clock when Mrs. Dennis pulled into the drive-way, tired but triumphant. After spending hours combing the stores, she'd finally found a perfect Batman costume for Josh. She couldn't wait to see his face! She was only a little surprised to see that they weren't home yet. Certainly, they were just running a few minutes late.

She was gathering the shopping bags to carry into the house when a neighbor ran up to the car. "Janeen!" she panted. "Where have you been? We've been paging you at all the malls."

Mrs. Dennis stared at her. "Why? What's the matter?"

"It's Josh." Her voice was shaking." The police department has been here looking for you. Terry called them a couple of hours ago. Oh Janeen, they can't find Josh!"

Mrs. Dennis froze. "What do you mean?"

"They think he's down in some mine. He went in last night and never came back out."

"He's been gone since *last night?*" Mrs. Dennis exclaimed in horror. "Oh, no!"

Now, racing toward the Hidden Treasure Mine with several close friends, she stared blindly out the passenger window. *Please, God,* she prayed. *Wherever Josh is, don't let him be scared. Send Your angels to be with him.*

Angels.

For some reason, Josh suddenly found himself thinking about them. It was a funny thing to think about, sitting all alone in the dark. He remembered his mom talked about angels a few weeks ear-lier during a family devotional.[6] She didn't think they had wings and harps; she said they were messengers who helped people.

Maybe, he thought in amusement, *an angel is sitting beside me right now!*

He stretched his eyes wide, peering into the blackness. If an angel was there, he'd never know—it wouldn't even have to be invisible. He even smiled, picturing a friendly angel keeping him company in the dark. It really *felt* like somebody was there with him, and he didn't feel lonely.

He settled back sleepily, burrowing his icy hands inside his jacket for warmth. He wished he'd brought along a canteen; his mouth was getting really dry. What was taking his dad so long?

---

6. **devotional** religious event

Sunday morning dawned clear and cold over the craggy slope outside the Hidden Treasure mine. The rest of the Boy Scout troop had gone home as scheduled the previous afternoon, but Mr. and Mrs. Dennis had stayed behind, waiting for word about Josh. He had now been missing for more than thirty-six hours.

A few miles away, Mr. and Mrs. Skinner were getting ready for church. Ever since the deputy had refused his help, Mr. Skinner had been trying not to worry about the boy. But he just couldn't help thinking about him, all alone in the dark like that. What a nightmare!

At church that morning, he prayed for Josh. Afterward, though, unable to stand it any longer, he drove out to the mine. He stopped at the roadblock and planted himself squarely in front of the deputy.

"I'm John Skinner," he said. "I've been in that mine hundreds of times, and I've been thinking about it. I know several places where the boy might be. I'd like to go in and check it out."

The young deputy shook his head. "I'm sorry, sir, but we've already got too many people up here as it is. We have to keep the search effort controlled. The best thing you can do is go on back home."

Mr. Skinner argued, but finally turned away in frustration. What was wrong with these people?

Monday morning passed with no sign of Josh, and by late afternoon Sheriff Proctor called his officers together.

"I think we've pretty much eliminated the mine," he said. "We've been through it from one end to the other. The boy *must* have come out and wandered off somewhere. Let's scale down the search inside and start concentrating on the mountain instead."

By mid-afternoon a massive manhunt was underway. The sheriff had set up a temporary "command post" just outside the mine from which he directed the rescue efforts.

Tracking dogs crisscrossed the rugged slopes, noses to the ground, while hundreds of searchers, including Mr. Weaver and other friends of the family, explored every tree, rock, and bush. Three helicopters also joined the search, their rotors chopping the air overhead with a rhythmic whup-whup sound.

There was a flurry of excitement when one of the dogs sniffed out a blue Cub Scout pocketknife near a bush. But then Mr. Weaver told them that one of the younger Scouts had reported losing his knife while playing on the mountainside. The search was resumed.

Late that afternoon, Mr. Skinner decided in frustration to join the search whether the Sheriff's Department liked it or not. There was another old mine, the Buckhorn, which connected to the Hidden Treasure. He planned to sneak in through the Buckhorn and do his best to find the boy.

He drove his Ford Ranger around the back way, through Ophir Canyon and then hiked up the slope. It took him only a few minutes to find the Buckhorn entrance. Once inside, however, he discovered that the old tunnel connecting to the Hidden Treasure had collapsed in a pile of rotten timbers and broken rocks. Discouraged, he had to turn back. The mine was too unsafe to risk shifting things around.

He drove home slowly. The thought kept gnawing at him that if he could just get inside the mine, he might find Joshua Dennis. He remembered how the area around Resolute Stope was filled with dozens of small ore pockets that could easily be missed. If only they'd let him look!

"Mr. Dennis, can you explain why you ignored 'No Trespassing' signs to take young boys into a dangerous mine?"

"Mr. Dennis, why did you take your son's flashlight and leave him in there by himself?"

"Mr. Dennis, we've heard that Joshua argued with you right before he ran off. Is that true?"

Each time Mr. Dennis appeared at the mine site, newspaper and television reporters clustered around him to thrust microphones in his face. Many of the questions were cruel.

"They keep asking me how I could've taken Josh's flashlight like that," Mr. Dennis said later, pacing back and forth in the cramped hotel room as he talked to his wife. "And they're right! How could I have been so stupid? I *knew* better!"

"It was an accident," Mrs. Dennis said helplessly, putting her arms around him. "You're a good father, Terry, you know that. *Josh* knows that!"

Josh was sleeping fitfully on the cold, dusty floor of the mine. "Dad?" he mumbled.

The strange sound of his own voice jolted him awake. He sat up slowly, rubbing his eyes. Where was he?

It was so dark and cold. *Really* cold. The damp, frigid air burned his nose with each breath he took, and his feet and hands felt numb.

He flexed his fingers and then tried to wiggle his toes. He couldn't feel his feet anymore.

Realization came back to him slowly. He was in the Hidden Treasure Mine. Without a watch to gauge time by, he had no idea how long he'd been there. Probably only a few hours, even though it seemed like forever. His mouth tasted really bad. He'd been sleeping a lot.

"Dad?" he called again in a hoarse voice. "You there?"

Nothing. Not even the faraway voices he'd heard a few times. His stomach rumbled loudly. He licked his lips, feeling how cracked and dry they were. Each time he swallowed it felt as if he had a dry lump stuck in his throat. *Heavenly Father,* he prayed, *could You please let them hurry up and find me soon? I want to get out of here.*

It was strange, but somehow the simple prayer made him feel better. He shook off his gloomy thoughts. Maybe it would cheer him up to think about some of the songs he'd been learning in school. One of his favorites was about heroes—just what he needed right now!

As he sang, the cheerful words seemed to penetrate the darkness, making him feel less lonely. Feeling around, he scooped back together the mound of soft dirt he'd been using as a pillow and then stretched back out on the floor.

Whoever gets me out of here, he told himself as he drifted off to sleep, *is going to be my hero.*

Four Days Lost

Tuesday morning, the overcast sky looked gray and threatening. After yet another sleepless night, Mr. and Mrs. Dennis left their hotel and drove up to the mine. It was now the fourth day since Josh had disappeared. Although nobody would say it, hope was rapidly fading that he'd be found alive.

Mrs. Dennis sat watching the search efforts in a kind of daze. A specially trained mine-search crew had been called in to make a final, thorough sweep through the mine. She watched the fifteen men of the Utah Power & Light Mine Rescue team disappear into the hole one by one. They were wearing hard hats with lights and carried climbing gear and oxygen tanks. They looked efficient.

Most of the mine's honeycomb passages were decorated with brightly-colored paint or tape strips, showing that they'd already been searched. But the UP&L searchers started all over again, splitting up into three teams and spreading out to work their way down each shaft.

It was late that afternoon when they wearily gave it up for the day. But they assured Mr. and Mrs. Dennis that they'd come back the next day.

"We're not giving up hope yet, so you don't either," said Ray Guymon, the leader of the UP&L team. Mr. and Mrs. Dennis thanked them and went back to their hotel.

That night, the Dennises listened in numb silence as a TV news announcer said the official search for Josh was "winding down." Authorities were talking about sealing off the entrance to the mine as soon as the search was called off—possibly as early as the next day. If Josh was still in the cold depths of the Hidden Treasure Mine, it was almost certain that, by now, he was dead.

Mr. and Mrs. Dennis turned off the TV and tried to go to sleep, but neither of them could settle down.

"Do you think he's dead?" Mrs. Dennis finally asked.

Mr. Dennis replied, "I don't know. I keep praying for him, but I don't know anymore." He swallowed hard. "It looks like he probably is."

There was a long silence. "Do you think the sheriff would let us put up a memorial plaque for Josh at the entrance to the mine?" Mrs. Dennis asked painfully. "I mean, if they can't find his body—"her voice broke and she closed her eyes.

"We can ask." Mr. Dennis drew a shaky breath. "I'd like Kevin Weaver to speak at the funeral. Josh is—was crazy about him. I think he'd like that."

They held each other tight as they tried to decide how to say their final good-byes to their son.

A hamburger! Josh stared and then reached out with trembling hands to pick it up. It seemed like there was some reason he wasn't supposed to have a hamburger now, but he couldn't remember what it was. Anyway, he was so hungry he really didn't care. He lifted it to his lips—then realized in confusion that the juicy "hamburger" in his hand was just a cold, dusty rock.

Another dream.

The disappointment made his heart sink. He dropped the rock and sighed. He didn't feel very good, kind of weak and mixed up. Whenever he tried to think now it was as if his brain moved in slow motion. And something was wrong with his eyes; he kept "seeing" little flashes of light that weren't there. They stayed even when his eyes were closed.

He tried to wet his cracked lips, but his tongue felt like a wooden stick. His eyes were getting heavy again. He yawned and then slumped back against the rock. It was funny, but he still felt like someone was sitting right there beside him, watching over him. Funny . . .

The thought slowly faded as he dozed off again.

John Skinner stared up through the darkness at the ceiling, unable to sleep. He, too, had heard the TV news report about the mine entrance being blasted closed the next day. He was appalled. What if the boy was still inside? They'd be burying him alive!

If Josh had survived this long he would be dehydrated, and the cold air would be making his body temperature drop. He'd feel sleepy and confused. Eventually, if they didn't find him, he'd fall asleep and never wake up.

Mr. Skinner rolled over and stuffed his face into his pillow, trying to blot out the depressing thoughts. He sent up another silent prayer for the boy before drifting off into a restless sleep.

On Wednesday morning the mountain outside the Hidden Treasure was unusually quiet. Although the skies had cleared, only a handful of people still lingered at the mine site. Sheriff Proctor, exhausted and with dark circles under his eyes, remained at the nearly deserted command post. It had been a long and disheartening five days.

He nodded a weary greeting when the UP&L team showed up to search the mine one last time. He was glad that Mr. and Mrs. Dennis had decided to stay at their hotel and try to rest. They'd been through a lot.

A few miles away, Mr. Skinner was pulling on jeans and a warm wool shirt. He reflected that he felt surprisingly cheerful for having slept only a few hours. For some reason, he'd awakened that morning sure that Josh Dennis was still alive—and that he'd be found.

I'm going up there this morning, he thought. *And this time, no matter what anybody says, I'm going inside.*

On the way to the mine, he stopped for lunch. He might not get another chance at food until dinnertime. Pulling into the Penney's

Service diner, he sat down at the counter, motioning to Mary Peterson, the manager.

"Hi, Mary. How about a cheeseburger and a Sprite?"

She nodded. "Where you off to this morning?"

"I'm going up to the Hidden Treasure. I've been trying to get in there for days to look for that boy, but they wouldn't let me in. Craziest thing you've ever seen."

"I read in the paper that they're abandoning the search today. I feel so sorry for the parents." She shook her head. "What a nightmare."

"The thing is, I think I know where he might be." Mr. Skinner took his napkin and spread it open on the counter. "Can I use your pen?"

"Sure."

He quickly sketched the inside of the mine from memory, noting three places he felt Josh might be found. "See this?" he said, tapping one area with the pen. "That's Resolute Stope. There are lots of places back in there a ten-year-old could squeeze into. I bet that's where he is."

"Think he's still alive after all this time?"

"I think so. I *hope* so!"

After paying for his cheeseburger, he started toward the mine. When he reached the roadblock, he saw that the officer on duty was an old friend, so John Skinner quickly explained what he wanted to do.

The officer nodded and waved him through. "I don't see why they didn't let you in here before," he said. "You could've been a big help."

"Yeah, well, that's what I kept saying. Anyway, thanks."

Up at the mine site Mr. Skinner found Sheriff Proctor at the command post talking quietly with Ray Guymon. The UP&L team had been through every inch of the mine—twice—without finding Josh.

Mr. Skinner introduced himself. "Listen," he said, "have you guys checked the Resolute Stope area? That spot back off the main tunnel about two thousand feet in?"

Mr. Guymon looked at the sheriff, and they both raised their eyebrows. This guy seemed to know what he was talking about!

"We checked it," Mr. Guymon said. "But if you know your way around, I wouldn't mind checking it one more time. Okay with you, Sheriff?"

"Might as well. Just don't get yourself hurt."

Mr. Guymon tossed Mr. Skinner a hard hat and then motioned to another teammate, Gary Christensen, to come along. The three dropped down the hole into the mine.

Mr. Skinner quickly led the others back to one area where he thought Josh might be. They searched a small ore pocket and called Josh's name repeatedly. Nothing.

"There's another pocket right back here," Mr. Skinner said, pushing on. Again, there was no sign of Josh. Discouraged, the men paused to get a drink of water.

He's just got to be here somewhere, Mr. Skinner thought desperately. *Please, God, help us find that boy before it's too late.*

Suddenly, Mr. Guymon became alert. "What was that?"

The other two men listened, straining their ears in the darkness. Mr. Guymon was hard of hearing, so it wasn't likely that he'd heard something they'd missed.

But then they all heard it—a faint, faraway whisper of sound. They froze, afraid to even breathe.

"*Help!*"

Mr. Skinner's face split into an incredulous grin. "Josh?" he shouted. "Josh Dennis! Is that you?"

Rescued at Last!

Josh blinked slowly, his eyes sore from the dryness and dust. In the tomblike silence of the mine shaft, the only sound was his own labored breathing. What had awakened him?

Then he heard the voices. They were faint and faraway, but they were voices. With a great effort he sat up.

"Help!" he called. The sound came out like a whispered croak. He cleared his throat and tried again. "Help! Help!"

The effort left him tired and weak. He slumped back against the rock again. He was just so sleepy.

"*Josh!*" The voice was clearer this time.

Josh snapped back to attention, his cracked and swollen lips stretching into a smile. "Over here!" he yelled. He tried shakily to stand up, but his numb, swollen feet wouldn't support him.

"*Josh!*" They were getting close. "If you hear us, keep yelling so we can find you!"

A light suddenly reflected on some rocks far below. Josh squinted, dazzled by the glare. After all the hours in total darkness, it looked as bright as a spotlight.

"I'm up here!" he shouted. By the flickering light he could see the steep, gravelly slope he'd climbed, and the small ore pocket where he was sitting. He was surprised to discover that he was tucked in a cramped area surrounded by rocks. No wonder the others hadn't been able to hear him!

With a sudden burst of energy he scooted forward on his behind and started down, feet first, toward the light. He was still sliding in a shower of gravel when a sturdy-looking blond man scrambled up the slope toward him.

Reaching him, the man, Mr. Christensen, swept him up in a bear hug, and then quickly helped him the rest of the way down to where two other men—he'd later learn they were Mr. Skinner and Mr. Guymon—stepped forward, their dust-blackened faces streaked with tears.

"Boy, are we glad to see you!" Mr. Skinner said, patting his back. "Come on. We'll take you out to your mom and dad!"

"My dad is outside, but my mom's at home," Josh said in confusion. "She didn't come with us."

Mr. Skinner raised an eyebrow. "Your mom's here, too. She's been really worried." Josh didn't have the strength to argue. Why would his mom be here? He'd thought it was Saturday, but maybe he'd been in here longer than he thought. Could it already be Sunday? If so, he'd missed the whole campout!

Since his feet were too swollen to walk, Mr. Christensen carried him on his back. Mr. Skinner ran ahead to tell the others outside the good news.

Minutes later Josh, Mr. Guymon, and Mr. Christensen emerged to face a small crowd of cheering people. Sheriff Proctor had tears running down his cheeks. He gave Josh a drink of water and then had him whisked away to the hospital for a joyful reunion with his parents. Josh was astonished to learn that five days had passed since he'd lost his way in the darkness of the mine.

"It didn't seem that long," he said disbelievingly. "I thought it was just overnight!"

"That's good," Mrs. Dennis said, hugging him close. "We were praying that you wouldn't suffer or be lonely."

"I wasn't lonely," Josh said. "I think angels were with me. It felt like they were sitting beside me the whole time."

A few days later, pale and thin but otherwise okay, Josh was allowed to go home. When his dad turned the car onto their block, Josh was surprised to find that the neighborhood was decorated with yellow ribbons and balloons in his honor. A huge banner was draped across his street, saying, "Welcome Home, Josh!" Hundreds of friends and neighbors were standing outside, waiting to greet him.

Josh stared around him, stunned into silence. All of this was for *him*?

He was relieved to go inside the house. He hugged Jake and his two little sisters. For some reason he felt older now than when he had left. He hugged them all again, glad to be home.

Then he remembered Striper.

"Where's Striper?" he asked, suddenly afraid the cage would be empty. If Striper had died while he was gone—

"He's still hanging on," Mrs. Dennis assured him. They'd decided to keep calling the hamster a "he" since they were used to it. "But he's pretty sick. I don't think he's going to last much longer."

"I'm going to see him."

In his room, Josh lifted Striper out of the cage and rubbed him gently against his cheek. The tiny animal was barely skin and bones, too exhausted to even try to play, but he fixed Josh trustingly with his small, beady eyes. Josh felt a lump rising in his throat.

"I'm here now," he whispered. "I'm with you." He knew what it was like to need company.

Striper didn't hold out much longer. Josh wrapped the small body carefully and buried him in a box in the backyard.

A couple of days later the doorbell rang. Mrs. Dennis answered the door and saw a little boy standing beside his father. His father was holding a large wire cage.

"Is Josh here?" the boy asked shyly.

"I'll go get him," Mrs. Dennis said.

Josh came to the door. "Yeah?" he said curiously.

"My name's Brandon. I heard about what happened to you in that mine, and a friend told me about your hamster dying. I brought you something, if you want it." He added, "It's a baby guinea pig. It was born the same day you were found.

Josh bent down to look into the cage. There was a hollow log

lying on top of the shredded litter, and just visible inside was a tiny, quivering ball of brown and white fur.

"He hides in that log all the time," Brandon said. "He's really cute. You can keep the cage." He looked up at his father. "My dad made it for him."

Josh turned to his mother. She was smiling. "Okay, okay," she said. "You took good care of Striper, and I'm sure you'll take good care of this one, too."

Josh nodded enthusiastically. "I've already picked a name for him." He grinned at Brandon. "Since he likes to hide in the log, I'll call him . . . Hidden Treasure!"

Some time later when Mr. and Mrs. Skinner came to visit, Josh hugged them both warmly.

"Thanks for looking for me," he told Mr. Skinner. "There was a song I kept thinking about while I was waiting. It was, 'Ev'rybody's Got to Have a Hero.' You and Mr. Guymon and Mr. Christensen were all my heroes!"

Mr. and Mrs. Dennis also hugged Mr. Skinner and then invited the couple to visit with them for a few minutes. They discussed the amazing string of "coincidences" that led to Josh being found at—literally—the last minute.

There were many questions that couldn't be answered. Why had Mr. Skinner felt compelled to come back to the mine, even though he'd been warned not to?

What made him wake up that Wednesday morning suddenly convinced that Josh was alive?

Why did the rescuers choose to stop for a drink in the exact spot where Josh could finally be heard?

How did hard-of-hearing Ray Guymon hear Josh's tiny cry for help when the others didn't?

And what about Josh's strange sense of a friendly presence in the darkness with him? And the fact that, despite going five whole days without food or water, he had come out in pretty good shape?

"The whole thing was just a miracle," Mr. Skinner said. The others quickly agreed—all except Josh.

"I wouldn't really call it a *miracle*," he said, shrugging. "I asked God to send somebody—and He did!"

John D. Evans

Getting the Bugs Out of Tom Sawyer:

An Entomologist's View of a Classic

A chance meeting between a teacher and an entomologist reveals the universal appeal of The Adventures of Tom Sawyer.

I COULD TELL that the gentleman sitting next to me was trying to see what I was reading. His head was pulled back and tilted slightly to the side to get a better view into the valley formed by the book in my lap. He was trying to be subtle but he failed miserably. I glanced over and acknowledged him with a polite smile. He nodded and smiled back, a little embarrassed at being caught. In that quick glance, I got the impression of a giant, benevolent bird—a stork perhaps. His arms and legs were long and thin, and the head above the equally thin neck was crowned with a crest of white unkempt hair. A pair of gold rimmed glasses perched at the end of a beak-like nose and his eyes twinkled intelligently behind them. The quick movement of his head as he nodded was decidedly bird-like—a robin listening for a worm.

As I resumed my reading, he resumed his attempt to peek into my book. I had been in enough airport waiting areas stuck in delays to know how to pass the time. A good book was always my first choice; casual conversation with a complete stranger, my second. The latter was risky, for there was always the possibility of becoming hopelessly entangled in a conversation about Aunt Alma's gall bladder operation or Cousin Twilly's rotten second marriage. On the other hand, I have met some interesting people with some equally interesting stories. This gentleman had a unique quality about him that made me decide to take a chance—I tilted the book open in his direction. His head snapped up, but the startled look melted into a smile as he saw that I was not offended by his curiosity. He then unashamedly leaned forward, his neck extending, as he cocked his head and stuck his beak into my book.

"Ahh, *Tom Sawyer,*" he said, nodding his approval. "One of my favorites." His voice was soft and melodious, his enunciation precise. "You're reading it for the first time perhaps?"

I closed the book on my index finger. "For the hundredth," I exaggerated.

He looked at me silently—patiently. I don't know what reaction I was expecting—shock, surprise, awe, but I didn't get them. He simply waited for the explanation that was due after such a comment. Perhaps there were books he had read countless times.

"I'm a teacher," I explained, and he nodded his head in understanding. "I read it year after year with my classes." I rolled the book over in my hand to expose the title. "I try to find some new approach, a new focus every once in a while. It keeps me fresh. I've studied it from just about every angle. This year I'm leaning toward a biographical approach—many of those adventures were Twain's. Right now I'm just trying to get the bugs out."

He threw his head back and let out a short, explosive laugh of delight that startled me.

"Wonderful!" he chirped. "What a marvelous way to phrase it: 'Getting the bugs out.'" He stroked his chin as he turned that phrase over in his mind, perhaps storing it away for future use.

"Are you a teacher also?" I asked.

"No," he smiled, "I'm an entomologist[1]—insects are my game."

We fell silent for an awkward moment, neither of us sure what to say next.

"I wouldn't think *The Adventures of Tom Sawyer* would be your kind of reading." I said picking up the thread of our mutual interest.

"Quite the contrary! *Tom Sawyer* is teeming with insect life of the most extraordinary variety!" He seemed shocked that one who has read *Tom Sawyer* so often could be blind to such an obvious fact.

---

1. **entomologist** scientist who studies insects

In a race to preserve my professional integrity, my mind buzzed through the plot in search of this teeming horde of insects, but I came up woefully short.

"You must be referring to the tick Tom played with in school—the tick he traded his tooth for with Huckleberry Finn."

"Well, yes," he said softly and there was something in his tone that told me that I had blundered. "There was that tick, yes. Technically it isn't an insect—it's in the class *arachnida*. It's a spider of sorts. Interesting nevertheless. Huckleberry Finn must have captured a common wood tick, *Dermacentor variabilis*. They like to crawl out on the tips of leaves and then . . ." he extended his arms like a giant crab, spread the fingers of his hands out like talons, and gently rocked back and forth, "they wait for a host to brush by. They grab the host," (his fingers snapped into tight fists) "and they feed on the blood of the victim. Once a mated female has gorged herself, she drops from the host, lays her eggs, and crawls out on another leaf. If the victim is a human, there is always the danger of Rocky Mountain spotted fever and tularemia, or rabbit fever. Nasty diseases. Nasty."

He shook his head sadly for a moment and then his face lit. "But if you want a disease carrier, you have to go to that fly Tom caught in church just as the minister ended his prayer. It was probably a common house fly, *Musca domestica*. I guarantee that Tom didn't know what he had in his hand besides that fly. It's been calculated that a single house fly carries with it as many as 33 million microorganisms in its gut, and perhaps a half billion more on its feet, legs, body. It's a wonder the damned thing can fly!" He chuckled softly to himself. I smiled weakly.

"But they do," he continued, "and at a top speed of about five miles per hour. That's quite a feat with all that cargo. They can't land anywhere without leaving some of those bacteria behind. Tuberculosis, typhoid, cholera, diarrhea and many other diseases can travel around with that fly, and they do travel—up to twenty miles from the place where they were born. And everywhere they land, they drop off some of those nasty little bacteria." He leaned in confidentially. "You see, the problem is that they can't chew."

I raised my eyebrows, and he smiled. "They can only suck up liquids. When they find some solid food, they must first dissolve it. They spit out some saliva which turns the solid into a liquid, and then they suck it up—most of it anyway. It's what they leave behind that contains the bacteria.

"Their feet present another problem. Their feet are equipped with sticky pads that give them the ability to walk on walls and ceilings. It also gives them the ability to pick up germs: leprosy, gonorrhea, scarlet fever, polio, gangrene—the list goes on. And flies have no social conscience. They'll land on a rotting carcass or piece of filth and then go directly to your sugar bowl. And in spite of all the filth they contact, they are rather meticulous[2] about their personal grooming, always rubbing their legs together, smoothing out their wings, dusting off their heads. And, of course, that helps deposit more germs wherever they land."

He paused reflectively. "I was always sorry Aunt Polly made Tom let that fly go. That one fly could lay 100 to 150 eggs at a time. The maggots that hatch mature in about two weeks, and then the females can begin to reproduce. One scientist calculated that a single pair of flies have the potential to produce five and a half *quintillion* offspring in a single summer! That's a 55 with seventeen zeros after it. Of course, that's supposing that every single fly survives to reproduce."

He looked over his eyeglasses and leaned in close. "Imagine how many offspring that fly of Tom Sawyer's was responsible for over the last 150 years!

"Of course, not all the insects in *Tom Sawyer* are harmful to man. The cricket is relatively harmless."

"Cricket?" I asked. "There's a cricket in *Tom Sawyer?*"

"Oh, absolutely. A field cricket, most likely—*Gryllus*." He reached over and gently removed the book from my hand. "May I?"

I nodded and he leafed through the pages.

"There is a house cricket, *Acheta domesticus*, which was introduced from Europe. That's the one Dickens labeled the 'Cricket on the Hearth.' One would assume that a cricket found in the house would be a house cricket, but that's not necessarily the case. Most of the time, the crickets you find in your house are field crickets that sneak in in the autumn. Besides, I doubt if *Acheta domesticus* would have ranged into Mississippi by the 1840s, but you never know. My best guess is that it was a common field cricket—a male. Here it is," he said pointing to a passage in my book. "Chapter nine: 'And now the

---

2. **meticulous** careful

tiresome chirping of a cricket, that no human ingenuity[3] could locate, began.' Actually, it doesn't take much ingenuity to locate a cricket, but it does take patience. You see, the difficulty in locating a cricket is that it is one of nature's great ventriloquists. The chirping is made using the same principle as the violin. The male has a rough surface on the edge of his wing on the underside. On the upper side is a scraper." He placed his hands together and, pivoting them at the wrist, he rubbed his palms together. "When the wings slide over each other it is like a bow drawing across a violin string. It produces that familiar chirp. Usually the field cricket holds his wings up at a 45 degree angle for maximum projection." He held his hand out flat and tilted it up and down like the flap of an airplane wing. "But it will also lower it to produce a more muffled, distant sound. To us humans, the cricket's songs sound pretty much alike, but the field cricket has two classes of song. One is a common song, a series of triple chirps, and the other is the all important courtship song, a continuous trill.[4] When he wants to attract a female, he increases the vibration frequency from 4,900 cycles a second to 17,000 cycles a second. Only the males make the chirping (we call it stridulations). The female hears it through tiny holes in her forelegs—no ears. It would be like you listening to music through your wrists. Hard to imagine, isn't it?"

I nodded.

"The field cricket has a cousin, the snowy tree cricket whose chirp can be used to tell the temperature. Count the number of chirps it makes in 15 seconds, add 40, and you'll have the temperature with amazing accuracy."

"Fahrenheit or Celsius?" I asked.

"Oh my! Fahrenheit, of course!" He seemed shocked. "Crickets only chirp when the temperature is above 55 degrees and below 100 degrees—Fahrenheit, that is. On the Celsius scale they would positively roast!"

He paused. My ignorance seemed to put him off for a moment and he returned to the book. He pointed to the same page as before and his face took on a serious cast. "There was another insect at work in Tom's bedroom that night." He lowered his head and craned his neck into the book as he read, "'Next the ghastly ticking of a death-watch

---

3. **ingenuity** cleverness
4. **trill** high-pitched sound

in the wall at the bed's head made Tom shudder. It meant that some-body's days were numbered.'"

He looked at me gravely. "It's easy to understand how that super-stition arose. What Tom was hearing was a death-watch beetle in the family *Anobiidae*. They like seasoned wood—furniture or timber. The one in Tom's room may have been boring into the headboard itself. It emits a ticking sound in its burrow by bobbing its head up and down—tapping the wood in search of a mate. In an active house, this ticking goes unnoticed, drowned out by other noises."

He leaned closer, his eyes widened, and he whispered, "Imagine, now, sitting by the bedside of a gravely ill person. Quiet pervades the room as the relatives wait for death to come. And then," his eyes moved from side to side and he pulled his head into his shoulders, "Tick! . . . tick! . . . tick! A mysterious noise from the dark shadows of the room seems to be counting off the last minutes of the dying. Supernatural forces must be at work!"

His features relaxed, and he continued in a normal conversational tone, "Of course after the person has died, the death-watch beetle continues to bore. Later on when his clicks are noticed deep in the middle of some sleepless night, the active imagination would natu-rally assume that someone else's last minutes are being counted—'Somebody's days are numbered' as Twain put it."

His brow wrinkled as if a troublesome thought came to him. "It's a wonder Tom heard the death-watch beetle with that cricket chirping away. Of course, if it was a cool night, its stridulations would be mini-mal. I suppose he could have heard it."

That must have satisfied him, because his face lit once again, and he continued happily: "They make wonderful pets, crickets. Give them a little place to live, some water, and feed them anything. They are omnivorous. They have the same diet you do. They eat all the same food groups plus some things that you may not want to eat like rubber, leather, and other insects. In fact, they'll even eat other crick-ets. They eat all the time; they are constantly hungry. Constantly! You don't have to walk them, and they make wonderful music. The Chinese and the Japanese have made an art form of carving cricket cages just so they can enjoy their songs." He shifted in his seat and threw one long leg over the other. "I've seen cages with covers of carved ivory and jade, and the Chicago Museum of Natural History has one on display carved from a walnut shell!

"Of course, their songs are not the only reason crickets are kept. For centuries the Chinese used them for sport—fighting crickets. They even had weight classes and personal trainers to make sure they were in proper trim before a fight. And just like the professional athletes, their diets were strictly watched. They were fed boiled chestnuts, mosquitoes, and, of course, rice". . . .

It was at this point that my long delayed flight was announced. My friend handed me my copy of *Tom Sawyer* and as we gathered our belongings he continued his enthusiastic chatter.

"There are many other insects mentioned in that book: inchworms measuring for Tom's pirate uniform, butterflies. . . ." He was standing now, and his face took on a troubled look. "Twain was shamefully vague in his description of them, and with over 12,000 species found in North America, there is no telling what species Tom was seeing."

He fell in beside me as I walked toward the boarding gate. "And then there was that procession of ants on Jackson's Island. According to Twain, one of those ants was struggling with a spider 'five times as big as itself' and 'lugged it straight up a tree trunk.' It was probably a procession of black carpenter ants, *Camponotus pennsylvanicus*. You see, most ants nest underground, but the carpenter ant will nest in the dead wood of a tree trunk.

"Twain really missed the boat there. If he had only concentrated more upon those ants and how they got that dead spider, he would have really had something!"

The attendant took our tickets and we marched down the covered ramp to the plane. I offered a silent prayer that our seats were far removed from each other.

"Now that inchworm that crawled on Tom's leg—it really wasn't a worm. It was the larva of a geometer moth, one of 1,200 species found all over North America. The reason they rear up and go 'sniffing around,' as Twain put it, is because. . . ."

John Ciardi

Sometimes I Feel This Way

*What motivates children like Tom Sawyer to take
certain actions? Poet John Ciardi offers the reader a
view inside a child's head, as the child makes a
decision whether to be good or bad.*

I have one head that wants to be good,
  And one that wants to be bad.
And always, as soon as I get up,
  One of my heads is sad.

5 "Be bad," says one head. "Don't you know
  It's fun to be bad. Be as bad as you like.
Put sand in your brother's shoe—that's fun.
  Put gum on the seat of your sister's bike."

"What fun is that?" says my other head.
10   "Why not go down before the rest
And set things out for breakfast? My,
  That would please Mother. Be good—that's best."

"What! Better than putting frogs in the sink?
  Or salt in the tea-pot? Have some fun.
15 Be bad, be bad, be good and bad.
  You know it is good to be bad," says One.

"Is it good to make Sister and Brother sad?
  And Mother and Daddy? And when you do,
Is it good to get spanked? Is it good to cry?
20 No, no. Be good—that's best," says Two.

So one by one they say what they say,
   And what they say is "Be Good—Be Bad."
And if One is happy that makes Two cry.
   And if Two is happy that makes One sad.

25 Someday maybe, when I grow up,
   I shall wake and find I have just one—
The happy head. But which will it be?
   I wish I knew. They are both *some* fun.

Susan Neiburg Terkel

from
Ethics

This reading by author Susan Neiburg Terkel offers criteria for evaluating right and wrong.

What Is Ethics?

Because ethics is about the meaning of life and the search for right from wrong, it is abstract[1] and difficult to define. Words limit what we can convey about moral living. Like the joy of a sunlit day or the power of riding a huge wave, it must be experienced to be fully understood. Nevertheless, much has been written about ethics and added to our understanding of it.

Ethics began as unwritten rules. From the time that humans lived together in groups and established rules for the way they treated one another, people engaged in ethical inquiry. The first incidents requiring moral consideration probably led to rules about killing and about property, which determined when it was right or wrong to kill another person or for people to protect what they owned.

Although all ancient societies and religions had moral codes— rules for behavior—it was during the fifth century B.C. in Greece that the philosopher Socrates gave ethics its formal beginning. In fact, the word ethics comes from the Greek word *ethos*, which means "character."

Socrates asked his fellow Greeks to look at *why* they did what they did and thought what they thought. Questioning the meaning and value of life, he asked: What is justice? What is a good life? Can virtue[2] be taught?

Socrates's student, Plato, and Plato's student, Aristotle, further

---

1. **abstract** complex
2. **virtue** goodness; moral excellence

developed Socrates's philosophy of ethics. Their thinking was so profound and complete that some philosophers comment that nothing new has been said since Plato or Aristotle. For centuries, many scholars have searched for fresh insight into the same basic questions explored by the Greek philosophers. What is the purpose of life and how can we live a good one?

The Good Life

By helping us determine what is important in life, ethics helps us set goals for what we can and ought to achieve. In devoting themselves to the attainment of human rights, for example, Abraham Lincoln, Rosa Parks (a black woman who refused to give up her seat on a bus in Montgomery, Alabama, in 1955, thereby instigating the Civil Rights movement), and Andrei Sakharov (Soviet Nobel Peace Prize winner who championed human rights in his country) all led morally good lives—full, rich, purposeful lives. So did Samantha Smith from Maine, who was only thirteen when she died in a tragic airplane crash.

In 1983, when the Soviets and Americans were still carrying on the Cold War, Samantha wrote to Soviet leader Yuri Andropov about her concern over nuclear war. When he received her letter, President Andropov invited her to visit the Soviet Union, which she did in July 1984. There she fostered[3] a friendship between the two nations and became a national heroine of goodwill.

Regardless of circumstances, setting a moral goal is available to anyone. Viktor Frankl, author of *Man's Search for Meaning*, discovered that even in the hellish confines of a concentration camp like Auschwitz, where people could no longer hold onto familiar goals, they could still choose to have a moral reason for living.

Recipe for Living

Ethics guides us to the "good life" by giving us a recipe for living. This includes rules, principles, and values about how we all can and should conduct ourselves.

Thou shalt not's. Certain moral rules set limits on our behavior and provide us with a "floor of decency." By telling us what we should *not* do, they prohibit us from abusing the rights of others or causing harm.

---

3. **fostered** encouraged; promoted

One such moral rule is: "Do not harm an innocent person." Another is: "Do not bear false witness."

Thou shalt's. From principles about what we *should* do, we acquire moral duties and learn what is expected of us, as members of families, communities, professions, and even the human race. Treat others as you would have them treat you, respect the rights of others, play fair, be loyal to your country, and give to charity. These are just a few examples of moral duties we learn in our American culture.

Beyond the call of duty. Ethics inspires us to what Mary Mahowald, a medical ethicist at the University of Chicago, calls virtue, or *moral excellence.* "Virtue," Mahowald suggests, "means going beyond what we are obliged to do."

For example, we have no duty, either legal or moral, to donate our bone marrow, kidneys, or blood to anyone, not even a close relative. Nor do we have a duty to send money to flood victims or even help the elderly across a street. That we do, however, is a virtue—"beyond the call of duty."

In All the Right Places

Morality[4] is not a "thing apart," a separate area of life. It is a part of everything, from our personal lives to public affairs and global concerns.

At home and school, it helps us decide how to treat our family and friends. At work, it helps us decide how honestly and how earnestly to perform our jobs, and even what kind of professions we choose. It shapes our public agenda and the way we treat members of our society. . . .

By helping us make wise decisions, adding purpose to our lives, and teaching us to be fair and kind, ethics deepens our understanding of ourselves and the world we live in. It also provides a challenge to the way we think and act.

---

4. **morality** honesty; integrity